The Mortal Groove

The Mortal Groove

ELLEN HART

ST. MARTIN'S MINOTAUR ✚ NEW YORK

This is a work of fiction. All of the characters, organizations, and events portrayed in this novel are either products of the author's imagination or are used fictitiously.

www.minotaurbooks.com

Library of Congress Cataloging-in-Publication Data

Hart, Ellen.
  The mortal groove / Ellen Hart. — 1st St. Martin's Minotaur paperback ed.
    p. cm.
  ISBN-13: 978-0-312-37787-8

  1. Lawless, Jane (Fictitious character)—Fiction. 2. Women detectives—Minnesota—Minneapolis—Fiction. 3. Restaurateurs—Fiction. 4. Minneapolis (Minn.)—Fiction. 5. Lesbians—Fiction. 6. Fathers—Fiction. I. Title.

PS3558.A6775M67 2007
813'.54—dc22

                                                    2007033534

First St. Martin's Minotaur Paperback Edition: November 2008

Cast of Characters

Jane Lawless: Owner of the Lyme House Restaurant and the Xanadu Club in Minneapolis. Peter's sister. Raymond's daughter.

Cordelia Thorn: Creative Director for the Allen Grimby Repertory Theater in St. Paul.

Raymond Lawless: Semiretired criminal lawyer. Jane and Peter's father.

Peter Lawless: Cameraman/photographer. Jane's brother. Raymond's son.

Sigrid Lawless: Psychologist. Peter's wife.

Delavon (Del) Green: Raymond's campaign manager. Randy and Larry's old army friend.

Randy Turk: Civil rights and poverty law attorney in St. Paul. Ethan's younger brother. Del and Larry's old army friend.

Ethan Turk: Randy's older brother.

Larry Wilton: Bartender. Randy and Del's old army friend.

Melanie Gunderson: Reporter/teacher. Cordelia's ex-girlfriend.

Emily Bouchard: Randy's old girlfriend.

A. J. Nolan: Retired cop. Private investigator. Good friend of Jane's.

I shall tell you a great secret, my friend.
Do not wait for the last judgment,
it takes place every day.

—Albert Camus

Prologue

Late Summer, 1971

*T*hree young men in a northern Iowa field. They could be college kids home for the summer or farmhands taking a break on a hot August afternoon, but they aren't. All three are outwardly good boys. They love their mothers. They don't swear in front of children. They know how to behave appropriately. But one, though he still has the face of sweet youth, is a time bomb—a bomb that has gone off once already, and threatens to do so again.

Within the last four months, all of these boys, now men, have come home from a tour in Vietnam. One is standing, smoking a joint; the other two sit with their backs against the trunk of an oak. All are wearing battered boots, army field pants, and T-shirts. The one standing, Larry Wilton, is watching a crow perched at the top of the tree. The two men on the ground pass a fifth of rum between them.

"I am so totally stoked," says the one called Larry. "The jury acquitted him. We're all in the clear."

Randy, the blond curly haired kid, the one who invited his two best buddies up to visit him on the vast, flat, Iowa prairie because he doesn't feel comfortable around his old high school friends anymore, shakes his head. "We'll never be in the clear."

"Don't be such a pessimist," says Larry. "Your brother's a free man and so are we. I think that calls for some fireworks." He leans over, reaches into his duffel bag, and comes out with a semiautomatic pistol, a new purchase. He tells anyone who's interested that he needs it because he just don't feel right if he ain't got no firepower. After a year in hell, a gun is as much a part of his body as his lungs. He fires several rounds into the air, then begins to dance his rendition of an Irish jig. He looks ridiculous and stoned, which he is.

Randy stares at him, takes another hit off the bottle, then hands it to Delavon. Delavon is a black man from Detroit. The biggest human being Randy had ever seen—before Vietnam. Randy believes that his life will forever be defined by two acronyms—B.N. and A.N. Before Nam and After Nam.

Larry lands on his knees in the dirt in front of Randy, grinning like a gargoyle. "Man, I love this life," he says, taking a deep breath. "I purely do."

"Nothin' pure about us," says Delavon.

"You guys fry me. We took care of business, right?"

With his eyes half lowered, Randy considers Larry's hair. Each man's hair is still short, not quite army issue, but Larry has been out the longest, so his has grown the most. Randy tries to decide what color it is. He comes to the conclusion that it has no color. It's anticolor. Like dust.

"That cunt deserved to die," says Larry.

Randy erupts at him, arm cocked, hand balled into a fist. He wants to annihilate him for saying that.

Delavon just watches from his position by the tree. He wishes he had a cigarette. When Larry and Randy have both rolled on their backs, grunting and sweating like hogs in a pen, Delavon, who fancies himself a preacher of sorts, offers his take on the matter.

2

"We gotta stop fighting like little kids, you understand me? We gotta become the brothers we always say we are. Like, maybe we do some serious voodoo shit. Cut our fingers and blend the blood in a cup. Or butcher ourselves a snake and swear an oath over it in a graveyard. 'Cause brothers, hear me well. If one of us ever talks, we be dead men."

New Year's Eve
The Present

Jane Lawless stood under the arch in her dad's living room, holding a tray of champagne flutes. Everyone was waiting for her, the bearer of the booze, but she couldn't bring herself to move because she was staring at a piece of magic. The firelight had collected itself around her family just like the glow in a Rembrandt painting. Maybe she was seeing things, or maybe she'd had one too many, but she could sense her mind taking a snapshot of the scene, knowing it would live inside her for the rest of her life. This was the center of her world—these six people.

"Get in here, Janey," called her father. "We're all dying of thirst."

"Coming," she said, stepping down into the sunken living room and passing out the glasses.

Jane was in her early forties, a successful restaurateur. For the past couple of years, she'd been working night and day developing a second restaurant in the Twin Cities. The Xanadu Club was located in the Uptown area of Minneapolis. In the year it had been open, it had already established itself as the premier nightclub in town. She was proud of her accomplishments, not that she intended to dwell on any of that tonight. All she wanted from this New Year's Eve was to enjoy the flow, have a few too many glasses of champagne, and then take a cab home with her partner, Kenzie Mullroy.

Jane's oldest and best friend, Cordelia Thorn, stood across the room, directly under one of the track lights near the fireplace. If there was a spotlight anywhere in the vicinity, Cordelia usually found it. She would, no doubt, have appreciated the fact that her red sequined evening gown glittered like rubies. Cordelia enjoyed glittering. In fact, she insisted on it. She was the creative director of the Allen Grimby Repertory Theater in St. Paul.

Adjusting the feather boa around her plunging neckline, Cordelia draped an arm around the shoulders of a tall, attractive woman standing next to her. Kenzie didn't have Hollywood looks, but she had the kind of presence that made people turn and stare when she entered a room. It seemed amazing to Jane that they'd already been together for over two years. Kenzie lived in Chadwick, Nebraska, where she taught cultural anthropology at Chadwick State College. She'd come up for the holidays. Long-distance relationships were hard, but Jane and Kenzie were trying their best to make it work. Still, the time apart weighed heavily on them both.

Kenzie and Cordelia were listening to Peter, Jane's brother. They appeared to be laughing and grimacing as he told a joke. Peter was a cameraman at WTWN-TV in Minneapolis. He was eight years younger than Jane, bearded, handsome, with the same thick chestnut hair and the same blue-violet eyes.

6

Sigrid, Peter's wife, sat on the sofa between Jane's dad and Elizabeth Piper, her father's girlfriend. Thanks to Cordelia's weird taste, a Roy Rogers CD crooned inanely from the stereo speakers on the bookcase. Roy had just finished singing "Don't Fence Me In" and had moved on to Cordelia's favorite, "The Gay Ranchero," when Cordelia turned, looking as if she'd just swallowed ground glass, and bolted from the room. As she rushed past Jane, her boa drifted to the floor.

"Cordelia? Hey?" Jane picked up the boa and followed her upstairs. She found her in the bathroom, the door closed and locked.

"Cordelia, open up."

Her crying became one long wail.

"Let me in." She banged on the door. "Cordelia?"

Several seconds passed. Finally, the door opened and Cordelia fell into Jane's arms, weeping. "I can't go on."

"Why?"

"Didn't you hear Roy singing about 'little chicos'?"

"I was doing my best to ignore him."

Cordelia backed up and sank down on the edge of the tub, pulled the toilet paper up to her nose, and blew hard.

Jane sat down next to her. "It's Hattie, isn't it. You're thinking about her."

"Of course it's Hattie!"

Hattie Thorn Lester was Cordelia's four-year-old niece—her sister Octavia's child. Hattie had lived with Cordelia for the last two years. From the start, it had been an odd pairing—a precocious kid bonding with a woman who generally referred to children, when she referred to them at all, as rug rats and carpet creepers. But Octavia, a graduate of the Joan Crawford school of mothering, was an actress with a hard-on, as it were, to make

7

it big in movies. With little time for a child, she'd allowed Cordelia to shoulder the responsibility. Cordelia had, against her will, fallen in love with Hattie. Everything was going swimmingly until Octavia had swooped in and whisked Hattie off to England. Octavia's first pronouncement stated that Cordelia could write or call as much as she wanted, but by Thanksgiving, that olive branch had been withdrawn.

Cordelia hit bottom so hard she didn't even bounce. She hired a lawyer to sue for custody, but she was told that as long as Hattie lived in England, there wasn't much she could do. And so began the long travail.

In early December, Cordelia suffered a total meltdown. She couldn't work, wouldn't eat—which, for her, was behavior worthy of a locked psych ward. She moved from her downtown loft into Jane's house because she couldn't stand to be alone. Not that she had to be. At least six women, all pursuing her romantically, came to the house at various intervals to rub her back, cook her meals, bring her boxes of candy, videos, books, and enough glitzy bargain-basement bling to fill a treasure chest.

It was a well-known fact that Cordelia adored cheap bling.

By late December, she seemed to have pulled herself together. As she and Jane were trimming the tree one evening, a few days before Christmas, Cordelia announced that if she continued with her funk, it would be like letting Octavia win— something she refused to do. She went back to work. She'd already gone back to eating. And she began talking about moving back to her loft. Thus far, however, she was still comfortably ensconced in Jane's guest bedroom.

Cordelia's biggest move was to change lawyers. The new one encouraged her to hire a British PI to watch the house in Northumberland where Hattie was now living. If Cordelia could prove negligence—or worse—she might have a shot at getting Hattie back.

"It was the 'little chicos' thing that got to me," said Cordelia, sniffing. She hiccuped a couple of times. "Hattie's my little chico."

"Chica."

"Whatever."

"Maybe you shouldn't play that song right now."

"But Roy is all I listen to these days! He's on my iPod. On a CD in my car. The music is . . . totally hot. It gets me going, makes me want to get up in the morning."

Jane gave her a sideways glance. "Are we talking about the same music that's playing downstairs? Roy *Rogers?*"

"Yes, Roy rocks, Jane. He kicks ass!"

"Let me ask you a question. Did Hattie like Roy Rogers?"

"Adored him. We have the same tastes, Hattie and me."

"You and a four-year-old?"

"What's your point?"

Jane was uncomfortable sitting on the edge of the bathtub. Cordelia, being as megasized as two Mae Wests, made her feel as if she was being squeezed against the wall.

"We're all down there laughing and enjoying ourselves," said Cordelia, sniffing some more, "while Hattie is probably standing in some cold, dark, drafty kitchen, asking some evil nanny if she can have another cup of gruel."

"That's Oliver Twist."

"What. *Ever!* If that PI I hired is any good at his job, I'll have the report soon. All the proof I need." A tear leaked out of the corner of her eye.

"I know it hurts," said Jane, patting Cordelia's knee.

"If it hurts, how can I be enjoying myself? Laughing at your brother's stupid jokes?"

9

"Laughter doesn't deny pain."

"Just what I need. A philosophy lesson."

"You know, Cordelia, it's almost midnight."

"So?"

"Don't you want to go downstairs and drink a toast with the rest of the family?"

"Say what you really mean. You want to be with Kenzie when the clock strikes twelve, not with me. You're afraid I'll turn into a pumpkin."

"I can't leave you, not when you're feeling so low."

Cordelia blew her nose again, then yanked the boa back from Jane and wrapped it around her neck. "It was just a momentary crash. You go down. I'll be there in a second."

Jane stood and held out her hand. "Come on. I can't ring in the new year without you. And besides, Hattie wouldn't want you to be up here all by yourself."

Cordelia thought about it. "She does love a good party."

"We'll drink a toast to her. To the two of you—that you'll be together soon."

"And one to Octavia," said Cordelia, following Jane back down the stairs. "May her inflated ego finally rupture and take the rest of her body with it."

At the stroke of midnight, everyone cried, "Happy New Year!"

Jane tugged Kenzie into the rear hallway. "Happy New Year," she whispered, an ache in her voice. She backed Kenzie up against the wall and kissed her.

When they finally came up for air, Kenzie rested her hands on Jane's shoulders. "How long we gonna stick around here?"

"Maybe another hour. That okay with you?"

"Fine." Kenzie stifled a yawn.

"You tired?"

"Dead on my feet."

"Liar," said Jane, grinning.

As they returned to the living room, the doorbell rang.

Jane's dad was just coming in from the kitchen with a fresh bottle of champagne. "Who the hell——," he grumbled, pulling a U-turn and stepping back up into the front foyer.

Silence descended as half a dozen men in heavy topcoats and two women in long formal wraps moved into the house like an ominous storm front. Jane recognized Randy Turk's curly blond head. He was a lawyer and an old friend of her father's. Everyone else was a stranger.

Ray conferred quietly with Randy for a few seconds, then turned and faced the group. "Well, everybody, it appears these people need to talk to me. Privately."

"Now?" said Jane.

"We're sorry to burst in on your celebration," said Randy, unbuttoning his coat. "But this can't wait. It won't take long. When we're done, we'll let your dad explain why we've come."

2

Ray Lawless was about to turn sixty-six. He'd been a criminal defense lawyer in St. Paul for most of his adult life. Last year, however, he'd pulled back. He'd called it semiretirement, and in terms of his caseload, that was accurate. And yet he'd been busier than ever.

Ray had finally allowed himself to nurture certain interests he'd put on the back burner for years—interests such as accepting invitations to speak at colleges and universities around the country on the topic of ending the death penalty in the United States; agreeing to chair local committees on senior housing and health care. New doors were opening to him all the time. If only someone had impressed upon him the fact that not every new goddamn door was one he needed to walk through.

Ray led the group upstairs to his study. He was curious why they'd come, but also annoyed at having his party interrupted. He'd always been ridiculously superstitious about ringing in the new year—so goes New Year's Eve, so goes the year. As he turned on the overhead light in his study, he tried to imagine why a mixed group of friends and strangers had burst in unannounced.

After sitting down behind his desk, Ray felt a little more convivial because he'd assumed the power position in the room. He couldn't offer them all chairs, so he just let it go.

Glancing at the faces, he recognized only one of the two women—Dorthea Land, a retired Episcopal bishop. Ray had known Dorthea for years, loved to argue ethics and politics with her over one of her famous homemade dinners. The man over by the window was Andrew Youngquist, CEO of AmTec, one of Minnesota's largest homegrown corporations. The fellow closing the door behind the group was Ted Azel, chairman of Azel, Lund, Malton, Feld and Snyder, the largest and most powerful corporate law firm in the state. Ray assumed the rest were equally well connected.

Randy Turk stood at the front of the pack. He'd started out as a corporate lawyer, discovered he had a gift for litigation, and made a small fortune by the time he was in his midforties. A few years ago he'd moved into civil rights and poverty law, and he was currently the chairman of Minnesota's new VoteFair Task Force. Randy was a good ten years younger than Ray. In court, he was a tiger, full of passion and conviction. Out of the spotlight, he was a quiet guy, a man with a profoundly good heart.

Randy took the lead. He briefly introduced the five men and two women, then turned back to Ray with a serious look on his face. "We're here to ask you an important question. I know this may seem a little melodramatic—"

"Just a tad," said Ray, easing back in his chair. "Why don't you cut to the chase."

13

"Fair enough," said Randy. "Did you read in the papers this morning about Theo Ludtke?"

"Our next governor? No. What about him?"

Ludtke had tossed his hat into Minnesota's political arena a year ago. He was pushing hard to win the Democratic-Farmer-Labor Party endorsement next June. Ray figured he was a shoo-in. He was charismatic, smart, politically connected, and rich.

"He had a stroke last night," said Randy. "The doctors think he'll recover, but it will take time. That means he's out of the race."

"I'm sorry to hear it. But what's it got to do with me?"

"We came here tonight because, as coincidence would have it, we were all at the same New Year's party over at the St. Paul Hotel. We got to talking about Theo, what will happen to the DFL now that we don't have a solid front-runner. We began kicking names around. Yours came up. Of course, there are others in the race, but nobody we believe who's strong enough to win."

"That's a judgment call."

"It is. In our judgment, we need someone new to step up. The eight of us, plus four others, were the ones who went to Theo last year and convinced him to run. We're hoping we can do the same with you."

"Me?" said Ray, almost laughing. "Have you lost your minds? I'm a *criminal* defense attorney. We're the scum of the earth."

"Stop it," piped up Dorthea Land. "Give people more credit. They know the legal system is based on checks and balances. Besides, you've got a reputation around this state as an honest man when it comes to ethics and the law. That's no small thing, Ray. Especially in a political campaign."

"The point is," said Ted Azel, standing next to the closed door, "what you've got to decide is, is it something you want.

14

You've got to have the fire in your gut to run. It will change your life, allow you to really make a difference in the way citizens live their lives in this state. On the other hand, it will open yours up to intense scrutiny. It will have an impact on your family, too, not all of it positive."

"Okay, just wait a damn minute here," said Ray, sitting forward and folding his hands on the desk. "I mean, sure this is flattering, but, hell, come on. Me? Why don't you run, Ted?"

"Too many skeletons in my closet. I'd never get past the door."

"What makes you think I don't have skeletons in my closet?"

"Do you?" asked Dorthea, her intense gray eyes fixed on Ray's.

"Look," said Randy. "In the past year, you've been out talking to people about things that matter to you. It's obvious you know how to create a buzz. We need that combination of qualities—your ideas, the force of your personality, your ability to move a crowd of strangers. Your ideas are all bedrock democratic ideals and you come at problems with a practical mind and a moral spirit. You get people excited. Most important, you're a born leader and everyone knows it."

"And that pretty face of yours belongs on a monument," said Ted.

Everyone laughed.

Ray shook his head. It wasn't that he'd never considered running for office. There had been a state senate seat open a few years ago that had interested him. But he knew better than to get mixed up in state politics. He'd seen other men disappear down that rabbit hole never to return.

"We realize we're taking a chance," continued Randy. "You may have no interest at all. And if that's the case, fine. But we had to find out. Whoever steps in will need to hit the ground running. We only have two months before the precinct caucuses."

"I'm not a multimillionaire like Ludtke," said Ray.

"Let us worry about the money," said Ted Azel. "Take some time. Tomorrow, the next day. Talk it over with your family. But one question we have to get an answer to tonight. Right now. It's a deal breaker. Dorthea alluded to it a second ago. Do you have anything in your life now—or your past—that would preclude you from running? We don't have much time, so you've got to be absolutely honest."

The champagne wasn't helping Ray think. "No, not that I remember. My first wife died. My second wife and I divorced last year. I'm dating someone now, but that shouldn't be an issue. I'm not a womanizer."

"Taxes?" said Ted. "Arrests? Alcohol or drug problems?"

Ray shook his head. "Never swindled anyone. Never murdered a client. On the other hand, I'm not a saint."

"Not a requirement," said Dorthea.

"I've got two great kids. One's married, one isn't. Well . . . not that my daughter wouldn't have married if our laws allowed it. She's gay. I suppose that could be a problem for some."

"Again, not an issue," said Randy.

"I'm healthy, walk two miles a day. I'm sixty-five, not getting any younger." Ray admitted to having an ego, maybe bigger than most, but he felt it had served him well. If he took something on, no matter what the final outcome, he intended to win. But politics? "I don't know."

"Think about it," said Randy.

Hearing a scratching noise behind the door, everyone turned to look.

"It's probably my dog," said Ray. "Go ahead and let him in."

When Ted drew back the door, Cordelia was crouched outside holding a drinking glass against her ear. She'd obviously been listening in on the conversation, trying to find the best spot to get the clearest sound.

"Why don't you come in and join us?" said Ray with an amused smile.

Looking like a deer caught in the headlights, Cordelia slowly stood up. "I . . . ah . . . ah . . . Oh hell. Everyone downstairs is a total wuss. They all want to know what's going on up here, but don't have the guts to do anything about it. So I said I would."

"And what did you learn?" asked Ray.

Casually tossing her boa over her shoulder, she said, "It was a little garbled, but I mainly got that you haven't swindled or murdered anyone, and that you walk two miles a day. Kind of an odd juxtaposition of facts. What I wanna know is why these people needed to come and ruin our party just to find that out. I mean, h-e-l-l-o. Haven't any of you ever heard of *phones*?"

Ray laughed, though nobody else seemed to find it funny. "You want to know why these people are here?"

"Damn straight," she said, adjusting her plunging neckline so that it didn't plunge quite so precipitously.

"These folks want me to run for governor."

"Governor of what?" she asked, still working on her dress.

"Minnesota."

She looked up. Her eyes grew huge. "That's fabulous news!" she shrieked.

Hearing the shriek, everyone who'd been waiting patiently in the living room was now rushing upstairs into the hallway.

"What's going on?" asked Jane, making her way to the front.

"Can I tell them?" asked Cordelia, looking like she was about to burst.

17

Ray smiled and shook his head. "I haven't made a decision yet, so it's probably a bit premature."

"Screw premature. Ladies and gentlemen." She turned around. "May I present to you the next governor of the great state of Minnesota, the honorable, the dashing, the father of my best friend . . . Raymond Patrick Lawless!"

Four Months Later
Early May

The Xanadu Club stopped serving lunch at two on weekdays. By three-thirty, the dining room was generally clear of customers. That's when Jane called her staff meetings, as she had today. As she stood near one of the wait stations, one of the bartenders walked up to her and said that there was a woman in the bar—Tia Masters—who said she needed to talk to Jane asap.

Jane knew who she was. Several weeks ago, Tia, a freelance feature writer for *Minnesota Today*, a major glossy monthly magazine, had contacted her about doing a story. Tia pitched the idea by saying that she wanted to concentrate on Jane Lawless, local restaurateur and general business phenom, and her two high-profile restaurants. The Lyme House, Jane's first restaurant, had been covered in several local and regional magazines, but never by *Minnesota Today*. This would also be the first feature article that would include the Xanadu Club.

Jane was thrilled, but she was also realistic. Because her dad

19

was running for governor, some of the attention focused on him was spilling over onto her. In the past two months, she'd received more requests for interviews than she had in the last ten years. It was great for business, but with each interview it seemed the personal and political questions grew more probing. She'd talked to her dad about it, but he'd kept his advice to a minimum. He'd told her to answer the questions she felt comfortable with, and pass on the rest. Be honest, he'd said, but let everyone know that she was speaking for herself, not her father. Clear boundaries. Seemed easy enough—in theory.

Jane wasn't quite sure why Tia had come today. As far as she knew, they were scheduled to meet tomorrow.

"Maybe I got my dates mixed up," Jane said, giving her business partner, Judah Johanson, a perplexed look.

Judah was more of a silent partner these days. He made it to meetings every now and then, and he spent whatever time he could at the club in the evenings, but Jane was in charge of the day-to-day functioning. Judah Johanson, as his name suggested, was a study in odd pairings. He was an anesthesiologist and an entrepreneur, half Jewish, half Norwegian, a guy who looked like a six-foot-three cross between Woody Allen and Max Von Sydow.

"You go deal with her," said Judah. "Tony and I can handle the meeting today. It will be good for me."

Tony Inazio was her executive chef. Since these staff meetings often took on a kind of rah-rah quality, with the one doing the talking taking the position of cheerleader, Jane was glad that Tony would be coming up from the kitchen in a few minutes. Judah was wonderful when it came to ideas, and even better when it came to finances, but he didn't have a lot of personal magnetism.

"If you run into any problems," said Jane, "just come get me."
Carrying her cup of coffee into the bar, she surveyed the early
happy hour crowd. She had no idea what Tia looked like, but
when she glanced over at the bartender, he nodded to an older
redheaded woman standing just inside the door.

"You must be Jane," said the woman, looking her up and down
as Jane approached.

"I thought our meeting was tomorrow."

"Oh, gosh, did I get it wrong?" She pulled her Franklin Plan-
ner out of her briefcase. "No, Tuesday, May 9th, 3:30 PM. Is this
okay? Do we need to reschedule?"

"It's fine," said Jane. "Why don't you come up to my office.
Or would you rather get a tour of the club first?"

"My husband and I came for dinner last night, so I've already
looked around. It used to be a theater, right? I remember coming
here as a child." She talked quickly and didn't wait for answers.

"Would you like something to drink before we start? Coffee?
A glass of wine?"

"Thanks, no."

Jane led the way up the curved stairway to her second-floor
office. She tried to ignore the nervous knot in her stomach, but
it wouldn't go away.

"This is nice," said Tia as she entered the small room. She immediately walked over to the round window that overlooked the
dining room below.

"That used to be the projection window," said Jane. "I had the
architect who did the redesign enlarge it so I could keep an eye
on what's happening downstairs when I'm working up here."
Viewed from the dining room, the window appeared to be part
of a large starburst pattern, all in keeping with the Art Deco
style.

21

"Did you ever see the movie *The Aviator?*" asked Tia.

"No, I don't think so."

"The decorating reminds me of the restaurant in that movie. The large palms, the colors—burgundy, chartreuse, and just a touch of turquoise."

Jane nodded for Tia to sit on a restored Biedermeier love seat, then pulled out her desk chair and turned it around. "So," she said, "what would you like to know?"

"First, would you mind if I taped the interview?" She removed a recorder from her purse and set it on a painted antique Chinese chest. "That way I don't have to take notes. I can concentrate on our conversation."

"Sure," said Jane. Only now did she realize that her clothes left something to be desired. Tomorrow she would have worn linen slacks and a blazer, or maybe leather. Today she had on frayed jeans, an old U of M T-shirt, and a pair of white Nikes. At least her hair was pulled back into a French braid.

Tia peeled the cellophane off a new audio tape. "Did you know that Jim Oberstar officially endorsed your father a few hours ago?"

James Oberstar was one of Minnesota's most influential members of the U.S. Congress.

"That's fabulous news," said Jane.

"Your dad's picking up a lot of support."

Jane couldn't tell from Tia's tone whether she was happy about it or not.

"After Ludtke dropped out," said Jane, "a lot of people claimed the front-runner status. But right now it's anybody's call who's going to win the party endorsement in June." Not that her father was counting on it, or even cared that much about it. Truth was, not since Paul Wellstone won his U.S. Senate seat in

1990 had the State Democratic Party endorsement helped a nonencumbant candidate get elected to a major office.

"Your dad seems to appeal to both party faithfuls and independents," said Tia. "That's quite a trick."

"A lot can change between now and November, but I hope he wins," said Jane. "I think he'd make a great governor."

"Spoken like a loyal daughter."

"No, it's more than that, but maybe we should move on."

After Tia pushed the tape into the recorder, she seemed to hesitate. She scrutinized Jane's face for a few seconds, and only then did she remove a small notebook from her purse and open it. "Okay," she said, slipping on her reading glasses. She pressed the Record button. "In doing my research, I found out that you've been a restaurateur for eighteen years. How did it all start? What drew you to the business?"

Jane shifted in her chair. "Well, I lived in England until I was nine, and then we moved back to the States—to Minnesota. My mother died when I was thirteen. Right after that, I went back to England. I spent the next couple of years living with my aunt Beryl and uncle Jimmy. Jimmy had a restaurant in Poole. I worked there after school and on weekends. I started by running errands, stocking, doing some salad prep, but before I left to come back home, I was working the line. It wasn't elegant food, just basic restaurant fare, but I learned a lot—loved every minute of it. Initially, I was put off by the crazy mix of people who worked for my uncle, but in time, they became friends. I still write to some of them. The restaurant business seems to attract people who don't fit anywhere else. Cowboys, loners, extreme extroverts or introverts, people who'd rather die than work your basic nine-to-five."

"Does that include you?" asked Tia.

23

"I suppose, although a forty-hour workweek would look pretty good to me right about now."

"I do all the cooking at home. My husband likes it that way. Sometimes, just between you and me, I get a little sick of it. I think of cooking as a truly feminine occupation. You know, something a woman should know how to do. But you're more of a business-woman than you are a cook, aren't you. I assume you don't spend much time in the kitchen. It's not really in your nature."

"My *nature*? Actually, I feel more at home in a commercial kitchen than I do anywhere else on earth. I don't know how to explain it to you, but . . . the smell of a commercial kitchen, it's something I can't describe, but it excites me."

"Did your father put up the financial backing for your first restaurant?"

"No," said Jane. It was a common misconception. "After I graduated from college, I cooked at an upscale restaurant in downtown Minneapolis for a couple of years, just to see if I was really serious about restaurant work. Again, I loved it. I knew nothing about the realities of running a restaurant, so I spoke to the owner and he agreed to let me work the front of the house. I stayed there for two more years, and at the same time I got my cheffing degree and took a bunch of business classes. I talked to dozens of people, all experts in the field. I designed a business plan I thought would not only work, but would get me the money I needed when I applied for a loan."

"All smooth sailing?" asked Tia.

Jane laughed. "Everything—and I mean *everything*—has been a struggle. I've made tons of mistakes over the years, but I've also learned. That's partly why I wanted to create a new restaurant."

"You found an . . . interesting . . . location for the club," said Tia. "Seems you've got a large gay following. Of course, Uptown is known as a local gay Mecca."

"I suppose. There are lots of ethnic restaurants, too. And it's become sort of a hot spot for great indie shops, indie movies. If you walk around here at night, you'll see a little of everything. I guess I'd call it culturally diverse."

"I'm sure that's more politically correct."

"Actually, I think it's just more accurate," said Jane.

"You're gay, right?" asked Tina.

She nodded.

"I'm curious. Your father is running for the highest political office in the state. Has your sexual orientation presented him with any problems?"

"You'd have to ask him."

"Okay. But . . . what's your father's opinion of say, gay marriage? I've never heard him make a comment about it."

Tia had gone through the motions of interviewing her, but now she was headed where she really wanted to go. Jane's instincts had been right to be wary.

"Again, you'd have to ask him."

"But surely you know."

She shrugged. "I can only speak for myself."

"Fine, then tell me your opinion."

"I'm not sure what this has to do with my restaurants, but I'd be happy to tell you. I think it's beyond ridiculous that rapists and murderers, child molesters and torturers can marry and I can't."

Tia cleared her throat. "But doesn't it ever bother you that being a homosexual is, well, simply not normal?"

"That's an opinion."

"It's happens to be *God's* opinion."

25

"Then maybe you should go interview God." She started to get up.

"I'm sorry, Jane. Please. I didn't mean to upset you."

Like hell. "Being gay is a variation, Tia. Like left-handedness. Or color blindness. I think Alfred Kinsey proved that a long time ago."

"Oh, yes, Kinsey. I saw the movie. I know you may not like what I'm saying, but . . . how can you people call yourselves 'gay'? I mean, you can't be happy."

There was so much to respond to in that question, Jane didn't even know where to start. "Do you have any gay friends or family members?"

"Are you suggesting that if I got to know some of you, that I'd change my mind?"

"No. Actually, I don't think that."

"Since we've moved to a more personal level, let's keep it there for a minute. Do you have a . . . significant other?"

"Yes."

"Have you been together long?"

"A couple years."

"When did you first choose the gay lifestyle?"

"When did you first choose the straight lifestyle?"

Tia looked at her over the top rim of her glasses. "Cute."

"It's a valid question."

"I didn't choose to be straight. You know that."

"I didn't choose to be gay. And by the way, it's not a lifestyle. It's my *life*."

Tia adjusted her glasses. "You people are so sensitive."

Jane had just about had enough. "Look, if this interview is going to be nothing more than a veiled attack on my sexuality, we can stop right now."

26

Tia held up her hand. "We'll table that thread. But I still have a couple more questions. Growing up, did you feel your dad was a good father? Did he make time for you and your brother?"

Jane's eyes rose to the ceiling. "Yes. Always."

"How would you describe your dad?"

"Decent," said Jane. "Human. Unsentimental. A guy who likes a good fight."

"Do you think you're like him?"

"In some ways."

"More like him than your mother?"

Talk about an agenda. Jane almost laughed out loud, not that it was funny. "No."

"You have a brother, Peter. Would you say your family is close?"

"Yes."

Tia pulled off her glasses. "One-word answers don't make for interesting interviews, Jane."

She forced herself to relax. "You have to understand, I've always been a very private person. With my dad running for office, I know I should get used to people asking a lot of personal questions, but I doubt I ever will. And when it comes to my father's views—on anything—if you've got questions, you'll have to ask him."

"All right. Fair enough. But could you talk a little more about your family life when you were growing up?"

Jane took a deep breath. "I guess I feel incredibly blessed. We lived in St. Paul. My dad still lives in the house my brother and I grew up in. As a family, we had our disagreements, our ups and downs, but we loved each other. I think that's what being a family teaches you. You can disagree, but you can still love."

"Now there's a nice quote. Good for you, Jane." She flipped

27

to the next page of her notes. She asked a few more questions about Jane's early life, then moved on to the Lyme House. Ten minutes later, she announced, "I think I've got some great information here, but if you'd indulge me one more minute for one last question?" Tapping a long red fingernail against her notebook, she said, "Do you think your father will support things like the Gay Pride Parade?"

Jane's eyes slid right. "We're done."

Around seven, Jane left the club, headed for the airport. Cordelia's plane was scheduled to arrive at 7:35. This was Cordelia's second trip across the pond since the beginning of the year. Her first trip to England, in early February, had been a spur-of-the-moment decision, which turned into a disaster. Octavia, her husband, Radley, and Hattie were gone from the house in Northumberland, the only address Cordelia had. The staff refused to give out any information about the family, where they were, when they would be back. Cordelia had booked a room in the nearest town and waited for over a week. She eventually gave up and flew home.

This time, however, her private investigator had been monitoring the Northumberland house. It was still a Cordelia-esque last-minute decision to get on the plane, but at least there was a better chance the family would be there. Jane offered to make the flight with her, but alas, Cordelia had booked the last seat. That was three days ago. Jane had received an e-mail from her this morning. It contained nothing but the return flight number and her time of arrival.

The traffic on the Crosstown was worse than Jane had expected, so when she pulled up to the curb on the arrival deck, Cordelia was already waiting outside, looking exhausted and utterly forlorn.

"I thought you'd never get here," she muttered, hoisting her bag into the backseat.

"Traffic." Jane studied her friend as she got herself settled. "How did you get those scratches on your face? Did Octavia do that?"

"No."

"Then what happened? Did you see Hattie? Did you get Octavia to change her mind?"

Cordelia pinched the bridge of her nose and leaned her head back. "None of the above." She motioned with her arm. "Drive on. I will tell all."

As they eased back into traffic, Cordelia sighed. "At least the PI had it right. They were home this time. I rented a car and drove up from London, got there just before nine in the evening— whenever that was. I'm all turned around for time. I knocked on the front door and believe it or not, Octavia answered. She rushed at me like a she-devil! Refused to let me in. You would have been proud of me, Jane. I started off trying to be conciliatory, but that's wasted on my sister.

"She pushed me out onto the steps and closed the door. Said that Hattie was in bed and she wouldn't wake her. I said fine, I'd come back in the morning. But oh, no. That wasn't going to happen. She insisted that I was responsible for turning Hattie into a weird little kid. That she kept asking for things like Brie, cornichons, fondu, foie gras, Steak Diane, fuffernutter 'sandwishes.' I responded that I took Hattie's culinary education seriously. That's when Octavia said, 'And what's all this crap about Mildred Pierce? And Bette, and Katherine?' "

"Bette Davis and Katherine Hepburn," said Jane.

"Of course," said Cordelia, flinging her arms in the air. "Any nincompoop should know who she was talking about. I told

Octavia that film noir was very important to Hattie. That's when she said my influence was pernicious. Pernicious! Me! That I'd turned Hattie into a Goth. Well, you and I both know that Hattie's love of black is only rivaled by her love of pink. That's who she is. I didn't *make* her that way. But Octavia thinks Hattie needs time away from me so that she can develop normally. She admitted that Hattie had cried for days when they brought her to England. That she talked about me nonstop. I mean, is this woman insane? Of course she did. She missed me. I'd been her mother figure for two freakin' years. But Octavia thought it was a sign of some sort of terrible instability or mental weakness. She's jealous, Jane. I could see the green glowing in her evil little eyes."

"You're probably right."

"Of course I'm right."

"So what happened?"

"She told me to leave and slammed the door in my face. Well, I wasn't going to let her stop me. I'd come all that way, I was *going* to see Hattie. There was a trellis on the side of the house that led up to a second-floor balcony. Don't you find it annoying that trellises are always so sturdy in movies but that in real life they aren't? I started to climb it, determined to get inside, but halfway up it gave way and I ended up in some brambles that Octavia had planted just for me!"

"I doubt that she——"

"After I picked myself up and dusted myself off, I drove to the nearest hospital to get my cuts treated. And then I drove back to London."

"Did you get any sleep?"

"On the plane."

"Have you eaten?"

"I don't remember."

30

A bad sign. "Do you want to come back to my house, or should I drop you off at your loft?"

"I can't be alone right now, Jane. Let's go to your place."

After a hot soak in the bathtub, a stiff glass of black cherry soda, and a bowl of homemade chicken soup, Cordelia was feeling a bit better. Jane could tell because she wasn't clenching and unclenching her fists every few seconds.

"What's your next move?" asked Jane, cleaning the dishes off the kitchen table.

"I don't know. Honestly, Janey, I'm not sure I have one."

"What about the investigator?"

"He hasn't been able to dig up anything I can use. I should probably fire him."

It did seem pretty hopeless, although Jane knew enough not to say that out loud.

Cordelia drifted off to her bedroom a few minutes later, saying it had been a long day and she had a headache.

While the dog did his final duties of the night out in the backyard, Jane wiped down the kitchen counters and turned on the light above the stove. Once Mouse was back inside, she checked to make sure everything was locked up tight and then went upstairs to take a shower. On her way past Cordelia's room she heard a sound so soft and muffled that at first, she wasn't sure what it was. And then she realized it was crying. She pressed a hand to the door and closed her eyes.

"It's not nice to listen at other people's doors," came Cordelia's voice.

"Are you okay? Can I get you anything?"

"No." She sniffed. "But thanks."

"If you need me—"

"Go to bed, Janey. I love you."

4

Just checking in," hollered Cordelia. "Are you at the club?"

"No, the Lyme House," Jane hollered back, holding the cell phone away from her ear. She was sitting cross-legged on the hood of her Mini in the back parking lot. She could hardly hear Cordelia over all the background noise. "What are you listening to? Iron Butterfly?"

"I sometimes play 'In-A-Gadda-Da-Vida' when I'm setting up for poker night. Gets me in the mood."

"You're going ahead with it? I thought maybe you'd cancel."

The second Tuesday of every month, Cordelia played poker with her theater pals. Jane didn't like card games so she rarely attended.

"Why? I can't spend all my time crying. Besides, being around friends will be good for me. By the way, you're invited," she yelled.

"Gee thanks," Jane yelled back. Considering it was her house, it was extremely kind of her. "But I'll be home late. FYI, I liked Roy Rogers better."

"No you didn't." As the song in the background changed to "Smoke on the Water" by Deep Purple, Cordelia said, "Better go. I've got some of my famous black bean chili on the stove. Wouldn't want it to burn. Bye, babe."

"Don't you give any of that to Mouse," yelled Jane, clutching the phone tight to her ear. "Did you hear me? *No chili for the dog!*"

As Jane trotted down the restaurant's back steps to her basement office, her cell phone rang again. This time it was her father.

"Janey, I need to talk to you and your brother, tonight if possible."

"You sound upset."

"It's nothing we can't handle. I asked Peter to meet us at the Lyme House pub at seven. That work for you?"

"That's perfect."

"See you soon."

Jane scooped fresh popcorn into a paper bowl as she led Peter to her favorite table in the back room, the one nearest the fire. This early in the evening, the table was still free. A waiter appeared almost instantly with two longneck Grain Belts. He set them on the table and then asked if Jane wanted anything else.

"Thanks, Rich. We're great," she said, giving him a smile.

Jane and her brother sat and talked until their father finally breezed in a few minutes after seven.

For all his traveling around the state, the late nights and bad food, Jane thought he looked great. Campaigning clearly agreed with him.

Ray gave them each a kiss on the tops of their heads, then

pulled out a chair and sat down. His silver hair, usually a little shaggy, had been styled. He'd also lost a little weight.

For the past four months, he'd been crisscrossing the state, making speeches and doing radio and TV interviews. Sometime in the next couple of weeks, he was scheduled to tour southern Minnesota again. To save money, he was using his Cessna to get himself around, usually taking along his press secretary and sometimes his campaign manager. He always had people on the ground ready to meet him and whisk him off somewhere for a speech or dinner.

"You want something to drink?" asked Jane.

He glanced at the beers. "No, I better not. I've got a meeting later."

"So, give us an update," said Peter, pulling the popcorn closer. "Oh, hey, I heard about the Oberstar endorsement. Congratulations."

"This is really happening, isn't it," said Jane.

"You bet it is," said her father. "I hopped a train a few months ago that's picking up steam. It surprises me, too. Coming in late the way I did has proved to be an unexpected advantage. I took the media off guard. It's taking my opponents some time to lock and load, but it will get nasty before we're all done, you can count on that."

Jane thought back to her interview with Tia Masters. She had no idea how she'd be painted in the article, and no control over it. The lack of control drove her nuts.

"Actually, " said Ray, "we had our first shot across the bow today."

"What?" asked Peter.

Ray's gaze roamed the room. "Look, you're going to hear this sooner or later, so I wanted it to come from me, not some newspaper. I'd completely forgotten about it. It happened over thirty

34

years ago—and it's never happened again. It was shortly after your mother died. I was so depressed," said Ray. "It was a terrible time—for all of us, I know. I should have handled things better."

"Don't," said Jane.

"No, let me say this, Janey. I need to take responsibility. I was the adult and I blew it, in so many ways. I started drinking too much. It was stupid, I know, but I suppose I'm not the first guy who's used alcohol to anesthetize his pain. Not that I'm excusing myself. I got stopped a couple of times for drunk driving. And now some reporter who checked my records is about to print a story in one of the local papers. I don't think it will hurt me much, because, like I said, it was so long ago and it never happened again, but it could hurt you two if you heard about it in the wrong way. I care about you more than anything else in my life. So," he said, leaning in to the table, "there it is. That's my story. I'm sorry if it embarrasses you."

"Good grief, Dad," said Peter, pushing his beer away. "You're human. Don't give it another thought."

Ray pressed his lips together and nodded. "Enough said. We don't need to dredge that awful time back up again."

"Do you know which paper the story will appear in?" asked Jane.

"The *Star Tribune*. Probably tomorrow."

They sat for a moment, all of them gazing into the fire.

"Either of you hungry?" asked Jane. "We've got some great shepherd's pie on the menu tonight."

Peter rubbed the back of his neck. "Actually, since we're in truth-telling mode here, I've got something I need to get off my chest. I'm afraid it's not good news." Pulling his beer back in front of him, he said, "I lost my job."

Jane turned to face him. "When? Why?"

"It happened in late February."

"What happened?" said Ray. "Be specific."

35

"They're downsizing at the station. It's the economy, partly, and partly the new general manager. We didn't exactly hit it off."

"Did they give you some kind of severance package?" asked Jane.

"Yeah, I'm okay for now."

"What are your plans?" asked Ray.

"I've been looking for a cameraman job in this market but it just isn't going to happen. The reason I'm telling you now is that I've been offered a job in Oklahoma City. It doesn't pay all that well, and Sigrid isn't exactly thrilled to move to Oklahoma, but I'm thinking of taking it."

"What about her job?" asked Jane. "She's been at that family practice clinic for quite a few years now."

"To be honest"—he looked down at his hands—"I'm not sure she's coming with me."

Jane and her dad exchanged glances.

"I thought you two had worked out your problems," said Ray.

"We called a cease-fire, but no, we never really settled anything. It's hard to talk about, Dad. There are things you don't know, things I can't tell either of you."

"Because Sigrid asked you not to?" said Jane.

Peter nodded.

What Jane did know was that a couple years ago, Peter and Sigrid had split up. Peter desperately wanted to start a family, but Sigrid didn't. They loved each other—that was never in question—but they were at an impasse. There was no middle ground in this kind of decision. If they stayed together, one of them would eventually have to give up or give in.

"What if you didn't take that job?" asked Ray, removing his glasses and using Jane's paper napkin to polish the lenses. "If you stayed in town, would you and Sigrid still split up?"

"I don't know. But I've got to make a living. And I'd like to

36

continue doing it as a photographer. There's nothing in town for me at any of the stations. Believe me, I've looked."

Ray finished cleaning his glasses and put them back on. Folding his arms over his chest, he said, "What if I asked you to come work on the campaign with me?"

Peter laughed. "Right. I'm sure you need your son, the unemployed cameraman, to follow you around."

"Actually, it might be worth thinking about. But beyond that, maybe we could figure out something more hands on, like working in the press office, or hey—Del's been screaming about needing an assistant."

Delavon Green was Ray's campaign manager. Randy Turk had suggested him because he'd been working on the Ludtke campaign so he already knew the political terrain. Jane had met him a couple times and was impressed by his professionalism and his political savvy. He was also charming as hell, which came in handy when you had to deal with people all day long. Delavon was African American, had grown up in the projects in Detroit. He'd worked on a number of other political campaigns—several in Illinois, a few in Michigan and Ohio, and the last two in Minnesota.

"I'd have to think about it—ask Sigrid what she thought," said Peter.

"Fine," said Ray. "But just remember, I'm not talking volunteer here, I'm talking paid position."

"Does the word 'nepotism' mean anything to you?" asked Jane, laughing.

"It's the way the world works," said Ray. "You get hired for jobs two ways. You either know somebody or you stand in line and pray. Let me talk to Del." He checked his watch. "I've gotta run, but I'll get back to you in a day or two. Don't make any final decisions until you hear from me."

37

5

Randy couldn't remember a time when he wasn't lonely. As a kid growing up in a small prairie town in the northwestern part of Iowa, he didn't have many friends. Partly, it was his own nature. He never felt as if he fit anywhere. But mostly it was because he spent so much of his time defending his brother, Ethan, who was, in the parlance of the day, considered "slow."

Ethan was big for his age, three years older than Randy, and he looked like he could crush rocks with his bare hands. Nobody dared say anything to his face, but behind his back it was a free-for-all.

Ethan had trouble with math and English, didn't always understand the rules to certain games. He was such an easy target, such a big fat joke, that kids Randy did call friends would eventually say something nasty about him. Many nights Randy came home bruised from a fight, or furious after an argument. People said he had a temper, but that wasn't it. He just couldn't stand it when his brother was the punch line to every joke.

After a while, Randy assumed that loneliness was simply the price he had to pay for protecting someone he loved. And yet he ached to have friends like other kids did. He wasn't athletic. Didn't like sports. By the time he was in high school, there were a few other misfits he palled around with, but it was all pretty superficial. What Randy wouldn't understand, couldn't until years later, was that this yearning for a deeper connection with other guys his age would set his life on a course he might have fled from had he understood the ramifications.

Around seven on Tuesday evening, Randy pulled his white Volvo into the gravel drive next to his home on the outskirts of Marine on St. Croix. He sat for a moment with the engine running, gazing at the house. It was four stories of glass and steel nestled into the woods on nine acres. Several decks jutted off the sides. He'd worked with an architect to get his dream down on paper—an adult version of a tree house. This was to be the home he and his wife would live in for the rest of their lives. But the house was empty now. Sherrie had moved out a month ago, taking with her not only their teenage daughter, but most of what was left of his heart. Since that time, he and his brother had knocked around the place like two aimless drifters, coming together occasionally for meals and then going their separate ways.

As Randy cut the motor and got out, his cell phone rang. Flipping it open, he leaned against the front fender and said hello.

"Randy, it's Del. We got a problem."

"You mean the drunk driving thing? I've already heard. I don't think it will be a big issue. Happened too long ago."

"Not that. Something else. We gotta talk—and not on the phone."

"When?"

"Now. Where are you?"

"I just got home."

"Stay there. I'm not far away. I'll be there in a few minutes."

Randy removed his briefcase from the backseat, stopped for a moment to make sure he'd brought home one particular file, then headed up the walk to the front door. It was a cool spring evening, the sky above him a vault of deep blue. Loosening his tie, he dashed up the stairs to the silent kitchen and grabbed a beer from the refrigerator. On his way out to the deck, he checked to see if he had any voice mail messages. There was no blinking red light.

Randy thought about going down to the deck off the living room with his drink. His favorite chaise was down there, but he decided against it. Upstairs, he could watch the sun set over the meadow. Besides, Del would be here soon. Ethan was probably around somewhere, up in his room watching TV, or down in his workshop working on a bird feeder. He sold them at the local hardware store. Not that he needed the money. Randy made more money than he knew what to do with. He'd offered the house to his wife, but she didn't want it—probably because she didn't want anything that reminded her of him.

Randy was angry, but then he had a right to be. His carefully constructed life had come apart and he didn't even know why. He'd been a faithful husband, a good father. Sure, he was moody sometimes, but who the hell wasn't.

Hearing footsteps on the deck stairs, he glanced down at the three-stall garage, but the only car in the drive was his own. It had to be his brother. Except when he looked over at the steps, the man coming up wasn't Ethan. "Larry?" said Randy, standing, surprise and delight spreading across his face.

"If it ain't the professor," said Larry with a grin.

They grabbed each other, slapped backs, then moved apart.

"Let me look at you," said Larry, holding Randy at arm's length. "How you been, man? Seems like life's been treatin' you pretty good. Where's Sherrie? I got a present for her. A new perfume she's gonna love."

Randy wiped a hand across his mouth. "She left me."

"No. When?"

"A month ago."

"Fuck, man, that stinks." He knocked Randy on the shoulder. "She'll be back."

"I don't know."

"Sure she will. Listen, I'm six months older than you are, boy. Trust your elders. She'll be back. Hey, maybe I should go talk to her. Me and Sherrie are tight. I could put in a good word for you."

"I don't think so. She's pretty angry right now."

"Well, then, best to give her some time to cool off."

Randy leaned against the railing, studying his old friend. Larry was rail thin inside his leather biker jacket. He had a graying pony tail, a long Fu Manchu mustache, and a surly look on his long, pockmarked face. "What are you doing in Minnesota?"

"Just travelin' through. I got sick of the heat, thought I'd come see my old buddies."

"You're still in Phoenix, right?"

"Yeah, but I gave up the apartment. I need a change. Thought I might settle somewhere in the North Country. Clean air. Clean water. Clean living."

"Right," said Randy. "That'll be the day."

Larry had been bartending for the last few years, not a particularly smart choice for a guy with a drinking and drug problem. He'd fought the good fight against his demons trying to get clean, attending AA meetings, doing an occasional stint in rehab, but nothing seemed to work. In the early nineties, he'd served four years in Douglas State Prison for aggravated assault. He had a temper that he didn't control very well, especially when he was high.

But none of that mattered to Randy. The blast-furnace pressure of war had formed powerful bonds. When he returned home from his tour in Vietnam, Randy was no longer a friendless loner. His new buddies might not have been the kind of guys he would have chosen under normal circumstances, but Nam had been a time in his life when none of the old rules mattered and nothing made sense except staying alive.

"Del's on his way over."

"No shit?" said Larry with a crooked grin. "That's cool."

They both leaned against the railing, looking out across the meadow. Larry lit a cigarette and offered the pack to Randy, but Randy shook his head.

"Quit."

"Yeah, I should, too, but I gotta have some vices or it wouldn't be me."

"Where are you staying?"

"With you."

"Perfect," said Randy, looking back at the house looming above them. "Take two or three bedrooms. I got nothing but space."

"One'll be fine," said Larry, blowing smoke circles into the twilight air. "Honest, I needed a·break bad. There's a woman down in Phoenix thinks I'm gonna marry her. You and I both know that ain't gonna happen."

Randy laughed. "You're running from a marriage ceremony?"

"Damn straight, I am. No shame in that." As his eyes panned

more carefully across the meadow, he took a deep hit off the cigarette. "What's it been? Three years since we last seen each other?"

"Sounds about right."

He fell silent, staring at the glowing tip of his smoke. "You're gonna think old Larry's gone soft, but I missed you, man. You and Del. I know this seems weird, but I miss the old days—our time in Nam. You ever go back there in your mind?"

"It still wakes me up at night."

"Yeah. I hear you."

"My wife told me I'm stuck in the past. Makes me awfully quiet sometimes. I guess I'm not much fun to be around."

"Hell, you're a hoot. Best drinking buddy I ever had."

Randy looked away.

"We were the lucky ones," said Larry. "We came back. We survived."

They both turned at the sound of a car motor.

Del was pulling his black Highlander up next to Randy's Volvo. As he opened the door to get out, the automatic floodlight on the side of the garage came on.

"I don't believe it," whispered Larry. "His hair's almost as gray as mine. We're gettin' old, man. I hate it. I wanna live forever."

As Del trudged up the steps to the deck, Larry pressed his fingers around the lit end of the cigarette, pocketing what was left of it. "Hey there, my brutha," he said, opening his arms wide.

Del took one look at him and broke into a hearty laugh. "You old piece of dog meat, what are you doin' here?"

They did some backslapping, some hand shaking.

"Just passin' through," said Larry. "Just passin' through."

"Anybody hungry?" asked Randy. "I could order us a pizza. Seems like we should celebrate."

"You mean somebody actually delivers way out here in the boonies?" asked Larry. "They do it by horse and buggy?"

Del laid a hand on the back of Larry's neck. At six foot seven, Del towered over everyone. "Can you believe it? All these years later and we're still standing. We must be made of kryptonite to live through what we did."

"Purely true," said Larry, shaking his head.

"And you two are still my best friends. My brothers," said Randy.

"Mom always liked you best," said Larry, punching Del's arm, putting up his fists.

Watching them spar, Randy felt something familiar stir inside. The gray hair didn't matter, neither did the years. Around these guys he was young again. He wanted to laugh, to drink too much, sleep too late, smoke and swear and argue. He wanted to suck in the sweet night air and never forget how much he owed them.

They talked for a few more minutes, swapped a few old stories, laughed at a few old jokes. When they finally came inside they found Randy's brother, Ethan, in the kitchen standing by the refrigerator eating refried beans from a Tupperware bowl. He'd turned on the light under the stove, but the rest of the house was dark.

"Hey, Ethan," said Larry, closing the sliding door behind him.

Ethan had grown into a bear of a man. Six four, 260 pounds. He looked like an aging linebacker. His hair was still thick and blond, like Randy's, only Ethan's hair was straight, no waves. He kept active because Randy had helped him organize a lawn and snow service. He took care of several dozen properties in the area. He couldn't do the billing, but he loved to be outside doing the work. And he lived to drive his truck.

44

"Hi," said Ethan, talking and chewing at the same time.

"Say, Ethan," said Randy, moving behind the island counter. "Why don't you take Larry upstairs and get him settled in one of the guest bedrooms. Del and I need a few minutes to discuss some business."

"He's staying?" said Ethan, nodding to Larry as he stuffed more beans into his mouth.

"For a while," said Randy.

"I want Sherrie to come home," said Ethan, sounding like a little boy who'd lost his mom.

"I know. I do, too. Now come on, help me out here. Maybe you could give Larry a hand with his bags."

"I only got one," said Larry. "Left it down by the front door."

"Where'd you put your car?" asked Randy.

"I hitchhiked."

"All the way from Arizona?"

"Had to sell my wheels a while back."

"Come on, Larry," said Ethan, pivoting with a tired sigh and walking out of the kitchen. "Maybe you better take a shower 'cause you sure smell like a lawn mower."

Larry turned back to Randy and Del and shrugged.

"We got new towels," said Ethan's disappearing voice. "Blue and green ones. I like the green ones best."

Randy's office was on the first level, on the other side of the house from the living room. It was comfortably furnished with leather chairs and an Indian ivory and ebony desk, one Randy had found in an antiques store in New Orleans. The room was small enough to seem warm even with the abandoned feel of the rest of the house. Three walls were filled with books, most of them law books. Across from the desk, a glass wall looked out on the woods, where blue twilight had finally deepened into night.

Randy switched on the desk lamp and found his address book. He phoned the pizza place and ordered two extra-large extra-everything pizzas. As he set the phone down, he said, "So tell me what's so important that you had to drive all the way out here."

Del dropped into a chair. "We got a reporter on our tail."

"*Our* tail? This isn't about the campaign?"

Del ran a weary hand over his hair. "No. I don't know the details, but from what I hear, it could be bad."

"We got so many ways for things to be bad, you better be more specific." Randy sat down himself, eased back into the darkness.

"Sue."

It was the one word Randy feared more than any other. "It's just an old story, Del. Nothing happened then and nothing will happen now." Unconsciously, he began to knead his wedding ring between his fingers.

"I wish I had your confidence."

It wasn't confidence, thought Randy. It felt more like desperation.

"The reporter's name is Melanie Gunderson. She works for *City Beat*—that weekly pulp. That's all I know about her, but I've got a bunch of feelers out. I'll have more by tomorrow morning. Man, I don't need this. I'm already up to my ears in campaign shit. We gotta do something."

"Like what? What are you suggesting? That we have her whacked?" He laughed.

Del didn't. "I got a bad feeling about this. Nobody's touched that story since the trial. And now this."

"Sounds like you boys got some heavy problems," said Larry,

leaning against the open office door. He ambled into the room and took the chair next to Del.

"How much of that did you hear?" asked Randy.

"Enough. Look, boys, if I understand it right, this concerns me, too."

Randy gave a slow nod.

"Either of you got any serious cash?"

"Why?" asked Del. "You think we can buy her off?"

"It's worth a try. She don't know me from Adam. I don't look nothing like I did back then. What if I contact her and offer her, say, twenty thousand to back away from the story. All I'd tell her is that I'm an interested party, a guy who don't wanna see innocent people get hurt." He shrugged. "Everybody's got a price."

Inside his perfectly pressed Oxford cloth shirt, Randy was beginning to sweat. He glanced at Del. "What do you think?"

"I haven't got twenty thousand dollars."

"But I do," said Randy. And yet his gut reaction was that it was a mistake.

"You boys mull it over," said Larry, stretching his arms high over his head. "I'll be kickin' around here for a few days. Whatever you decide is fine by me."

6

Is that you, honey?" called Sigrid from the bathroom.

Peter had just come through the front door of their apartment. "How come you're home so early," he called back, feeling momentarily panicked. He searched the top of the credenza in the dining room, looking for the day's mail.

"My last client canceled," called Sigrid. "Hey, what do you say we go out for a drink, maybe some food. I know it's late—"

"Sounds good to me."

"I just got out of the shower. I'll be there in a sec."

Peter darted into the kitchen, looked around, then returned to the dining room. His eyes cruised the living room until he saw the stack of letters on the coffee table. Sweeping them up, he turned away from the hallway door and flipped through them. If Sigrid had brought the mail in, she might have already found the letter— if it had come. On the other hand, if she'd seen it, read the contents, she would've been waiting for him with a loaded shotgun.

The letter he'd been waiting for was at the bottom of the stack—unopened. He quickly stuffed it in his pants pocket, then sat down on the couch, depositing the rest of the mail on the end table next to him. He couldn't believe he'd nearly blown it. Retrieving the mail before Sigrid got home wasn't usually a problem. When his dad had called and asked to meet him at the Lyme House, he'd assumed that he'd still get home before she did. So much for dumb assumptions. If Sigrid discovered what he was up to, he wasn't sure what she'd do. That's why he couldn't let her find out, not until he had all the information he needed.

"Did you see the letter from that TV station in Maine?" asked Sigrid, coming into the room. She was wearing a blue terry cloth bathrobe, drying her short blond hair with a towel. "I didn't open it. I thought it might be another job offer."

A muscle twitched in his neck.

"Something wrong?" asked Sigrid, standing over him. She let the towel drop to her shoulders.

"I glanced at the mail, but I didn't see it."

"Here," she said. She bent over the stack and found it for him.

"Maine, huh?" He worked to keep his hands steady as he opened it. After reading the letter, he handed it to her. "You want to move to Bangor?"

"Sounds better than Oklahoma. I hate hot weather."

"Are you saying you'd actually consider moving out East?" It sounded like the end of the earth to him.

Sigrid rubbed the back of his hair with the towel. "I don't know, Peter."

"Let's not go there tonight, okay?"

"There was another letter for you. I think the postmark was New Jersey."

As she reached for the stack again, he caught her arm. "And

49

no more talking about my lack of employment, either. Let's just have a nice, relaxing evening."

Her expression softened. She sat down next to him, laid her head on his chest. "That's sounds good to me. How come you're home so late?"

"My dad wanted to meet with me and Jane at the Lyme House. Hey, get this. What if I told you I might have a job offer here in town?"

She gazed up at him with a puzzled look. "That would be great, but I thought you'd checked out every station and nobody was hiring."

"I wouldn't be working for a TV station. Dad wants me to come work for his campaign. He said he has to check it out, but he's pretty sure he can offer me a paid position."

"Wow, Peter, that would be a fantastic opportunity for you."

He pulled her closer to him, felt the warmth of her body through the thin fabric of his shirt. "I love you, Siggy. I don't ever want to lose you." He tipped her chin up. And then he kissed her.

Right about then they both forgot about dinner.

The clock on the nightstand read 3:27 AM. Easing out of bed, Peter found his pants hanging over a chair. He carried them into the bathroom and turned on the light. Digging the letter out of his pocket, he tore the back flap open and removed an invoice with a scribbled note attached.

"Shit," whispered Peter, reading through it quickly. This wasn't what he'd expected. He'd hired a private investigator to locate and then send him a copy of the adoption papers Sigrid had signed ten years ago. The lawyer who'd brokered the deal in New Jersey, Vaughn Cabot, had drawn them up. Sigrid said she would never forget the names of the people who'd adopted her baby—Matt and Carrie Tanhauer, residents of New York. Cabot told her they'd named the baby Margaret. Peter had never met Cabot, but it didn't matter. He loathed him on general principle.

Glancing back down at the note, he read it again:

No birth certificate on record. And no adoption record in either New Jersey or New York. That means whatever your wife signed was never filed. Found an address for Matthew Tanhauer in Manhattan. Don't know if it's the same guy who adopted Margaret, but will investigate further if you want. Tanhauer's address is—
570 Parkway West
New York, NY 10010
Unlisted phone number. I included an invoice, in case you don't want to pursue this further.

—Shifflet

The invoice was for five hours' work at $125 an hour.

"Margaret," whispered Peter, sitting down on the side of the tub. In the past few months, with little to do but brood about his life, finding Margaret had become an obsession. Margaret was the reason Sigrid refused to have another child. Nobody in the family knew about the baby Sigrid had given birth to while living in New York—nobody except Peter. Everyone thought Sigrid had gone off to the Big Apple after graduating from high school to "find herself." It was such a hopeless cliché, people laughed and then let it go. Sigrid had returned home the following year, entered the University of Minnesota in the spring, and gone on with her public life as if nothing had happened. But privately, it was a different matter.

51

Because of Margaret, Peter and Sigrid would never have a child together. That knowledge clawed at his insides until he felt like screaming. The one thing he wanted most in the world—a child with the woman he loved—was never going to happen.

It wasn't that Peter was angry at Sigrid. Far from it. When she'd come clean, told him why she refused to get pregnant, he was horrified to hear how her high school boyfriend had treated her, how Sigrid had agonized over her decision, whether to abort or give birth to the child, whether to keep her or put her up for adoption. In the end, Sigrid said she found the best family she could to raise her child and had given her up. Peter tried to make her see that what she'd done was the best thing possible for both of them, but Sigrid didn't agree. Of course she knew that as a young, single mother with no skills and no education, she could easily have ruined the child's life. Or the child could have ruined hers. She'd done the best with the cards she'd been dealt, tried to act responsibly, but she also said she had to be honest. Her decision was selfish. She'd put herself and her future before her child's.

Sigrid had only seen Margaret briefly in the hospital, but after carrying her for nine months, the sight of her cemented an already strong bond. The idea of hurting her a second time was too much. She asked Peter a question. What if Margaret came looking for her one day and found her. And what if Sigrid was living with Peter and their child. The idea of looking into Margaret's eyes and seeing the pain and rejection just stopped her cold. At least, if she didn't have another child, it would present a different picture. Maybe Margaret would think that Sigrid wasn't the maternal type. That she'd done her a favor. But if Margaret saw her with a child—or children—around her, children she loved and who loved her in return, what could Sigrid say? Gee, too bad about that, Margaret. Bad timing. Hope you had a nice childhood. Sorry I didn't have time to be around.

It was impossible.

Peter tried to get her to see that she could simply ask Margaret to forgive the seventeen-year-old girl she'd once been, that her decision had been the right one for both of them, but nothing he said made a dent in her resolve. Sigrid insisted that giving Margaret up was the biggest mistake of her life, that Margaret should be with *her*—not the Tanhauers, no matter how super a set of parents they turned out to be.

And that's what got Peter to thinking. If, for some reason, the Tanhauer family hadn't turned out to be the Brady Bunch, then maybe there was a chance he could reunite Margaret and Sigrid. He didn't have a clue how it would actually happen, but before he could come up with a plan, he had to find Margaret. He'd hired the PI in New York five days ago. He still had money from his severance package and he intended to use it to find the little girl. It made no rational sense, but he'd pretty much come to the conclusion that the Tanhauers were poison. He didn't like to think that Margaret had spent the last ten years living with monsters, but he'd convinced himself it was the truth. Peter felt a sense of urgency now.

"I'm coming, Margaret," he whispered, closing his eyes. "Just hold on a little while longer."

7

On Wednesday morning, Jane opened her eyes to a wet brown nose. Mouse, her chocolate lab, was standing by her bed, his chin on her pillow, whining softly.

"What's wrong, baby?" She stroked his head. Struggling out of her blankets, she glanced over at his bed in the corner. Lucifer, one of Cordelia's cats, was curled up in it, licking his paw. It was the third morning in a row Lucifer had decided to evict Mouse. Jane had had enough.

She pulled on a robe and loomed over the nasty feline. "You're evil, you know that? You belong in an Anne Rice novel. I don't care what Cordelia says. No more fun and games with my dog." She scooped him up, walked across the hall to Cordelia's bedroom, and dropped him on top of her sleeping form.

Cordelia barely moved.

Lucifer, being a practiced suck-up, nestled right down next to her and closed his eyes.

"As if," said Jane, hands rising to her hips. "You think I don't know what you're up to? These little games of yours have got to stop."

Cordelia gave a snort, pulled the quilt up over her head, and turned over.

"That's it," said Jane, checking the clock on the nightstand. It was just after eight. "I'm going to take a shower now, Cordelia." She said it loudly. "When I'm done, I expect you to be downstairs cleaning up the mess you and your poker friends made last night." Sure, Cordelia was hurting because of Hattie, but if she felt well enough to throw a party, then she was well enough to clean up after herself.

Jane stormed out. Fifteen minutes later she was back with Mouse by her side.

Cordelia hadn't moved.

"Get up," said Jane.

No response.

"Come on, boy. Let's go look up recipes for fried cat."

After letting Mouse out into the backyard, she fixed him a bowl of kibble. The kitchen was such a disaster that she could barely find a clean space on the counter to set the bowl. Since Mouse seemed to be taking his old sweet time in the yard, she crossed through the dining room, glancing at the beer bottle collection on the table, and headed for the stereo in the living room. It only took her a second to find what she was looking for.

As the opening strains of "In-A-Gadda-Da-Vida" shattered the silence, Jane smiled to herself. She waited at the bottom of the stairs, arms crossed.

It took the better part of two minutes, but Cordelia finally stumbled into view. She still had on her one-piece red flannel PJs and her striped red-and-white nightcap with the seven-foot-long tail. Her auburn curls were a tangled mess under the cap and her eyes looked scrambled.

"Not funny!" Cordelia yelled. She thumped down the stairs, one step at a time, dragging the round furry ball at the end of her hat after her.

"Morning," yelled Jane.

Cordelia tossed visual thunderbolts at her as she marched past into the living room and snapped off the music. "Well, alert the friggin' media," she shouted. "Cordelia Thorn made a mess."

"You're going to clean this up all by yourself."

"Can't we call a maid service or something?"

"You've been here for what? Four months? Have you ever seen a maid?"

Cordelia shrugged.

"Get busy. Start with the living room and dining room."

Generally, Cordelia was a great houseguest, but she got an F when it came to cleaning up after parties—and she loved giving parties.

Jane let Mouse in the back door and fed him his kibble. As she was bagging up some garbage—in an effort to look a little less like Simon Legree—she heard the opening strains to a John Philip Sousa march roar in from the living room. A little better than Iron Butterfly, but not much.

An hour later, Cordelia was in the kitchen putting the last dish in the dishwasher. "In case you're interested, I fired that English PI yesterday—and hired another."

This made an even half dozen. "What about Cecily?" asked Jane.

Cecily Finch was Hattie's nanny. Cordelia had hired her to help out when Octavia had first dropped Hattie on Cordelia's doorstep. She'd moved to England to continue to care for the little girl.

"She's useless. I thought she was my friend, but she doesn't write, hasn't called in months."

"Maybe Octavia told her not to."

"Of course she did. But Cecily is sufficiently conniving. She could figure something out."

"You think this new PI will be any better?"

"God knows. She said she had a plan, but didn't want to get my hopes up, just in case it doesn't work." Cordelia closed the dishwasher. "Every lawyer I talk to tells me the same thing. I've got no rights when it comes to Hattie." As she switched the dishwasher on, the doorbell rang. "You expecting visitors?"

"Not that I know of."

"Well, I'm done, so I'm outta here. I need to get to the theater."

Jane put her arms around Cordelia, gave her a hug. She wished she could say something to make it all better, but they both knew Octavia held all the cards.

On their way through the dining room, Cordelia eyed Jane with a glimmer of humor. "Think I need to change my outfit?"

"Red flannel pajamas are a good look for you."

"What about the apron?"

"Very Martha Stewart."

"It's not really *me*, though. I usually go for drama—for *va voom*."

"Wear your stiletto heels," said Jane, drawing back the door.

A familiar looking woman stood outside on the front steps. One of her hands fidgeted with a cigarette, the other was hooked on to a shoulder-strap purse. She was dressed in a pin-striped navy jacket over a pair of tight black jeans, her short coffee brown hair brushed back over her ears.

"Melanie?" said Jane.

"For a minute there, I thought you might not remember me."

"Of course I remember you."

Melanie Gunderson and Cordelia had lived together for five years, the longest serious relationship in Cordelia's long line of daytime drama. To say that it was stormy would be an understatement. When they first met, Cordelia had just been hired as the creative director at the Blackburn Playhouse and Melanie was working on her dissertation for her doctorate in journalism and mass communications at the University of Minnesota.

"Can I come in?" she asked, dropping the cigarette to the steps and crushing it out with her flip-flop.

"What am I thinking? Of course you can." Jane had always been a little bit in love with Melanie. Everyone had. She was flat-out smart and flat-out sexy, an irresistible combination.

Cordelia was three-quarters of the way up the stairs when she bellowed, "My god, Gunderson? Is that *you*?"

Melanie looked a little startled. "What are you doing here?" she asked, watching Cordelia rush back down the stairs.

"I could ask you the same thing."

"You look sufficiently odd," said Melanie, her gaze dropping to the apron. "You're sure I'm not interrupting . . . something?"

"Nah," said Cordelia. "Jane and I are just friends, you know that. I been staying here for a while. Long story."

"Why don't we sit in the living room?" said Jane. "I assume you dropped by for a reason."

"Thanks." Melanie edged past Cordelia, who partially blocked her entrance but didn't seem inclined to move.

"Why'd we break up?" asked Cordelia.

"Beats me."

"It was love at first sight."

"Love and lust can look disgracefully identical to the untrained eye."

"That's how you remember it? Four years of lust?"

"Five," said Melanie.

"What?"

"We were together for five years. How flattering that you remember our time together so clearly."

"What are you doing now?" asked Jane, trying to head off a potential disaster. She sat down in the rocker by the fireplace.

Melanie chose the couch. "I teach journalism at St. Cloud State. But I'm on sabbatical. Believe it or not, I took a job with *City Beat*. I interned at the *Star Trib* for a while after college, but what I really wanted to do was teach. Now I'm so sick of it I could puke."

"Why *City Beat?*" asked Jane.

"Because for the last couple years I've been dying to do some real-life, hands-on investigative journalism. I broke that story last February about Arnold Hammond, one of our fine local judges who was selling crack out of the trunk of his car."

Cordelia sat down next to Melanie and slipped her arm across the back of the couch—behind Melanie's back.

Melanie noted the arm with a nod of her head. "You haven't changed much."

"I am the Sphinx. Waiting and watching."

"And hustling women."

"Not everyone. I discriminate."

"Consider me unhustleable."

"I'm just stretching out," said Cordelia. "Don't take the arm personally."

"Why'd you come by?" asked Jane.

"Well, actually, I wanted to talk to you about your dad's campaign manager."

"Delavon Green?"

59

"Green, yeah, and two others. Randall Turk and his brother, Ethan."

"Why?"

"It's part of some research I'm doing."

"What research?" asked Cordelia, eyeing her with a kind of grim concentration.

"Well, since you're interested, a friend sent me some information recently on a cold murder case in Iowa, one that happened back in the early seventies. The name Delavon Green came up. I knew that was the name of your dad's campaign manager, Jane, but I didn't know if it was the same guy. Turns out it is. I think there's an important story there that was never told—a murder that was never solved. And if my instincts are right, it might also have some contemporary relevance."

"Go on," said Cordelia, arching an eyebrow.

Melanie stared at her a moment, then continued. "Well, I think most people would agree that America is involved in another Vietnam, another endless war that grinds men and women up and then spits them out, expecting them to just pick up and go on with their lives when they get home as if the brutality they witnessed never happened. I'm becoming convinced that the murder in Iowa back in '71 had its roots in Vietnam, and if so, it may be a cautionary tale for us today." She removed a small notebook from her pocket. "If you don't mind talking to me, Jane, why don't we start with Randall Turk? Give me your impressions of him."

"Well, he's a longtime friend of my dad's. He and his wife used to throw a lot of dinner parties, so I've been to their house many times. I don't know Randy all that well, but I mean, he's quiet, and I suspect he's also pretty intense. My dad thinks the world of him. He's known for his aggressiveness in the courtroom."

60

"He and his wife recently split," said Melanie.

"Really. That surprises me."

"Why?"

"I don't know. They seemed like such a great couple."

"Close? Happy?"

"Yes."

"Randy ever talk to you about his tour in Vietnam? Or after he came home?"

"No, not that I remember."

"Does he have any close friends? Other people I could talk to?"

"Sorry. Like I said, I don't know him that well. You might talk to my dad about him. Not that he has a lot of time at the moment, but I'm sure I could connect you somehow."

"That would be terrific," said Melanie. "Thanks. Now, what about Green? What's your impression of him?"

"I've only met him a few times. He strikes me as competent, professional, good with people. *Very* tall. My dad mentioned that he grew up in Detroit, had a rough time of it as a kid, but he's turned it to his advantage. He has a real common touch. The staff adores him."

"How'd your dad get hooked up with Green?"

"Del had been working on Theo Ludtke's campaign. I think Randy suggested him to my father, said he'd make a great campaign manager."

"And your dad's happy with him?"

"Very."

"What about Ethan Turk, Randy's brother?"

"I like Ethan. He's a few years older than Randy. I don't know if he'd be considered developmentally disabled or what, but he knows everything there is to know about cars and trucks. I think

61

he could build one from the ground up. Randy helped him set up a lawn and snow business out near Stillwater. He likes being outside."

"Did you know Ethan was on trial for murder back in the early seventies? It's the case I'm investigating."

Jane looked up sharply.

"He was acquitted, but there are a lot of people who still believe he did it."

"Did what?" asked Cordelia.

"A young woman, Susan Bouchard, was strangled in a field just outside Waldo, Iowa. It happened shortly after Randy got out of the army. He returned home in the spring of '71 with two of his army buddies—Delavon Green, and a guy named Larry Wilton. Sue was Randy's girlfriend."

"God, I can't believe it," said Jane. "But Ethan was acquitted. Are you saying he shouldn't have been?"

"I'm saying there was a cover-up. Of what, I'm not sure. As I said, Sue was Randy's girl, but Green had some kind of connection, too, possibly romantic. I don't know what it all means, but the situation was clearly a powder keg that went off, killing Susan."

"What happened to the other guy—Wilton?"

"He lives in Arizona now. That's all I've been able to find out."

"I'm sure my dad doesn't know about any of this." Jane couldn't help but wonder what it would mean for his political future if it came out that his campaign manager had been involved in a homicide.

When Jane looked back at Melanie she could tell she'd read her mind.

"Exactly, Jane. This could blow up in a big way. And the fallout could hurt your dad. I'm sorry about that, but as I said, I think there's an important story here, and also a major injustice. A young woman was brutally murdered and her killer has gone free all these years. It's possible I won't develop enough info to break the story until after the election, but I have to go where the story leads."

"I understand," said Jane.

"I don't," said Cordelia, sitting up, full of indignation. "You may never find enough information to break the case. And if you print a bunch of innuendoes, you could ruin an incredibly fine man's chance at public office."

"*This* is why we broke up," muttered Melanie.

"Listen to me," said Cordelia. "It's simple. If you don't find anything the police can use to make an arrest, don't go public with it. If you find something, then sit on it until after the election next November."

"I wouldn't smear someone for no reason," said Melanie, pushing off the couch. "But I won't back off just because it's politically sensitive. Besides, printing something that's true, even if it doesn't lead to an arrest, is completely ethical. If Woodward and Bernstein's bosses had told them not to go public with what they were learning about the Watergate scandal, we might never haven known what Nixon and his cronies were up to. They started the ball rolling by what they printed."

"You aren't Woodward and Bernstein," said Cordelia, standing and glaring at her.

"I should have known better than to talk to Jane with you around."

"We won't help you destroy Ray's chance of becoming governor."

"Fine."

"Fine."

"Traitor," shouted Cordelia as Melanie slammed the front door on her way out.

8

Late Wednesday afternoon, Randy sat behind the desk in his home office doing some paperwork when he heard a car pull into the driveway. A few seconds later, Larry appeared in the doorway, a cigarette dangling from his lips.

"You shaved off your mustache," said Randy, tossing down his pen and leaning back.

"Had to," said Larry. "Didn't want Gunderson to be able to ID me to the police—if worst came to worst." He took off his baseball cap and let his pony tail drop down his back.

Against his better judgment, Randy had allowed Del to talk him into giving the bribe idea a shot. He reasoned that nobody could tie them to Larry. And if Larry did get caught, he'd promised to say it was his idea, that Randy and Del had nothing to do with it. At the very least, that gave them deniability. "So? You talked to her?"

"Yup. Met her at a bar in downtown Minneapolis."

"How'd it go?"

Larry walked over and set the attaché case next to the desk. Instead of taking one of the chairs close to Randy, he chose the leather couch across the room. Stretching out, he took a drag from his cigarette. "She's smart," he said, smoke billowing from his nostrils. "The offer got her attention, I guarantee you that. But she played it cool, tried to make me think she was insulted. It took me a minute to get the point. She wants more money."

"How much more?"

"Fifty thousand. The woman was a real piece of work. She maintained she had high ethical standards, but then it came out that she also had some nasty debts. For fifty large, we'll not only get her silence, but the file she's worked up."

"She said that?"

"Not in so many words, but we understood each other. Once we get our hands on the info, we'll know where the holes are. We need to plug them, if you catch my drift. Hope you've got deep pockets, bro, 'cause that's what it's gonna take."

Randy's head sank to his chest. "I thought it was all over years ago."

"Well, it ain't, so get used to it."

"If I give you the fifty, do you trust this woman to play ball with us?"

"Yeah, I do. Fifty thousand's a bunch of cash. I told her I'd need some time. I didn't know whether you'd go for it or not."

Randy blew out a heavy breath. "I've got the money. I'm just . . . worried. If we get caught offering a bribe to a member of the press, we'll all go down in flames."

"I understand, man. But look, if I get nailed, I'd never rat you and Del out, you know that. It's your call. But one way or another, she's gotta be dealt with."

66

"Did she give you any indication what she has?"

"She's been digging into the Sue thing—you know, the *trial*."

The *Sue thing*, thought Randy. He'd never put it that way, not in a million years. But then Larry had never known Sue all that well. When they were in Nam, Randy would read certain parts of the letters she wrote him to Larry and Del, but mainly he kept her locked away in his heart. Safe. Away from the flies and the heat, the boredom and the terror. She was his secret weapon. He kept her gold locket in his pocket the entire time he was in country. She'd given it to him the day he got on the bus to leave for boot camp. Inside was a tiny pressed violet. He was positive it was the reason he could walk through a firefight and not get shot, walk down a road laced with Bouncing Betties and not get his legs blown off. Lots of guys were superstitious. It was hard not to be. He still had the locket in a desk drawer, not that he ever looked at it anymore. It was too painful now. And besides, the magic was gone. She'd taken it with her when she died.

"Okay," said Randy. "I'll get the money to you by tomorrow."

"You gotta go to a bank?"

"Just let me take care of it."

"Whatever you say, man." He stretched his arms over his head. "I'm famished. Thought maybe I'd eat what was left of last night's pizza."

"Bad idea," said Randy, glancing at the time. It was going on five. "Let me take you out. After what you did today, I owe you big. But I'd like to go running first. You're welcome to come along."

"Christ, no," said Larry, choking on the smoke as he let out a laugh. "I get all the exercise my lungs can handle just walkin' around. Think I'll just mosey on upstairs and help myself to a

67

beer. Maybe do up last night's dishes. Take your time. I'm happy to hang out."

Ethan appeared in Randy's bedroom doorway just as Randy was pulling on his sweatpants. He didn't say anything, he just stood there, hands at his sides, looking morose.

"What's up?" asked Randy. He sat down on the bed to put on his running shoes.

"I heard you and Larry downstairs. You were talking about Sue."

Randy stopped tying his shoelace and looked up. "It's nothing for you to worry about."

"Why'd you say her name?"

"We were just talking."

"Something's going on. Why's Larry here? I don't want it to be about Sue."

"It's not. He just came to Minnesota for a little vacation."

"I loved her."

"I know you did."

"I didn't hurt her, did I?"

"No, of course not."

"But those people . . . they all said I did." He began to rock from side to side.

"You didn't," said Randy. "We've been through this a million times."

"But I can't *remember*," said Ethan, his voice deep yet soft.

"Come in here. Sit down on the bed with me."

"No."

Randy could tell his brother was starting to cry. "Ethan, you didn't do anything wrong. You have to trust me."

"But why can't I *remember*?"

"You had too much to drink. You blacked out."

"I drank, yeah. I was scared."

"Scared of what?"

Ethan shook his head.

"Sue's in heaven now. You don't have to worry anymore."

"Is she with Mom?" he said, wiping a hand across his eyes.

"Yes, Ethan, she's with Mom and Dad. They're taking good care of her."

"But I was supposed to do that! You told me to take care of her when you left to go be a soldier."

Randy regretted ever saying those words. "You did take care of her."

"Not the way you wanted. I screwed up. More than you know."

"You always say that, but you *didn't*, Ethan."

"You don't know. You don't understand. I'd never hurt her, Randy."

Randy put his head down and tried to breathe through the pain. "I know, Ethan. All you did was help her."

Ethan stood in the doorway a moment more, then turned and walked away.

Randy ran full out for well over a mile. He didn't want to think, he just wanted to sink into the sensations of his body, exhaust himself until nothing mattered but the next breath. And yet no matter how fast and how far he went, he couldn't run away from himself. Stopping finally, he bent over and rested his hands on his knees, then looked up at the hard, slate-colored clouds drifting across the sky from the west. In the distance came a rumble of thunder. He hadn't listened to the weather report, but it looked like a storm was brewing. Easing upright, he unzipped his jacket, then took off again, this time more slowly. He was working out the kinks in his legs when he saw it, the charred wreckage of a car down in a deep ditch.

"What the hell," he whispered. Moving sideways down the embankment to get a closer look, he saw that it was a newer car. A Mazda or a Honda. There was no sign of the driver inside, so hopefully he'd gotten out. Randy tried to imagine what had happened. An overheated engine? Or maybe the gas tank had caught fire when the car hit the ditch.

Walking through the wet, matted weeds, he saw that some of the brush around the car was blackened, but thankfully it had been a wet spring, otherwise the flames might have caused a grass fire.

Randy stood for a moment more, wondering if he should call the cops. There was no rational reason not to, except that every time he reached for the cell phone in the pocket of his jacket, something stopped him.

"This is ridiculous," he said finally. He tapped in 411 and asked to be connected to the police. He reported the car, gave his name and address, the approximate location along Potter Road, then hung up.

"Stupid," he said as he climbed back up to the road and continued with his run.

Cordelia waited outside the the two-story building on Lyndale Avenue, where *City Beat*'s offices were located. She'd been there for all of two minutes when Melanie walked out.

"Hey, Gunderson," she called, her back pressed against the side of her Hummer.

Melanie gave her an annoyed look and walked in the opposite direction.

70

"You can outrun me, but I'll hunt you down. You know I will."

Melanie stopped, turned around. "I'm not interested in an argument."

Cordelia held up her hands. "Just wanna talk. Nice and friendly."

"Yeah, I'll bet."

"Come on. Do I look *that* disagreeable?" She'd worn her favorite new outfit—brown gaucho pants that ended just below the knee, long black leather boots with one-inch heels, a blousey embroidered silk tunic tied at the waist, and to top it off, a flat-brimmed black gaucho hat. She looked spectacular, if she did say so herself.

"I've got an appointment," said Melanie.

"Yeah. With me."

"You are so frustrating!"

"Can't we just talk about your investigation like two adults?"

"I'm an adult. Where are we gonna get the other one?"

"Funny." Cordelia wiped a spot off the hood of her Hummer.

"That thing belong to you?"

"Yup."

"What's wrong with you?"

"I suppose you drive a Prius."

"As a matter of fact, I do."

"Boy, I can see why we split. We've got nothing in common."

"Amen."

"I make all the stupid choices and you make all the smart ones. Like smoking."

"I'm not having this conversation." She turned, but before she got more than a few feet, Cordelia was next to her.

"You hungry?" she asked.

71

"As a matter of fact, I'm starving."

"Well, there. We agree on that. There's a restaurant just up the street. I'll buy you dinner."

Melanie groaned. "If I have dinner with you, will you leave me alone, not bother me anymore?"

"Deal."

Over tapas, they talked turkey about Melanie's investigation. After a good hour of heated conversation, they agreed that they were unlikely to reach a détente, but by then they were both in much better moods due to the bottle of red wine they'd consumed. The discussion moved back to their breakup—how different they were, and why they could never live together.

"We were so young," said Cordelia.

"And pigheaded."

"Want some dessert?"

"Maybe we could split something. You like crème brûlée?"

Cordelia turned up her nose. "How about the molten chocolate cake."

"I can't eat chocolate anymore. It gives me heartburn."

"That's it in a nutshell." She played with her napkin.

Melanie picked up the small dessert menu, looked it over. "I should probably just get home. I'm into the second season of *Six Feet Under*. Have to say I'm kind of addicted."

"Wow," said Cordelia. "I loved that show. I've never seen anything I thought was more brilliantly written, acted, or directed."

"Really?"

"What's the best book you've read recently?"

"I'd have to think." She picked up her wineglass, swirled the dregs. "Probably . . . oh, *The Time Traveler's Wife*. By a woman named Niffenegger. I think it was a first book. I loved it."

"Amazing," said Cordelia, looking deep into Melanie's eyes. "I adored that book."

"I'm stunned."

They eventually moved the conversation back to Cordelia's loft. Melanie was impressed by the space, but she said she didn't like Swedish modern furniture.

"Me either," said Cordelia.

"Then why's the loft filled with it?"

"It's my current idiom. It's so functionally boring, it kind of appeals to me."

"You really are strange, you know that?" Melanie drifted around the living room. Picking up a picture of Hattie, she said, "Who's this?"

"My sister's daughter, Hattie Thorn Lester. She lived with me for two years. I've been more of a mother to her than Octavia ever has."

"I remember your sister. I can't imagine her with a kid."

"Takes a special person."

"You hate kids."

"Not anymore. Hattie is the most important person in my life. She'll be back, just wait and see."

When Melanie turned around to look at Cordelia, her eyes had softened. "This is a whole new side to you."

"I am *truly* multifaceted. Can't remember if you're a kid person or not."

"I adore children."

They sat down on the couch, entranced by each other.

"You should do something different with your hair," said Melanie.

"Think so?"

She touched it.

They polished off another bottle of wine, just sitting and talking. And later, in the wee hours of the morning, after a long, fierce argument about the merits of oaked versus unoaked Chardonnay, they put their relationship back on track.

9

Late the following morning, Peter was on his third cup of coffee, reading the paper at the kitchen table, when he got a call
from the private investigator he'd hired.

"It's Shifflet. You get my invoice?"

"We're not done."

Shifflet laughed. "You got that right, pal. I dug up some new
info."

"Give." Sigrid had already left for work, so Peter could talk
freely.

"I checked out the Tanhauer who lives on the Upper West
Side. No other Matt Tanhauer in Manhattan, and this man's
wife's name is Carrie, so I think we got the right guy. He's been
working his way up the investment banking ladder for years.
He's a VP now at BKL."

"What's that?"

"Benson, Klug and Lockhart. Not big into investment allocation, are we?"

"Just give me the information."

"Tanhauer was a financial analyst when Margaret was adopted."

"They *bought* her," said Peter. "There *was* no legal adoption."

"Right. Whatever. So I go to the address. It's a pricey apartment building a few blocks west of Central Park. I talked to the doorman and he says the Tanhauers moved out to the Hamptons about six months ago. He figured they left a forwarding address, but he didn't know what it was. I asked him how long they'd been living in the apartment and he told me a few years. Said they seemed nice enough—always gave him a great tip at Christmas. Then I asked him about Margaret. That's where the story gets a little strange. He says the Tanhauers had two kids, but they were both boys."

All expression died on Peter's face. "Then you've got the wrong couple."

"No, these are the right folks, I'm sure of it."

"How old are the two boys?"

"One is maybe four, the other is in school, so he's older."

Peter struggled to come up with an answer. "They're rich, right?"

"By my standards they're royalty."

"Okay, so maybe they sent her away to school."

"Suppose that's possible, but why wouldn't she come home for Christmas?"

"Maybe she's in Switzerland or something and didn't want to leave her friends. Look, I want you to go out to the Hamptons, find their house, and talk to them. She can't have just disappeared."

"Okay, pal. It's your money. I'll cross the doorman's hand with some cash, see if he can dig up the address for me. But it may take some time."

"Just call me back when you have something," said Peter. "Hey, before you go, did you ever hear back from Vaughn Cabot?"

"Nobody ever answers his damn phone. I've left half a dozen messages, but he never returns them."

"All right," said Peter. "Thanks."

After hanging up, he sat for a moment, running a hand over his beard, thinking about what Shifflet had said, then picked up his cell phone again and called directory assistance. A few seconds later he had Cabot's number in New Jersey. He wrote it on the edge of the newspaper. Tapping in the number, he listened as the answering machine asked him to state his name, phone number, and the reason for his call. Peter decided to take a chance.

"Mr. Cabot, my name is Peter . . . Johnson. I hope I've got the right guy. My wife and I want to adopt a child, but for . . . well, for certain reasons I don't want to get into, we haven't been able to find the . . . right situation. I'm told you might be able to help us. Call me back and let's talk. Money isn't a problem. Let me underline that, Mr. Cabot. Money is not a problem. My number is 555-839-2911. Hope to hear from you soon."

Peter had been reading up on adoption fraud. The number one red flag to look for was money. If Cabot hadn't filed any adoption papers, the chances were that he was an illegal baby broker. That meant the good old American dollar sign was the easiest way to rouse the snake from his hole.

Randy sat on the lower deck at his house, waiting for his wife to drop off his daughter. They hadn't firmed up any custody arrangements, mainly because Randy was dragging his feet, hoping to convince Sherrie that before they called it quits, they should talk to a marriage counselor. Sherrie had been after him for years to do couples counseling, but Randy couldn't see himself sitting in some office, spilling his guts to a stranger. Except now, it was the only card he had left to play.

Ethan had given Larry a lift into Stillwater right after breakfast. Larry had found a truck he wanted to buy. Nothing fancy, just some wheels. He'd hit Randy up for a small loan—a couple thousand dollars. Randy was happy to help out, especially after last night. He and Larry had sat up late, smoking weed and passing a bottle of tequila between them as they sat under the stars in the meadow next to the house. Nine years Randy had lived in this place, and not once had he ever done anything like that. Sure, he had a massive headache this morning, but it was a small price to pay to feel alive again.

Larry planned to meet with Melanie Gunderson again tonight. Randy's stomach vanished every time he thought about that woman scrutinizing his past. He prayed that she'd take the money and back off, because if she didn't, he was afraid Del and Larry would push for something more drastic. He was even more afraid that he might go along with it. Randy had tried to bury his past, but in the process, he'd come to the conclusion that he'd buried himself along with it. Maybe that's why Sherrie had left him. She couldn't stand to live with the smell of a stinking corpse.

"Am I alive or am I the walking dead?" he whispered. He really wanted to know. "I'm good at my job. I've made a difference in the world. But what's that prove when I won't let myself ever feel anything. My wife's left me and I'm depressed, but hell, I'm always depressed." Except, this morning, the blood pumped in his veins a little harder. Last night had been good for him. He felt opened up today, the sun hotter, the sky bluer, his skin alive. It wasn't just Larry's sudden appearance, although that may have been part of the catalyst. This morning, as he walked around the house, it was as if he was waking from a long sleep. Sherrie was mere inches from being lost to him forever. He wanted her back, wanted forgiveness and absolution for his past. He wanted a goddamn second chance.

When Sherrie's Lexus pulled into the drive a few minutes later, he trotted down the steps to meet her.

"Hi," he said, smiling and opening the passenger door for his daughter, Katie. He gave her an extralong hug. It meant more to him than just the usual hug, but it didn't even put a dent in her sullenness. She'd made her feelings very clear weeks ago. She didn't want to be dragged from house to house for the next two years. If her parents were gonna get all stupid on her and ditch their marriage, she wanted to live with her mother until she finished her senior year of high school, and then she'd be off to college somewhere, hopefully far far away.

Grabbing an overnight bag from the trunk, Katie disappeared up the steps. Randy moved around to the driver's side. "You coming in?" he asked Sherrie, trying to look serious, even though he felt like pulling her out of the car and spinning her around.

"No," she said. She looked about as cheerful as Katie.

"We should talk," he said. "Come on, just sit on the deck with me for a few minutes."

She seemed torn.

"Please?" he asked, hoping that he still had some pull with her.

Finally relenting, she turned off the motor and got out.

Sherrie and Katie were both brunettes, although Sherrie's hair was short and Katie's was long. Both were slim and athletic. Randy hadn't seen either of them in a couple of weeks. Was it possible that they'd grown even more beautiful in that short period of time?

"You want something to drink?" he asked on his way up the steps to the upper deck. "I think the coffee's still on from breakfast. Or I could fix us a drink."

79

"A little early in the day for that."

"Come in the house for a second," he said. "There's something I want you to see." Entering through the second-floor patio doors, he could tell that Katie had already made it up to her bedroom because he could hear Blue October blasting from the speakers in her room. She was trying to erase her parents' existence. He didn't blame her.

When he turned around, Sherrie was walking silently around the kitchen—her kitchen—a tentative, almost forlorn look on her face. She was living in a small apartment now. He'd only seen it from the outside, but he knew it was small because Katie had told him about it one night on the phone.

"What do you want to show me?" she asked.

Randy moved toward her. "Don't freak, okay?" Drawing her against his chest, he said, "I miss you so much." She felt stiff in his arms. He'd done that to her. He'd made her that way. "I love you more than you know. Maybe I never said that enough."

"That's an understatement," she said, but she didn't push him away.

He wanted so badly to show her how much he loved her. He kissed her as softly as he knew how. That was another thing missing from his marriage. Tenderness. When had he stopped allowing himself to feel that emotion? He knew the answer. All roads led back to Sue, and before that, to Vietnam.

Randy backed up, saw the tears in his wife's eyes. "I'm sorry. I've made so many mistakes."

She just stood there, wiping her eyes.

"Have you thought any more about seeing a couples counselor?" he asked.

"Why are you doing this?"

"What?"

"I've been after you for years to go to counseling. The answer was always no. I get it that you don't like having your life messed with. You like things neat and clean. No hassles. When things get messy, you always walk out the door and then you stay at work until the mess resolves itself. But you know, Randy, the chaos you leave behind never really resolves. It might go away for a while, but it's still there, festering. If you think counseling is just a quick fix, think again. Our marriage is broken. It has been for years. Maybe it was never any good and I just refused to see it. But I can't live with coldness anymore. I'm done. Finished. I may not find someone else to love in this life, but I'm nowhere near as lonely since we separated as I was living with you."

She might as well have slugged him in the stomach. He was struggling for a way to respond when the front doorbell rang. Whoever it was, it was the worst possible timing.

"I better go," said Sherrie.

"No, please. I'll get rid of them. You can't just leave. You have to give me a chance to explain."

She stood next to the kitchen counter while he dashed downstairs. Two police officers stood outside the front door.

"Are you Randy Turk?" asked the shorter man.

"Yes?"

"We need to talk to you about that car you found in the ditch yesterday afternoon."

Randy looked back at the stairs. Sherrie was on her way down.

"I'll talk to you later, Randy," she said, passing the officers on her way out.

There was nothing he could do but watch her go.

10

The officers introduced themselves as Sergeant Williams and Patrolman Vessi. Their eyes swept the interior of the house—and Randy—as they sat down on the Italian-leather sectional in the living room.

"I'm an attorney," said Randy. In jeans and an old red polo shirt, he didn't look all that professional, so he decided to state it up front.

Williams started in without preamble. "The information we were given said that you were jogging along Potter Road last night when you saw the burned car. Is that correct?"

Randy nodded.

"Is that your usual route when you go jogging?"

"Yes."

"How often do you run?"

"As often as I can. Two or three times a week, sometimes

more." Randy wondered where Williams was going with his questions.

"I'd like you to go through it again with us. What you saw. Any details you remember that you might not have reported last night."

Randy had assumed the wreck was the result of an engine malfunction or an accident. It occurred to him later that someone might have torched the vehicle for the insurance money. Either way, it wasn't a big deal. So why were the cops all over it? "Well, it was around five in the afternoon when I went out. Like I told the guy on the phone, I saw this burned car off to the side of the road in a ditch. I climbed down to take a closer look, just in case someone had been in it when it went off the road, but it was empty. I assume the driver got out."

"Did you touch anything when you examined the car?"

"Maybe I put my hand on the door. It was pretty charred."

"Did you move anything? Or remove anything?"

"Hell, no. Have you found the owner? The plates weren't local."

"No they weren't," said Williams. He glanced at his partner. "The car was from Colorado. The owner's name is Carlos Xavier. Ever heard of him?"

Randy shook his head. "You think he set it on fire himself?"

Williams sat forward, rested his arms on his knees. "We found a body in the trunk, Mr. Turk."

"Oh," said Randy. "I see."

"The man was dead before the car blew. We're still checking it out, but we think the body may be Mr. Xavier. There was evidence that an accelerant was used."

"So you're thinking it was a homicide?"

"Did you see anyone else out last night? A neighbor? A stranger?"

"No, no one. The car was cold, so it must have happened a while ago."

"When was the last time you went out for a run along Potter Road?"

It was a good question. An answer would go a long way toward helping them establish a time line. "Let's see. Sunday, I think. I was home early that night, so I went jogging around seven."

"Was the car there that night?"

"No. It was still light, so I would have seen it. If the car was cold last night, it must have happened sometime between late Sunday and early Wednesday morning."

"Did anything unusual happen around here during that period?"

"No." Larry had arrived on Tuesday night. He'd been on foot, which gave Randy a moment's pause, but he pushed the thought aside. He understood now why the police were asking him so many questions. It wasn't unusual for the person who reports a crime to be the one who committed it. "I wish I could be more help, but that's all I know."

Right then, Larry came in the front door. He stopped dead when he saw the two cops sitting in the living room. "Something wrong?" he asked, flashing them an uncertain smile.

"This is an old friend of mine," said Randy, standing. "Larry Wilton."

"You live around here, Mr. Wilton?" asked Williams.

"Arizona," said Larry. He pulled a pack of cigarettes out of his shirt pocket and fired one up. "I'm here on vacation."

"How long you been in Minnesota?" asked Williams.

"Couple of weeks. I been staying with Randy."

84

"Is that correct, Mr. Turk?"

Randy blinked. "Yes. That's right."

Williams looked Larry up and down. "How'd you get here? Did you fly? Drive?"

"The bus," said Larry. "Why? What's going on?"

"You know anything about a car in the ditch on Potter Road?"

"Where's Potter Road?"

Williams glanced back at Randy. After a few tense seconds, he said, "Okay, I guess that's it for now. We may have more questions later."

"Anything I can do, just ask," said Randy as he walked them back to the door.

The officers nodded to Larry on their way out.

Once they were alone, Randy turned on Larry. "Why the hell'd you do that? You forced me to lie to them."

Larry shrugged, blew smoke out his nose. "Don't like cops. I lie to them on principle. I mean, what the hell went down?"

"They found a body in the trunk of a burned car. The guy was murdered."

"Wow. Guess this ain't Shangri-la after all."

Randy felt the banging in his head dial up to detonate. "Tell me the truth, Larry. No bullshit. Did you do it? Did you kill that guy? Swear—on our friendship."

"No, man, I swear. But bad shit follows me around like a homeless dog. And that's God's honest truth. I got one of them guilty faces. I'm always gettin' accused of crap I didn't do."

Randy backed up and sat down on the arm of a chair. "You're right about your face."

"I know. It's just the luck of the draw. Hey, did you get that money yet? I'm meeting with Gunderson tonight, remember? I'm anxious to get this thing settled."

85

Randy looked at him hard. "Yeah, I got it." He held Larry's eyes for another few seconds, then got up and headed into his office.

Peter had just entered the grocery store to shop for dinner when his cell phone rang. He hadn't heard back yet from his dad about that potential job offer with the campaign. He was getting a little antsy, wondering if it had fallen through. When he checked his caller ID, he saw the word "Unknown" pop up.

"Hello?" he said, pausing by the shopping carts.

"I'm calling for Peter Johnson." The voice was thin and high, but definitely a man's voice.

"This is Peter."

"Vaughn Cabot. Is this a convenient time?"

Peter turned away from the people coming into the store. "Absolutely," he said, lowering his voice. "You got my message?"

"I'm curious how you found my name."

It was a question Peter should have anticipated, but hadn't. "Well, actually, the man I talked to asked me to keep his name out of it. It was someone you helped years ago."

"A private adoption."

"Yes," said Peter, forcing the coldness out of his voice. "Private."

"And he explained to you what my services are?"

"Yeah. My question is, do you have anyone right now who might be suitable for us—my wife and me. We're anxious to adopt as soon as possible. We'd be willing to pay whatever it costs."

"You understand about supporting the birth mother, picking up all the medical fees until she delivers."

"Yes."

"And my fee, of course."

"Of course."

"Do you have special needs? Race? Sex? Age?"

"White, for sure."

"I assumed."

"Sex doesn't matter. So, do we have a deal?"

"Mr. Johnson, we need to take this one step at a time. I can cut through a lot of red tape for you—that's a big part of the service I provide—but this is still a delicate kind of negotiation. I work with a number of clients who pass on needy young women to me when they . . . well, require a special kind of help. You understand."

"I do."

"I would need to meet with you and your wife—"

"That's a deal breaker, Mr. Cabot. I'd be happy to meet with you, but my wife, for personal reasons, has to remain out of it."

"That's unusual, Mr. Johnson, but I realize people have different needs, different personal . . . situations. I do bend my rules—I'm not heartless. But I don't place babies with just anybody. No ethical lawyer would. I will need to talk to you personally, have you fill out a financial statement."

It was crystal clear that all the guy really cared about was money. Peter could be buying a kid for sex for all Cabot cared. "When we meet, is there anything I need to bring other than my financial records?"

"No," said Cabot. "Finances are primary, in my opinion. If you can't care for the child comfortably, I couldn't possibly consider you for a placement. I'll have some other questions for you, and some forms to fill out, but nothing that should present a significant hurdle. It's my job to make sure the process is as easy as possible for you."

"I think we understand each other."

"Yes, Mr. Johnson. I think we do. Now, when could we meet?"

Another thing Peter hadn't considered. "I live in the Midwest. It will take me a day or two to tie up some business here. Why don't I give you a call when I can free up some time?"

"May I ask what you do for a living?"

"I work in investments."

"Have you worked in the field long?"

"Fourteen years."

"Well, then, I'll wait for your call. If you have a pen handy, I'll give you a different number where it will be easier for you to reach me."

Peter pulled a pen out of the pocket of his bomber jacket and wrote the number on the edge of a flyer tacked up on the grocery store's bulletin board. No wonder Shifflet hadn't been able to get Cabot on the line. He wasn't asking the right questions. Cabot had a public number he used to screen calls and a public office he used as a front, but his real dealings were performed off the radar.

Peter wasn't sure what he'd expected to come out of their conversation, but he'd never anticipated that he would need to fly to New Jersey. He'd stumbled into it, but he knew instantly that this was his best chance to get the information he needed. He'd have to figure out some excuse so that Sigrid wouldn't ask too many questions, but that wouldn't be difficult. He was, after all, in the middle of a job search. He was glad now that his father hadn't called him back about that job offer. Peter wanted to work for the campaign, but the meeting with Cabot came first. One way or another, he intended to find out what had happened to Margaret and bring her home where she belonged.

11

Cordelia scanned the dim bar looking for Melanie. It was going on 1:30 in the morning, but for Cordelia, whose life in the theater had made her a creature of the night, her evening was just getting started. The Unicorn bar was a mixed scene; gay, bi, lots of straight bikers, the usual after-theater suspects, and a few brave suburbanites out for a murky urban experience.

The place was also a dive. In the cold light of day, the dirt, the fungus growing in between the cracks in the wood floor, and the stink of stale beer and even staler sweat would chase anyone with normal sanitary requirements out. But at night, with loud music pumping, the darkness disinfecting the local color, and lots of colored lights reflected in the mirrors behind the bar, it was as good a place as any.

The bar itself was in the shape of a "U," with tables crammed close together around it, and one long row of booths that spread across the back of the room. There was no pool table or dance floor. People who came to the Unicorn came to drink, talk, or hustle. As it happened, Cordelia was interested in all three.

Melanie had called her around six and they'd agreed to meet at the Unicorn. It was an odd choice. Melanie's tastes were usually a little more upscale. Standing just inside the door, Cordelia surveyed the room, finally spying her sitting at the bar nursing a beer. She moved up behind her and whispered into her ear, "Turn around slowly."

As usual, Melanie did the exact opposite. She whipped her head around. "Good God, woman!"

Cordelia touched her newly cut and died hair. "Do you like it?"

"Like it, I love it!"

"Thought you would."

"You look incredibly hot."

"I know."

She nuzzled in close, gave Cordelia a long, lingering kiss. "You want something to drink?"

"Actually, I thought maybe you'd like to go back to my place."

"Can't," said Melanie, easing off the stool and moving her drink and briefcase over to an empty table. "Not just yet?"

"Why?" Cordelia pulled out a chair and sat down next to her.

"I promised to meet a guy here. He said his name was Smith, but I doubt that's for real. He's got some information for me about Sue Bouchard."

Cordelia's eyes flashed.

"Calm down. If some of the feelers I put out there pay off, I'm not going to look the other way. I'm still gathering facts, *okay*. Speaking of which, Del Green called me today. He's another one who wants to talk to me."

"About Sue?"

"Didn't say that precisely, but that would be my guess."

"News travels fast."

"When highly placed interests are at stake, it does. Which isn't always a good thing. I like to work quietly. On the other hand, all this attention makes me think I've hit the mother lode."

"You think Green will spill something important?"

Melanie shrugged. "No idea. But I can tell you this much. The man is scared. I think he was trying get a feel for how much I've dug up. I'm pretty good at faking people out, making them think I know more than I do. If a person thinks I already know something, that's when you really get an earful."

"You're good."

"You're just saying that to get me in bed."

"Maybe, but it's also true."

Looking down into her beer, Melanie added, "I might be making a mountain out of a molehill, but I think somebody's been following me. I've seen this truck several times today in my rearview mirror. And it was parked outside my duplex late this afternoon." She gave an involuntary shiver.

"Move in with me," said Cordelia. "Linden Lofts is a security building."

Melanie laughed. "God, that's such a lesbian cliché. One date and the movers arrive."

"Feels right to me."

"It's a big step."

"Okay, don't move in. But come stay with me, just until your life feels safer."

"But you're living at Jane's house now, right?"

"No, I'm not. Not if you need me."

Melanie's smile was almost shy. "I'm a coward, Cordelia. When we broke up all those years ago, I really hit bottom.

You're a hard person to forget. I guess . . . what I'm saying is, I don't want to get hurt again."

"If you're worried about the pain, Mel, you'll never find your soul mate. Life's a party, a banquet. Sure, you get ptomaine every now and then, but I'm asking you to dance with me. I've learned some since the last time we tried it. I suspect you have, too. Here," she said, taking an extra key off her key ring and pushing it across the table. "Now you can come and go as you please."

"You're amazing, you know that?"

Cordelia lowered her eyes demurely.

"Okay," said Melanie, pulling her own key ring out of her jeans. "You should have one of mine, too, just so that we both have something to throw at each other in a few days."

"We've mellowed," said Cordelia. "Aged, like fine wines."

Melanie laughed. "Right. Maybe we should buy each other flak jackets instead of rings this time."

"I really, really want to give this another shot," said Cordelia, her expression growing serious. "Years ago, when we were first together, I knew we had something special, but then we had that awful knock-down-drag-out fight about God knows what, and we just gave up on each other. I think that was a mistake. Am I alone here? Didn't you feel that way, too?"

Melanie rolled the beer glass between her hands. "Sure, I did. But I figured I'd blown it and there was no turning back."

"Look, I'll be honest with you. I've dated a lot of women since we were together. I'm never hard up for female companionship. But none of those women have your—"

"Sensuality?"

"I was going to say complexity."

"Complexity is good."

"We owe it to each other to give it another try."

Melanie glanced over at the door as a man came in. "That's him," she whispered, moving instantly into reporter mode. "He said he'd be wearing an Oakland Raider's cap." Rising from her chair, she slipped a tape recorder out of her briefcase and said, "I won't be long. Wait for me, okay?"

As she walked over to him, Cordelia tried to get a look at his face, but with so little light in the bar, it was impossible. They disappeared outside, leaving Cordelia alone with nothing but Melanie's beer and her briefcase. She pulled the glass in front of her and inspected the room.

Five minutes went by. Then ten. Fifteen minutes later she was still waiting and the beer was gone. She was about to go outside and see if she could hurry things along when she heard the sound of an approaching siren. Then another. Several of the customers raced to the windows to look outside. With a bunch of squirming bodies blocking her line of sight, Cordelia couldn't see very much, except for the reflected flashing lights from the cruisers as they sped past.

A moment later, a woman stumbled in through the glut of curiosity seekers about to head out the door. "There's a woman in the parking lot who's down on the ground," she gasped. "I think she's hurt."

Cordelia grabbed the briefcase and flew off her chair, shoving her way through the crowd. Once outside, she rushed around to the back lot, but halfway there a cop blocked her way.

"Back up, lady. Let us do our job."

"I think that might be a friend of mine. Is it a woman?" She described Melanie, what she was wearing, what she looked like.

Right then, a fight broke out between two of the bar patrons.

"Stay here. I'll be back," said the cop, racing over to break up the scuffle.

"Forget that," said Cordelia, skirting around one of the parked squad cars. Just as she broke through a gawker jam, she was stopped again, this time by a cop with a baton. "This is a crime scene. Nobody allowed in." Another cop was winding yellow tape around the perimeter. People were shouting. Cordelia stood on her tiptoes and searched the crowd, but Melanie was nowhere to be found.

"I know the victim!" she shouted. "She's my girlfriend!"

A couple of the biker types turned to stare at her, but the cops were busy with crowd control. "You've got to listen to me," she yelled.

The longer she stood there, helpless in the growing mass of onlookers, the more frantic she became. "I am Cordelia M. Thorn!" she shouted. It was her trump card. She assumed the very mention of her name could stop a roaring locomotive.

But nobody seemed interested.

A man oozed up to her and stuck out his hand. "You're that theater director, right?" He eyed her for a second, then said, "Am I wrong, or do you look different than you used to?"

"I am a *work* in *progress*."

"What?" He couldn't hear her over all the shouting.

"I cut my hair!"

"I liked it the old way better."

"Everyone's a critic," she snarled. Backing her way through the great honking gaggle, she reached the street. "Melanie?" she hollered, stomping her foot. "If you're out here, you better let me know right now, because if you don't, I'm gonna have a heart attack right here in the friggin' street!"

Nothing.

"Melanie!"

As she surveyed the scene, her eyes locked on the glowing

neon pyramid high atop the Xanadu Club less than a block away. That was it. Jane would know what to do. Jane always knew what to do. Picking up the hem of her evening gown, she rushed down the sidewalk toward the building.

Jane was working at her desk in her upstairs office when Cordelia burst in.

"You gotta come," she said, yanking Jane out of her chair.

"Hey," said Jane, feeling her arm almost wrenched out of its socket. "Where's the fire?" When she looked up, she did a double take. "What happened to you?"

Cordelia appeared wild eyed in her slinky midnight blue evening gown, but it was the magenta, blue and green hair spiking in every direction that caught Jane's attention.

"Just come!" She dragged Jane down the stairs, through the long bar and out onto the street. "Look!" she cried, pointing at the police cruisers, their lights flashing in the darkness.

Released from Cordelia's iron grip, Jane straightened her clothes. "I thought I heard sirens a few minutes ago," she said, rubbing her shoulder. "Something happen down at the Unicorn?"

"It's Melanie! She's hurt."

That's all Jane needed to hear. She cut around a group of people who'd gathered to watch the scene from a safe distance and ran flat out to the alley behind the bar. Ducking into the shadows, she took a moment to get her bearings. A paramedic van had pulled into the space between the parked cars. Just as Cordelia lumbered up next to her, Jane spied a cop she knew. "Hey, Michael?" She waved at him, hoping he'd see her and come over.

Michael Chen had bartended at the Lyme House a couple years ago while he was getting his law enforcement degree at North Hennepin Community College.

"Is that Chen over there?" asked Cordelia, pressing a hand to her chest as she tried to catch her breath.

Michael finished talking to one of the other cops, then drifted over. "What are you two doing here?" He was tall, dark, extremely good looking, and always had a grim look on his face. Cordelia thought he was a self-important jerk. Jane merely saw him as determined.

"Cordelia thinks she knows who was attacked," said Jane. "Her name is Melanie Gunderson. She's about five-six, brown hair."

"She was wearing a brown leather jacket over black jeans," said Cordelia. "Is it her? Is she okay?"

Chen moved up next to them. "What else do you know about her?"

"Was she badly hurt?" asked Jane.

"She's lost a lot of blood."

Cordelia's eyes opened wide. "But she's going to be okay, right?"

"Whoever knifed her knew right where to cause the most damage. But she's still breathing. We're transporting her to HCMC. Don't get your hopes up. From what I saw, I wouldn't hold my breath that she'll even make it to the emergency room."

Cordelia collapsed against the side of the building and sank to the ground.

Jane bent down to make sure she was okay.

"She was the love of my life," cried Cordelia, covering her face with her hands.

Jane looked up at Michael. "They were an item once, years ago."

"No, no, we're back together," cried Cordelia. "We just made up."

Chen crouched down on the other side of her. "Do you have any idea what happened?"

"She was supposed to meet a guy. His name was Smith, but—but she didn't think he was telling the truth. He promised to give her some information about a story she was working on. He showed up a little after one-thirty and they went outside to talk."

"She's a reporter?"

"She works for *City Beat*," said Jane.

"That artsy-fartsy weekly?"

"It's not artsy-fartsy," snapped Cordelia. It's *independent*. Counterculture."

"Can you describe the guy?" asked Chen.

Cordelia rubbed the tears out of her eyes. "God, it was so dark in the bar. I remember he had on a black baseball cap. The Raiders, I think. That's a baseball team, right?"

"Football," said Chen.

"Whatever. I'm sure that's what it was. I couldn't see his face very well. I can't believe—I mean, I was just talking to her a few minutes ago. And now—"

"Can you describe the man physically? Was he white, black—"

"White," said Cordelia, glancing down at the briefcase slung over her shoulder. "And sort of, well, really, he was basically just kind of nondescript. Not fat, not skinny, not tall, not short, although maybe more on the thin side. He was wearing a dark jacket and dark pants."

Except for the cap and the fact that he was white, nothing Cordelia had said was very helpful. Jane had a bunch of questions of her own, but decided to let Michael take the lead.

"Do you know what your friend was working on? What kind of story?"

97

Cordelia glanced at Jane, then looked away as if she were thinking the question over. Speaking in a tight voice that Jane new was fake, but Chen probably didn't, she said, "No, not really. She didn't talk about that kind of thing with me."

Jane stared at her, blank-faced.

Standing up, Chen adjusted his cap and looked around. "I need you to talk to my sergeant. Wait here, okay?"

As he angled back through the crowd, Jane got right up into Cordelia's face. "Why'd you do that? You lied to him!"

"I'm protecting your dad!"

"That's great, Cordelia. But what about Melanie? Somebody just tried to kill her."

"You think I somehow failed to grasp that point?"

"So how do the police find Mr. White Nondescript with the Raider's cap if they don't know where to look?"

"I don't know! I'm working on it, okay." She closed her eyes and tipped her head back as a flood of helpless tears rolled down her cheeks.

12

It was almost three in the morning. Randy and Del sat on the lower deck at Randy's house, waiting for Larry to return from his meeting with Gunderson. The night was chilly and windy, with a brilliant canopy of stars overhead.

"He shoulda been back by now," said Del, pressing the light on his wristwatch to check the time. "You think he ran into problems?"

Randy took a swig of beer. "Hope not." The possible negative outcomes were so numerous, he couldn't even begin to anticipate them all. As a lawyer, Randy was used to working his way through each potential issue in a lawsuit. Before he entered a courtroom, he had all his bases covered. Everything was ordered, considered to the last detail. He was a man who craved order the way other men might crave alcohol or sex. It was survival coding, the only way he knew to keep the horror-stained semireality of his past at bay. But in a situation like this, order was impossible.

They resumed their restless silence, heads tilted up toward the sky.

"I hated the moon when we were in Nam," said Del.

"Yeah," said Randy, remembering how bright the nights could be. "I never felt that way when I was a kid. Night was just . . . like *dark*. Didn't matter if the moon was there or not."

"There are so many kinds of dark," muttered Del, leaning over and setting his empty beer bottle next to his chair. He kicked open the cooler and grabbed himself another—his third. Twisting off the cap, he said, "You know, when I was up in Grand Rapids a few weeks ago with the campaign, I met this old guy, an Ojibwe leader. We got to talking after Ray's speech. One thing led to another and he eventually brought up the subject of the Ojibwe Vision Quest. Ever heard of it?"

Randy shook his head.

"When I was in junior high, I was given this assignment on how boys become men in different cultures. I remember it because it touched a nerve in me. A lot of cultures make boys go through a rite of passage. I was supposed to pick one of them and write a two-page paper on it. I never wrote the paper, of course, but I did do some of the reading. I thought it was all pretty interesting stuff. So, I guess, I was curious what this guy had to say."

"And?"

"Well, the Ojibwe look at life a lot differently than we do. They think the world is filled with spirits that inhabit birds, rocks, trees, animals, the wind, the moon, everything really. Each person gets a personal vision to help him navigate his life. They receive it when they're young—teenagers, usually. In fact, an Ojibwe's life doesn't really begin until he's acquired his guiding vision."

"Is it just for boys?" asked Randy.

"No, girls, too. They make this journey into the wilderness, where they fast and wait for their personal animal spirit guide to reveal to them the central truth of their life. When they know what it is, then they go back home and take on the mantle of adulthood."

"Sounds . . . civilized."

"Yeah, it does—compared to what we went through. I mean, we were just kids when we were sent to Vietnam. I figure that's where we grew up, where we received our vision."

"God, I hope not," said Randy, finally seeing where Del was headed. "I suppose I had a few visions while I was there, usually when I was fucked up on something. But they weren't anything I'd want to build my life around."

"But don't you get it? It's not just the fact of the vision that makes the whole thing work, it's the time in your life that's important. When you're young, you're open to the world, to experience, to idealism, or as the Ojibwe call it, a vision quest."

"Okay. I'll play along. What do you suppose the animals and trees in Vietnam were trying to tell us?"

"Waste or be wasted," said Del. "The world is a rotting sinkhole. Corpses are heavy. Leaders are arrogant assholes at best, at worst, insane. We came home with that crap lodged in our souls. That was our vision."

And so much more, thought Randy. "Larry always said we were there for righteous reasons. Me, I thought it was wrong, but I went anyway. I was drafted and I was too ashamed to let my family think I was a coward—but that's what I was. That's what I learned about myself over there. I was scared the entire time."

"You weren't any different than any other guy. We were all

grunts, peeing in the bushes or our pants, hoping the next bullet that came along didn't have our name on it."

"Not Larry," said Randy.

"No," said Del softly. "Not Larry. But we'd both be dead if it weren't for him. If I ever saw a real hero, it was Larry Wilton."

Randy didn't like to think about it too hard. Larry had saved his life, for sure, but usually that's as far as the conversation in his head got. Nam wasn't the movies. Larry wasn't a hero because he was a deeply principled man, a natural leader who used his moral superiority to motivate men. No, Larry was just an average guy that, for whatever reason, hadn't been saddled with the same kind of paralyzing fear Randy had felt from the moment he set foot in country. In so many ways, Larry was in his element in Nam. He'd been such a great soldier that Randy had been a little surprised when he hadn't made a success out of his life back home. Obviously, the requirements were different, although Randy hadn't known that as a young man. Larry had gone from being a kind of god in Randy's life to a screwup—but through it all, Larry always seemed to maintain a positive outlook. For Larry, the world was an exciting place, where possibilities abounded. Maybe, in some odd way, he was a hero after all.

"The worst part for me," said Del, "was seeing my buddies die. That's what got me in the end. Not the bullshit about the importance of our mission, but the need to protect the only people I cared about. For *that* I was willing to kill—and die." He tipped his beer bottle back and took a few swallows. "The world is a graveyard, man. Another vision to live by."

"Hey, remember that old papa san who got the drop on us up near Phong Dien? Man, I thought we were dead meat for sure."

"But then Larry drops out of a tree right on top of the guy, making *uga uga* sounds like a gorilla. I remember thinking, hell, if I was gonna die, at least I'd die laughing."

"You know, if something had happened to you or Larry, if I hadn't had your friendship to lean on all these years, I don't—" Randy couldn't finish the sentence. Even now, the emotion was still so close to the surface that it choked off words. Looking away, he tried to stuff the feelings back down inside him.

"Hey, I see headlights," said Del, standing and moving over to the railing. "This one's gotta be Larry."

They watched as a red Dodge Dakota pulled into the drive.

"That's Ethan's truck," said Randy.

"What's he doing out this late?"

As Ethan walked up to the house, Randy called to him from the deck. "Where you been?"

Ethan squinted into the darkness. "Oh, hi, Randy. I was . . . just out driving around."

"Any particular reason?"

He inched his way toward the front door. "Nope. Just couldn't sleep. But I'm tired now. Think I'll go to bed."

"Okay," said Randy, shrugging at Del. "See you in the morning."

They heard the door open and then shut.

"He doing okay?" asked Del, sitting back down.

"He misses Sherrie."

"You and her . . . talking?"

"Not much."

"My heart goes out to you, man. Kesia and my kids, they're why I get up in the morning."

Randy didn't look at him. Instead, he walked over to the ice chest and grabbed himself a can of Coke.

"More headlights," said Del, pointing at two pinpricks of light in the distance.

They both waited as the truck pulled into the drive.

"We're on the deck," called Del, as Larry cracked the door.

"Be right there." He cut across the grass and climbed the short stairway, rubbing his hands together. "Hey boys. The brewskies would be where?"

"In the cooler," said Randy. "What happened?"

Larry leaned over and grabbed himself a bottle. "All is well, my brothers."

"She take the money?" asked Randy.

"Yup."

"Where's the file?"

Larry reached into the pocket of his jacket and pulled out a key.

"What's that?" asked Del.

"It's for a locker at the YWCA on Lake Street. We gotta wait until tomorrow morning to go get it."

Del grabbed Larry by his jacket, backed him up against the rail. "You're telling me you gave her all that money and all you got was a lousy key?"

"Don't worry, man. I made it real clear that I knew where she lived. If she messed with me even a little, she'd be hearin' from me again."

"Jesus H. Christ," said Randy, tossing the full can of Coke over his shoulder. "We got nothing."

"Back the hell off, you guys. We'll have the entire file in the morning, I promise."

"Did she tell you what she found out?" asked Randy, raking a hand through his hair.

"She talked to some people down in Waldo. Folks who re-membered the night in question. I think one was the bartender at Big Chick's Lounge. And maybe your uncle, too."

"It doesn't end here," said Del, turning away from them and staring out across the dark meadow. "Not if these people are so willing to talk."

"Let's just wait and see," said Larry. "Believe me, I'm all over this one. Nothin' to worry your pretty little heads about. I'll take care of business, just like always."

Early the next morning, Randy's eyes blinked open to the sound of a closing door. Sunlight streamed in through an open shade. Glancing at the clock on the nightstand, he saw that it was just after six. He turned over on his back and listened to a truck engine cough a couple of times and then catch. It had to be Larry's new junker, an '84 Silverado.

Randy rubbed his eyes and then glanced over at the empty space next to him. He doubted he'd ever get used to sleeping alone. It was awfully early for Larry to be up, but then Randy figured Larry was as anxious to see the contents of that reporter's file as he was. Closing his eyes, he tried to clear his mind and go back to sleep, but once his mind engaged, it was all over. He might as well get up.

For a second he considered shouting to Larry from the bedroom window to wait, that he'd toss on some clothes and go with him. But then he remembered that Katie was asleep in her room downstairs. He didn't want to wake her. Instead, he slipped into his bathrobe and headed two flights down to the kitchen to make coffee.

Larry would be back soon enough.

13

On Friday morning, Peter made it to the airport by 7:20, and boarded an MD-80 headed for New Jersey at 9:15. His appointment with Cabot was scheduled for 2:00, which meant that if all went as planned, he'd be back home by late evening.

In the past few months, Peter had spent so much time waiting for something to happen—for a job offer, for Sigrid to leave him, for his money to run out—that actual movement felt exhilarating.

He stuffed his bag in the overhead bin, then sat down in his aisle seat. Cabot might not be able to do much other than confirm that Shifflet had found the right couple, but at least it was something concrete. Beyond that, Peter wanted to get a good look at the man who'd created so much havoc in his life.

As the plane took off, he closed his eyes. He usually slept when he flew, but he was too keyed up today. When the seat belt sign went off, he got up and opened the storage bin. Several days ago, his father had messengered over some papers he wanted Peter to read.

Peter pulled the file folder out of the side pocket, then closed the bin and sat back down. Flipping through the contents, he saw that it was a bunch of position papers on various political topics, as well as a few of his dad's campaign speeches.

Because of his work as a cameraman at WTWN, Peter was familiar with most of the important issues in state and local politics. He'd also been present for several of his father's local appearances, so most of the speeches were variations on a theme. It wasn't something he'd ever expressed to his dad, but he was repelled by politics and politicians, although he understood the need for intelligent, decent, committed people to take on the job. He wasn't sure how well he'd do working for a political campaign, but he figured he owed it a shot, especially since he wasn't being inundated with marvelous job offers.

Even as a young child, Peter had been aware that he came from a family of overachievers. He wasn't one of them. For all practical purposes, his dad might as well have been Perry Mason and his sister Julia Child. Well, maybe it wasn't that bad, but sometimes it felt that way. And it wasn't just about personal achievement, either.

Both Peter's dad and his sister had an amazing inner strength—at least it sure seemed that way to him. All he really knew was that he didn't have the same kind of certainty about who he was or where he was going. Maybe it was partly because he'd lost his mother at such a young age. He'd wondered about that. But Jane had lost a mother, too. In her case, it seemed to focus her energy. She'd needed to grow up fast and she had.

Peter, on the other hand, had felt like a balloon filled with helium. If someone wasn't physically holding on to him at all times, he was afraid he'd float away over the rooftops and be lost forever. He couldn't sleep in his bedroom after his mom was gone. He became terrified of the dark. Either he slept with Jane, or on the sofa in the basement rec room, where he could keep the TV on all night. Entering his parents' bedroom was impossible. The scent of his mother lingered in there and made him cry. Crying embarrassed him so he stayed away. And then Jane left to go back to England. One more tether to the earth came unstuck.

At five years old, Peter Lawless lost his faith in happy endings and slowly morphed into the kid who stood in the shadows, waiting for someone older to tell him what to do. He loved his dad, but he'd always been closer to his mom. She was the one who represented safety, tenderness, stability, all the things he craved. His father taught him right from wrong, but it was his mother who told him stories, helping him to understand the difference.

Long about seventh grade, Peter's dad began calling him a "people person." It may not have been meant as a slam, but to Peter, who'd become supersensitive to attacks on his character, it seemed like a nice way of saying he was weak. Only weak people liked to have friends or family around all the time. Only weak people hated to be alone.

Peter didn't think he'd changed much from the little boy he'd once been. He didn't blame his family. His dad had always been there for him. He looked up to both his dad and his sister. But Peter wanted someone to look up to *him*. Jane always said how much she loved his gentle soul, but Peter read gentle as another flaw, another deficit. He wanted to be a man, like his dad. He wanted to take charge, be strong, make a difference. Maybe that was one reason he'd become so obsessed with finding

Margaret. He needed to prove he could succeed at something important.

Wood-Ridge, New Jersey, the town where Cabot lived, was about thirty minutes northeast of the Newark airport. Cabot suggested they meet at his house instead of his office in Jersey City because it was more comfortable. Peter didn't care where they met, as long as he got the information he'd come for.

As he pulled his rented Chevy into the wide drive in front of the three-car garage, his cell phone trilled. Sliding it out of his pocket, he checked the caller ID. It was Shifflet.

"This is Peter," he said, glancing up at the expensive two-story colonial. The curtains in the living room parted slightly at the center, but because of the glare on the glass, he couldn't see who was inside.

"You got a minute for an update?"

"You bet."

"I waited until Tanhauer left for work this morning," said Shifflet. "That's when I talked to his wife. I figured I could get more out of her if she was alone. I asked her about Margaret right up front. At first she denied knowing anything about her."

Peter's heart sank. He was hoping for a simple explanation. "She's lying."

"I know. She finally came clean after I showed her a copy of the adoption papers."

"What adoption papers? There aren't any."

"Sure there are. Looked pretty official, too. I included the Tanhauers' names and the street address where they were living when they adopted her."

"How'd you find that?"

"It's what you pay me for, pal. It was a row house in the Village. Nice place. I checked it out last night. Anyway, she gave up pretty quick when she looked at those fake papers. I put in a bunch of legal mumbo jumbo, then signed Cabot's name at the bottom, and Sigrid's."

"You're a genius."

"I like to think so, but mainly she was scared. That was clear from the moment I mentioned Margaret's name. I told her I was a PI, gave her my card. Said I was trying to find Margaret—for a client. She wanted to know who, but I told her it was private."

"So where is Margaret?"

"You sitting down?"

"Just tell me."

"Mrs. Tanhauer said she died."

A tremor rippled across Peter's cheek. "When? How?"

"SIDS. When she was eight months old."

Peter bowed his head, rested it against the steering wheel. "I don't believe it."

"Neither did I. That's part of what I been doing all day. Looking for her death certificate. The long and short of it is, there isn't one. So I went back to the house, but by the time I got there, Mr. Tanhauer was home. He wouldn't even let me in the door, so I stood on the front steps and asked him about Margaret, told him there was no death certificate on record and asked why that was. He said it was my problem if I couldn't find it. Then he slammed the door in my face."

Peter smacked his fist against the steering wheel.

"Just wait. It gets better. As I was about to drive away, I get this call from the lady who lived next to the Tanhauers in the Village. Like I said, I drove down there last night, talked to a bunch of people. A few remembered them, but not very well. One guy told me to go talk to the woman who owned the row house next to the one the Tanhauers rented. Apparently, she'd been there since the Declaration of Independence was signed, knew everything that happened in the neighborhood. I knocked on her door, but she either wasn't home or wasn't answering. So I wrote a message on the back of my card and stuffed it under her door. Her name is Disalvatore. Lucia Disalvatore. She's the one who called. And get this. She not only remembered the Tanhauers, she remembered Margaret. Said she used to baby-sit her, that she was a sweet little girl, but very quiet. Actually, she said she never spoke. The woman thought it was odd because the kid was almost two."

"What?"

"Carrie Tanhauer was lying, Lawless. Margaret didn't die of SIDS. But she did disappear from their lives right around the time they moved to the Upper East Side—the place they lived before they moved to that apartment on the West Side. I plan to check out the East Side address this afternoon. My guess is that they moved for a reason. I'm bettin' that nobody at the East Side address will have ever heard of Margaret. Whatever happened to her happened during that move. We've got to find out what. If you've got another minute, I'll tell you what I think."

"Go ahead."

"People like the Tanhauers, folks who are willing to buy a kid, well, there's something wrong with them in my book. What if they get a kid that turns out to be defective in some way? What do you think they'd do?"

"You're saying there was something wrong with Margaret?"

"She's *two* and she doesn't talk? When my kid was two he never shut up."

"You think they did something to her?"

"I'm not saying they offed her, but I'll bet you anything they got rid of her. I mean, they paid good money for damaged goods. Rich people don't stand for that. If either of us ever does talk to that lawyer who brokered the deal, that's the first question that should get asked.. If Margaret turned out not to be a perfectly healthy child, I figure there's a good chance they took her back to the lawyer and demanded a refund."

"But what about Margaret? What happened to her?"

"Hope you got a lot of money, pal, because this investigation is gonna take time."

The fact was, each morning Peter opened up his laptop and looked at the numbers in his dwindling checking account. At the rate Shifflet charged, it wouldn't be long before he was broke. "Call me after you check out the East Side address. And then send me another invoice. This time, use my Yahoo address."

"Will do, sport. Later."

With a sinking feeling in his stomach, Peter tossed the cell on the passenger's seat, then got out of the car. If Margaret was still alive, and he prayed she was, her fate could easily rest on the conversation he was about to have with Vaughn Cabot.

He removed his briefcase from the backseat, locked the car, then approached the front of the house. The curtains were no longer parted. After ringing the bell, he waited. It didn't take long for the door to be opened.

A thin, almost frail-looking man stood before him. His skin appeared leather hard from way too many hours spent on the golf course. Flat gray hair sat on top of his head like a saucer. He was dressed in a yellow shirt, striped tie, gray slacks, and white shoes, and looked for all the world like a man who'd been hermetically sealed inside the Sands Hotel in Vegas since the days of Sinatra and Dean Martin.

"Mr. Johnson?" said Cabot, flashing his baby white teeth.

"Yes," said Peter.

They shook hands.

Cabot led him to an office in the back of the house. The interior was silent. No one else seemed to be around. Cabot sat down behind his sleek, immaculately empty desk and motioned for Peter to take one of the Bauhaus-inspired chairs. The furniture looked expensive, but Peter had the sense that everything in the room was a cheap knockoff.

"I trust you had a good flight?" said Cabot, leaning back and lacing his fingers over his stomach.

"Fine," said Peter.

"May I see your financial records first, please?" He leaned forward.

Clenching his jaw, Peter said, "That's not why I came."

"I beg your pardon?"

"I'm here to find out what happened to Margaret Tanhauer. Don't play dumb, Mr. Cabot. Don't waste my time. You know who she is. You know Matt and Carrie Tanhauer. You placed Margaret with them ten years ago."

Cabot looked momentarily flustered. He stood up. "I—"

"Sit down!" demanded Peter.

Cabot's eyes narrowed.

"We can have a civil conversation or I can beat the information out of you. Your call." He saw Cabot's eyes move toward the top drawer.

In a flash, Peter was behind the desk. He slammed the drawer shut on Cabot's hand.

Cabot shrieked, falling back against his chair.

Peter grabbed the revolver and pointed it at him.

"You're not going to shoot me," said Cabot, regaining some of his composure.

"You don't know me from Adam. You have no idea what I'm capable of."

That put some doubt in his eyes. "All right. What do you want to know?"

"Where is she?"

"Dead. She died of SIDS when she was eight months old."

"Wrong. You lie to me again and you lose a kneecap. Lie a third time and the other knee goes. We've got a lot of anatomy to work through before we get to your brain." Peter didn't know where that came from. Too much TV, probably. And yet, when he said the words, he realized he meant them.

"She . . ."

"She what?" said Peter. "Tell me!"

"She had a learning problem. Carrie Tanhauer nearly had a breakdown over it. Matt brought Margaret back, said if I didn't find them another child—a healthy one—he'd report me to the police and the New Jersey Bar Association. But he didn't need to get nasty, Mr. Johnson—or, whatever your name is. I tell all my customers up front that I guarantee all my placements. It's part of the service I provide, which, in my opinion, is both necessary and unavoidable in this day and age. The Tanhauers now have two thriving young boys, thanks to me."

"What happened to Margaret!"

Cabot gave his head an irritated shake. "I assume she's in foster care."

"You *assume?*" Peter cocked the hammer.

"Look. I took her to Jersey City Child Protective Services and told them that I found her wandering the streets. That was a lie, of course, but I had to say something."

"Did you give them her name?"

"No, I didn't give them a name. From that point on, she was in the system and no longer my concern."

"Then how am I supposed to find her?"

"Not my problem," said Cabot.

"When did you leave her there? I want the exact date."

He stood and opened a filing cabinet.

"Take it slow," said Peter. "Just in case you've got more guns lying around."

"No more guns," said Cabot, removing a date book. He flipped through it, back and forth, until he came to the correct page. "February 17th. Eight years ago this past February."

Peter's mind started to race. If he had any other questions, he needed to ask them now. "What did she look like?"

Cabot raised his eyes in thought. "Platinum blond. Blue eyes, I think. Yes, blue. Pretty little girl. Actually, she was the spitting image of her mother, if I recall correctly."

The words were like a knife twisting in Peter's stomach.

Closing his eyes, Cabot continued. "Her facial features were rounded, I'd say. Not the least bit angular. She was compact. Well muscled. The gymnast type, if you know what I mean. Sweet, but retarded."

Peter's heart was bleeding. "People like you don't deserve to live."

"If you needed my services," said Cabot, dropping the date book on his desk, "you might take a less righteously indignant view. Now, if that's all, I'd like you to leave."

14

Jane sat on the couch in her living room, legs tucked up under her, talking on the phone to Kenzie. Mouse was stretched out next to her, his head in her lap.

"So it was a long night," she said, her hand caressing the fur around Mouse's ears. "We sat in the emergency room until dawn. Melanie's holding her own, but that's all we know. She's still unconscious. The police are calling it an attempted murder. If she dies—"

"Is that possible?"

"At this point, I think anything is possible."

"Where's Cordelia now?"

"Upstairs trying to catch a little sleep."

"That's what you should probably be doing."

"No, I'd rather talk to you. I can sleep later." Jane dropped her head back against the pillow. "Melanie's mother should be here soon. Cordelia called her from the waiting room last night."

"Where does she live?"

"Kansas City, Missouri. That's where Melanie grew up."

"So let me get this straight. You think Melanie was attacked because of the story she was working on. That old murder case in Iowa."

"That's my theory. I think we should tell the police everything we know, but Cordelia's convinced it would hurt my dad's campaign. She may be right, and if she is, I guess it's something we should consider, but still . . . I met a guy last fall who works as a bodyguard. Cordelia and I are paying him and a friend of his to sit by Mel's door at the hospital, 24/7."

"You think that's really necessary?"

"If we don't go to the police and something happened to her, I couldn't live with myself."

"I guess you better make a decision then—and fast."

"Yeah."

"You sound beat."

"I am."

"Would you like to change the subject for a few minutes?"

"Boy, would I."

"We're still on for the Memorial Day party, right? You're coming down on the 28th? Will you be able to use your dad's plane?"

"Not sure yet, but I'd say it's unlikely."

"Well, here's the big news. We're riding in the Chadwick Memorial Day parade. The college organizes one every year. It's a big deal around here. I told them we'd carry a banner between us."

"We're *riding?*"

"Yeah, my horses. You on Ben, me on Rocket."

Jane was actually starting to feel at ease on a horse. Kenzie had been a good teacher.

117

"I bought us each fringed suede jackets. Yours is black—with a line of red and white embroidery on the front—and mine is buckskin, with turquoise and yellow embroidery. They're gorgeous. And, of course, we'll each wear cowboy hats. We can buy those when you get down here. But the jackets arrived yesterday. I guessed at your size—we're pretty similar. I sent it to you this morning, just in case it needs some alterations."

"You're really going all out."

"Do you realize this will be our first big party together at the ranch? You and me—as a couple. But remember, you promised to do the food. I'm leaving that all to you."

"Not a problem."

"I am so excited. You *promise* me that nothing will come up at work, right?"

"I've already got it handled." Jane had disappointed Kenzie on more than one occasion over the last couple of years, always because of her work schedule. She'd had to cancel a few long weekends in Chadwick, and once she'd even had to back out of a planned vacation. Kenzie was still smarting over that one.

"Hey, look at the time," said Kenzie. "I've got a class in half an hour and I'm not even dressed."

"Call me later," said Jane.

"Love you, babe. Bye."

Jane sat for a moment and tried to rub the tiredness out of her shoulders. On her way to the kitchen to make herself a sandwich, she looked up and saw Cordelia slumping down the stairs from the second floor.

"Melanie's mother just called." She held up her cell phone, then let her hand flop to her side.

"And?"

"Mel's officially in a coma. Her vitals are getting stronger, but they think she may've hit her head when she fell. They're doing tests."

"And that's why she's still unconscious?"

"The doctors aren't being terribly specific."

"Do they have a prognosis?"

"Not according to Tammy. That's Melanie's mother. She seems like a nice enough woman, but she has a voice like a frog with a bad head cold." Cordelia sank down on one of the dining-room chairs.

"Where will she stay while she's here?" asked Jane.

"At Melanie's place. She's renting a duplex over on 34th Avenue. Her mom was asking about a key."

"Do you have one?"

"As it happens, I do."

Jane moved over behind Cordelia and began to rub the back of her neck.

"I told Tammy that I'd put a key under a flower pot by the back door. You'll have to drive me back to the Unicorn so I can get my car."

Cordelia had been too upset to drive herself to the hospital last night. Normally, she refused to ride in Jane's Mini because, as a plus-sized person, she found it Lilliputian.

Jane sat down next to her. "I could drive you over to Melanie's first."

"Fine," said Cordelia, her voice a dull monotone. "I got to thinking after I told her about the key. Melanie's mom doesn't know she's gay."

"That's awkward."

"Yeah. But this might not be the best time to drop it on her. I think we should go over and de-dyke the place. Melanie would thank us, believe me. What do you say? You wanna help me get rid of her ten copies of *Curious Wine*—or whatever?"

119

"I'm there," said Jane, covering Cordelia's hand with her own. "Whatever you need."

Half an hour later, they pulled up in front of a cocoa brown stucco building with white trim. There wasn't much of a yard because the house was so big.

"She rents the first floor," said Cordelia, struggling to get out of the Mini. "The couple who own it live in the top half. Two gay guys."

"You don't think her mother is going to get the message?"

"Nope," said Cordelia. "You know the way it is. Most straight people only see what they want to see. That's why they can live in the world and never think they've met a gay person."

Jane agreed that it was a strange kind of blindness.

When Cordelia opened the front door, an odd little white critter slithered past. Jane caught it as it darted between her legs.

"What is it?" she asked, holding it up to get a better look.

"Oh, Bones! I forgot about him. He's Melanie's cat. She's had him forever."

"What kind is he?" Jane had never seen anything like him before. He had batlike large brownish ears that stuck out at an upright angle, big round gray eyes, and a tight, white, wavy coat. His paws almost looked like fingers.

"He's a Cornish Rex," said Cordelia. "Poor thing. I wonder if he has any food or water."

While Cordelia busied herself in the kitchen, making sure the cat was cared for, Jane drifted through the house. "She likes antiques. And books."

"Two of her finer qualities."

Jane scooped up several copies of *Lavender,* the local GLBT paper, off the coffee table in the living room. On top of an old upright piano she found a bunch of back issues of Lambda Book Report. On the piano bench was a stack of books. Most were current affairs. *American Theocracy*, by Kevin Phillips. *The Battle for God—A History of Fundamentalism*, by Karen Armstrong. *The Smartest Guys in the Room: The Amazing Rise and Scandalous Fall of Enron*, by Bethany McLean and Peter Elkind. And two novels: *One Hundred Years of Solitude*, by Gabriel Garcia Marquez. And *The Remains of the Day*, by Kazuo Ishiguro.

"There's a Fran Lebowitz Reader here," called Jane. "Think I should bag it?"

"Nah," said Cordelia, coming through the kitchen door cuddling Bones in her arms.

"She's not really into light reading," said Jane.

"Actually, she loves a good mystery or romance, but she reads everything."

Jane walked into the study. Sitting down at Melanie's desk, she picked up several old newspaper clippings and read through them while Cordelia searched the bookcase behind her.

"This is what I was afraid of," said Cordelia with a groan. "Here's the cache. We'll need a semi to get all these books out of here. Karin Kallmaker. Andrew Holleran. Val McDermid. Armistead Maupin. J. M. Redmann. Michael Cunningham. Sarah Waters. Jim Grimsley. Lori L. Lake. Augusten Burroughs. Radclyffe. Ellen Hart. Hey, maybe I'll have to borrow that last one."

"Listen to this," said Jane. "It's from the *Fort Dodge Messenger*. May 21, 1971."

"Local Woman Found Dead

On Wednesday morning, the body of Susan Bouchard, daughter of Rod and Grace Bouchard, longtime residents of Waldo, Iowa, was found along County Road 6. Mark

Trumble, another resident of Waldo, was on his way to work in Fort Dodge when he spied two people slumped against a weeping willow along the County Rd. Being a good samaritan, Mr. Trumble stopped his car to make sure everything was okay. It was later determined that the woman, Susan Bouchard, 20, had been strangled to death sometime during the night. The police were immediately summoned.

"The man with Miss Bouchard, Ethan Turk, 24, the son of Harold and Bernice Turk of Waldo, was suffering from a hangover, but was otherwise unharmed. Turk had been sleeping with his arm around Miss Bouchard's stomach and appeared to have no idea how he got there or what had happened.

"Mr. Turk has been taken into police custody for further questioning."

"This is incredible," said Jane. "I had no idea about any of this."

"Are there more clippings?" asked Cordelia, moving over to a window overlooking the front yard.

"A bunch of them. All from the *Fort Dodge Messenger*." She moved on to the next.

"May 22, 1971

Ethan Turk Arrested

Ethan Turk, 24, son of Harold and Bernice Turk of Waldo, Iowa, was arrested yesterday for the murder of Susan Bouchard, 20, daughter of Rod and Grace Bouchard, also residents of Waldo. Miss Bouchard's body was discovered in a field along County Road 6 the morning of May 20th.

"In a statement to the press, Mr. Turk's lawyer, Irwin Bernstadt of Des Moines, said that his client was entirely innocent of the murder charge and would plead not guilty at an
arraignment later today. Bernstadt added that the police had
no proof whatsoever that his client had strangled Miss
Bouchard. He made no comment about the fact that Mr.
Turk had been found with her the morning her body was discovered.

"Before her death, Sue Bouchard was in her second year of a
prelaw program at Drake University in Des Moines. She was
considered an outstanding student with a bright future. Miss
Bouchard had been dating Randall Turk, Ethan Turk's
brother, before he left to serve in Vietnam. Randall had returned home less than two weeks before her death. In a
statement to this paper, Randall Turk said that he believed
his brother to be entirely innocent and would be proved so at
the trial."

Jane skipped the next two articles because they were simply a
rehash of the first two. "Here's the verdict," she said.

"August 29, 1971
Jury Acquits Turk of Murder
Ethan Turk, resident of Waldo, Iowa, was acquitted yester-
day of the murder of Susan Bouchard, daughter of Rod and
Grace Bouchard, also of Waldo.

"A jury spokesperson gave a statement at the courthouse after the trial: 'The bottom line was, the prosecution didn't
prove its case. Simple as that. In my opinion, Ethan's biggest

123

error was being at the scene of the crime. He's slow, for sure, but he understands right from wrong. He's a responsible young man with a good future at Casin's Auto Shop. And he had no motive to kill Sue that I could discern. I think the police jumped the gun when they arrested him. I pray he can put this part of his life behind him and move on.'

"The parents of Susan Bouchard were asked to make a statement, but left the courthouse without comment." '

Jane picked up the last article. "This final one's from the op-ed section." She read out loud:

"September 11, 1971

Getting Away with Patriotic Murder

"As a resident of Waldo, I've had my doubts all along that Ethan Turk murdered Sue Bouchard in cold blood—mainly because I've known Ethan since he was a little boy. He's a decent kid, slow but kindhearted. What bothers me isn't that he was acquitted. I believe that in the last few months, we have witnessed a travesty of justice being perpetrated against Sue and her family—and against the good citizens of Waldo. I refer to the way in which this murder investigation was handled from the outset.

"The police saw Ethan as an easy target, so with little else to go on, they accused him of the crime. But let me tell you, the story goes a lot deeper than that. People have been reticent to tell what they saw or heard, some of us may even be afraid, but there's much more to the story than ever came out at the trial.

"This is a deeply patriotic community. We abhor the war protesters we see every night on the evening news. We aren't like that. We choose to honor the men and women who have served this country—even in unpopular wars. But in the last couple of days, I've come to the unhappy conclusion that it is *that* desire to honor and protect our heroes which has blinded us in our pursuit of justice.

"Now that Ethan has been declared innocent, we feel we can go back to our normal lives, content in the notion that justice has been done. But in doing so we forget that there is still a murderer loose in our midst—a murderer that may have come home to us wearing the uniform we revere so deeply.

"If we refuse to look past our own patriotic needs, if we are afraid to scratch beneath the surface of that uniform we honor so passionately, if we let our patriotic reverence blind us to the kind of ugliness that exists in the human soul— even a hero's soul—then we are guilty of just what the so-called hippies accuse us of: My country, right or wrong. That is a banner that should never fly over any home in this nation. It is our own patriotic cowardice that has led us to this refusal to dig deeper into this horrific homicide. But nothing less than the truth should ever satisfy any of us.
Signed,
Alf Trotter
A Proud World War II Vet"

"Boy," said Jane, sitting back and letting the clipping fall to the desk, "I wonder what happened to him. If he's still alive, I'll bet he'd give us an earful about what really went down all those years ago." She turned to get Cordelia's reaction, but Cordelia's attention seemed to be focused on something outside the house. "What are you looking at?"

"A truck."

"What's so interesting about a truck?"

"I wish I had a pair of binoculars. I think the person sitting inside is watching the house. He looks a lot like the guy I saw in the bar last night, black cap and thin face."

"You never said he had a thin face."

Cordelia bent closer to the window. "I didn't remember it until right now. I'm positive that's him."

"Can you see the license plate?"

Cordelia squinted. "Too far away."

"Maybe I can see it," said Jane, edging in next to her. "It's a Minnesota plate. CKB—"

"169."

"No, GKE 789," said Jane. "Or—"

"Hell, we need to get a closer look."

"Wait," said Jane.

Before she could stop her, Cordelia had dashed back through the house and burst out the front door. "Damn," she said, watching the truck speed off down the street. She stood in the middle of the sidewalk, hands stuffed into the pockets of her new black-and-white football referee's jacket. "Who the hell *is* that guy?"

"Well, if he's the man Melanie met last night, we know one thing for sure. He's dangerous." Jane stood on the front steps, one hand shading her eyes from the sun. "Rushing out here wasn't exactly smart. Now he's seen you twice."

Cordelia hugged herself and shivered. "Lord, someone should have my head examined!"

"I'd be happy to make the appointment. Look, I think we better call the cops. Let them know about the truck, and that you think it was the same guy."

"Absolutely not," said Cordelia, stomping back up the front steps. "Let me say this once more—slowly—so you get it. If Randy Turk and Delavon Green are pulled into this, it could wreck your father's chance at becoming our next governor. Use your little gray cells, Janey. This is an old murder case—a *cold case*."

"But what about Melanie? That's not a cold case—unless we let it become one." Normally, if Jane wanted to do something, she just did it. She didn't need Cordelia's approval. But on this one, she was truly conflicted. Certainty gave a person the edge—whether she was right or wrong. Cordelia had it. Jane didn't.

"You want Dinosaur Don Pettyjohn to be our next governor? Think, Janey! He's owned by every corporation in the state—hell, the universe. You give those sharks an opening and they'll eat your dad alive. Listen to me. Are you listening?"

"Yes."

"I had a friend in Arizona tell me once about a great candidate she was supporting for the U.S. Congress. The guy's campaign manager got caught doing drugs with a prostitute seven months before the election and, of course, it made all the papers. It wasn't like the candidate had anything to do with it, but his opponents made the rest of the election all about this guy's lack of judgment. How could he hire a man like that to run his campaign? Would you want a man with judgment like that working for you in Washington?"

"Did he lose in the general election?"

"By a landslide. And that's exactly what will happen to your dad if Del Green's name is associated with an old murder. Hell, Randy is one of his biggest backers. They'll use that to annihilate Ray."

"I see your point, but——"

"This is bigger than just Melanie. There was a third guy, right? Can't remember his name, but——"

"Wilton," said Jane. "Larry Wilton. Maybe he's the one who murdered Sue Bouchard. Could be he's the guy in the truck. If we could just prove he did it, my dad——and Del and Randy—— would be off the hook. And then we could tell the police what we know."

"That's a huge *if*. Hey, I've got an idea." Cordelia pulled a quarter out of her jacket pocket. "Let's toss a coin."

"Oh, great. I love it. You always come up with such innovative *mature* solutions."

"Creative to the core."

Jane thought about it for a second. "Okay. Sure, I'll play. Heads we don't tell the cops. Tails we throw caution to the wind and tell them everything we know."

"No," said Cordelia, cupping the coin in her hands and blowing on it. "Heads we don't tell the cops. Tails, you and me, we drive down to Waldo for a little R & R. Maybe talk to the guy who wrote that op-ed piece."

"You'd do that?"

"It's what you want, right?"

"Yeah, actually, it is."

"Fine. To shut you up, I'd do just about anything. And besides, there's a fifty-fifty chance it will be heads and"——she poked Jane in the chest——"that means you have to shut up about talking to the cops for the duration."

"All right. Toss it."

Cordelia launched the coin into the air, caught it, and flipped it onto the arm of her jacket. Raising her hand to look at it, one eyebrow shot upward. "Well well. Seems like we're headed down to Waldo on a little fact-finding mission."

"What about Melanie? You can't just leave her."

"We won't be gone long. And until we go, I plan to spend every waking minute by her side."

15

Peter tried a smile, but it wasn't returned. The woman with the thick Jersey accent standing behind the counter at Child Protective Services in Newark instructed him to take a seat in the waiting room. She might have added, but didn't, that since he had chosen to come in without an appointment he was royally screwing up her day. In a tight voice, she told him she couldn't promise anything, but that she'd see if her supervisor could squeeze him in.

Peter took the chair next to the door. There were at least thirty other people in the room, some with children, some trying to ignore the din by reading a magazine, others looking bored, anxious, confused, or a combination of all three.

By the time Peter was finally allowed in to see someone, the room had all but cleared out. It was going on five-thirty. He ran a quick hand over his hair, wished he had some gum. He hadn't eaten since breakfast. He'd stopped at a gas station after leaving Cabot's place and searched the yellow pages for the address he wanted in Newark. He was still hoping he wouldn't have to spend the night.

"How can I help you, Mr. . . . Johnson?" The woman looked down at a yellow Post-it note, then removed her glasses and stared up at him. She had iodine-colored skin, a slippery spray of black bangs, and kind eyes.

He explained what he knew about Margaret, said she'd been dropped off somewhere in Jersey City on February 17th—eight years ago.

"And you have no name, just a description."

"That's right."

"You have to understand, Mr. Johnson, that even if I could help you, I simply don't have the time." She nodded to the foot-high stack of files on her desk. "The system is already severely overloaded. Every one of these cases needs my immediate attention. There aren't enough hours in the day to take care of all the kids—or parents—who are in trouble and need help. If I were to stop, spend all my efforts looking for your wife's little girl, what would happen to all these people?"

"Don't you have someone on your staff who might be less busy?"

"Everyone here is as backed up as I am."

"But—" His eyes locked on hers. "I mean, isn't there any way I could do the searching myself? Don't you have records I could look through?"

"All our records are confidential. I'd like to help you, but it's just not possible."

"The fact that she was learning disabled, doesn't that make her case stand out, even a little?"

She gave a mirthless laugh, shook her head. "Not in the slightest."

131

"So there's nothing I can do to find her."

She gazed across the desk at him with sad eyes. "I'm afraid not. I'm truly sorry."

"I don't accept that," said Peter, shooting to his feet.

"If I were you, I wouldn't either." She stood and extended her hand. "Good luck, Mr. Johnson. I wish you only the best."

16

When Randy entered the family room that same afternoon, he found his daughter, Katie, sitting on the floor with a bunch of his old phonograph records spread out in front of her. A Bob Dylan song played softly from the stereo—"My Back Pages," one of his favorites.

"What's up, honey?" he asked, a soft smile playing on his face as he sat down on the edge of the couch. "This music is prehistoric. Not exactly your style."

Katie's attention was focused on the back of a Procol Harum album. "Just looking around," she said, with an indifferent shrug.

"You like Dylan?"

"Not really."

Randy had been anxiously waiting all day for Larry to get back with Melanie Gunderson's file. Del had phoned at least four times, but there was nothing either of them could do. Randy envisioned Larry stopping at a bar to hoist a few and losing track of time. Larry was a talker. An extrovert. Get him started and he could go on for hours. On the other hand, Randy could come up with dozens of other scenarios for what had happened, each worse than the one before it. Sure, Larry could be a flake, but it wasn't like him to just forget about Randy and Del, not when the stakes were this high.

"Something wrong?" asked Katie, her blue eyes fixed on her father.

"No, honey. Just wondering where Larry is."

"You know, Dad, I don't know why he's even your friend. He smells. He's a mooch. He tries to help around the house, but he always ends up making an even bigger mess. He's like . . . this weird person who appears every few years, drinks your booze, makes you stay up late laughing at his raunchy jokes, and then disappears. And you . . . you get all goofy around him, like he's some kind of guru, when anybody with a brain can see he's, like, this total loser."

. She seemed angry. "He do something to upset you?"

She chewed on her lower lip, set the Procol Harum album down and picked up a Grateful Dead. "I don't get you at all, Dad. You fall all over yourself to be nice to that man. Why can't you be nice like that to Mom? It's like you care more about Del and him than you do about Mom and me."

"Never," said Randy, the word catching in his throat. "That's not true."

"Feels that way to me."

"Honey, I love you and your mother more than anything."

"Then why'd you split up with her?"

"It's . . . complicated. You're so young."

"Oh, right. The kid wouldn't understand."

Randy desperately wanted to get up and go do something else, make an excuse that he had work to do and they'd talk about it later, but they both knew that wouldn't cut it. Not this time. "It wasn't just the war, Katie, but what came after. It was like . . . you know that saying I hear people use every now and then. About getting their 'groove on,' or getting their 'groove back.' It was like we were in our own kind of groove over there—a mortal groove. Death—the possibility of dying or killing—was our reality. I don't know if you can truly understand what that feels like."

"I'm not a baby." She seemed so indignant.

"One instant you could be walking next to a guy, a friend, talking casually about nothing in particular, actually being kind of bored, and the next second you'd still be walking along but what was left of your buddy was hanging from a tree. After a while, I got used to living that way. We all did. The flies and the heat, the horror and the stink, it became our norm. And this is the tricky part, honey. When we came home, we were still in that groove. It wasn't like we could turn a switch and go back to our old way of living. We'd seen things no human being should ever have to see. Our reactions—our instincts—had been honed to keep us alive, but they didn't work for us back here. They were so *incredibly* wrong. We tried to slip back into our old selves, but some part of our brains was still stuck back there."

"But . . . like . . . how did that work?"

She really seemed to want to know, and that presented Randy with a problem. He felt obliged to give her a piece of the truth without getting himself in too deep.

"Well, for example. When I got home, your grandmother sent me to buy some groceries. I remember being in the store with all these other people who seemed so intent on what cereal

136

they were going to buy. What brand of milk. I wanted to scream at the top of my lungs that men were fighting and dying a world away. How could they even care about cereal brands. It was insane."

Randy watched his daughter go through a silent reassessment. "That makes sense."

"I was so angry all the time. People were living their normal lives and it just made me furious."

"Maybe it still does."

Randy lowered his head. "Yeah, maybe you're right."

"What else?"

She had no idea how hard this was for him. "Well, when Larry and Delavon came to Waldo to visit me, my mother told us to sleep in the basement. You remember the house, right? It was small, only two bedrooms. I'd always bunked with Ethan, but it didn't seem fair for us to take over his room. The first night we were all there, Larry kept getting up. He was driving Del and me crazy. The next night, after dinner, we found him out back. He was digging himself a foxhole. He'd set up a perimeter, like we'd been taught to do. He had a bunch of gear—night vision binoculars, rifle, extra ammo, poncho, field jacket, a couple knives, a boonie hat. He wore that boonie hat for years, until it rotted right off his head. Anyway, he was all set to crawl in for the night. Neither Del nor I even asked him why. We knew. He just didn't feel safe in the basement."

"But you didn't do that, right?"

"No, honey. Everybody reacted differently. We just knew enough to leave him alone, let him take care of his own business." Randy laughed, remembering his mother's reaction. "My mom thought he was nuts. And, of course, since Waldo is a pretty small community, word got around. When the three of us would go into town for some reason, or stop at a bar for a beer, Larry would get some strange looks."

"So, did you just kind of hang out? Do nothing?"

"For a while, yeah. I had a year of college behind me before I was sent over. I was an English major. I'd always thought I'd be a writer."

"Why didn't you?"

"I guess my priorities changed somewhere along the line. Larry had worked as a mechanic for a while out of high school. He's from southern Ohio. Had no interest in college. Del, well, he was on his way to gang oblivion before Nam. For him, the war was a real turning point. When he came home, he was determined to make something of himself. He never thought he was very smart, but he'd learned otherwise. Eventually, he got his GED—he'd quit school when he was fifteen. And then he earned his undergrad degree in political science at the University of Minnesota. He could have gone on for a master's, but he wanted to get out into the real world and see what he could do to change things."

The doorbell chimed.

"That's probably Mom," said Katie. She seemed crestfallen.

Randy glanced at his watch. It was almost six. "Seems kind of early."

"Can we talk about this again?"

"Sure, honey. Anytime you want."

"Promise?"

"I promise." He stood and walked over to the window. Instead of his wife's car in the drive, he saw a police cruiser. "Honey, I want you to stay here while I go down and talk to the police."

"What are they doing here? Why can't I come?"

"I'm not sure what this is about. Please, Katie. Just stay here, okay?"

He rushed down the steps, his mind racing in a million differ- ent directions. When he pulled back the door, he found the same two cops who'd come by the house yesterday.

"Hi. Can I help you?"

"We need to talk to your houseguest, Larry Wilton."

"He's, ah, not here at the moment."

"When do you expect him back?"

"To be honest, I don't know."

"But he's still staying with you?"

Randy nodded.

The shorter one, Sergeant Williams, pulled some papers out of his shirt pocket, handed them to Randy. "We've got a search warrant here—"

Randy instantly began to sweat. He took a desperate stab, hoping this wasn't about the bribe Larry had offered Gunderson last night. "Is this about the car you found in the ditch?"

"We need you to show us Mr. Wilton's room."

"Well, sure. Of course."

They followed him up the stairs to the third level.

Ethan came out of his room, stood in the doorway in his Skivvies and a gray sweatshirt. "What's going on, Randy? Hey, they shouldn't be in here. You guys go away."

"Ethan's my brother," said Randy, nodding to the cops. "He lives with me."

The officers eyed Ethan warily as they walked past.

Randy opened the door to Larry's room and flipped on the overhead light. Inside, the bed was a mass of tangled sheets and blankets, the ashtray on the nightstand overflowing with ciga- rette butts. An empty bottle of vodka poked out from under a pillow. The room stank of unwashed flesh and just a hint of weed.

The sergeant walked to the closet and opened the door.

Randy stood behind him, working on what he'd tell him if he asked about the marijuana. But as he looked over the cop's shoulder, his surprise disconnected his thought process. "His clothes," he said, moving closer. "They're gone. And his duffel. What the—"

"You didn't know he'd taken all his stuff?"

"No. He's coming back, I'm sure of it."

"When did he leave?"

"This morning. Early. I was still in bed."

"So you didn't talk to him?"

"No."

"And you haven't seen or heard from him since?"

He shook his head.

The cops proceeded to take the room apart.

"He told us the other day that he arrived by bus," said the sergeant, flipping the mattress off the box springs.

"That's right," said Randy.

"Did you pick him up at the bus station?"

"No, he walked here—or hitchhiked. I mean, he must have. He just showed up."

"Then how did he leave this morning?"

"He bought a truck."

"You have any of the paperwork? The license number?"

"Sorry."

"Know who he bought it from?"

"No idea."

"What kind of truck?"

"Brown and white '84 Silverado with a topper on the back."

As the cops finished up, Williams gave Randy an appraising look. "Tell me the truth, Mr. Turk. How well do you really know this guy?"

"We were in Nam together."

"But since then?"

"We get together every few years to catch up. What's going on?" He asked the question again about the burned-out car. "You think Larry had something to do with it?"

"He got a temper, this friend of yours?"

"Sometimes. Who doesn't in the right circumstance?"

"Likes bars, does he? Drugs?"

"I'm sure you've run a background check on him. You know he did time for assault."

"You hear from him, you call us."

"Of course."

"You don't call us and we find out you've had contact with him, we pull your license."

"You don't have to threaten me."

"Just a word to the wise, Mr. Turk."

Randy walked them back down to the front door.

Before they left, Williams turned to him one last time. "I know Wilton is your friend, but I suggest you be careful. And again, notify us if he contacts you."

"I will," said Randy.

"You take care now," said Williams as he and his partner walked back out to their cruiser.

Randy had no sooner closed and locked the door than his cell phone rang. Pulling it out of his back pocket, he checked the caller ID. It was Del.

"I still haven't heard from him," said Randy. "But I do have some news."

"So do I. Go turn on the TV."

"What?"

"Do it now."

Randy dashed up the stairs and switched on the 13" in the kitchen.

"Turn to Channel 5."

The local early evening news was just beginning.

"What am I supposed to see?" asked Randy.

"Just wait."

Katie walked out of the family room, stood behind him. "Who's on the phone?" she asked.

"Del," he whispered.

A moment later, he watched in stunned silence as the anchor moved to a story about an attempted murder that had taken place last night at the Unicorn bar in Uptown. Melanie Gunderson, forty, a reporter for *City Beat,* had been stabbed several times in the chest in the bar's parking lot. She'd been taken to HCMC, where she was now in a coma, fighting for her life.

Still holding the cell phone to his ear, Randy heard Del say, "We are fucked so many ways, man, we'll never see the light of day again."

It was Monday morning. Standing on the Lyme House deck with the fog rolling in off the lake, Jane felt momentarily suspended. On mornings like these, when the world turned indistinct, when the outside blurred and forced her to look inward, she would often feel a quick, powerful rush, a sense that Christine, her partner now gone for so many years, was hovering just outside her vision. She couldn't explain it. She had no proof. But Christine was there, her angel, her guide. Jane felt certain that one day she would turn her head too fast and Christine would be there, the threshold separating them momentarily breached. Maybe it would be a cosmic mistake, or maybe it was allowed. Jane had no real idea about any of these things. She wasn't religious, but she knew it would happen, she would see Christine again, look into her clear, smiling eyes.

Jane wondered why these visitations never left her feeling guilty. After all, she had a new love now and a life very different from the one she'd shared with Christine. But these moments were out of time, on a different plane.

Looking out at the water, she saw that the sun was beginning to burn its way through the fog. The mist was rising, gathering itself at the tops of the trees. The corners of Jane's eyes finally relaxed. She stood on the deck in that rare in-between state, her mind drifting, until a door behind her opened and then closed and she felt the familiar squeeze to her insides that told her the world was back in place. She turned to find her brother smiling at her.

"Am I interrupting something?" he asked. "You look so peaceful."

"I love it out here," she said. She had a busy life, too busy most of the time. That's why she craved quiet. The Lyme House deck, early, before the restaurant opened, or late, after the restaurant had closed for the night, was one of her favorite places to just sit and think. "You're back from New Jersey. How did the job interview go?"

Peter moved up next to her, leaned his arms on the wooden rail, and looked out at the dark, choppy water. "Actually, that's what I came to talk to you about."

"Don't tell me you're moving to New Jersey."

He shook his head. "No, I'm taking the job Dad offered."

"That's great news."

"I talked to him last night. We're leaving this afternoon, flying down to Worthington. It's the kickoff for another southern Minnesota swing. I've gotta run by his campaign office this morning, sign some papers. I'm already packed."

"Sigrid okay with all this?"

"Yeah. Fine." His lips parted in a grimace.

"Peter? What's wrong?"

He looked up through the shifting mist, leaned farther out over the railing. "If I tell you, do you promise to keep it to yourself?"

She slipped her arm across his back. "Sure, kiddo. You know you can trust me."

"You can tell Cordelia if you want, but nobody else."

"Okay."

"I didn't have a job interview in New Jersey. You know about Sigrid and me . . . the problems we've been having?"

"I know you'd like to start a family and that she doesn't want to have children."

He hesitated. "Last year she confided something to me—something she's never told another living soul. She got pregnant towards the end of her senior year in high school. She'd saved up some money, so she went to New York to live for a while, had the baby, but then gave it up for adoption." He went on to explain all the struggles he'd had with her over Margaret, how he'd tried to get her to see that just because she'd given one child up didn't mean she couldn't have another. It took him nearly an hour to unload the frustration and accumulated bile in his stomach. By the time he was done, they were sitting at one of the tables, the sun burning hot over their heads.

"So that's why you went to New Jersey on Friday, to talk to her adoption lawyer."

He nodded, then launched into the conversation he'd had with the woman at Child Protective Services in Newark. "She basically told me it was hopeless, that I could never find Margaret. All the records are private."

"What about this PI you hired?"

"That's one of my problems, Janey. He's expensive and I'm running out of cash. I refuse to believe that she can't be found, but I'm not so out of touch with reality that I don't realize it could take years. I just don't see how I can afford it."

"You haven't told Sigrid any of this?"

"How can I? She'll be angry, for sure, but then maybe she'll get into it. If I raise her hopes only to dash them when Margaret can't be found—I couldn't live with that. No, I can't tell her about any of this until I find the little girl. All this time I felt in my gut that she's not in a good situation. And now more than ever, I think I'm right."

"Have you thought about the kind of effort it takes to raise a special-needs child?"

"Of course I have." Now he was indignant. "But it doesn't change anything. I've never set eyes on that kid, but I already love her. Can you understand that?"

"To be honest, I'm not sure I do, but I believe you mean it."

He leaned forward, spread his arms on the table. "While I was waiting for my plane to leave, I stopped at a bookstore, found a book on foster care. I read it coming home on the plane. I mean, did you know that over half a million children are part of that vile system? Less than half of them will finish high school. Two-thirds of the girls will get pregnant in their teens. Without a stable childhood, these kids don't have a prayer, they just repeat the cycle. If they stay with their biological parents, the problems are poverty, neglect. Bad enough, but the problems in foster homes are even worse—sexual and physical abuse. One study found that abuse of all kinds was, like, seven times greater in a foster home than in a biological home—and the person doing the abusing was generally one of the foster parents. I know it's not everybody. I'm sure there are good foster homes, but what if Margaret ended up in a bad one? And then there are 'children's homes'—the PC word for orphanages. They can even be worse."

"It sounds awful."

"It's a fucking game of Russian roulette." He yanked a paper out of the pocket of his tan chinos. "I did some searching on the Web last night, looking for information on the New Jersey child welfare system. Turns out, the rate of abuse and neglect for children in the adoption resource centers—the kids who have the best chance of being adopted—is thirty times the national average. And get this. According to a press release about the foster care system in New Jersey, the system has 'egregiously failed the children in its care on a long-term, routine basis.' " He tossed the paper at her. "They need to hire, like, three hundred more social workers just to begin to dig out. It's a national disgrace. And that's the system Margaret ended up in. Do you see now why I have to do this? I have to find her before it's too late. Shit, it might already be too late."

She picked up the paper, read through it quickly.

"I know I seem like I'm hyperventilating all over you, but I needed to talk to someone, and I thought maybe you'd help me."

"Anything. Do you want money?"

"No. But you've got that friend—the PI."

"Nolan?"

"Yeah, him. All the way home on the plane, I kept trying to figure out a way to keep the ball moving. You think, maybe, he might help me?"

Jane had met A. J. Nolan during a particularly difficult time in her life. In the last few years, they'd become good friends. He was a retired homicide cop who'd started a PI business out of his

146

house. Since he wasn't hurting for money, he sometimes took cases that interested him from people who might normally have trouble paying. "Sure, I'll ask him."

"You think he'd do it? I mean, since he's your friend, I thought maybe he might cut me a break on his fee."

"He'll do it, Peter. And he won't charge you." Jane figured she could pay the expenses. But she'd keep that between her and Nolan.

"Could you call him?"

"Today?"

"Right now." He took his cell out of his pocket and pushed it across the table. Desperation flickered in his eyes.

Tapping in the number, Jane waited through several rings until Nolan's voice mail picked up. She left him a message, outlined briefly the situation, and then asked him to call her when he had a minute. "There," she said. "Done."

"You'll call me when you hear from him, right?"

"Either that or he'll call you directly."

"Thanks, Janey. You don't know how much this means to me."

As they got up, she put her hand on his back. "Good luck with Dad. Oh, by the way, I'm leaving town myself. Driving down to northern Iowa with Cordelia later today."

He turned and cocked his head. "What on earth could you two possibly have going on in northern Iowa?"

"Long story. We'll only be gone a couple of days. If there's anything interesting to tell, I promise, you'll be the first to hear."

17

Del lit a cigar with his brass Zippo. "If you want coffee, help yourself."

Randy set his briefcase on the kitchen table, waiting for Kesia to hustle the two kids out the back door of their town house on the river in downtown Minneapolis. Del usually picked them up from school, and Kesia dropped them off in the morning before work. She was a senior marketing manager in product development at Regent Sans, a cardiovascular medical device company located in Eagan. She was such a ball of energy that when she left a room, it felt as if all the air had been sucked out with her. Not only was she smart, she was beautiful. Randy didn't believe in the American Dream, but Delavon and Kesia came about as close to living it as anyone he'd ever met.

After Kesia and the two girls were gone, Randy went to the refrigerator and got out a carton of grapefruit juice. Nobody in Del's family drank the stuff, but they always stocked it in the refrigerator for him. Pouring himself a glass, he sat down at the table. "Okay, what do we do?"

"Don't suppose you've heard from Larry?"

Randy shook his head. "As I see it, he may have killed one person since he's been here——"

"The guy in the trunk of the burned car."

"——and tried to murder another."

"Not a very nice guy, is he." Del leaned back in his chair. "I figure he's either got the file, in which case, he may contact us again, or he lied to us about it. There never was one. He was just playing us so he could get his hands on the money."

"He'd wouldn't do that, Del."

"Wake up, Randy. It all depends on how desperate he is for cash. You know, man, we've always sort of pretended we know him. We don't really. Maybe his plan all along was to take the money in payment for getting rid of Gunderson. In his mind, he might even think it was fair. Except, he didn't get rid of her."

Randy stared at the glass of grapefruit juice in front of him. He couldn't bring himself to pick it up.

"Nothing's changed," said Del. "All our asses are on the line for Sue's murder. We colluded to keep the guilty party from going to prison. Any way you look at it, that's a felony."

Randy felt like a million fire ants were crawling around inside him. "What about Sue?"

"What about her?"

"Where's *her* justice?"

Del shot him a disgusted look. "You lawyers. Always talking about justice, like it's some rabbit you can pull out of a hat. It's bullshit, Randy. And I, for one, ain't goin' back there with you. You can wallow in your sins all you want, but I'm livin' in the here and now. I'm alive and free, man, and I'm happy about that.

149

You won't get no apologies from this guy, no matter what I did back in Waldo. I'm not the same man anymore. Hell, I mean, how long do I have to do penance for Sue Bouchard?"

Randy moved the juice glass closer, but still didn't pick it up.

"Course, we might get lucky. Maybe Larry will take the fall. If he goes down for the murder of the man in the car, who knows, he may come clean, cop to the whole thing—as a gift to us."

"When pigs fly."

"Yeah." Del drew in a little smoke, blew it into the air between them. Glancing at his watch, he said, "I'm heading down to Worthington this afternoon with Ray and his son."

"You finally hired Peter, huh?"

"We can use another guy. Hell, we could use a dozen more guys to go with us when we travel, but Peter will have to do for now."

It occurred to Randy right then that there was already so much acid in his stomach that adding more in the form of grapefruit juice might not be smart. He pushed the glass away.

"With Gunderson off our tail," said Del, "maybe the story will die a natural death."

"Not if she pulls out of her coma and points a finger at Larry, and by association, us."

Just then, Delavon's phone rang. He got up and grabbed the cordless on the kitchen counter, checking the caller ID.

"Who is it?" asked Randy.

"Just says 'wireless call.' Yeah?" he said, clicking the phone on as he stepped over to windows that overlooked the river. "Shit, man, why the hell are you calling me on a land line!" He put his hand over the mouthpiece. "Larry," he mouthed. He listened for a moment. Covering the mouthpiece again, he whispered, "It's one of those no-name cells with calling card. Untraceable, right?"

Randy nodded.

Moving back over to the counter, he said, "Let me put this on speakerphone. Randy's here, too. We might as well all talk." He pushed a button, then set the phone back in its cradle.

Larry's voice poured over the line. "You boys havin' yourself a mess of flapjacks for breakfast? Wish I was there with ya."

"Where the hell are you?" demanded Randy.

"Now, now. Calm down. I'm handlin' things."

"Yeah, like you handled the guy in the back of that burned car."

"That's why I took off. I figured the police were about to come knockin' on your door to have a little come-to-Jesus meetin' with me."

"They did," said Randy. "What the hell is *wrong* with you? You lied to me! You murdered him!"

"Come on, fellas. We all know the world's a scary place. See, I hoisted a few too many in a bar outside of Steamboat Springs, got into a car with a dude who said he'd take me down to Denver. Except, halfway there, he tries to jack my wallet. We had a little disagreement about it, if you catch my drift. He had a pipe wrench in the backseat, so I showed him a little cowboy justice. And then I drove his car all the way to Minnesota. Figured he owed me that much."

Randy felt sick to his stomach.

Del leaned over the speaker. "You tried to murder Gunderson. You think that was what we wanted? I'd say you're not handling things very well at all."

The line went silent.

"You still there?" asked Del.

"You think *I* was the one who knifed her?"

"You're tellin' us you weren't?"

151

"Hell no! You guys are off your rocker. I gave her the cash, she gave me the key, just like I said. I didn't find out about the knifin' till yesterday afternoon. I was havin' a few beers with a friend because I was so pissed at her. That's when I saw it on TV."

"Pissed at what?" asked Randy.

"That key. It worked in the lock, all right, but there weren't nothin' in the box. She stiffed us, boys. Can you beat that?"

"You're saying she took the money?" said Randy.

"I figure that's why she got knifed," said Larry. "Somebody saw the transfer and came down on her after I left."

"You believe him?" whispered Delavon.

Randy gave him a bewildered shrug.

"But don't you worry yourselves, I've got it covered. I'm headed down to Waldo even as we speak. If there's any loose ends that need lookin' after, I'll take care of it."

Randy peeled himself off the chair and shouted at the speaker, "No. Stay here."

"Can't," said Larry. "The cops are lookin' for me, remember?"

"Don't you hurt anyone!" shouted Randy.

"Hey, I don't go killin' people just for fun, you know. This is *me*, Larry. I'm just tryin' to cover our naked asses. Don't worry, my brothers, I'll be careful. Now, gotta go. I'll be in touch."

18

Jane had already packed an overnight case for the trip to Iowa. Cordelia said she'd be by around eleven. She also said not to worry about maps. She had it all handled.

By ten to eleven, Jane was dressed in her best worn jeans, a faded long-sleeved chambray shirt, a brown leather vest, and the boots Kenzie had bought for her on her first visit to Nebraska. Returning downstairs to her study, she wrote Kenzie a quick e-mail, saying that the suede jacket had arrived and fit perfectly. She added that she was thinking about the menu for the Memorial Day party and would call her later to discuss it. She still hadn't heard back from Nolan about Peter's problem, but it had only been a couple of hours. She knew he'd call as soon as he could.

Jane assumed Cordelia would be late. But just as she was about to go into the kitchen, she heard a horn honk outside.

"That's her, buddy," she said, feeling in her back pocket for

Mouse's leash. He loved the open road almost as much as she did. And Cordelia's Hummer was a lot like sitting in a traveling living room.

But as Jane stepped outside with her bag in hand and her new black suede coat over her shoulder, she did a double take. "Where'd you get *that?*"

Cordelia waved proudly from a shiny new silver convertible. "Just bought it," she said.

"This morning?"

"Saturday night, right after I left Mel at the hospital. Used the Hummer for a trade-in."

Jane locked the door behind her, then she and Mouse walked out to the curb to take a closer look. "Why? I thought you adored your Hummer."

"I did. But I'm sick of all the nasty comments I keep getting from friends and total strangers—the gas mileage thing, the size. Apparently a Hummer is insidious, idiotic, impractical, illogical, and totally irrational. I guess that's why I liked it. But the last straw was the other night. I was just driving down the street, minding my own business, when this guy yells, 'Hey, you off to a Bush youth rally?' I mean, that was The End."

Jane tried not to laugh.

Looking away, Cordelia added, "I also promised Melanie I'd get rid of it. Had to keep my promise, didn't I?"

Jane opened the door so that Mouse could climb in the back. "What kind of car is it?"

"A BMW 650i. Totally tricked out. GPS. Automatic everything. I've always wanted a convertible." She caressed the cream-colored leather seats. "And it gets pretty good gas mileage, has a bunch of air bags. It also has plenty of room for a child safety seat in the back—for Hattie. When she gets home."

Jane put her overnight bag and coat in the small trunk, then slipped into the passenger's seat. "This thing is pretty luxurious. Must have cost some bucks."

"Not with the trade-in. And it's used, last year's model, but it's only got about seventeen thousand miles on it."

"Is it big enough for you?"

"We all have to sacrifice, Janey—for the good of the environment."

"Sacrifice. Right."

Cordelia put the car in gear and they were off—not quite in a cloud of dust, but almost.

"It's a four-hour trip, give or take," she said, turning onto West Lake Harriet Parkway, headed for I-35.

Jane looked over her shoulder to make sure Mouse was all settled in. Instead of lying down, he was sitting up, ears pinned back by the stiff breeze, eyes squinting at the joggers running around the lake. The backseat was exceptionally roomy, and Mouse appeared to be in his element with all the fresh air.

"I think this car was a good choice," said Jane, strapping on her seat belt. "Well done."

"Thank you. I've been at the hospital all morning."

"How's Melanie doing today?"

"No change. She's still in a coma. Her mother was there, but she did leave us alone for a few seconds, so I got a chance to tell her I loved her, you know, all the mushy stuff—I won't elaborate—and that I'd be gone for a couple of days. I hate leaving her. This is so hard. I mean, if she were awake, I'd call her every hour on the hour. Or I'd send her cards. You know how much I love Hallmark."

"Cheap, trashy sentiment."

"Exactly."

"Did you mention where you were going?"

"No way. We probably won't find anything anyway, so what's the point of getting her hopes up. If she can hear me. I'm proceeding on the assumption that she can."

Jane wondered what the good people of Waldo would make of a middle-aged woman with spiky magenta, blue, and green hair, arriving in town driving a flashy silver convertible. Cordelia always made a visual impact, that was a given, but Jane doubted her current "look" would go over terribly well with the Iowa locals.

As they pulled into a run-down drive-in for lunch, Cordelia said, "Here's the big news."

"You've been holding out on me?"

They each ordered burgers and fries before Cordelia would agree to continue. She adored the pregnant pause.

"The other night when Melanie went outside to talk to that lethal goon, she left her leather briefcase with me. I dumped it in the back of my Hummer before you drove me to the hospital, and of course, I promptly forgot about it. But then, Saturday evening, when I was cleaning the truck out so it would look great as a trade-in, I came across the bag. Her laptop was inside. After I got home from the BMW dealership, I opened it up to see if there was anything on it about her investigation in Iowa. But, of·course, all her work was protected by a password."

Jane threw up her hands. "So close."

"Do not despair, dearheart. Cordelia M. Thorn was on the case." Mischief danced in her eyes. "It took some time, but I figured it out. I finally remembered a nickname I'd given her way back when, when we were first together. It touched me deeply, Janey, that she used it as her password."

"What was it?"

"The General. She acted like one, always issuing orders like she was in charge of the world."

Her description of Melanie sounded painfully similar to how Jane might describe Cordelia, which made her wonder if they really were meant to be together. Two generals in one relationship was probably one too many.

"I printed out the file for you." She glanced in the rearview mirror. "Mouse is sitting on it."

Jane turned around and pulled it out from under him. "Have you read through it?"

"Of course. Lost some beauty sleep over it, too." She patted the underside of her chin, then smoothed her red lipstick with the tip of her pinky.

By the time they were done eating, Jane had read through it twice. She now had a list of people she wanted to talk to before they drove back home. Melanie had even included phone numbers and addresses, but the only person she'd actually contacted so far was Alf Trotter, the "proud WWII vet" who'd written that op-ed piece for the *Fort Dodge Messenger*.

"This is amazing luck," said Jane.

"No, it's Cordelia Thorn on the case."

"I forgot."

"I forgive you. Just don't let it happen again."

Waldo, Iowa's population had grown since the early seventies. Instead of 1400 and some odd people, there were now 2153, according to the sign on the outskirts of town.

As they drove along the main drag, Jane judged that the business district wasn't much more than three blocks long, although several of the side streets that led back to the residential sections were

157

dotted with businesses. They passed by a couple bars, a Laundromat, a large Ben Franklin store, a pizza parlor, a dilapidated cafe with a Closed sign in the front window, an ice cream parlor/candy shop, a garage with a bunch of dusty cars sitting out front, and a tiny gift shop/bookstore. Dean's Feed Bin had greeted them as they came into town, and on the other end was a gas station on one side of the road and a grocery store on the other.

"*That* was the town?" said Cordelia, lowering her shades.

Jane pointed at the speed limit sign. "We're back to sixty-five."

She twisted around. "I figured there would be at least a couple of hotels to choose from."

"The only one I saw—a motel—was the Dreamland Motor Court about a half mile back."

"The dump? The one with the junker cars parked in some of the slots to make it look less like a ghost motel?"

Jane shrugged. "They may not have all been junkers."

"I do not stay in fleabags, Jane. No no no."

"Fine. We'll find something else. But don't expect a Hilton experience out here in the middle of farm country."

Cordelia pulled a U-turn and headed back to the grocery store.

"We can always drive back to Fort Dodge," said Jane.

"Too far. I'm beat. I need a chocolate milk fix."

Cordelia came out of the grocery store a few minutes later carrying a quart of Nestle's Quik and talking on her cell phone. She stood outside the car while she finished the call, then slipped into the driver's seat.

"Any change?" asked Jane.

"She's holding steady, but no better. Want a swig?" She handed the chocolate milk carton across to Jane.

"I'll pass, thanks."

They spent the next few minutes locating the field where the murder had taken place. Jane wanted to see it. She had no idea what she thought it would tell her, it just seemed important. Half a mile or so out of town, they took a left on County Road 6, drove another quarter of a mile until they spotted the weeping willow.

"That's it," said Jane. "Stop the car."

It was just an ordinary field. Because the land was so flat, Jane had the sense the she could see for miles. The only thing that set the place apart was the willow and the stone Sue's family had placed next to it as a memorial.

Cordelia pulled off onto the shoulder and turned off the motor. "Kind of quiet out here. Too quiet."

"That sounds like dialogue from a B movie."

"So? If it fits, it fits."

Jane let Mouse out of the car to run. He'd been cooped up for hours and needed the exercise. They both did. She passed through the scrub brush up to the tree and squatted down. Pulling a long blade of sweet grass out of the soil, she chewed the end and looked around. "I wonder what really happened here all those years ago."

Cordelia came up behind her. "I'll bet it gets pretty spooky out here at night. No streetlights."

"Not much of a country girl, are you."

"Give me pavement and the smell of car exhaust any day."

Jane smiled. There was never any doubt who Cordelia was.

She waited while Mouse sniffed his way toward her, then clapped her hands. As he jumped back into the car, she said, "Let's go see if Randy's uncle is around."

"Good idea. I'll bet he'll know where we can find a decent motel—and a place to have dinner."

The sun was beginning to set when Jane and Cordelia finally found the mailbox with the name Mortonsen painted on the side. The white, wood-frame farmhouse was sheltered from the road by a line of pine trees. They turned off the highway onto a dirt drive and rolled slowly into a yard filled with odd, welded metal sculptures.

"They almost look like buildings," said Cordelia. "They remind me of the ones in the movie *Metropolis*."

Gus Mortonsen was sitting on the porch smoking a pipe, enjoying the spring night. "Can I help you?" he asked, standing up as they got out of the car and approached. He was dressed in a wool Pendleton shirt tucked into a pair of brown trousers. His expression was open and friendly.

Jane introduced herself and then Cordelia, explaining that they'd driven down from Minneapolis. "I'm a friend of your nephew, Randy."

"My lord, haven't seen that boy in years. Not since my sister died—Randy's mother—back in '94." He invited them to sit down. As he talked, he kept sneaking peeks at Cordelia's hair. He puffed on his pipe a couple more times, then seemed to reach a decision. Clearing his throat, he said, "Mind if I ask a personal question? Was that hard to do?"

She blinked. "What? My hair?"

"Yeah."

"No, not really. I just went to the salon and told them what I wanted."

"The salon, huh? Wish we had one of them in town. There's a kid that works part-time at the grocery store. His hair's bright

160

orange. I think it's damn beautiful, if you'll pardon my French. I had the guts, I'd do it myself. I hate this old white hair of mine. Makes me seem more ancient than I already am."

"You an artist?" asked Cordelia, nodding to the sculptures.

"Yes, ma'am, I guess I am. My wife, God rest her soul, thought I was deranged. But a man needs a hobby. When I make a new one, I put it in the yard. I've actually sold a few. Can you beat that?" He laughed, then squinted at the car. "That a dog you've got out there?"

"A lab," said Jane. "He's mine."

"Let him out. I'll get him some water." He opened the screen door and shuffled off into the house.

"My kind of guy," said Cordelia, patting the back of her hair. "Artistic type."

Jane returned to the car and opened the door. Mouse jumped out, his nose working furiously to figure out all the new smells. They reached the porch just as Gus returned with a bowl of water and a beef bone.

"What's his name?" asked Gus, watching him lap up the water. He held the bone back until Mouse walked over to him.

"M. Mouse."

"No!"

"He was a stray. That's what was on his collar."

"Well, if that don't beat all." He gave Mouse the bone. "I guess Mouse is a name as well as a thing. Kinda like 'John.'" He winked.

"Do you have a few minutes to talk to us?" asked Jane. The remnants of his supper—a bowl of chili and a glass of milk—sat on a rickety TV tray next to him.

"Got all the time in the world," he said, his teeth clamped around the pipe. "Especially for a friend of the family. How's Randy doing these days?"

161

Jane didn't want to pass on bad news. "He's fine. Busy as ever."

"So what are you two young lasses doing down here in the middle of nowhere?"

"Well," said Jane, "Cordelia and I have a mutual friend, Melanie Gunderson. She's a journalism professor, and also a reporter. She was attacked in a parking lot a few nights ago."

"Mercy," he said, pulling the pipe out of his mouth. "Is she okay?"

"She's in a coma," said Cordelia, looking down at the rings on her fingers. "The doctors don't know if she'll recover."

"The thing is," continued Jane, "we believe she was attacked because she was digging into an old murder case. Susan Bouchard's murder."

He digested that for a few seconds.

"We're here in her place," said Jane.

"Are the two of you reporters for the same paper?"

"No," said Jane. "I own a couple of restaurants in the Twin Cities."

"And I'm a theater director," said Cordelia.

"Then, I don't understand."

"We're doing it for Melanie," said Cordelia, looking over at Jane.

Gus just smoked his pipe.

"We were hoping you could tell us what you remember about the night it happened," said Jane. "I know it was a long time ago, but anything you remember could be important."

"The police investigated the whole thing, you know."

"But Sue's murderer was never caught." From the pained look on his face, Jane could tell her words had opened an old wound.

162

"I don't know what I can tell you," he said, his eyes drawn to a large oak in the yard. He crossed his arms over his chest, shifted in his chair, drew an invisible line on the floor with the toe of his shoe. "I don't even know where to start."

19

Gus brought them all coffee before he sat back down to begin his story. Jane figured he wanted a little more time to think about what he wanted to say. She wondered at his reticence, but then this wasn't a big city, where murders happened if not daily, then at least frequently. The fact that a family member had been arrested for the crime undoubtedly added to his sense of unease. And also, they'd pretty much walked in and blindsided him with their request to talk about the old murder case.

Gus took a sip of coffee, then held the mug in his hands. He seemed to relish the warmth against his gnarled fingers. "You gotta understand one thing up front. Ethan and Randy were always good kids. Ethan, contrary to popular opinion, wasn't stupid. And back in his early years, he was as handsome as they come. Fact is, around here, people thought he looked a lot like Robert Redford. Lots of girls liked him, too. He had a sweetness about him, a kind of innocence that appealed to the ladies.

I know when my wife saw him comin', she got out the pie and put the coffeepot on real fast."

Jane smiled.

"Randy asked Ethan to look after Sue while he was gone to war and Ethan took that seriously. I know because he talked to me about it. He wanted my advice on how to do it just right. Some people saw them together and got the wrong idea— humans being what they are. Always made me mad when I saw people whispering about them behind their backs. It was just plain stupid."

This was a twist Jane hadn't heard before. Gus was working so hard to make sure Jane and Cordelia didn't have the wrong impression that she wondered if there was something to it.

"Ethan didn't kill Sue. He couldn't have. He was the gentlest boy I ever knew. Why, he'd see a baby robin fall from its nest and he'd care for the little thing until it was strong enough to fly away. I can't say the same thing about his brother. Randy had lots of fine qualities, but gentleness wasn't one of them. He had a temper, especially when he was younger. I'm not saying he had anything to do with Sue's death, mind you. Don't take that the wrong way."

"A bad temper can be like a loaded gun," said Jane. "Especially when you mix it with alcohol."

"Well, I'll give you that much," said Gus, stretching his legs out in front of him. "He and his buddies were all drunk as skunks that night. So was Ethan, sad to say. And he wasn't used to drinking." He turned the cup around in his hands, looked past the barn at the horizon line, where the peach-colored sky was quickly fading to a deep blue. "I'll tell you one thing I never told anyone before. There was somethin' goin' on with those boys the day it happened. Some tension they wouldn't talk about. I happened to be over at my sister's house that afternoon. There was a plumbing problem, and like always, I get the phone call to come fix it. Randy was in one of his black moods. He was sitting at the kitchen table. Didn't do more than grunt at me when I walked in. His friends were out in the yard, sitting under a tree, smoking cigarettes. Nobody looked very happy."

"You have no idea what it was about?"

"None. That was a Tuesday, which meant there were few people out and about that evening. Randy's two friends walked into town to get themselves a drink after dinner. Randy arrived a few minutes later with Sue. They all sat at the same table, and somewhere in there, Ethan joined them. I guess they played some pool, even did a little dancing to the jukebox music. The talk around town was that Sue left the bar around twelve thirty with the black kid. They walked down the center of the street, laughing and grabbing at each other, really making a spectacle of themselves. You have to understand, in a small Midwestern town in the early seventies, there were lots of people who thought a black man with a white woman was just plain wrong."

"We're talking sexual 'grabbing'?" said Cordelia.

Gus nodded.

"Where was Randy when all this was going on?" asked Jane.

"Still in the bar, with his other buddy."

"Larry Wilton."

"Wilton, yeah. And with Ethan."

"What did you think of Larry Wilton?" asked Cordelia, swatting a fly away from her face.

"He was real friendly, had a pretty good sense of humor. See, Randy and his two buddies came over to the house for dinner a couple times that summer. The only thing I had against Wilton was that he drank like the dickens. We usually had beer around

166

the house, but after he left, it was all gone. My wife thought he had atrocious manners at the table, like he'd been raised with the pigs and chickens."

"Staying with that bucolic image——," said Cordelia, unwrapping a stick of gum.

"But I liked him," continued Gus, cutting her off. "The black kid, on the other hand——"

"Delavon," said Jane.

"Yeah, Del. He was more quiet. Acted real uncomfortable around us. I liked Wilton better, not that I got to know either of them very well."

"We know the bare outline of what happened that night," said Jane. "What was reported in the papers. Ethan and Sue were found in a field early the next morning. Ethan had a hangover, said he didn't remember how he'd gotten there. Sue was dead. She'd been strangled."

"I always figured Ethan was headed home," said Gus. "The Turk house wasn't far from where they were found. I suppose he saw Sue by the tree. He just lay down with her and fell asleep."

"You think she was already dead?" asked Jane.

He shrugged. "That's the conclusion most of the jurors came to at trial."

"But it's just not logical to think Sue was strangled by a total stranger for no apparent reason," said Cordelia, chewing thoughtfully. "Homicide victims generally know their attackers. Crimes are motivated."

"True," said Gus.

"So, the next question seems to be," said Jane, "could Randy or one of his friends have done it? Did anybody ever investigate that possibility?"

Gus set his coffee mug on the TV tray, then leaned forward and pressed his hands together. "Honestly, ladies, I don't know the answer to that."

"But think about it," said Cordelia. "Three guys home from Vietnam. One with an admittedly bad temper. A young woman who had a romantic connection to him, and maybe one of his buddies. And then there's Ethan, wherever he comes in. It was like a firecracker waiting for a match."

"Could be," said Gus. "Or maybe it just looked that way from the outside, when in reality, it was nothing at all."

"*Nothing at all* doesn't get somebody killed," said Jane.

"Okay. Point taken. But the problem with all that is, if you're right, if Randy or one of his pals did murder her, the only people who know what really happened that night—Randy, the black kid, and the motormouth—all gave statements at trial that they had nothing to do with it. You can propose any theory you want, but the police needed proof, solid evidence, and they didn't have any."

"Do you remember what they said at trial?" asked Jane. "Specifically?"

"Del said he walked Sue back to her house, left her there on the front steps, and said good night. He returned to the Turk home around one AM. Randy and Larry had a few more drinks at the bar, and then walked home themselves. They left Ethan behind, all by himself. He said he left about half an hour later. If they all took the main road out of town and then cut across the field like they usually did, they would have passed right by the spot where Sue died, right about the time she died."

"What time was that?" asked Cordelia, chewing her gum way too eagerly.

"We heard that the police put it at sometime between one and three in the morning. On the witness stand, the boys said they didn't see a thing. They came home and went to bed—that the black guy was already in the basement, dead to the world."

"And you believe that?" asked Jane. In the darkness, she could sense him staring at her. "If you know something—"

He ran his fingers over the stubble on his face. "This is awfully hard for me."

She could feel agitation coming off him in waves.

After almost a minute, he leaned back and picked up his pipe, tapped the cold ash into the chili bowl. That small act of normality seemed to release something inside him. "Before my sister died, she told me a secret, made me swear to never tell another living soul. I refused, because, well, I don't believe in that sort of thing. But she went ahead and told me anyway. She said that the boys never came home that night. What they told the police—and repeated at trial—was a lie."

"Where were they?" asked Jane.

"They never said. I don't think she ever asked. They didn't come home until the next morning. Alice wasn't able to sleep that night, for some reason, so she was up drinking a cup of tea on the front porch when they walked into the yard just after sunup. She backed up their story, lied to protect them. But she didn't want to die with that lie on her conscience. I think what she wanted from me was forgiveness."

"Did you give it to her?" asked Cordelia. Her gum chewing stopped midchew.

"I did," he said. "Unreservedly."

20

Jane was just about to check her cell phone messages when Cordelia opened the bathroom door and emerged looking like Cleopatra after tussling with the asp. A towel surrounded her head like a royal turban.

"Feeling better?" asked Jane. "You were kind of drooping there when we left the Mortonsen place."

Sitting down primly on the other double bed in the room, she turned her impassive gaze on the offending bathroom. "It was nothing six steaming jets couldn't have fixed. But there's only *one* in that shower and it barely spits, let alone sprays."

"This isn't the Ritz."

"You think?"

"We could have driven to Conner's Mills, booked a room at the Trail's End Motor Court instead of this place. Gus said they were about the same. Clean and cheap."

"But the one in Conner's Mills was fifteen miles away. This one was just up the road."

Jane shrugged.

"I am *not* in a good mood. I haven't eaten since lunch and it's almost nine."

"Except for that quart of Nestle's Quik."

"That wasn't food."

"No, it wasn't." Jane saw that she had four new calls. They'd all come in while she was talking to Gus Mortonsen. "The pizza should be here any minute."

"How good could pizza be from *Bjorn's* Pizzeria?" She whipped the towel off her hair. "And they don't even have a TV in this room. Or a phone."

"But there's a refrigerator."

"Odd priorities. By the way, while you were out walking Mouse, I called the hospital again. Still no change."

"Did you talk to Melanie's mother?"

"No, the charge nurse. Tammy had gone home for the night."

Jane listened to her voice messages. One was from the club, asking if she'd spoken to a particular vendor before leaving town. Two were from Kenzie. It sounded like she was going great guns with her party preparations. She wanted Jane's opinion on how many people to invite. The last message was from Nolan. All he said was, "Let's talk about your brother. Call me."

"You know," said Cordelia, setting a framed picture of Hattie on the nightstand between the two beds, "I've been thinking about what Gus told us. If Randy's mother hadn't backed up his story, we might not even be here. Melanie might never have been attacked."

"She was protecting her son."

"Yeah, I get that. But at what cost? It doesn't take a trained bloodhound to figure out that something monstrous went on that night. If Randy wasn't the murderer, he certainly knew who was. I mean, if you'd been his mother, what would you have done?"

Jane stared down at her boots. "Hard to say."

"No way. You're St. Jane."

She laughed, flipping on her back and pulling a pillow over her chest. "I'm hardly that. I've bent a few rules in my day. More than a few. But I think if you lie about something as important as that—if the truth never comes out—it's always going to be there ready to eat you alive."

Mouse, who was lying on Jane's bed, lifted his head and barked at the door.

"Speaking of eating," said Cordelia, taking out her pocketbook, "I think our pizza delivery is here. That was a nice segue, didn't you think?"

"Very smooth," said Jane.

Cordelia paid the delivery guy in cash. She was about to come back into the motel room when her attention was drawn outside.

"Something wrong?" asked Jane, sitting up.

Cordelia stood with the door open another few seconds, then ducked her head and came back inside. She locked the door behind her, then rushed around snapping off all the lights.

"What's going on?" said Jane. She felt Cordelia plunk down next to her in the darkness.

"Remember that truck we saw outside Melanie's apartment? It was brown and white with a topper on the back."

"Yeah."

"It's parked out there, just a few spaces down from us."

Jane's immediate response was to dismiss it. "There have to be lots of trucks like that, Cordelia."

"But this one is *exact*. Rust across the hood. Chevy insignia on that wide front grill. It's even got Minnesota plates, and those big-ass tires that make it sit up real high. You remember? I'll bet you anything it's Larry Wilton's truck. Maybe he even followed us down here."

"Jesus," said Jane under her breath, her eyes drawn to the open window. One similarity might mean nothing. But this did seem like a lot.

"What should we do?" whispered Cordelia.

"I doubt he knows we're here."

"Unless he saw us."

"Well, let's hope he didn't. In this instance, getting the hell out of Dodge is probably the better part of valor."

"My feelings exactly."

They repacked their suitcases by flashlight and carried them out to the trunk. "I'll get Mouse," whispered Jane. "You grab the pizza."

"We're headed home, right?" She glanced at the light in the window of Room 14, Larry's room.

"Nope. Not yet. We'll spend the night in Conner's Mills."

"Oh, goodie. Why can't we just leave?"

"Remember why we're doing this?"

"For Melanie and your father. But Melanie won't be attracted to me anymore if I get my head blown off. I think having a head is, well, sort of a minimum requirement for a committed relationship, don't you?"

"One more day and night should do it, and then we're out of here."

"Unless Lethal Larry finds us first."

"I know it may not seem like a good omen," said Jane, buckling her seat belt, "but knowing he's down here sniffing around makes me realize we're on to something important."

Cordelia backed the car slowly out of the parking space. She rolled to the edge of the lot, looked both ways down the silent highway, then let out a whoop, pressed the pedal to the metal, and sped off.

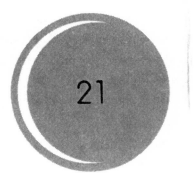

21

After checking in to the Trail's End Motor Court in Conner's Mills, Jane and Cordelia attempted to wind down by staying up late, watching an old Charlie Chan movie, and eating their cold Bjorn's Special, an extralarge potato sausage, lingonberry, and Havarti pizza. The new motel believed in televisions, but no refrigerators. The logic behind these decisions would forever remain a mystery.

Jane was up the next morning by ten. By ten thirty, she and Mouse had walked the length of the town's business district and had checked out all the potential eateries. It was slim pickings.

The day was overcast, with a stiff wind blowing leaves across the road. Waldo and Conner's Mills were approximately the same size, but the two small towns felt surprisingly different. While Waldo's business district was spread out and appeared decades newer, Conner's Mills's main street ran along both sides of two blocks. It looked like the town had hit its zenith in the twenties and thirties and had been on the downslide ever since. Weeds sprung up from cracks in the sidewalk and many of the windows appeared to be held together by duct tape. It felt like the town was, if not dying, then in serious decay.

Finding a bench outside the barber shop, Jane sat down to make a couple phone calls. She hadn't been able to reach Nolan last night, but this morning he answered on the first ring.

"It's me," she said, crossing her legs to get more comfortable on the stiff wood slats.

"Hey," he said, his deep voice rumbling across the line. "Glad we finally connected. I talked to your brother last night. He filled me in on the entire story."

"Think you can help him?"

"I told him I'd do whatever I could."

"He hasn't got much money."

"Not a problem. You can always work off the debt."

"Oh, that's how we're going to play it."

"You're a natural PI, Jane."

"I'm a natural restaurateur."

"Who should come to work for me. How many times do I have to tell you, I'll teach you everything I know. You're wasting your talents in the restaurant business."

He knew Jane had always been pulled in that direction and liked to apply pressure whenever the moment seemed right.

"You have any connections in New Jersey?" asked Jane.

"You're changing the subject."

"For the moment, yes."

"Okay, yeah, I do have some connections. Like I told Peter, I'll get back to you when I know something. It may take a while. Or I may hit a dead end. No promises."

"Anything you can do to help him—"

"Yeah, I hear you. He's very determined to find that kid. I never pass judgments on other men's crusades. He said he'd be gone for a week or so with your father's campaign, but it would be a big help if I could get my hands on a picture of his wife when she was Margaret's age. The sooner the better. Since Peter can't get it to me, he thought you might have something."

Jane had to think. All her family albums were in her study at home. But she was pretty sure she didn't have any of Sigrid when she was a child. "Wait. Peter made a big deal out of Siggy's last birthday. Had a party at their apartment for about thirty people. He sent out these funny invitations with a picture of Sigrid as a young kid on the front. It's not the best-quality photo, but it's something."

"When can I come get it?"

"Well, that's kind of a problem. I'm down in Iowa at the moment."

"What the hell are you doing in Iowa?"

"Long story."

"I'll bet."

"Listen, the card is in my study. I think I stuffed it in a folder labeled 'Family.' It's in the bottom left-hand drawer of my desk."

"How do I get in?"

"There's a neighbor—Evelyn Bratrude—who lives directly across the street. White house with dark green trim. She's got a key. I'll call and tell her you'll be coming by."

"Perfect. What are you doing in Iowa, Jane?"

"Just a little vacation."

"Your nose is growing."

"Probably. Thanks, kiddo. I owe you big-time."

"And I won't forget it. I'll be in touch."

After hanging up, Jane phoned Evelyn and left her a message. Her last call was to Kenzie.

"Hey, babe. It's me."

"I'm so glad you called, Lawless. I'm really missing you this morning. I hate this long-distance crap."

"I'll be there soon."

"I'm glad the jacket fits."

"Like a glove. Hey, I've been thinking about the kind of food we should serve at the party. We can either be really casual, grill burgers, brats, chicken, that sort of thing. Beans, potato salad, corn on the cob, apple pies. Homemade sangría. Or, we could do something a little more elegant. Like, say, an appetizer buffet. Champagne. Lots of spring flowers on the buffet table."

"They both sound great. I'll let you choose, okay?"

"Fine with me. Look, I'm sorry, but I can't talk long this morning. Cordelia and I are just about to leave. But I'll call you later."

"I'll be gone late tonight. And tomorrow I'm going antiquing with some friends."

"No problem. I'll talk to you soon. I miss you."

"I can't wait until you come."

"Me either. Bye, sweetheart."

Jane sat for a moment watching a few cars pass, then got up and walked across the street. She tied Mouse up outside a bakery. The one thing Conner's Mills had going for it that Waldo didn't was Mona's Bake Shoppe. Jane bought a half dozen pastries and two cups of coffee.

When she got back to the motel, Cordelia was, of course, still asleep, but the smell of coffee seemed to rouse her.

"I had bad dreams," she said, turning on her back and groaning. "I woke a few minutes ago and thought I'd been transformed into a large Chinese water beetle."

"You're mixing up Charlie Chan with Kafka," said Jane, sitting cross-legged on the bed.

"I suppose, or it was Bjorn's Special." One skeptical eye peered at the interior of the room. The other one remained closed. "Life doesn't get any more surreal than waking up in the Trail's End Motor Court in Conner's Mills, Iowa." She hoisted herself up, stuffed another pillow behind her back. "Say, what time is it?"

"A little after eleven."

"No way." She grabbed her cell phone and punched in some numbers. After talking to Melanie's mom and getting the morning update, she closed the phone and leaned back. "She's about the same."

"Wish it was better news," said Jane.

"Yeah." She nodded at the sack.

"I've got two bear claws, two slices of banana loaf, and two raised glazed." Jane tossed it to her. "All fresh from the oven."

"And coffee, yes?"

"Black and strong."

"What's on today's itinerary?"

"I called Alf Trotter on the way back from the bakery. He's agreed to meet with us this afternoon. Didn't get an answer at Sue's brother's place, so I tried her mother's. From what Melanie said in her notes, I would imagine she's in her late eighties. Anyway, she was a little wary, but she finally agreed to let us come by tomorrow morning, as long as we promise not to stay long. After we're done talking to her, I figure we'll head back to the cities."

"Splendid."

"I'm also hoping we can talk to the guy who owns Big Chick's Lounge in Waldo, the one where everyone got drunk the night of the murder. Melanie's notes said the same guy has owned it since the midsixties, but according to what I found out this morning, his son runs it now. Name's Bob Nelson. Thought we'd stop by there this evening."

"What about Lethal Larry Wilton?"

"Assuming we're right and he's the guy who owns the Silverado, we'll just have to keep our eyes peeled for the truck. The biggest problem I see is that we don't know what he looks like. Since we've got some time before we talk to Trotter, I suggest we find you a baseball cap to cover your hair. You're like a walking neon sign. He could pick you out of a crowd a hundred yards away."

Cordelia selected a bear claw, sniffed it, and then took a bite. "Ambrosia! As I see it, Janey, there's only one problem with your hat suggestion. Cordelia Thorn does not wear baseball caps. It's not part of my idiom."

"Look, I don't care if you cover your head with a doily. Before we go back to Waldo, the hair issue *will* be handled."

Conner's Mills wasn't exactly a hat-shopping paradise. After a couple hours of mad searching, they found two hats that Cordelia said she might be willing to wear. One was a battered green St. Patrick's Day felt derby. It covered her hair, all right, but it didn't do much to mute her odd appearance. The other was a child's white yacht hat with gold braids and a black brim. They found it at a garage sale. It didn't quite cover all her hair, but by then, Jane was losing patience.

"Just buy it," she said. "It's better than nothing."

Cordelia tried to rub a stain out of the cloth, then put it back on. "It's me, isn't it?"

"Absolutely."

"But it squishes my head."

Jane yanked it off and threw it back on the table. "Come on. You can stay in the car with the top up and the tinted windows to protect you from prying eyes. We'll drive back to Waldo and I'll go get you something from the Ben Franklin store. They're bound to have a better selection than this."

Forty-five minutes later, Jane came out of the store waving a sack. She'd bought three hats. If Cordelia didn't like any of them, she could either shave her head or stay at the motel for the duration. Presented with those two options, Jane figured she'd go for at least one of them.

"I'll close my eyes," said Cordelia. "Surprise me."

Jane handed her a pith helmut. She had to give Cordelia the opportunity to say no—and this was the one she was hoping she'd say no to.

Cordelia studied it for a moment, then handed it back and said, "One word. *Yawn.* I am *so over* pith helmets."

"Okay, then how about this." She pulled out a black beret.

Cordelia tried it on. "It fits. I've never really been the beret sort. I don't suppose they have it in gold lamé."

Jane ripped it off her head. "One more," she said. She'd bought the last one as a joke. "Maybe you better close your eyes again."

"Why?"

"All right. Don't." She took out a red and black plaid man's hunting cap and held it up.

"Janey, I love it!" cried Cordelia, grabbing it away from her. "This is it! It's me me me! It's even got earflaps. How did you know I've *always* wanted one of these? None of the designer shops in the Twin Cities carry them, God knows why." She placed it on her head with great reverence, pulled down the visor, and flipped up the mirror. "Oh, this is too fabulous."

"You're telling me you've always wanted to look like an old Minnesota farmer standing in a cornfield?"

"Always!"

Jane wasn't sure it was a good idea for Cordelia to go wandering around with that hat on her head. On the other hand, red buffalo plaid wasn't exactly unheard of in these parts. Now that it was attached to her, it wasn't likely to come off anytime soon.

"It's not exactly hunting season," said Jane.

"I'm not a slave to fashion rules, Janey, you know that. I wear white after Labor Day all the time."

"Well, at least it covers your colored spikes."

"Do you like it with the flaps up or down?"

"Up, I think." Jane turned and looked out the window at the bar across the street.

"I'm ready for anything now," said Cordelia. "Bring on the day."

"Welcome to my home," said Alf Trotter, leading them into the living room and spreading his arms wide. "Sit anywhere."

The room was tiny. Two brown corduroy La-Z-Boys flanked a matching love seat. Along the opposite wall was a massive oak entertainment unit, where the TV, VCR, DVD, and stereo system were located. Cordelia edged her way between the wall unit and one of the chairs and sat down.

"Thanks for seeing us on such short notice," said Jane, lowering herself onto the end of the love seat nearest Cordelia.

"I was sorry to hear about Melanie," said Alf. A bowl of peanuts sat on a glass-topped coffee table. He pushed it toward them. "Hope she recovers quickly."

Alf Trotter was was about five eight, heavily built, with a halo of wispy white hair surrounding an otherwise bald head.

"Can I get you something to drink?" he asked. "Coffee? Tea?"

"Nothing, thanks," said Jane.

Cordelia tried a peanut.

"Well, all right then." He slapped his hands together and sat down. "Let's get down to business, shall we? I'm not the kind to beat around the bush. You're here because of that opinion piece I wrote in the *Fort Dodge Messenger*. Tell you the truth, I got a lot of hate mail after I wrote it."

"Why?" asked Jane.

"It was a politically charged time, much like it is today. We all like to think we're patriotic Americans. I served my country in a just war, and I'm proud to say that to anyone. But Vietnam, well, that was another matter entirely. And so's this new travesty in Iraq. Don't get me started."

"Correct me if I'm wrong," said Jane, "but in your op-ed piece you seemed to suggest that the authorities around here gave Randy Turk and his friends a pass when it came to the murder investigation because they'd just come back from serving in the military."

"I did indeed," said Alf, flipping up the foot of the La-Z-Boy. "And I still believe that today. I taught history for thirty-two years at Buena Vista University in Storm Lake, so I know how difficult it is to get at the truth. There are always a lot of pressures that try to shape something this way or that. Take, for instance, our view of the Ottoman Empire, specifically, the Siege of Vienna in 1529."

For the next fifteen minutes, he gave them a history lesson. It was interesting, sort of, but Jane thought it came under the heading of "beating around the bush." On the other hand, she was sure that, to Alf, it was right on point.

"So you see," he said, crossing his ankles, "what gets recorded isn't always the full story. Take the sixties and early seventies here in the U.S. It was an explosive time. People were polarized into two camps: those who supported the war, and those who opposed it. Around these parts, people generally felt our reasons for being in Vietnam were valid. In Waldo, specifically, we'd sent off three of our sons to war. The kid who left before Randy came back in a body bag, so when Randy returned, he was treated like a hero. We gave him a parade down the center of town. We gave him a dinner at the local Lutheran church. The high school over in Prairie River asked him to come talk to the students. People couldn't seem to get enough of him. He was a quiet boy, and I think all the attention kind of overwhelmed him. A week or so after he got back, his two buddies showed up. They weren't quite as presentable as Randy, but to most of us, they were vets who deserved our admiration and gratitude. After a while, things quieted down. But Randy remained the kid we all wanted to see succeed in life in every way possible. And it's in that context that you have to put the murder investigation. Nobody wanted to believe that Randy or his friends could have murdered Sue. It was simply easier on our consciences, our sense of right and wrong, our understanding of how the world should work, to point the finger at Ethan."

"Do you think Ethan did it?" asked Cordelia.

"No, never. But the county deputies who were the first ones on the scene that morning, they concluded Ethan was guilty. It wasn't a big leap. Ethan was there, and he was mightily confused, had a terrible hangover. He's not the most articulate guy in the world. And from what I hear, he told the police he didn't know what had happened. He even said that maybe he had done it. That was all it took. Word got around. People liked Ethan, but he was different. For many people, that made him an easy target."

"What he said, was that considered an admission of guilt?" asked Jane.

"It wasn't admissible, but the police assumed it would be. A friend of mine on the force let me take a look at the initial police report. I saw the photographs that were taken at the scene. Believe me, you never get images like that out of your mind. Sue was on the ground, her legs splayed, her back was against the willow. Her head had rolled to the side, and you could see these wicked bruise marks around her neck. The doctors determined later that she hadn't been raped. But the truth is, we really don't know what happened."

"Because there were no witnesses," said Jane.

Alf nodded. "Although, of course, there were."

"You think Randy did it?"

"No. But I think he was there."

"Did something in the police report lead you to believe that?" asked Jane.

Again, he nodded. "The report I saw contained all the information the police assembled in the aftermath. Statements from people who knew Ethan and Sue. Teachers, employers, family. As you can imagine, there aren't many murders around here. I got the impression that the police left the in-depth interviewing to the prosecutors in Fort Dodge. But there was one extremely significant detail that should have been in the report that wasn't. It never became public knowledge. I only learned about it after the trial. The judge ruled that this piece of evidence was inadmissible, so the public defender wasn't allowed to use it in Ethan's defense. That's what I wanted to talk to your friend Melanie Gunderson about. I didn't mention it in the op-ed piece that I wrote because I couldn't. I had no physical proof—just the word of someone I trusted."

"Your police officer friend?"

"She wasn't an officer, Ms. Lawless. She worked in the department. That's all I can say."

"What was this extremely significant detail?"

"One of the deputies on the scene that morning found Delavon Green's dog tags in the dirt not three feet from Sue's body."

"Uffda," said Cordelia, sitting forward. "How could they cover that up?"

"In my opinion, it was a classic case of telescopic thinking. The police had their theory of the crime, and this didn't fit. Apparently, Green was called in and questioned about it. He said that he and Larry Wilton had cut across the field where Sue was found on the night in question. They were on their way to a bar in town. He stated for the record that he and Wilton—and Randy, too—often wrestled each other, partly to burn off energy, and partly because Green was so big that Wilton liked the satisfaction of pinning him. Wilton backed up the story. They said they'd been wrestling that night in the field, and that Green's tags had come off. They tried to find them, but eventually gave up and walked into town. They figured they'd come back in the morning, when the light was better, and look again. Randy backed up the story, too, said that Green had made the comment in the bar that he'd lost his tags, that he was pretty bummed."

"So the police let it die right there," said Cordelia.

"They did."

"Del Green's story seems awfully convenient," said Jane.

"Doesn't it," said Alf.

"Do you think Green killed Sue?"

"That's exactly what I think happened."

"Why?"

"I think he was in love with Sue and she rebuffed him. He was drunk, and he got angry. Next thing he knew, she was dead and he was on the hook for murder. His two buddies rallied around him, came up with a cover story. The reasons for the murder may have been a bit more complex than that, but I think I've hit the high points."

"But you have no proof," said Jane.

"None. Except for the dog tags."

"You think that Randy let his brother go to trial, knowing he wasn't guilty? Are you suggesting he was willing to sacrifice Ethan to save his buddy?"

"Nobody ever thought Ethan would be convicted," said Alf. "I think Randy was willing to take a calculated risk. And it paid off. In the end, none of them went to jail."

"But Sue was Randy's girl," said Cordelia. "He loved her, right? Why didn't he stand up for her—point a finger at the guilty party?"

Alf shrugged. "Depends on a man's fundamental allegiances, I guess. War forms potent bonds. Randy must have felt more deeply connected to his buddies than he did to his girlfriend, because the fact is, on that warm May night in 1971, Sue Bouchard slipped from the world and has been largely forgotten. With her last breath, we not only lost a young woman with a brilliant future, but we also lost any chance of finding her murderer."

22

Let's get out of here," said Cordelia on the way back to the car. "Go somewhere else for dinner. I don't want to stay in this town a minute more than we need to." She scanned the quiet neighborhood, then ducked into the car. "Wilton could be watching us right now, for all we know."

"Dinner sounds fine," said Jane, reaching into the backseat to give Mouse a scratch. "But first, we have to pay a visit to Big Chick's Lounge."

"Rats. I forgot." She waited for Jane to get settled in the front seat, then started the engine. "Let's make it quick."

It was going on six when they finally entered through the battered front door. They'd spent some time driving around town, looking for the two-tone Chevy truck, but thankfully, it was nowhere to be found. Cordelia called the hospital again. After she hung up, she said, "I'm going to take the position that no news is good news."

A sign in Big Chick's window said that they now served burgers and fries. The smell of grill grease assaulted them as they sat down at the bar.

A middle-aged, heavyset guy set a couple of napkins in front of them. "What'll it be?"

Cordelia slipped her sunglasses down to the tip of her nose. "I'd like a nice wheat beer and a slice of lemon Stilton, please."

Jane kicked her under the table.

"Ouch! Don't—"

Jane gave her a hard stare.

"Oh, I mean, anything you have on tap will be fine."

"You?" asked the bartender, switching his gaze to Jane.

Jane glanced at the row of beer pulls. "Give me the Sam Adams." She took a moment to look around as the man pulled the brews.

It was a fairly large room. Black linoleum from the fifties covered the floor, knotty pine the walls. Toward the back were a couple of pool tables that looked like they'd seen better days. Just inside the door was an old-fashioned Wurlitzer jukebox. At the moment, it was playing the Percy Sledge golden oldie, "When a Man Loves a Woman." Most of the tables were empty, except for a gray-haired guy and a young woman enjoying their hamburgers, and two middle-aged men playing pool. Seated at the other end of the bar under a large TV was another customer, his attention glued to the basketball game above him.

The bartender set their beers on the napkins. "Four bucks."

Jane assumed this wasn't the kind of place that ran a tab, not that it mattered. She took a fifty out of her wallet, set it on the bar, then covered it with her hand. "I'm hoping you can help us."

The guy's eyes dropped impassively to the fifty.

"I'm looking for Bob Nelson."

"Why?"

"Are you Bob?"

"It's possible."

"I need some information. I understand your father used to own the bar."

"He did."

"Ever heard the name Sue Bouchard?"

He bent over, rested his elbows on the counter. "Yeah. Went to school with her as a matter of fact."

"Was your father here the night she died?"

"I imagine. He was usually around back then."

"I'd like to talk to him."

"About what went on in here with the 'Turk Party of Five'?"

She nodded.

"Then you should ask me. I was the one serving drinks that night. I knew Turk, too, in case you were wondering. He was a year ahead of me in school."

Jane pulled her hand away from the fifty.

Nelson didn't pick it up.

"Can you tell me what you remember? Anything would be helpful."

"You cops?"

"We look like cops?" asked Cordelia.

He shrugged. "I'll tell you the same thing I told the investigators. Turk's two army buddies came in first. They ordered beers and played a round of pool. Ethan came in a few minutes later. He seemed kind of nervous to me, but that might've been my imagination. Anyway, Turk waltzes in a while later with Sue. They all order beers and sit at a table in the back."

"How much did they have to drink that night?"

"They stuck with beers until around eleven, then started in on boilermakers."

"Sue, too?"

"Nah. She wasn't that stupid."

"What did the five of them do all evening?" asked Jane.

"They talked, played some more pool, fed the jukebox. I think Sue might've danced with the black guy, but I'm not positive. They seemed pretty friendly. Around eleven thirty, Turk got up. He was so pissed, I thought he was going to put the black guy through the front window, but his brother broke it up."

"Do you know what he was angry about?"

"It was a busy night, lady. I had better things to do than keep track of their bullshit."

"You didn't like them?"

"After Turk got back from Nam, he acted like he was too good for his old pals. Didn't have time for us anymore. I wasn't going to bow down to him just because he'd been some army grunt. I didn't even agree with the war. If my number had come up, I would've run. Canada seemed like a better choice to me than fighting and dying in a rice paddy for God knows what reason."

"That night," said Jane, trying to nudge him back on track, "who left first?"

"The black guy and Sue walked out together. A while later I saw that Turk and Wilton had left. Didn't actually see them go. Ethan stuck around until closing. Sat by himself at the table and drank a bunch more beers. He was in bad shape when he left. He fell off the curb outside. I helped him up, dusted him off, asked him if he wanted me to call someone to come get him, but he just staggered away. And that's the sum and total of all I know, lady." He picked up the fifty and crushed it in his fist. "Anything else?"

"Thank you, no," said Cordelia. "You've been an immense help, but we have to leave now. Places to go, things to do. I'm sure you understand." She yanked Jane off the stool.

"You aren't gonna drink your beers?"

"No, but thanks," said Jane.

The guy watching TV at the end of the bar pushed his beer bottle away and looked over at them with disinterest. He motioned for Nelson to bring him another, belched, then went back to watching the game.

On the way back to Conner's Mills, Jane didn't say much. She was thinking about Sue. She knew, of course, that there were people who could take a human life and not lose a minute's sleep over it, but neither Randy nor Del seemed like that kind of man. The only one in the group who might fit the profile was Larry Wilton, but nobody had pointed a finger at him. In fact, Gus had said he liked him, that he was friendly, even funny. The only red flag Gus had raised was his drinking.

Twenty minutes later, Cordelia turned off the highway into a gas station at the edge of Conner's Mills. While she was filling the tank, Jane talked to the attendant inside, asked him if he could recommend a place to have dinner.

The guy suggested the pizza shop over in Waldo. Jane said pizza wouldn't work.

"What about a roadhouse or a supper club?" she asked. "Someplace where we can get a drink with our meal."

"There's a nice supper club just outside Hollandale, but that's a good forty miles away."

"Do we stay on the highway?"

"Yup. All the way. You can't miss it. It's on your right as you come into town."

She thanked him, paid for the gas, and then trotted back out to the car. "You up for a drive?"

"If it means dinner, yah, you betcha."

"Stop it."

"Sorry. It's the hat."

By the time Jane and Cordelia returned to the motor court that evening, a purple twilight had settled over the countryside.

"I like getting out of the city," said Jane as she flipped back the front seat so Mouse could jump out. "Breathing a little fresh air doesn't damage our city lungs."

"It's just too friggin' dark out here. Gives me the creeps."

"Kenzie seems to thrive on it."

"Then go down to Chadwick and thrive on it with her."

"I will. I'm supposed to be there for the Memorial Day parade." She hesitated a moment, then said, "You know, Cordelia, I've never seen this side of Kenzie before. She's so anxious about the party. She's usually so laid-back."

They stood on the sidewalk in front of their room, neither one of them all that anxious to go inside.

"Has she ever done a big party before?" asked Cordelia, swatting away the mosquitos.

"Don't know."

"Well there you have it. She's nervous, and for good reason. In my mind, entertaining ranks right up there with other sacred rites. It takes skill, experience, and a certain reverence for the form to do it right."

"I suppose."

"You think she's anxious about something else?"

193

"She has been leaning on me pretty hard lately about my erratic work schedule."

"You *are* the boss."

"True, but that also means there are times when everyday personal matters have to take a backseat to business. The kind of life she leads is very different. It's regimented. She knows in advance what her day—her month, her year—will be like. I have to go with the flow, wherever it takes me. When she wants to nail things down, it makes me feel a little crazy because I know I might have to disappoint her."

"That kind of stuff always causes stress. But you'll figure it out. True love conquers all."

"You actually believe that?"

"Nah, but it sounds like something I'd say. Let's put it this way. I wish I believed it."

Jane opened the door for Cordelia, but instead of going in, she bent over and clipped Mouse's leash to his collar.

Cordelia flipped on the overhead light and stared bleakly at the room. "Ah, our little hovel away from home. Think I'll take a shower and then call the hospital again. God, wouldn't it be fabulous if Mel was awake?"

Jane squeezed her hand. "We have to hang in there for her."

"Are you going for your nightly run?"

"Are you kidding? I just ate a prime rib dinner. No, we'll just do a short walk."

"Don't be gone long. I generally don't *do* intimidated, but this Larry Wilton has me worried."

"We only have one more person to see in the morning and then we can head for home."

"Home," said Cordelia. Staggering over to the bed, she struck a dramatic pose. " 'Though it be but a dream—' "

"Don't quote Shakespeare," said Jane. "When you start, you never stop."

She held the pose. " 'If it were done, when 'tis done, then 'twere well it were done quickly.' "

"I'm leaving. Bye."

" 'Farewell the neighing steed and the shrill trump—' "

Jane shut the door.

There were times when Jane thought beds asked too much. If you took off your clothes and got under the covers, the deal was, you had to fall asleep. That's why she sometimes slept on her living-room couch at home. It wasn't such a big commitment.

When she finally returned to the motel, later than she'd expected because the night air was simply too sweet, the town too peaceful, Cordelia was already asleep, snoring softly, lying on her stomach. Jane gave Mouse some fresh water, then lay down on her bed fully clothed. She knew her mind was unlikely to shut down long enough to give her any rest. Mouse seemed to be as restless as she was. Maybe he was picking up her vibe. She patted the bed, but he seemed to want to stay by the door. She'd just closed her eyes, which she felt, under the circumstances, was a bold act of faith, when he began to growl.

"It's okay, boy," she said, patting the bed again. There were lots of noises outside that were new to him. The growling deepened. He seemed so upset that she got up and walked over to him. She squatted down and stroked his fur. "We'll be home tomorrow," she whispered, giving him a hug. "You can come sleep with me if you want."

Just then, the window exploded inward and the bedspread on Jane's bed erupted in flame. Mouse dug at the base of the door. She held him tight, watching in stunned horror as two more burning balls crashed through what was left of the glass, one landing on the floor between the beds, the other hitting Jane's suitcase dead center.

"Cordelia," she screamed, holding on to Mouse's collar with one hand and shaking Cordelia's leg through the blankets with the other. "Wake up! Move it!" She yanked the covers off to the side. "Come on!"

Cordelia twisted around. As soon as the fire registered, she recoiled to the other side of the bed.

"There's glass on the floor," said Jane. "Be careful." She turned and cracked the door just as the rusted Silverado pulled past the room and roared out of the lot. She opened the screen, still holding on to Mouse.

"I gotta get my bag," cried Cordelia.

"Forget it," called Jane, but Cordelia had already grabbed it. They rushed out to the car.

"Back it up," said Jane. Flames were starting to shoot out the broken window. "Hurry!"

Cordelia pulled a piece of paper out from under the windshield wipers, jumped in, cranked up the motor, and then put it in reverse.

Jane yanked Mouse a safe distance away from the building. His barking had alerted the other two people staying at the motel. Two middle-aged guys came out of their rooms, looking frazzled, sleepy, confused. They each stood by their cars to watch.

A woman rushed out of the office. Jane hollered to her to call the police and the fire department.

"Look at this," said Cordelia, coming up beside Jane. She was wearing her nightgown, but had wrapped the car blanket around her shoulders. "It's a note from guess who."

196

Jane tore her eyes away from the burning building long
enough to read:

You get one warning.
This is it.

"I'd say we're in deep shit," said Cordelia, shivering under the
blanket.
"I'd say you're right."

Conner's Mills didn't have a professional fire department, but
the volunteers did their jobs like they'd been at it all their lives.
The sheriff's department sent two cruisers and an ambulance,
but when it was determined that no one had been hurt, the ambulance left.

One of the deputies talked to Jane and Cordelia for a few
minutes, took a statement, then excused himself. He said he
needed to call it in.

For the next hour and a half, Jane sat on the ground, hugging
Mouse against her and watching the scene. A crowd began to
gather as soon as the town's fire whistle had gone off. By two, it
was pretty much over. Three of the motel rooms were a total
loss. Several of the others had been damaged by smoke and water.

Jane whispered in Mouse's ear, thanking him for growling,
for getting her off that bed. "You saved my life, boy. I'll never ·
forget that." It was hard for her to isolate a single emotion, so
many feelings were coiled and twisting inside her. Mainly, she
was just glad that they'd all made it out safely.

Cordelia had put on some jeans and a jacket, but looked no
less bedraggled than she had when she'd been wearing nothing

but a nightgown and a blanket. She was walking around the parking lot like a bird unsure where to land. She'd left her hunting cap on the car's dash. With her spiky hair, she got a lot of pitying looks. There wasn't much that was funny about what had just happened, but Jane found herself almost laughing, her mouth pressed to Mouse's neck. She was pretty sure that people thought Cordelia's unfortunate hairdo was a direct result of the fire.

Just as the firemen were finishing up, another cruiser pulled into the lot. She watched a tall guy with a jock's build get out. From the way the other cops treated him, he was apparently the man in charge.

"Boy, that's one hefty side of beef," said Cordelia. She was standing, leaning against the hood of the car.

One of the deputies pointed in their direction, and the jock walked over.

"Ms. Lawless?" he said, looking at Cordelia.

"That's me," said Jane.

"By process of elimination, you must be Ms. Thorn."

Cordelia crossed her arms over her chest and nodded.

"I'm Sheriff Lang. I've got the statement here that you gave one of my deputies. You mention a name that interests me. Larry Wilton. You say you have no proof that he was the one who set fire to your room, but he's the one you suspect."

"That's right," said Cordelia.

"Why?"

Jane cleared her throat. "We're from the Twin Cities. A friend of ours—a reporter—was looking into the death of a young woman in Waldo, Sue Bouchard. It happened back in 1971."

"I know the story," said Lang.

198

"Our friend was attacked a few nights ago. We're pretty sure she met with Wilton and he was the one who knifed her."

"Because she was looking into the old murder case?"

"Exactly," said Jane. "She was planning to drive down here and do some research—"

"And you two decided, that since she couldn't, you'd do it for her."

"Something like that," said Cordelia.

"Again, my question is why."

"Because I love her," said Cordelia, pushing off the hood of the car and meeting his hard gaze. "And I'm not talking about platonic friendship either. I want to see Wilton get what's coming to him."

"So you've been looking into that old murder case. I checked before I drove over here. Larry Wilton has been living in Phoenix for the last dozen or so years. But he recently spent some time in Minnesota, where he's currently wanted on a murder charge."

"What murder charge?" said Cordelia.

"Seems he bludgeoned a man from Colorado with a pipe wrench, stuffed the man in the trunk of a car, drove the car to Minnesota, and then set it on fire to cover his tracks."

"Good God," said Cordelia, looking away.

"Let me tell you ladies, this is not a man you want to mess with."

"We had no idea he'd be down here," said Jane.

"No, well, he obviously doesn't want anyone digging into that unsolved homicide."

"Because he did it," erupted Cordelia. "He was the one who killed Sue Bouchard."

"You found proof of that, did you?"

199

Cordelia's entire body deflated. "No."

Lang crouched down next to Jane, looked her in the eye. "This is important. You have to listen to me. Get in your car and go home. Forget about playing amateur detective. Wilton is a scary man. He's running from a murder investigation. If Ms. Thorn's girlfriend dies, he'll be on the hook for two murders. He's already been in jail once for assault. Three strikes and he's looking at life in prison. That makes him a man who's got nothing to lose. Did you hear that? Do you understand what it means?"

Jane nodded.

"So you're leaving, right?"

"We're leaving," said Cordelia.

He stood up, his hands on his hips. "I'm sorry your trip to Iowa wasn't a pleasant experience. Have a safe trip home."

23

I'm exhausted," said Cordelia, driving slowly past the last of the gawkers still lingering along the street. "I can't make it home on one hour's sleep."

"Let's pull off somewhere, maybe take a short nap," said Jane.

A few miles out of Conner's Mills, they spied a gravel road. Cordelia backed the car in so they could see the highway, then told Jane to use the power switch to recline her seat. Once both seats were at a more comfortable angle, she switched off the engine and the lights.

Cordelia covered herself with the car blanket and Jane pulled her suede jacket up over her shoulders. She didn't think she'd actually sleep, but the next thing she knew, her eyes opened and it was morning.

Glancing over at Cordelia, she saw that she was already awake. "What time is it?" she asked, stretching her arms.

"A little after nine."

"Can you believe we slept this long?"

"Nine is *long*?"

Mouse loomed over Jane's head, sniffing her face. "Hi, boy," she said, reaching up and patting the sides of his neck. "I suppose you need to do your morning routine." She leaned over and turned the ignition key, then pulled the seat back up to a sitting position. She opened the door and Mouse jumped out. She let him do a little roaming, knowing he wouldn't go far.

"I'm starving," said Cordelia, checking in the glove compartment and finding nothing but empty candy wrappers.

"So here's what we do," said Jane. "I want you to drop me off at the Ben Franklin store in Waldo."

"Are you kidding me? I was planning to blow through that town in under a minute."

"And then you drive somewhere, anywhere you want, and find yourself a nice breakfast. Pancakes with fresh maple syrup, a nice fluffy omelet filled with ham and cheese, and some home-made country-fried potatoes. Sound good?"

"You forgot the ketchup for my potatoes."

Jane's stomach flipped over. "Of course, have all you want. Oh, and don't forget to give Mouse some water. Buy him something nice for breakfast, too. But no sweets, got it? And then you can call the hospital, get an update."

Cordelia's eyebrow arched upward. "And what will you be doing while Mouse and I are enjoying our sumptuous repast?"

"I'll hit the store and buy myself some different clothes and a cap to cover my hair. After I'm all decked out in my new duds, I'll walk over to Sue Bouchard's mother's house, talk to her for a few minutes, and then I'll call you. You can come pick me up along the highway. I'll just start out walking, heading east."

"And what if Larry Wilton sees you?"

Jane glanced over at her. "I'm counting on him laying low this morning after what he did last night. Look, Cordelia, I just want a few minutes with Sue's mom. That's all."

"We're not going to take Lang's advice—let this go?"

"Yes, we will take his advice, *after* I've spoken to Mrs. Bouchard."

Jane could tell Cordelia didn't believe her.

"You know, Jane dear, I love you like a sister, but sometimes you have this sick, insanely tenacious need to understand things that are none of your business."

"Nolan said almost the same thing to me once, although he left out the words *sick* and *insanely*."

"Well, he shouldn't have. If you've got an Achilles' heel, that's it."

"But will you do it, even if you don't agree it's the right thing?"

Her eyes rose to the roof of the car. "Oh, I suppose."

Jane leaned over and kissed her cheek. "You're a real mensch, you know that?"

"Oh, joy. I've always wanted to be a mensch."

Jane let Mouse back into the car. "Let's hit the road. The sooner we're done in Waldo, the sooner we can go home."

On the drive back, the gray day darkened and a cold rain began to fall. This actually made Jane's effort to disguise herself easier. It only took fifteen minutes to find a pair of lined logger pants, brown work boots, a brown hard hat, and a tan PVC raincoat with a hood. In small towns, Ben Franklin stores often took on the form of a mini-Cabela's. After paying for everything, she changed into her new gear in the unisex fitting room, stuffed her old clothes and boots into a sack, and headed out the back door.

On her way through town, nobody seemed to take much notice of her. She took back streets, kept her head down and stayed away from the main drag. By ten AM, she was standing on Mrs. Bouchard's side steps, ringing the doorbell.

The elderly woman who answered was stooped and seemed terribly frail. Her thin hair was curled away from a heart-shaped face, and she wore rimless glasses. She seemed somewhat taken aback by Jane's clothing, but she invited her in nonetheless, leading her through the kitchen into the living room. She walked slowly, as if she feared the consequence of putting a foot down wrong.

"I don't usually wear this kind of outfit," said Jane, taking off the hard hat.

"No?"

"It's kind of a long story."

Mrs. Bouchard sat on an antique couch. It was a beautiful piece, covered in a red, dark green and black Chinese-patterned silk. Much of the furniture in the living room was an Oriental style. She nodded for Jane to take the chair next to the couch. "You mentioned on the phone that you'd come down to Iowa to look into my daughter's death. You're doing research for a friend?"

"That's right," said Jane. "An investigative reporter."

"She wants the case reopened?"

"Possibly. But I don't want to get your hopes up."

"No," said Mrs. Bouchard, straightening her flowered housedress over her knees. "Believe me, I know nobody cares anymore. It happened too long ago. Ancient history."

"This may seem strange to you, Mrs. Bouchard, but I care."

The old woman pressed her lips together, then nodded. "Call me Grace."

"Thank you, Grace. I'm Jane."

204

"Just ask whatever questions you want. I'll try to answer them as honestly as I can."

"I'm sorry if this seems abrupt, but I don't have much time. Do you have any idea who might have done it?"

She gave her head a quick shake, looked around the room. "This just seems very strange to me. Nobody's ever been very interested in my opinion." She removed a handkerchief from her sleeve, touched it to her nose. "I *know* who did it, Jane. There's never been a doubt in my mind. Randy Turk murdered my daughter. He couldn't have her, so he took her life."

Jane inched forward in her chair. "What do you mean 'he couldn't have her'?"

"He couldn't stand the thought that Sue would turn his proposal down."

"He proposed marriage?"

"It was a couple of days before Sue died that Randy came over here with a ring. They sat on the back porch, on the swing, and talked for a while, then he got down on his knee and asked her for her hand in marriage. I'm ashamed to say that I was looking out the kitchen window at the time. I could tell by the look on Sue's face how pained she was."

"She just flat out turned him down?"

"I think so. But he talked her into waiting a couple of days. He thought if she gave it more thought, she'd change her mind."

"She talked to you about it?"

"Oh, yes."

"Why did she turn him down?"

Grace hesitated for a moment, then said, "Because she was in love with someone else."

"Do you know who?"

"Of course I do. It was Randy's brother. Ethan."

205

At Jane's surprised look, she added, "I know it seems like an odd match. My daughter was very bright. She wanted to become a lawyer, you know—and she would have, too. Ethan wasn't a smart man, but he was decent, kind, and had his own kind of intelligence. And he was handsome as all get out. He had a good job as a car mechanic. They fell in love while Randy was away in Vietnam. I'm not sure Sue was ever really that serious about Randy. She felt sorry for him because he was going off to war. She promised to write him every week—and she kept her promise. They'd gone steady in high school. She was a year behind him. When he went to college, they dated other people, but still kept in touch. He came home after he learned he would be sent over to fight. And that's when things heated up again. But it didn't last—not for Sue."

"So when Randy got home, he didn't know anything about the romance between his brother and his girlfriend?"

Grace shook her head. "They kept things very private. Ethan felt terrible about it, I could tell. It tormented him. I love him like a son, Jane. He was always so good to me." She took her glasses off and wiped at the edges of her eyes.

"The night your daughter died—"

"Yes, well, Randy came over. He wanted her to go have a beer with him and his army friends down at Big Chick's Lounge. Sue didn't want to go, but I think he pressured her."

"Had she broken it off yet?"

"No. I assume she told him that night, and that's what led to her death. From what I was told, Randy drank a great deal at the bar. I don't think he would have done it if he'd been sober. It was a combination of bad decisions."

"I've heard he had a terrible temper."

"I know people say that, but I never saw it. He could be

206

moody. And when he came back from Vietnam, he seemed changed somehow. He was so angry. He said the people in Waldo were small-minded and self-consumed."

"Did you ever meet his army buddies?"

"Yes, briefly."

"What did you think of them?"

"They were polite, but rather rough."

"And what did you think of Randy?"

"Oh," she said, sighing, "he was a responsible boy. I know he and Ethan were close, that he'd always stood up for his brother. I admired his loyalty. Children can be terribly mean and I imagine Ethan was an easy target. But there was a restiveness in Randy even before the war. All I knew for sure was, he wasn't right for my daughter."

"The police," said Jane. "You must have told them about Ethan and Sue. Didn't that cause them to look at Randy much more critically?"

Her gaze drifted out the picture window. "I never said anything. Ethan begged me not to."

"But . . . why would he do that?"

"Because he didn't want all of the details of his romance with my daughter brought up at trial. It might not have helped his case, and it would surely have hurt his brother. On the other hand, it was the truth. People should have been told. That's my one regret, Jane. I should have gone against Ethan's wishes and told the police what I knew."

It was a huge omission. Jane couldn't help believe that it would have had a significant impact on the outcome of the murder investigation. "I've heard that Delavon Green brought Sue home that night, sometime after midnight. Did you talk to her after she got back?"

207

"I'm sorry to say I didn't. I was already in bed, asleep. But Grant, my son, was out in the garage working on his car. He liked to do that when the weather was nice. He said he talked to Mr. Green briefly, but he never saw Sue."

"So she came in, then went out again?"

"Yes, she must have."

"Do you know why?"

Grace shook her head.

There were still things about that night that were a mystery. As much as Jane wanted to believe that she'd just heard the definitive word on who was guilty and who was innocent, she still had doubts.

"I was wondering, Grace. Do you have a photo of Sue I could look at? I've only seen one, and it wasn't very good."

"Of course." She pointed at a stack of old photograph albums sitting on the piano bench. "I look at them so often these days that I never get them put back in the closet. Bring me the dark green one."

Jane found the one Grace wanted and brought it back to her.

"Sit down next to me," said Grace, patting the couch. She opened the book and let one side fall across Jane's lap. "This album starts the Christmas before Sue died. You can see her here next to the tree. She still had on the dress she'd worn to church that morning."

The pictures turned Jane inside out. Sue's face was impossibly soft and young. She was dark-haired, tall, with a mischievous grin you could spot a mile away.

"She was always very athletic," said Grace, a wistful smile on her face. "She loved to swim. Ethan, he was a great swimmer, too. And they went hiking together whenever they could. They both loved the outdoors. On weekends, the summer after Randy left, Sue would ask me to pack a picnic lunch for her and Ethan and they'd be gone for hours. I think I knew she was in love with him even before she did."

Grace turned over a few pages. "Here she is with her brother and sister. Oh, and here's a photo of Randy and his army chums. Sue must have taken it."

Jane felt a sudden shiver of recognition. "My God," she whispered.

"What is it?" asked Grace, a concerned look on her face.

"That man. Larry. He's here in town. Right now." He was the man at Big Chick's last night, the one sitting at the bar watching the basketball game.

"It is strange that he just showed up," said Grace.

"You knew he was here?"

"He stopped by yesterday afternoon, said he was on his way up to the Twin Cities to see Randy and just wanted to pay his respects."

"You let him in your house?"

"No, we stood in the backyard for a few minutes and talked. I was out working in the garden. I try to do a little bit of that every week. He did ask me an odd question, though. He wanted to know if anyone ever came around asking about Sue's death."

"Did you tell him about me?"

"Yes, I hope that's not a problem. Since your call was so out of the blue, I suppose it was on my mind. He seemed to know who you were. I mean, he acted like you were friends."

Jane got up, making a huge effort to control herself and not run like hell over to the front window. "Did you tell him we were getting together this morning?"

"You know, I didn't. There was just something about the way he looked at me. To be honest, he frightened me a little."

Jane parted the sheers and looked outside. A new Honda Civic was parked halfway down the block. Other than that, the street was clear of both cars and people.

"Did I do something wrong?" asked Grace.

Jane scanned the street for a few more seconds, then turned around. "No, everything's fine. But I want you to promise me something. If Larry ever comes back, if there's any way you can avoid talking to him—"

"Oh, I'd already come to that conclusion."

Jane didn't want to scare her any more than she already was, but she had to ask. "Do you usually keep your doors locked?"

"No," she said, folding up the album. "Not always. My daughter—she lives in Des Moines now with her husband and two sons—she's always telling me I need to lock up at night. We never locked our doors when the kids were little. My husband and I couldn't even find the house key once when we were going on an extended vacation. I just don't know what this world is coming to."

"You need to listen to your daughter," said Jane, sitting down on the couch next to her.

"Yes, I'm sure you're right." Thinking about it a moment more, she added, "Do you think Mr. Wilton will come back again?"

"I don't know. But it's always good to be on the safe side." Judicious counsel, thought Jane, coming from a woman who seemed incapable of taking her own advice.

24

The day after Jane and Cordelia returned from Iowa, Melanie stopped breathing. Cordelia was sitting alone by her bedside when the monitor flatlined. Even before a scream could well up inside her, the room was filled with doctors and nurses. She was told to leave, but instead, she squeezed behind a narrow curtain and watched as electric paddles were used to shock Melanie's heart back to life. Cordelia's own heart was beating like a metronome set to hypersonic.

"Breathe," she whispered, closing her eyes and repeating the word over and over again. She peeked carefully around the curtain. The doctors were on the second round with the paddle. "Don't die on me," she pleaded wordlessly. "Not now. Not when we've just found each other again."

"We're back," said one of the doctors.

Cordelia watched the blip on the monitor zip back to life.

Releasing the breath she hadn't even realized she'd been holding, she said a silent prayer of thanks.

As soon as Melanie seemed stable, they moved the bed out.

"Where are you taking her?" demanded Cordelia.

"For tests," said one of the nurses.

Within seconds, the room emptied.

Cordelia sat back down in her chair, feeling dazed.

A nurse came in a few minutes later. She told Cordelia there was fresh coffee in the waiting room.

"What I'd really like is for someone to explain what just happened in here."

"Well," said the nurse, "we're not sure yet. It might have been something with her lung. The knife wounds were all to the chest. It's difficult sometimes to know what's cause and what's effect."

Which clarified exactly nothing.

Cordelia asked how long Melanie was likely to be gone and got another garbled response.

"If she's sent back to ICU, someone will come let you know."

Cordelia sat in the silent room a while longer, then drifted out into the hall. She nodded to the bodyguard sitting by the door, explaining that Melanie might be transferred to another room. She'd let him know. And then she headed to the waiting room to call Jane.

"She flatlined."

"No!"

"But she's okay. For now. I hid behind a curtain so they couldn't chase me out. I'm wearing my green dress. They were all so busy I figured that if one of them looked my way, they'd think I was a potted plant."

"Ah, right," said Jane. "I'm sure that's what they thought. Where's Melanie's mom?"

"Getting her hair done. It's the first time she's left the hospital—except to sleep at night. Poor woman. But she couldn't have known."

"You sound kind of funny."

"Funny how?"

"I don't know. Want me to come down?"

"No," said Cordelia. "I'm okay."

"You'll call me with updates, right?"

"I think it's just going to be a long day of waiting."

"I'll say a prayer."

"Light a candle, too. And some incense. God, Jane, what if she dies?"

"All we can do is take it one step at a time."

"Yeah."

"Don't catastrophize."

"But I'm so good at it."

Tammy arrived back at the hospital just after one. When she came into the room and saw that the bed was gone, she almost fainted. Cordelia filled her in on what had happened, and together they sat and talked until a nurse came in and informed them that Melanie had been returned to ICU, where she could be watched more carefully.

Cordelia felt relieved that a bullet had been dodged, and yet Melanie was still in a coma, and now back in critical condition. The doctors hadn't mentioned brain damage, but when her heart had stopped beating, her brain must have been deprived of oxygen. How much abuse could one brain take?

When Tammy went down to the cafeteria to eat dinner, Cordelia stood next to Melanie's bed, kissed her softly, and then took hold of her hand.

"I'm here, babe," she said bending down close to her ear, trying

213

to suck every ounce of fear out of her voice. "You're doing fine. Had a bit of a bumpy day, but the doctors say you'll be back to fighting shape in no time at all." It was a lie, of course, but what did Melanie know?

"Jane and I were in Iowa for a few days. Believe me, it was no vacation. The motels down there are, like, on the star rating system, maybe minus three or four. The shower heads haven't been replaced since before the Civil War. I am *not* a pioneer, dear-heart, in case you'd forgotten. Hey, but when you're feeling better, we can talk about some things we found out." She squeezed Melanie's hand, stroked her hair.

"I mean, who the hell knows what will happen to us, whether we'll be the love story of the century, or end up like we did last time—tossing verbal grenades at each other. But we deserve the chance, right? My heart is so full of you right now. All you've got to do is open your eyes. Come on, you can do that, can't you? Just a little flutter?" She straightened up to watch. "Come on, babe. Open those baby blues and tell me we'll always have Paris."

She just knew it was going to happen.

She waited, holding her breath until she nearly passed out.

"Okay," she said, gulping in air. "Maybe you're tired from such an exhausting day. It's okay. We'll try again tomorrow."

Cordelia stayed at the hospital until just after nine that night. When she got back to Linden Lofts, she took the ancient freight elevator up to the fifth floor and got off, feeling utterly ener-vated. At the end of the hall she could see a large lump on the floor near her door.

"Time to think about getting glasses," she muttered to herself.

The lump stood up. "What happened to your hair?"

214

"Cecily?" Cordelia squinted. "What are you doing here?" Her heart skipped a beat. "Where's Hattie? Did she come with you!"

"No," said Cecily. "I got sacked."

Once upon a time, in a galaxy far far away, Cecily had been a theater major. She'd never set out to become a nanny, although she was great with children. Mainly, she was awestruck by Cordelia Thorn, creative director. Cordelia suspected Cecily figured that if she could develop a personal connection it might lead to being asked to join the Allen Grimby Repertory Theater. And then, when Cecily met Octavia, a woman who was already the toast of the Great White Way and on her way to Switzerland to star opposite Michael Douglas in a movie thriller, well, Cecily was, like, *sign me up!*

"Why'd Octavia fire you?" asked Cordelia.

"Because she's a witch."

"Tell me something I don't know." She unlocked the door.

Cecily followed, dragging her luggage into the living room. "I'm bloody knackered," she said, falling backward onto the couch.

Cordelia tossed her purse and car keys on the dining-room table, then turned to study the new ex-nanny. "You've been in England for what? Five months? And you've already picked up the slang?"

"I'm an actor, in case you forgot. That means I'm a sponge. I soak up my surroundings so that I can use it in my art." She picked at a button on her red sweater. "And besides," she muttered, "Octavia's husband says it all the time."

"I don't want to hear about Radley," said Cordelia, stepping over to the drinks cart. "Tell me about Hattie. Is she okay? Have they been feeding her? Do they keep her locked in the cellar?"

"It's not that bad. She's fine really. She misses you like crazy

215

though. She doesn't understand where you are, why everything's changed and all of a sudden she's living with Mommy and Radley."

"You explained it to her, right? You told her it's not what I want."

"Sure, but I don't think she really gets it. She just knows that things are different now. She has a bigger room, a pool to swim in. But you know how much Hattie loves animals. Octavia is allergic to everything, so no cats or dogs. But Hattie has a closet full of new clothes."

"All black and pink?"

"No, Octavia put an end to her pink Goth period. For the first month, she took Hatts shopping all over London. I think she was showing her off. But she got tired of that pretty fast, handed her back to me."

"Is Hattie happy?"

Cecily shrugged. "She seems happy enough. But I don't think she likes Octavia very much. She might even be a little scared of her. Octavia has a nasty mouth. And she's been in a terrible mood ever since the Spielberg movie fell through."

Cordelia hadn't heard about that. "My heart weeps."

"Doesn't it just. When Radley's around, Hattie glows, but if it's just Octavia, she can get pretty sullen. She's developed quite a little pout. She is, after all, a Thorn."

"What's that supposed to mean?"

Cecily played with the button on her sweater, didn't respond.

"So tell me everything," said Cordelia, holding up a bottle of vodka. "Martini?"

"Make it a double." She pulled a pillow over her stomach and groaned. "I got canned because of a taped letter Hattie and I were making for you. Hattie didn't mean to, but she let the cat

216

out of the bag—told Octavia that she'd talked to you. Octavia demanded to know how *exactly* that had happened. Before I could explain, she found the tape recorder in my dresser drawer and threw it at a brick wall. Hattie wasn't there, thank God. Anyway, Octavia told me to pack my bags. Next thing I knew, I was in a limo headed to the airport in Newcastle. At least she paid my way back."

"How did Hattie take it?"

Cecily glanced down. "I don't know. She was in London with Radley. I left before she got back."

"You mean you didn't even get a chance to say good-bye?"

Cecily shook her head.

"She just sent you off? Doesn't that woman have any empathy at all? Doesn't she think Hattie has feelings? You don't just rip people out of a child's life."

"I don't think she was thinking about Hattie."

"What a stellar mother. If I ever get my hands on her—"

"You should have seen all the pictures of her and Hattie that appeared in the papers, even some magazines. Octavia Thorn Lester and her golden child. I mean, they look so much alike. The press is in love with Octavia right now. She's a wife, a mother, an actress, a humanitarian—"

"A what?"

"She gives a lot of money to various charities. Like it's any sweat off her back. Believe me, Octavia is loving every minute of it."

"She's evil incarnate."

"She's not that bad," said Cecily. "But she is a pretty crummy human being. She owed me a month's salary when I left. Said she'd put it in the mail."

"You'll never see it."

217

"I know. That's why I'm basically penniless."

"And that's why you came here," said Cordelia, shaking the martini as if she were trying to make butter out of whipping cream.

"I figured you owed me," said Cecily, sitting up as Cordelia handed her the drink. "On the way here, I stopped at a Best Buy. With my last few shekels I bought another tape recorder." She nodded to her carry-on bag. "Go head. It's in the side pocket. I've already put the batteries in. Just press it on. Octavia got the tape recorder, but in her fury to get rid of me, she forgot about the tape."

Cordelia's eyes bugged out. She took a swig of the martini, then grabbed the bag. She studied the recorder for a few seconds to find the Play button, then pushed it on.

"Hi, Deeya," came Hattie's wee little voice. In the background, Cordelia could hear Cecily encouraging her to talk. She closed her eyes, her heart nearly bursting.

"I miss you, Deeya. I want you to come here and then, I go home. We fry, on a pyane. Um, we have ducks. I feed them. Harry is the biggest. I yuv Harry the most. And . . . and I yuv Byance and Ucifer and . . . I miss my kitties. I have big cyouds here. Pretty cyouds. Mommy is mad at me. Sometimes. Um. Um. Do you know Radey? I . . . dance with him. And I sing songs. I, ah . . . Deeya! I want you to come. Okay? Come now. And I have a ring. It's pink and byack."

"It's actually red," whispered Cecily.

"And a pink room with a byack bed and byack curtains! And lots of byack shoes and socks. I need . . . I yike . . . and a furry bear I yuv so much. His name is Pinky. I named him. I put him in the pond to swim. With Harry. Mommy got mad at me and I got mad at Mommy. Um, um. I want you to read me a story." Long

218

pause. "Deeya, I can't see you." Her voice had turned to a whine. "I want to go home. I want a fuffernutter sanwich. You come, Deeya."

Cordelia's smile faded and then died. "That's all?" The tape continued to play, but all she could hear was a weak hiss.

"She wanted to sing you a song," said Cecily, "but we never got that far. She was getting kind of upset, so I said we'd finish it later."

Cordelia blinked hard to keep the tears out of her eyes, then bowed her head and pressed the tape recorder to her chest. She had no words. No words.

"I'm sorry," said Cecily. "It's the best I could do."

"No, it's great. Just hearing her voice . . . it's great."

They sat in silence for a few seconds.

"I was wondering," said Cecily, moving to the edge of the couch. "Could I stay here with you? Just until I get back on my feet financially."

The edges of Cordelia's mouth quivered. "Of course you'll stay. You're Hattie's nanny. She'll need you when she comes home."

"I don't think—"

Cordelia shot her a fierce look. *"When she comes home,"* she repeated.

"Right," said Cecily. "Right."

25

Every house had its own distinctive smell. The one Peter was in at the moment smelled like fried Spam, cigar smoke, and kitty litter. The one he'd been in yesterday morning had been a little harder to define. Miracle Whip, maybe, mixed with a hint of fish fertilizer and something sweet and herbal—some weird potpourri. He'd been on the road with his father's campaign now for four days. His general lack of enthusiasm for politics hadn't changed.

Peter thought his dad was doing a great job, giving dynamic speeches, shaking hands like a trooper, talking with small groups at private homes, generating lots of dialogue. He deserved to win the election, not just because of his endless energy, but because of his ideas. While it was fun to be along for the ride, the job Peter had been given was little more than a well-paid gopher. The house smell thing had amused him for a while, but it was getting old.

Peter missed Sigrid, missed his job as a TV cameraman, missed his old life. But the restlessness that was becoming as much a part of him as his skin came from his growing worry about Margaret. Every day he didn't hear from Nolan was a day that ratcheted up his anxiety another notch. His personal life hung by a thread and his professional life had already crashed and burned, and yet he held on to the belief that it was only a matter of time before he could present Sigrid with the greatest gift of her life—a reunion with her lost daughter.

"Get a picture of me with my son," called Peter's dad. He was standing in front of an ornate carved-wood fireplace in Belinda and Gary Brockaway's living room. Belinda was the mayor of Gibbon, Minnesota. They'd offered their home to the campaign entourage for the night. Gibbon was a moderate-sized town in the far southwestern part of the state. Peter thought it looked pretty much like the last town they'd visited.

Ray stood sans suit coat, his tie loosened, holding a mug of morning coffee. He was the picture of relaxed confidence. The heartiness in his voice almost made Peter cringe. His father was aware that Peter wasn't having the best experience. They'd touched on the subject yesterday evening after the potluck dinner in the basement of St. John's Lutheran, but, as usual, they'd been interrupted.

"Come on, Peter," called his dad, motioning for him to stand next to him. Ray proudly draped his arm around Peter's shoulders and they both said "cheese" for the camera.

Peter felt like he was four years old.

"Great," said Ray, clapping Peter on the back. "Well, this has been a wonderful stay, Madam Mayor, but I'm afraid it's about time we hit the road." While he conferred with Belinda and Del Green, Peter drifted outside to a van that was waiting to take them to the airstrip. The Cessna would be gassed up and ready by the time they arrived. Peter had already stowed his suitcase in the van, so he walked to the end of the block, then turned around to look back at the stately Victorian. It was a nice enough house, but it just didn't seem right that it should smell like Spam. Peter figured that if Cordelia were here, she'd have something deadly to say about it.

Pushing his hands into the pockets of his Dockers, he strolled slowly back to the van, watching Del Green and his dad saying their final good-byes to the mayor and her husband. His dad was so good at all this people stuff. Peter wished he'd inherited some of that competence. It wasn't that he had zero interpersonal skills, but his dad had something extra. Charisma, he supposed it was, though he'd never been entirely sure what the word meant. Whatever it was, Del Green had it, too.

Peter had stayed up way too late last night sitting on the front porch talking to Del and a couple of the mayor's aides. He should have gone to bed, but Del had such an obvious commitment to changing the face of Democratic politics that at one point, Peter had asked him why he didn't run for political office himself. It just seemed logical. Del had shaken his head, said it wasn't in the cards. Peter figured there was a story behind it, but he didn't press the point. He made a mental note to ask his father when they got a few seconds alone. Which might be next year, if this trip was any indication.

It was a humid, cloudy day. Storms were predicted for later in the afternoon. Peter had flown in plenty of rough weather when he was a cameraman, but he'd never gotten used to it.

They boarded the four-seater Cessna at 10:40 and landed at Rochester International approximately an hour and a half later. His father had radioed ahead and booked space in a hangar with Regent Aviation, just in case a storm actually hit.

As they were waiting for another van to arrive and take them to the high school, where his father was giving his afternoon stump speech, Peter's cell phone rang. He walked back into the hangar for some privacy.

"Peter Lawless," he said, removing his dark glasses.

"It's Nolan. How fast can you get to New Jersey?"

"Why?" said Peter, coming to a full stop. He pressed a hand to his other ear.

"I found her."

"You're kidding me."

"Where are you?"

"Down in Rochester at the moment with my dad's campaign."

"Okay, here's what you do. Catch a flight from there to Chicago. You might have a layover, but it shouldn't be long. I'll pick you up at Newark or LaGuardia—whichever is fastest."

"I'll call you when I've got the flight number."

"Good."

"Is she okay?"

Silence.

The hesitation made Peter's stomach vanish.

"Yeah, she's okay. More or less."

"What's that mean? Has she been adopted?"

"She's in foster care. I know you've got a lot of questions, but they don't have simple answers. Get on the plane, Lawless. I'll see you in a few hours."

Peter stood in the hangar, staring at the cell phone. The call had finally come. It was what he wanted. So why was he feeling such a sense of dread, like maybe he'd just made the biggest mistake of his life?

"Something wrong?" asked his dad, coming up behind him.

"Wrong?" repeated Peter, turning around. "No, it's good

news." He forced a smile. "That was, ah, a station manager in Chicago. I sent my resume there a few months ago. Never expected a call back. But the guy wants me to fly down—today if possible. They may have a job for me."

Peter could see the disappointment in his father's eyes.

"Look, Dad, you and I both know this isn't working." His gaze drifted to a car that had just arrived. Del was standing next to it, talking to the driver. He'd put his earpiece back in his ear, connected to a unit on his belt. He was back in his campaign manager mode.

"I'd hoped," said his father, "that this might work into something you could get behind, but I know this trip hasn't been the best experience. That's mostly my fault."

"No—"

"Look, if the Chicago job works out for you, that's great. But if not, I've been waiting for the right moment to tell you something. I guess I better do it now. Remember I mentioned to you that I was thinking of making a video documentary about my run for governor? Well, I've been talking to some people about actually pulling it together. Win or lose, I think it could make an interesting story. I've got a producer/director interested. A woman I know, Eva Manion, would do the writing. I'm looking for someone to handle the narration. The financing isn't a problem. And I wanted you to shoot it."

Under normal circumstances, Peter would kill to be part of a project like that. But at the moment, his attention was divided. "Let's talk when I get back."

"Sure," said his dad. He pressed a hand to Peter's shoulder, then pulled him into his arms. "I probably don't tell you this often enough, son, but I'm so proud of you."

———

Randy was working at his Cathedral Hill office when his secretary buzzed him.

"Mr. Turk, you've got a call from your brother in Arizona."

Randy was just about to say he didn't have a brother in Arizona when it dawned on him who it was. "Put him through."

A moment later he heard, "Hey, dog, how's it hangin'?"

"This is my office! If the police—"

"Don't worry, bro. I'm using another crap cell. Bought it at Target not ten minutes ago. Can't be traced."

"What do you want?"

"You could be a little nicer, you know. I been down in Waldo, working my ass off protecting yours. Good thing I was there, too, because two women were in town crawling all over that old homicide."

"Who?"

"One's name is Thorn. She's like this battleship with curves. A real solid sexy earth mama." He whistled. "She's a friend of Melanie Gunderson's. The other is . . . get this: Ray Lawless's daughter."

"Jane?"

"Yeah. I don't know what they found out, but they sure made the rounds. They're long gone now, though, thanks to me. I sent them a little present, told them to back off."

Randy dropped his pen. "What did you do?"

"Nothing much."

"Tell me."

"I tossed a brick through the window of their motel room. Attached a note."

"That's all?"

"If they do as they're told, keep their noses clean, nothing more will happen to them."

"You listen to me, Larry. You don't touch either of them. Got it? You hurt them and I'll hunt you down across time and space and make you sorry you were ever born."

"I'm already sorry."

"Promise me you won't touch them. On your honor."

Larry laughed. "You and I both know I ain't got any honor."

"Then swear on our friendship, on what we've meant to each other all these years."

He sighed. "Oh, all right."

"Say it."

"I promise I won't hurt either of them. But I'm still gonna watch them. If it looks like they're gonna keep digging—"

"No. Just leave them alone. I'll handle it."

Larry laughed again. Only this time, it was loud and mean. "You're the weak link, man. What you gonna do?"

Randy had always given Larry a huge pass when it came to his behavior. Maybe he was naive, but they were buddies and that's what buddies did. Sure, Larry tended to act without thinking and it got him in trouble, but then who hadn't acted without thinking? Randy believed that the good in Larry—his loyalty, humor, protectiveness—outweighed the bad. Until recently. Until that man was found murdered in his burned car. Against his will, Randy was beginning to see the shape of a consciousness that was both unnatural and violent. Not only was Larry a danger to himself and others, but he was looking more and more like he might be a danger to Randy—and Del. Even though Larry insisted he wasn't the one who'd knifed Melanie Gunderson, Randy's gut told told him a different story.

"I think you should leave town," said Randy. "Get as far away from here as fast as you can."

"Yeah, I thought about it."

226

"Do it," said Randy. He wanted Larry to evaporate. He never wanted to see or hear from him again.

"Hey, man, I know how much you and Del love the Big Ten. Iowa had a pretty decent team this year, so I bought you each a Hawkeye T-shirt. I'll mail them to you."

"Where are you staying?" asked Randy.

"Here and there."

"In town?"

"Last night, yeah. But I been on the road. I found me a real sweet deal."

"Where?"

"Not anywhere, really. Out in the woods. A place where a man can howl at the moon and nobody cares—away from the cops, away from everybody."

"You're camping?"

"Not quite that rustic." He laughed. "Look, I gotta go. Too many cop cars."

"Throw the cell phone away and just . . . just disappear, okay?"

"Be sweet, bro. I'll be in touch."

Peter landed at LaGuardia just after seven, New York time. He had to wait around for his bag at the baggage claim area, but once he was outside, he found Nolan standing next to the entrance, smoking a cigarette. Jane was right about Nolan still looking like a cop. He was a tall black man in his midsixties, with gray hair and a thick gray mustache, an imposing figure with his heavily muscled shoulders and arms—and those cop eyes that missed nothing.

"How was the flight?" Nolan took one last drag off the smoke, then dropped it to the ground and stepped on it.

"It landed. That's the best thing I can say about commercial airlines these days."

"Couldn't agree more," said Nolan with a thin smile. He motioned for Peter to follow him.

They walked through an endless sea of parked cars until they found Nolan's rented Ford Crown Vic.

"Get in," said Nolan, unlocking the car and hefting Peter's bag into the backseat. "I've got some papers I want you to take a look at."

As Nolan sipped a Dr Pepper, Peter read through the file.

Margaret—who had been given the name Mia Smith by her first caseworker—had been officially taken into New Jersey child protective custody on February 19th, two days after she'd been dropped off at a facility in Jersey City. She was placed in a group home and was registered as available for adoption.

Peter read silently, learning that Mia had initially appeared to be in good health, but that she didn't speak and didn't respond to sounds of any kind. She was examined by a doctor who found her to be severely hearing impaired. There was nothing in the written record about the cause of the impairment, and nothing was mentioned about other learning disabilities.

According the the record, Mia remained at the group home for two years. She adapted reasonably well, but kept to herself and didn't make friends. Further physical and psychological testing was done during that time, but everyone seemed to be in a wait-and-see mode—hoping she'd get adopted. When she was about to turn five, she was placed in a residential program for deaf and emotionally disturbed children and adolescents. She stayed there for four months. At that point, a notation appeared in the record about cost. The writing was almost illegible. When Peter turned the page, Mia had been placed in a foster home.

228

"God," said Peter. "The poor kid. She was kicked around like a football."

Nolan didn't respond.

Mia stayed with this foster parent until the age of eight. All the caseworker reports—seven in all—were essentially positive. Mia was attending a school for the hearing impaired and doing well, leaning how to sign. She'd formed a positive bond with her foster mom, although she still wasn't communicating much. But everything seemed to be going well enough until the woman suffered a stroke. Mia was moved out immediately to a group home, where she stayed for a period of three months. There were many notations about her emotional problems, her silences, her tantrums. At one point, she apparently stopped eating. She was eventually placed in another foster home—this time, with a family in East Orange.

For the first year, there were extensive caseworker visits. Mia was not doing well. The words ADD and ADHD started to appear in the notes. She was having difficulties at school, trouble with the other foster kids in the home. And then the records began to dwindle. When she was nine, there was only one visit made by a caseworker.

"Nobody's been out to see her for over a year," said Peter, flipping back and forth through the pages. "How can that be?"

Nolan shook his head. "Laws aren't written by people who care much about poor kids. Fact is, I hear more screaming in this country about protecting the unborn than I do about protecting the ones that are already here. We pat ourselves on the back all the time about what a great country we are—compassionate conservatism and all that crap. But kids aren't a political constituency. They have no political or financial clout, so they might as well be invisible. Our child care system is one of our dirty little secrets, but hell, children don't vote and don't start revolutions, so who the fuck cares?"

Peter returned to the file, looked through the last few pages again. "Have you driven out to East Orange to see her?"

"Yeah," said Nolan. "Yesterday."

"And?"

"It doesn't look like a good situation to me. I talked to a guy who shall remain nameless. Seems Mia ran away from home a few weeks ago, but the police caught her and brought her back. He said the foster father isn't around much. He comes home to collect an occasional welfare check, then takes off for God knows where. The mom is a drunk, although she has a steady job. Works in a supermarket. There are four other foster kids— the oldest, a fifteen-year-old boy, has been busted for drugs, petty theft. A girl at his school said he'd tried to rape her, but she couldn't prove it so nothing was done. He's a junior thug who's ready to graduate to the big leagues. He seems to be the dominant male in the family."

Peter closed his eyes. "What can I do?"

"Quickly? Nothing. You could start adoption proceedings, but that could take up to a year or more. In the meantime, Mia is at the mercy of a predator, an absent father figure, and a boozehound mother. I don't know much about the other three kids. At least they haven't had any run-ins with the law. I assume the parents pretty much live on the money that's supposed to go to support the kids. It's not unusual."

Peter checked his watch. "I suppose it's too late to go see her now."

"Best chance will be tomorrow afternoon. She lives about seven blocks from her school, usually walks home alone. It'll be tricky, but I think that's your best chance. I booked you a room at the Fairfield in East Rutherford. That's where I'm staying."

"Good," said Peter, his mind barely registering Nolan's words. All he could think about was Margaret—or Mia. On the plane from Chicago to New York, he'd struggled to understand why his enthusiasm to find her had been almost completely erased by an intense sense of dread. But now he saw it clearly. He was afraid. Against all odds, Mia had been found. But now that the miracle had happened, he was terrified that he might not be able to protect her.

And that would kill him.

26

The photos of Sue Bouchard had sealed it. Without a face, without a sense of the physical presence, the wires didn't quite connect. But now that Jane had seen the pictures of Sue in her mother's photo album, registered the enormity of what was lost, she couldn't forget. Sue's eyes haunted her, crying out for someone to care enough to bring the man who murdered her so violently to justice. And yet the difficulty of finding the truth this long after the fact seemed impossible. Add to that the possibility that Jane might die trying and the smart thing to do would be to let it go. And that's what she'd done. But when she forced the thoughts out of her mind, there was Sue's face again, inside her now, like a permanent weight in her chest.

Jane ended up leaving the club early on Thursday afternoon because she couldn't concentrate. Better to go make stupid mistakes somewhere else.

When she got home, she showered and changed into ratty

jeans and an old sweatshirt, and then she called Kenzie. She just needed to hear her voice. They ended up talking for almost an hour, which most of the time would seem like a long conversation but today seemed too short. Jane wanted nothing more than to be happy and unconcerned about anything other than the woman she loved. It hurt like hell to turn her back on Sue Bouchard, but it was the way it had to be.

As she lay on the couch, she closed her eyes. For a moment it was as if Kenzie were there, lying beside her in the darkness. But then Kenzie said she had to go. She had a meeting with a student in town. Jane said good-bye reluctantly, said she'd see her soon, the end of next week, that she'd be driving down. She lay on the couch for a long time, motionless as a lizard, listening to the street noises outside.

Later, when she was in the kitchen heating up some soup for dinner, her father called.

"Are you back?" she asked, pouring the soup into a bowl. Mouse was lying on the rug by the back door, chewing on a beef bone.

"Got back around three."

"How'd it go?"

"Have you talked to Peter?"

"Not yet. Hey, I had a dream the other night that you couldn't make one of your speaking engagements, so Peter went in place of you and he was such a smash that people started talking about running him for governor instead of you."

"Very funny."

"So has Peter become the total political animal?"

"What do you think?"

What Jane thought was that this was a terrible time for her brother, that his internal terrain had blurred and he couldn't get his bearings, so he'd turned his attention instead to rescuing a

233

child. None of which she could say to her dad. What she also couldn't say was that she thought Peter was too high strung, too easily wounded, too decent for the brutality of politics.

Her father continued, "Peter got a call from a station manager in Chicago, so he flew down there for an interview."

"Wow, that's great news."

"Yeah, I suppose so. I don't know, Janey. I guess I was hoping that he might really get into campaigning with me. You know, jump into the thick of it. Introduce himself to people, talk to them about our ideas, get them excited, take some initiative, look around and see what needed to be done and then do it. Instead, I mean, he just stood in the background, waiting for someone to tell him what to do."

"He's not like you, Dad. He doesn't like the spotlight. It's not a moral failing."

"Yeah, I know. I just wish he had more confidence."

"He's got plenty of confidence," said Jane. "Except when he's around you. You're kind of a tough act to follow."

"It doesn't seem to bother you."

"I'm not living in your shadow the way he is. He's your son. Like it or not, it makes a difference. And he's got different pressures on him—whether real or imagined, it's his reality."

"You're a good sister, Janey."

"It's funny, we were always pretty tight, but we've gotten even closer in the last few years."

"I know," said her father. "That's the way it should be. I don't mean to put him down. Maybe I do expect too much of him sometimes."

"Trust me, Dad. You do."

"Okay, enough said. I'm going home, take my beautiful girl-friend out to dinner, and spend the rest of the night relaxing."

"And tomorrow?"

"We don't hit the road again until next week. Memorial Day weekend will be the busiest so far. I don't remember how many stops I'm making. Ten, twelve. The state convention is just a few weeks away."

"Get some sleep."

The doorbell rang.

"Sounds like you've got visitors," said her dad.

"I'll talk to you later?"

"Let me know if you hear anything from Peter about the job in Chicago."

"Will do," said Jane.

"Bye, honey."

Jane rushed into the front hall and looked through the peephole. Cordelia was standing outside wearing one of her favorite costumes from the Allen Grimby costume department: a Julius Caesar red toga with gold trim and gold sash, gold wrist cuffs, and golden laurel crown. She only wore it on special occasions.

" 'Beware the ides of March,' " said Jane, opening the door.

Cordelia charged inside.

Mouse trotted out of the kitchen to greet her, but he stopped several feet away and sniffed the air. Apparently, he found Cordelia's Roman "idiom" suspicious.

"I've got news!" announced Cordelia, quivering with excitement. She drew Jane into the living room and made her sit on the couch. Standing over her, she said, "What's the best thing you can think of?"

There were so many possibilities that Jane found it a frustrating question. "World peace? An end to global warming?"

"Oh, come on. You can do better than that."

Jane wasn't sure she could. "Give me a hint?"

235

"I *am*," she screeched, pointing at her hyper open eyes.

"You finally decided to get glasses?"

She flung her arms in the air. Flopping down on the rug, she proceeded to do a dying scene—complete with clutching at her throat and thrashing around—and then she lay back, her breathing labored, one arm slightly raised, suggesting that death was imminent.

Jane couldn't help but laugh. It had to be Melanie, and from the excitement in Cordelia's eyes, it also had to be good news. But Cordelia was so into her game of charades that Jane decided to make her work for it. "How many words?"

Cordelia held up four fingers. She tapped the fourth finger to the wrist of her other arm and sat up.

"Fourth word," said Jane.

Cordelia nodded. She pointed to her eye.

"Eye," said Jane.

She pointed to both eyes.

"Eyes?"

Cordelia gave an eager nod. She held up her second finger.

"Second word."

She picked up a small wooden curio box off the end table, held it in front of Jane's nose, and opened it slowly.

"Wood box?"

Cordelia shook her head furiously. She closed the box again and opened it even more slowly.

"Open?"

She socked Jane on the arm and grinned. Next she held up her first finger.

"First word."

Cordelia took a pillow in her arms, gave it a slow, seductive smile, caressed it tenderly, and then kissed it with great passion.

"You're in love with my pillow?"

Cordelia threw it at her, turned away, and mimed banging her head on the mantelpiece. She whirled around and grabbed the pillow back. Again, she kissed it.

"Someone you love," said Jane.

Cordelia nodded. She pointed to her eyes and held up the box.

"Someone you love opened a box with their eyes?"

Cordelia dropped the pillow and the box on the floor and grabbed Jane by her sweatshirt. She shrieked with her lips pressed together.

"Give me a second to think about it," said Jane. "Someone you love open . . . opened their eyes?"

"Yes!"

"Melanie? Melanie's awake?"

"I've been at the hospital all day."

"Dressed like that?"

"What's wrong with the way I'm dressed?"

"Nothing," said Jane. "Nothing at all."

"Melanie opened her eyes four or five times before they stayed open. She's looking around now, moving her arms and legs. She even smiled at me."

"Is she talking?"

"A little. I think she's kind of confused. She doesn't remember what happened. The doctors said not to push her. Apparently, it may come back to her or it may not. Time will tell. I guess she's not entirely out of the woods, but this has to be a good sign."

"Cordelia, that's great news."

They looked at each other until their smiles faded.

"What about Larry Wilton?" said Cordelia.

"That's why we've got the bodyguard."

"When Mel does finally remember what happened, I mean, she can pick Larry out of a lineup. He'll go to prison for sure."

"Couldn't happen to a nicer guy."

"Yeah." Cordelia thought about it a minute more, then shot to her feet. "I'm going back to the hospital."

"Remember, you're not supposed to push."

"I won't. Well, not much. I just need to be with her right now."

Jane opened the door and followed her out to her new convertible.

"You be careful," said Cordelia, slipping into the front seat.

Just then, a truck pulled around the corner and drove slowly past them. Inside the house, Jane heard Mouse bark. She looked over and saw him pawing furiously at the front window.

"Evening, ladies," said Larry, nodding and smiling. "Nice night, isn't it?"

The truck turned at the corner and disappeared into the night.

"Well that does it," said Cordelia. "I am now completely and totally freaked."

"Want to move back in here? There's strength in numbers."

"Oh, I forgot to tell you. Cecily's back. Octavia kicked her out. She's moved in with me."

"Any word on Hattie?"

"Octavia's still dug in, so no change."

"What about the new PI you hired?"

"Nothing so far."

Jane looked around to make sure the truck wasn't coming back for a second pass.

"Remember, Janey. Linden Lofts is a security building. Why don't you and Mouse come stay with us until Wilton is arrested?"

"Maybe we will." The idea of a security door appealed to her right about now.

"You got a key, right? I'll see you when I get home. Ciao, babe."

"Give Melanie my love."

"Will do," shouted Cordelia as her car zoomed off, leaving Jane standing alone in the dark street.

Everyone in ICU knew that Cordelia was a famous local theater director. Most of the staff probably guessed at her relationship with Melanie. In Cordelia's mind, that was both good and bad news. The good part had to do with the fact that nobody had challenged her right to be with Melanie or had tried to toss her out when visiting hours were over. The bad part also had to do with the nurses hands-off policy. They obviously felt Melanie's condition was critical enough to warrant their decision not to deny her visitors. Maybe they even thought she might not make it. But Cordelia refused to give credence to that prognosis. Not only was Melanie going to get better, she would leave the hospital one day soon, move in with Cordelia, and live happily ever after.

"And the earth is flat," mumbled Cordelia, sitting by Melanie's bedside. It was going on one in the morning. Still early for Cordelia, although her usual wee-hour agenda generally meant partying, not sitting in a darkened hospital room. Hospitals were gloomy places. As hard as she tried, she couldn't keep the gloom from seeping inside her.

While she was finishing off the last of her Coke, Melanie opened her eyes.

Cordelia shot to her feet. "Want some water, sweetheart?"

"Cordelia?"

"It's me. How are you feeling?"

"Kind of . . . strange."

239

"Strange how?"

"Floaty."

"That's good. You're not in any pain, right?"

"Not much. Tell me . . . again. What . . . happened?"

"You were hurt. But you're going to be right as rain."

"Don't do that."

"Do what?"

"Don't talk to me . . . like I'm a child."

"I didn't mean—"

"I know it's bad."

"Okay. It's bad. But the doctors are taking great care of you. I really think—"

Melanie turned her head and looked at Cordelia full in the face. "We're back together, huh? Can you beat that."

"Do you remember our dinner together?"

"We . . . argued?"

"Yeah, well, sure. We argued. We always argue."

"I remember being at your loft. You have a little daughter. Can't remember her name."

"Not a daughter, a niece. Her name is Hattie."

"How did I mix that up? Why is everything so . . . garbled?"

"It must be the medication. You need to rest. That's how you'll get better."

"Rest. Right." She tried to wet her lips with her tongue.

"Here," said Cordelia, lifting the water glass closer, placing the straw in her mouth. "Better?"

"Yeah." She looked around with unfocused eyes. When she tried to move her arms, she grimaced.

"Don't," said Cordelia, leaning closer, stroking her face. "If you need something, I'll get a nurse."

"Where's my mom?"

"She went home. It's late. Night is the only time I can be with you when she isn't around."

When Melanie nodded that she understood, Cordelia thought she saw the briefest smile.

"I love you, Mel."

"I love you, too. Never stopped."

And then Melanie closed her eyes and fell back to sleep.

Cordelia stayed for another hour. Melanie didn't wake up again, but those few conscious minutes meant everything.

On the way back to her loft, Cordelia's cell phone began playing "The Stars and Stripes Forever." She couldn't imagine who would be calling her at this time of night.

"Thorn," she said, pulling over to the curb.

"Ms. Thorn, this is Nicola Stark, the private investigator you hired—the Berwick on Tweed Agency in Northumberland?"

"Oh, yeah." Her heart began to thump harder inside her chest. "What is it? Have you found something I can use?"

"Well, not sure about that. But here's what I know. I saw an advert in the local paper that your sister and her husband needed a new housekeeper. I used to do that sort of thing in my younger days, even had some references, so I applied. I didn't want to tell you about it until I knew I had the job."

"And?"

"I started Saturday. Believe me, Ms. Thorn, when I tell you it's a complete dog's dinner in that house."

"Pardon me?"

"The mum isn't very good with your Hattie. She's not abusive, mind you, just not very involved. The little girl sits in front of the telly most of the day. The Mr., now, he's a different story. He plays with her every chance he gets, takes her for walks, buys her presents. He's busy with his work, but he makes time for her. Apparently the old nanny got the sack. They've hired a temporary nanny, but she's more of a minder and between you and me, she's a tuppence short of a shilling."

"What else?" said Cordelia.

"Well, yes, the nitty-gritty as you call it. The Mr. and the Mrs. aren't getting along. For one thing, the Mr. wants to adopt the little girl, but the Mrs. is having none of it. They fight about it all the time. He wants to know why, if she loves him enough to marry him, she won't let him go a step further and adopt the child."

"Has Hattie heard any of this?"

"Expect so. They can get pretty loud. Yesterday was the worst. They had a huge row before lunch. I heard the whole thing with my own two ears. The Mr. said he was ready to call it quits. The Mrs. backed down a bit, but still wouldn't give on the adoption. And that's when he shouted something like, 'You never spend any time with her. What is it you're after? Ownership?' "

"What did Octavia say?"

"She just stood there and seethed. The Mr. stormed out. Didn't come back until late, as I understand it. The cook told me he had dinner sent up to one of the guest bedrooms, so I expect that's where he spent the night. But while he was gone, the Mrs. called a barrister. I didn't hear what she said to him, but I'll bet you anything she wants to see what's what financially before she files for divorce."

Cordelia's heart couldn't help but sing with jubilation. If her sister's marriage was coming apart, maybe she'd see the light, realize she couldn't handle Hattie on her own, and bring her back to Cordelia where she belonged. Cordelia felt sorry for Radley, of course, but it had been his choice to marry a woman who'd already divorced half a dozen other men. Caveat emptor, thought Cordelia. Caveat emptor in spades.

"Good work," said Cordelia. "Keep listening."

"Oh, I will. The Mrs. is traveling tomorrow to Italy for a month, leaving the child and husband behind."

"A month!"

"She says she needs time to clear her head."

"What's to clear?" said Cordelia. "It's empty."

"The Mr.'s set up a number of appointments with potential nannies tomorrow. I don't think much will happen until the Mrs. gets back, but you never know."

"Bravo, Ms. Stark. Excellent work. Keep me posted."

"Will do. Over and out."

27

Peter met Nolan the next day for a late lunch at a burger joint in East Orange. On the way to the Fairfield Inn the night before, he'd asked Nolan to drop him off at a car rental place. He'd begun to form a plan he hoped would work. Over fries and bacon cheeseburgers, they talked about Mia.

"I couldn't figure out from that file if she has a hearing problem, or she's retarded in some way." Peter gazed down at his lunch. Normally, he could eat a burger for breakfast, lunch, and dinner. Today the sight of it made his stomach lurch.

"That's because it wasn't clear." Nolan took a sip of his Dr Pepper.

"I don't understand why her caseworker doesn't visit that house more often."

"Could be a lot of things," said Nolan, taking another bite and chewing thoughtfully. "Like you said, Child Protective Services is overwhelmed. But I also know from experience that there's lots of ways people can play the system, if they want to dodge a visit. Hell, I even knew a guy back in the Twin Cities who paid off someone in the child protection office to let him know when the caseworker was scheduled. That way he could make sure everyone was out of the house."

Peter watched Nolan eat for a few seconds, then said, "What if I took her?"

"You mean, what if you kidnapped her? It's illegal."

"Yeah, but what if I did it anyway?"

"I could lose my license if I advised you——"

"Yeah, sure, but man to man. What would you do?"

Nolan finished chewing, dropped the half-eaten burger on his plate, and stared at Peter hard. "If she was my kid, she'd be gone from that hellhole before anybody missed her."

Peter nodded, pulled his Mountain Dew in front of him. "But I can't just grab her against her will."

"No, son, you can't."

He thought about it while Nolan resumed eating. "Look, let's say that Mia somehow gets to Minnesota."

"Uh-huh."

"How hard would it be to get her a fake ID?"

"Not hard."

"Could you help me?"

"Hell, no."

"But, I mean, do you know anyone who could?"

"I know lots of people, Peter. Not all of them are upright citizens."

"What about adoption papers? Could those be faked so that it would look like Sigrid and I adopted her—legally?"

"Anything can be faked."

"And you have lots of friends."

"Not friends, per se. Acquaintances." He wiped his hands on a napkin, then leaned into the table. "Listen, I can't tell you to break the law, but I'll be more than happy to look the other way."

After paying the tab, they walked out to their cars. Nolan did a double take when he glanced at Peter's Ford Taurus. "What's that in your backseat?"

Peter opened the door. A curly little black poodle jumped out. "Meet Teacake."

"God," said Nolan, squatting down as the dog jumped into his arms and licked his face. "Where'd you get him?"

"Her. I went to a bunch of shelters this morning. I needed to find a small dog that was superfriendly."

Nolan looked up at him. "Brilliant, kid. I can tell you and Jane are related."

"Thanks, but I've just read a bunch of stuff on how perverts lure kids into cars."

Nolan stood up and handed the dog back. "Hell of a sick world." He tapped a cigarette out of a package of Winstons and lit up. "Okay, follow me to the school. I'll show you the route she takes home. From there, you're on your own."

"Wish me luck?"

"All the luck in the world."

While Peter waited in his car, he called Sigrid. She was at work, which meant she might be in a counseling session. He'd phoned her last night from the motel room, lied about where he was and what he was doing. At one point, he almost broke down and told her the truth. But as much as he wanted to talk it all over with her, tell her that he'd found Margaret and explain what he planned to do today, as much as he craved her approval, this wasn't something he could drop on her over the phone. He hadn't slept much last night. He hated all this sneaking around and couldn't wait for it to be over.

The receptionist at the Heritage Family & Health Services told him that Sigrid was unavailable and asked if she could take a message. Peter's hands were sweating, his mouth was dry, and he felt like he was about to throw up. If he could just hear his wife's voice, he knew it would help settle him down, but even though it felt like an emergency to him, he couldn't say that to the receptionist. He thanked her, told her he'd call Sigrid later, and then turned off his cell phone and stuffed it in the glove compartment.

Teacake was sleeping in the passenger's seat. Peter had bought her a new collar and leash. Checking his watch, he cracked the door and pushed it all the way open with his foot. "Come on, girl. It's time." He led the dog around to the back of the car. Opening the trunk, he removed the sketchbook and black magic marker he'd prepared last night. He glanced over at Nolan's Crown Vic parked across the street. That was all. Just the glance. No indication that he knew who was sitting behind the wheel.

And then he walked. Up and down the block. Teacake didn't tug too much at the leash. She seemed happy just to be out of the car. And then he saw her. She'd just turned the corner, walking fast. He would have known her anywhere. She was a mini-Sigrid. Platinum blond hair pulled back into a messy ponytail. Small for her age. Beautiful beyond words. She had on frayed jeans, black shoes, a beat-up red backpack over a striped shirt. Her clothing looked worn, maybe even a little dirty. Her eyes were fastened on the sidewalk. She didn't look up.

Peter quickly turned, began walking in the same direction,

only he walked more slowly, let her catch up. When he could feel her just behind him, he let go of the leash. Teacake charged ahead.

"No," he yelled. "Come back here!" He turned and saw that Mia was watching. He knew she probably couldn't hear him, but he motioned for her to help him catch the dog.

She hesitated, then took the bait. They both took off after the dog, chased her half a block before Peter finally jumped on the end of the leash, ending Teacake's getaway. He smiled at Mia, gave her a thumbs-up.

Mia held her hand out for the dog to sniff, then crouched down and began to pet her.

Peter squatted down next to her. "Thanks for your help." He smiled.

She didn't respond. She didn't even look at him.

He removed the sketch pad from under his arm, flipped to the first page, then uncapped the Sharpie and wrote, "Thanks!"

Mia looked at it, then looked up at him.

He wrote, "Do you like dogs?"

She gave a shy nod.

Next he wrote, "My name is Peter. The dog is Teacake. I think she likes you."

She was clearly delighted by Teacake's enthusiasm. The dog was all over her, licking her hands and face, jumping up and putting her paws on her chest.

Peter sat down with his back against a tree and let them play for a few minutes. The two of them seemed to be made for each other. "Can you hear me, Mia?" he asked when her back was turned.

She made no response.

With the leash, he pulled Teacake closer to him, and Mia moved right along with her.

Peter flipped to a clean page in the sketchbook. "Mia," he wrote, "will you stay and talk to me for a minute?"

This time, she looked at him more closely. She didn't seem frightened, but a wariness crept into her eyes.

"I'm a friend of your mom's," he wrote. "Your *real* mom. She loves you very much, but could not find you. Her name is Sigrid and she wants to see you."

Mia read the words. She didn't look at Peter this time, but she didn't move away.

Peter handed her the pen, nodded for her to write something. Anything.

"Where does she live?" Mia wrote. She handed back the pen.

"Your real mom lives in Minnesota. Do you know where that is?" Mia nodded.

"I know you ran away from your house. Does that mean you are not happy there?"

Teacake turned on her back so that Mia could scratch her stomach. The dog's presence seemed to normalize what was anything but normal.

"*Not* happy," wrote Mia, underlining the word "not" three times.

"Will you let me help you?" Peter wrote. "I want to take you to see your mom. She's sad because she misses you so much. Will you help make her happy again?" He could feel her uncertainty, but there was something else, too. He tried to read her expression, but she was too good at covering up her emotions. "Teacake will come with us to keep us company," he wrote. "I promise to take very good care of you and Teacake."

She stood up and backed away.

Peter's heart stopped. He was sure she was going to bolt. If she did, that was the end of it.

Teacake struggled at the end of the leash. Peter let it go and Mia crouched low again so that Teacake could jump into her arms. At that moment, Peter realized it was the dog who was doing the negotiating.

Mia petted her, scratched her back, nuzzled her nose into her fur.

It was now or never. This was the moment. He stood up, held out his hand.

She stared up at him with a look of such blistering intensity that it nearly knocked him flat. But he didn't flinch. His arm remained outstretched.

And then the miracle happened. She didn't take his hand, but she stood up with the dog in her arms.

Peter got the message. She would go with him. It was the wrong thing to do, for all the wrong reasons, but Peter silently said a prayer of thanks. God willing, he would make it all right.

28

Three days later, on Monday morning, Jane was sitting at the breakfast table in Cordelia's kitchen, eating a bowl of oatmeal and reading the latest *Time Magazine,* when her cell phone went off. She pulled it out of the pocket of her brown cords and looked at the caller ID.

"Peter, hi!" she said, getting up to put the dirty dish in the sink. "Are you back?"

"Yeah," he said, sounding rushed. She could hear street noise in the background. "I need to see you, Janey. Right away."

"Actually, I'm staying at Cordelia's loft for a few days. Long story. I could meet you at the club."

"I'd rather come there. I'm not far away."

"Sure. But first, tell me what's up? Were you really in Chicago?"

"I'll explain everything when I get there."

Jane finished dressing while she waited. She buzzed her brother in a few minutes later, then stood in the outer hallway waiting for the freight elevator to lumber up from the first floor. When the door opened and Peter pushed back the wooden hoist-away gate, she could see that he wasn't alone. Not only did he have a small dog with him, but he also had a blond-haired girl.

"Oh my God," she whispered, knowing immediately who the child was. "You found her."

Peter's smile was so dazzling, it could have lit up the entire city. "Jane, I'd like you to meet Mia."

"Mia? Not Margaret?"

"It's the name she goes by now."

The little girl stopped and picked up the dog, who seemed to be right at home in her arms. Jane also assumed it was Mia's way of putting some space between herself and a total stranger.

"Hi, Mia," said Jane, bending down to her level.

Mia wouldn't meet her eyes.

Jane gazed up at Peter.

"She can't hear you, Janey."

"She's . . . deaf?"

"Yeah, but she can read lips. And she knows how to sign. Unfortunately, I don't. We've been communicating mostly by writing things down."

Jane held out her hand. When Mia finally met her eyes, she said very slowly, "I'm Jane. Peter's sister. I'm very happy to meet you."

Mia didn't respond.

"Nolan got me a copy of the file New Jersey Child Protection had on her," said Peter. "From what I read, I wasn't sure what was wrong. I thought maybe she might be retarded, or learning impaired. But she's incredibly smart."

And clearly in love with the little dog, thought Jane. "Can I pet him?" she asked, holding her hand over the dog's head.

252

Mia bit her lower lip and nodded.

"It's a *her*," said Peter. "Name's Teacake."

Jane shook the dog's paw.

Mia stepped back closer to Peter, grabbed hold of the sleeve of his jacket.

"She's very slow to let you in," said Peter. "But we're working on it."

Jane held the door open for them.

Once inside, Mia tiptoed forward, gazing around cautiously.

"Hope she's not terrified by Swedish modern furniture," said Peter, adding, "like I am."

Mia seemed to be fascinated by the floor-to-ceiling windows overlooking downtown Minneapolis. She walked up to them and stood looking outside for almost a minute, then turned and sat down on Cordelia's newest Ikea purchase, a white leather AR-ILD armchair. Teacake jumped into her arms as Mouse trotted out from the back of the loft, followed by Blanche, the matriarch of Cordelia's cat colony.

Mia set Teacake down so that she and Mouse could sniff each other.

"She's got a way with animals," said Peter, sitting down on an orange love seat that looked like it belonged in a bus terminal. "Seems to really understand them."

Mia let Mouse sniff her hands. When he seemed ready, she petted his head very softly, scratched under his chin. She didn't smile, but some of the hardness in her expression had disappeared.

Blanche, the most doglike cat Jane had ever known, jumped into Mia's lap and settled down, ready to be adored.

"If she likes animals," said Jane, "she's come to the right place. She's beautiful, Peter. But so serious."

"She's had a hellish life. I stole her—kidnapped her right off the street not three blocks from her foster home. And I don't regret it, not for a minute. The family she was living with was a nightmare. I don't know what Child Protective Services was thinking, letting her live in a situation like that. At night, while we were on the road, we'd sit on one of the beds in the motel room and write things to each other. I asked her about what it was like in her foster home, but she doesn't want to talk about it. It'll take time, I suppose."

Jane put her arms around her brother, squeezed him tight. But her joy was tempered by an even greater concern.

"Do you think I made a mistake?" he asked.

"I don't know," said Jane, stepping back. "I agree you rescued her, but what if the police come after you? Kidnapping across state lines is a federal offense."

"Believe me, Janey, nobody from New Jersey will ever come looking for her. Child Protective Services hasn't even checked on her in over a year. And besides, Mia tried to run away not too long ago. The cops brought her back. I figure that this time, they'll think she succeeded. She'll just be one more lost kid. Nobody's got the money or interest to go looking for all the lost kids in this country."

"But . . . if, all of a sudden, you and Sigrid just show up with a child, what will you tell people?"

"That we adopted her."

"But if you don't have the court papers—"

"We'll get them. You can buy them, Jane, it's not hard. We'll get away with it, I know we will. Mia is a throwaway kid. She was lost the minute she entered that child welfare system. I found her, Jane. And I'm not letting her go back there. Ever."

Considering the potential trouble Peter might be in, Jane felt more than a little conflicted, and yet he seemed so determined that, for the moment, she let the subject drop. "Have you talked to Sigrid?"

"No. I've kept her in the dark about all of this. I had to. I didn't know if I'd ever find Mia, so I never said anything, and then when Nolan located her, I couldn't break it to Siggy over the phone."

"Sure, that makes sense."

"Mia and I have been on the road for three days. Honestly, we've had a great time. We stopped at some stores in Pennsylvania and I bought her all new clothes, shoes, socks, hair barrettes. Even some perfume. She likes to read, so we found a children's bookstore along the way. Bought the first *Harry Potter*. One *Lemony Snicket*. And three from *The Black Stallion* series. That's her favorite so far. And Teacake, I mean, she's a great dog, good in the car, good in the motel rooms. She was a stray, but completely house-trained. I got lucky when I found her."

Cordelia appeared at the top of the stairs leading down from her bedroom. She'd been at the hospital late last night, so Jane was a little surprised to see her up so early. She glared a moment, then moved trancelike down the steps to the main level. "And who do we have here?" she intoned, sounding about as friendly as the wicked witch in *The Wizard of Oz*. She was wearing her red silk dragon robe, her arms folded over her ample bosom.

Mia didn't turn her head, but she did look at her sideways. She seemed more startled than frightened.

"Holy stars and garters!" said Peter, breaking into an amazed grin. "I leave for five minutes and someone steals your hair."

"How droll." She walked up to Mia, stared down at her with an austere look, then gave her a broad wink. "Thorn, Cordelia— with a C. And you are?"

Taking in Cordelia's height, size, and dress, Mia's jaw dropped at least an inch. She spelled her name using sign language.

Cordelia's eyebrow inched upward. "Ah, I see." She signed something back. They signed for a few more seconds, and then Cordelia sat down in the chair next to her. Teacake jumped into her lap.

"How is it possible that I never knew you could sign?" said Jane, hands rising to her hips.

"There are many things you do not know about me, Jane dear. I am multilayered. Labyrinthine in my complexity. Possibly even unknowable in all my infinite variety. And also, we got a woman at the theater who signs for the hearing impaired. She's been teaching me for years."

"Incredible," said Peter. "Maybe you can teach me."

"Little Miss Mia is adorable," said Cordelia. She winked at her again, her expression still dour.

This time, Mia almost smiled.

"You know," said Peter, "you're such a natural with kids it's amazing to me to think you spent most of your life hating them."

"So how are you planning to proceed?" said Jane. "I assume you're going to tell Sigrid right away."

"Tonight," said Peter. "I thought, if you didn't mind, I'd leave Mia here for a few hours. I know it's a lot to ask, but could one of you take care of her?"

Cecily walked sleepily out from the rear of the loft. She had on a light blue sweatshirt that came almost to her knees. "What's all the commotion?" Her eyes landed on Mia. "Who's that?"

"Long story," said Cordelia. "You didn't have anything planned for the rest of the day, did you?"

"Well, no, but—"

"Good. Then Cecily and I will take care of the child, Peter. Not to worry. I've taken a leave of absence from the theater for a couple of weeks, so my time is my own."

"Wonderful. Do you have a piece of paper and a pen? I need to explain this to Mia."

"Not necessary." Cordelia turned to the little girl. As she signed, she spoke out loud. "Mia, Peter has to run and do some errands, so I was hoping you could stay here with me for a few hours. I'm Peter's good friend. That funny-looking woman over there with the long brown hair is Jane, Peter's sister. The other woman wearing the blue sweatshirt is Cecily. While Peter is gone, we can play with the cats and dogs. And I've got a big-screen TV and lots of movies to watch. Oh, and games, too. Do you play checkers? Or we could make some chocolate chip cookies. Do you like cookies?"

Mia nodded. She seemed mesmerized by Cordelia.

"Great, then it's a deal." She held out her hand.

Mia shook it.

"God," said Peter. "You're amazing."

"I know."

"Okay, I'm going to call Siggy and tell her I'm home, then I'm off to buy flowers, champagne, and food to make her a fabulous dinner."

"She'll know something's up," said Jane.

"That's fine with me. After I tell her about Mia, we'll come by and pick her up."

"I want to be here when that happens," said Jane. "I have to be at the Lyme House for the rest of the day. One of my managers is sick. Maybe you could give me a heads-up when you think you're heading over."

"No problem," said Peter. He couched down next to Mia and

257

took her hand. "I love you," he said, making sure she was looking at his mouth. "I'll be back soon."

She scowled, shook her head.

"It's okay, Mia. I promise you—word of honor—that I'll be back in a few hours. And I'll bring your mother with me. These people are all kind and good. You'll have a fun day and then I'll come get you and take you and Teacake home." He hesitated, then said, "Will you let me hug you?"

She slid off her chair and threw her arms around his neck.

"Oh, my God," he said, hoisting her up. "She's never done that before." He kissed her and held her, closing his eyes, lost in the moment. When he finally set her back down, he reassured her again that he'd be back soon. "Cordelia will take good care of you," he said, brushing a strand of blond hair away from her eyes. "Will you wait for me?"

She patted his beard, gave him a serious nod.

"Good girl." He hugged her again, then said his good-byes to everyone else.

After he was gone, Mia picked up Teacake and sat down on the floor by the front door to do just what Peter had asked. Wait.

Jane's heart nearly broke.

"It'll be okay," said Cordelia. "I've got a lot of ammunition in this loft to entertain a kid. Besides, if nothing else"—she spread her arms wide—"there's always the stupendousness of me."

Jane was working the dining room at the restaurant that night, moving from table to table, greeting returning customers, welcoming new ones, when one of her waiters came up and told her she had a call that sounded urgent.

It had to be Peter. Jane quickly excused herself and returned to her downstairs office. She pushed the blinking light on her intercom and said hello.

"Jane? It's Sigrid."

"Oh, hi. How's—"

"Have you heard from Peter? He was supposed to be home tonight. He called me this morning before I left for work, said he'd fix us dinner. I got here around six, but his suitcase isn't in the closet, so I assume he's not back yet. I've called his cell at least half a dozen times, left messages, but he hasn't called back. Have you talked to him today? I think he was going to rent a car, drive back from Chicago. I'm starting to worry that something might have happened on the road. I mean, it's after eight."

Jane pulled out her desk chair and sat down. "Yes, I spoke to him this morning."

"Where was he?"

"I'm . . . not sure." She had no clue how to handle this.

"Maybe I should call Dad, see if he's heard from him."

"Sure, you could try that," said Jane. "You're positive Peter hasn't been home?"

"The mail hasn't been touched. I chilled some beer in the fridge. None of that's gone. No dirty clothes in the hamper."

"Huh," said Jane, her mind searching the possibilities. "I know how excited he was to see you tonight."

"Do you think he could've been in a car accident?"

"I suppose it's possible. But he had plenty of ID on him. If he was taken to a hospital, I'm sure one of us would've been contacted by now."

"I don't like this," said Sigrid. "Something's wrong. He would have called me if something had come up. He always lets me know where he is."

Jane had a bad feeling, too. Somewhere between Cordelia's

loft and Peter and Sigrid's apartment, something had happened.
"Look, I don't mean to jump the gun, but maybe we should start calling hospitals."

"Oh, lord."

"I'll do it," said Jane.

"No, let me. It's better than just sitting around worrying. He wouldn't have called Cordelia, would he?"

"I doubt it, but I'll check. If I hear anything, I'll call you back."

"Is Cordelia even home tonight?"

"Yes," said Jane, her heart sinking as she thought of Mia, of what would happen if something prevented Peter from coming to pick her up tonight.

Sigrid didn't say anything for a few seconds. "You don't think anything really bad happened to him, do you?"

"It's probably nothing. Just some mix-up. Maybe his cell phone is out of juice and he can't get to a phone."

"But where is he?"

"I wish I could tell you, Siggy, but honestly, I have no idea. If I find out, I'll let you know right away. You do the same."

"Sure," she said, then added, "Jane? I'm scared."

"He could sail through your front door any minute."

"You think so?"

"Absolutely. Let's give it a little more time before we hit the panic button."

29

Don't anybody bother me for at least two hours," shouted Katie Turk as she bounded up the stairs to her bedroom, holding her cell phone over her head.

"Why?" called Ethan, looking amused. He was standing in the kitchen with Randy and Sherrie.

"Because I'll be on my phone," she shouted back. "With *Chad*. And don't listen at my door either. You guys oughtta seriously look up the word *voyeur*."

Randy laughed. Having Katie back in the house again was like drinking a glass of sparkling water instead of the plain tap crap. Sherrie had called him a couple of hours ago and said that her boss had phoned her asking if she could fly to Seattle with him for a hastily arranged business meeting tomorrow. He'd never invited her to come on a business trip before, so in Sherrie's mind, this was a precursor to the promotion she'd been angling for.

"I'm sorry it's such short notice," said Sherrie.

"Not a problem," said Randy, wishing she hadn't planted herself halfway across the room.

"We love it," said Ethan. "I don't know why you both don't come back for good. This is your home, it's where you belong."

Randy cleared his throat, gave Sherrie a look.

"It's not that simple," she said.

"Yeah, right. And what does a retard know."

"Ethan!" said Sherrie.

He set his empty bottle of beer down on the counter. "I'll leave you guys so you can *not* talk to each other some more. Besides, I better get goin'. I don't want to miss another episode of *Katie and Chad.*" He winked as he left the room.

Sherrie shook her head. "Sometimes I forget what a great sense of humor he has."

Randy smiled at her. "Ethan is an optimist at heart, always thinks things are going to work out for the best." Looking away, he added, "Well, almost always."

"I got your message about the marriage counselor," said Sherrie. "What's her name?"

"Pearl Sarris. She's supposed to be good. So, are you willing to give it a shot?"

She kept her head down, pressed the toe of her shoe on the edge of the kitchen rug.

When she didn't answer, he spoke to fill the silence. "Katie and I had a great conversation the other day."

"Did you?"

"I think we really communicated. We talked about my past, about the war."

Under her breath, she said, "Why doesn't that surprise me?"

"She seemed really interested. Said she wanted to talk to me about it some more."

"Why don't you ask her how *her* life is going, Randy?"

"Are you saying I don't care?"

"No, but I am saying you rarely ask."

He caught her eye, didn't like what he saw so he looked away. "Come on, Sher. Don't be so hard on me."

"You know, Randy, when you try, you can be such a great guy. Early in our marriage, I couldn't believe how lucky I was."

"It can be that way again."

She shook her head. "Something's missing in you. You can be so incredibly focused, but you have no passion. Even in bed. It took me years to figure that out."

"That's not true."

"From the very beginning, I knew something was wrong, but I just couldn't put my finger on it. When we moved in here, I was just glad we could put Katie one floor down from our bedroom."

"Why?"

"Because of your bad dreams!"

"Everybody has bad dreams, Sherrie."

"Not like yours. Not everybody wakes up once or twice a month screaming, crying, drenched in sweat. I know you make light of it. You lie to me, tell me you were being chased by monster ants, grizzly bears, whatever. But give me *some* credit. I'm not that dumb. It's all tied to your past—the past you never talk about."

"You really want to hear a bunch of brutal war stories?"

"Is that it?" She searched his face. "Maybe you've got post-traumatic stress. If you do, you can get help. In fact, why don't you try getting some personal therapy. If you did that, I might consider couples counseling."

"Look, either our marriage is worth fighting for or it isn't."

"Fine. Fight for it. Find yourself a therapist and work on yourself for a while. I know you won't. You talk a good game, but when it comes right down to it, you're a coward."

"You don't know me at all."

"Don't I?" She held his gaze. "Prove me wrong."

After she left, Randy drifted into his study, sat down behind the desk, and tipped his seat back. As soon as he closed his eyes, the phone rang. He held the receiver to his ear, said hello. He knew he didn't sound very upbeat. The talk with Sherrie had left him feeling strung out.

"Something wrong in paradise?" came Larry's voice.

"I thought I told you to get the hell away from here."

"I been busy. Did you hear that Gunderson regained consciousness?"

"No," said Randy.

"Believe me, pal, you don't want her to remember the night she was knifed."

"Why? You said you had nothing to do with it."

"Oops. Guess I lied. But here's the kicker. Ethan helped me."

Randy's eyes opened. "What?"

"I told him what Gunderson was up to. He agreed that she needed to be stopped, so I asked him to come with me that night. Told him that I'd talk to her, impress on her the need for her to stop her nosin' around, and then he'd be waitin' in his truck with the engine runnin' so I could make a quick getaway. And that's just what happened. I left my truck about two miles away. He drove me back there and we parted company."

Randy recalled that Ethan had been out very late that night. He said he'd been driving around because he couldn't sleep. "You bastard! You didn't need to get my brother mixed up in this."

"He already is, did you forget that little tidbit? And anyway, I needed a little insurance policy just in case you didn't see eye to eye with my methods."

"Did Ethan know you planned to kill her?"

"Course not, man. He just thought I was gonna scare her a little."

Randy switched the desk lamp off and sat in the dark. "What happened to the money?"

"My cut for taking care of business."

"But you didn't take care of business, Larry. And now, what if she talks? She can ID you."

"Yeah, I know. But I think I've got it handled."

"Meaning?"

"I want you to do something for me. This is very important, so don't fail me, brother. You've got that hot-shit speakerphone in your office, right? I wanna do a conference call. Get hold of Del and tell him to come over."

"Now?"

"Yes, now, asshole. Tell him it's life or death. Then get Ray Lawless over to your place. I don't care how you do it. And his daughter, Jane, too."

"Why?"

"All part of the plan. Tell them they've got one hour."

"What if they won't do it? Or I can't find them?"

"You'll find them. Tell them that if they don't come, the fuckin' sky will fall on them in the worst possible way. I mean it. Get them to your house *or else*." He cut the line.

265

"What do you think he's up to?" asked Del.

The darkness in Randy's office moved around him like an eerie physical presence. "I don't know, but you better get your ass over here. You want to call Lawless, or should I?"

"No, I'll do it."

"What about Jane?"

"I'll get Ray to phone her. But, Jesus, Randy. He hasn't given us much time."

"I figure the one thing we've got going for us is that he's not the smartest guy in the room."

"That could work to our disadvantage."

Randy blew out some air. "I'm about ready to give up on this whole thing. Call the police and tell them everything I know."

"The hell you will."

"What are we *doing*, Del?"

"Saving our lives. *Surviving*. You want to go to jail? We made a deal all those years ago and we all swore we'd stick by it. You've got no right to mess with my life. Even if you're ready to throw in the towel, I'm not. I've got a lot of living left to do, a wife and two kids to support. Think about it, man. Is it worth it?"

"But other people are getting hurt. We never took that into consideration."

"Just stay sane a little while longer. I'll be there in thirty."

"If you can't find Ray or Jane, call me back."

"Ray's at home tonight. And I'll make sure he gets Jane there, one way or the other."

Ray had no idea what the summons was about, but Del made it sound like life or death, so reluctantly, he kissed Elizabeth good-bye and drove out to Marine on St. Croix. Sitting in Randy's study now, with Jane seated in a leather chair next to him, he demanded to know what was going on.

Randy, who stood ramrod straight behind his desk, glanced at Del with a tense look on his face. "An old army buddy of ours asked me to set this conference call up."

"Larry Wilton?" asked Jane.

A muscle pulsed in Randy's cheek. "Yes."

"Who the hell is Larry Wilton?" asked Ray. Everybody seemed to know more about what was going on than he did.

"He tried to kill a friend of mine," said Jane. "Melanie Gunderson. He knifed her outside the Unicorn bar in Uptown a few weeks ago. She's been in a coma, but she's doing better now. She's a reporter who was working on a story about a young woman who was murdered in Waldo, Iowa, back in the early seventies. Her name was Sue Bouchard. She was Randy's girlfriend."

Ray gave Randy a sharp look.

"Ethan was arrested and tried for the murder," said Jane.

"Your *brother,* Ethan?"

"Yeah," said Randy, looking away. "The whole thing was a travesty. Ethan had nothing to do with it."

"The jury acquitted him," said Jane. "And then, the case went cold."

Ray studied Randy, saw the worry in his eyes, the faint slick of perspiration on his upper lip, then turned to Del and saw the same thing. "What's going on here? What's this Larry Wilton got to do with Jane or me?" And even more to the point, thought Ray, why the hell did Jane know so much about it when he knew nothing?

The phone rang, echoing like a cannon shot in the silent room.

"I don't know what he wants," said Randy. "But I think we better find out." He picked up the phone, said hello. "Yeah, they're all here. Just a minute." He pressed the speakerphone button and set the receiver back on the hook.

"Well, well, well," came Larry's tinny voice. He sounded amused, almost leering. "Welcome to my little party."

"What do you want?" demanded Ray, impatient to get this over with.

"Hi, Jane," said Larry, using a sexy voice.

"Come on, asshole," said Del. "Spit it out."

"Okay, but you're spoiling my fun."

Ray looked over and saw that Jane's eyes were firmly fastened on the floor. Her intensity scared him more than anything else had.

"Here's the deal. I'm in a shitload of legal trouble, I guess you could say. The cops are after me for a small accident that happened not far from Randy's house. And now I hear that Melanie Gunderson has regained consciousness. Sorry to say, she can cause me even more problems if she goes to the cops. And then there's the little matter of that homicide in Waldo. I got lots of headaches here, people."

"I backed off," said Jane. "You have my word that I won't go to the police with anything I know."

"And what do you know? A big fat zero. Just a lot of conjecture from a bunch of people who belong in the Alzheimer's ward. FYI, vegetables don't make good witnesses in court."

"Right," said Jane. "So you've got nothing to worry about."

"Ah, but there's the rub. Sure, I got you to leave Waldo, but I don't trust you or your hefty friend. And then there's Melanie. Maybe you ain't gonna spill your guts to the police, but what if she does? It all gets really muddy here, folks, but if she did talk, it would look bad not only for me, but for my best buddies, Randy and Del. I can't have that."

"Larry, I don't—"

"Shut up, Randy! Shut the fuck up!"

Randy raised his eyes to Ray, then closed them.

"So, I went and bought myself an insurance policy. His name is Peter Lawless."

Jane roared out of her chair. "What have you done with him?"

"Well, that sure got a rise."

"You've . . . kidnapped my son?" said Ray, feeling dazed.

"Let's say I borrowed him for a while. Listen fast, Mr. Wannabe Governor. Your daughter and her friend have been poking their noses into matters that don't concern them. Gunderson started it all, so I had to take her out. Or I tried. Everybody has a bad day, know what I mean? Now that I got Peter, I believe your cooperation will follow. I need some time to get all my ducks in a row without the cops getting in my way. If you all don't keep your mouths shut, if you go to the cops about this or anything else that has to do with me, well, you may never see handsome young Petey again. It's really no skin off my nose. I'll erase him. You'll never find the body."

"You hurt my son and I'll—"

"You'll what, Mr. Hot Shit? Kill me?" He laughed. "That son of yours is a little soft, if you want my opinion. He needs hardening up. Don't worry. I'll make a good soldier out of him. You won't even recognize him when you get him back. *If* you get him back."

"What do you want?" said Jane. She sounded frantic. "Anything. Money? Drugs? Just name it. I'll give you anything I have if you'll just let him go."

"Sorry. But no thanks."

"You can have *me*. We'll make a switch. I'd be a lot more fun, wouldn't I? I'm sure you'd like to torture a woman."

"Now that ain't nice. And besides, I made Randy a promise. I said I wouldn't touch you or Cordelia. I swore on our friendship, the only thing that means anything to me in this rotten fucking world. Otherwise, yeah, you would have been my first choice."

"Don't hurt him," pleaded Jane.

"Larry," said Del. "You know this is crap. Let him go. If you do it now, we'll look the other way. We'll even help you run."

"No can do, dog. This is war. And you know how much I love a good war."

"He's nuts," whispered Randy.

"I don't believe you've got him," Ray piped up.

Larry laughed. "Good try."

"Prove it. Put him on the phone."

"Can't do that."

"Because it's all a lie."

"Shut up, old man. I got your goddamn son all right."

"Then you better offer me proof."

The line was silent. Then, "Yeah, I suppose I could do that. Might even be fun. A finger. A toe."

"Christ," said Randy. "This is just bullshit. Utter bullshit! What's wrong with you? How can you be like that?"

"Why bro, I've always been like this. Didn't you ever notice?"

Ray glanced up, saw Ethan move into the doorway.

"Well, folks, this has been real," said Larry. "But I gotta hit the bricks. Enjoy the rest of your evening. I know I will."

30

The silence in the room was broken by the deep rumble of thunder. Heavy rain began to pelt the trees outside the windows.

Randy watched Ethan back out of the doorway and disappear. He had to go talk to him, but he couldn't just bolt out of the room.

"What do we do?" asked Jane.

"We call the police," said her father.

"I'm not sure that's the wisest approach," said Del.

"He's my son," shouted Ray, looking hard at Del, then turning to Randy. "I make those decisions."

"I could talk to Nolan," said Jane. "See what he thinks."

"Who's Nolan?" Del had moved over to the windows, turned his back to them.

"He's a retired homicide cop," said Jane. "A friend of mine. Before we do anything, I'd like to get his opinion."

"Okay," said her dad. "I'll agree to that."

Jane stood up. "I've got to go talk to Sigrid."

"Oh, God, I forgot about her," said her father, rubbing the back of his neck. "Thanks, honey. But call Nolan on the way. And call me as soon as you've talked to him."

Jane kissed him and left.

"Okay, boys," said Ray, locking eyes with Randy. "I want the full story. Everything you know."

Del turned around.

"Look, my son's the innocent bystander here. I can't fight your buddy, Larry, if I'm in the dark."

"Come on, Ray," said Del, pressing a hand to his back. "Let's you and me go find ourselves a couple beers."

"Only if they come with some answers."

Randy thanked Del with his eyes as Del guided Ray out of the study. When Randy heard the front door close, he got up. He rushed up the stairs to Ethan's bedroom. The door was closed.

Randy knocked. "It's me. We have to talk."

"Go away," came Ethan's voice.

Randy knocked louder. "Come on, Ethan. Please!"

"Leave me alone."

Katie's door opened and she came out. "What's all the commotion?"

"Oh, hi, honey." Randy shoved his hands into the pockets of his dress slacks. "I just needed to talk to Ethan for a sec."

"Well, keep it down, okay? I gotta study for my geometry test."

"Sure, honey," said Randy, forcing a smile. "Sorry."

After she closed her door, he waited a few more seconds, then, cursing Larry under his breath, walked back down the stairs.

———

Ray followed Del back to Stillwater, where they stopped at a bar on South Main Street. Because the lift bridge to Wisconsin was temporarily shut down for repairs, Stillwater had briefly returned to a quiet small town with decent parking. Ray found a spot not far from the entrance to the bar and dashed across the street, holding a newspaper over his head to prevent himself from getting soaked.

Del was already waiting for him at a table by the windows. "I ordered us a couple of Leines."

Ray didn't care about the beer, he wanted to talk. He pulled out a chair and sat down. "First order of business. You're fired."

Del leaned back in his chair. He seemed startled.

"Now tell me about this psychopathic friend of yours."

"I never wanted any of this to happen, Ray. You must know that."

"Fine. But it did. And now we have to deal with it."

Del nodded, played with the salt shaker. "I never thought Larry was a psychopath. At least, not before tonight."

"He tried to *kill* a woman, Del, a friend of my daughter's. Did you know about that?"

Del leaned into the table. "Yeah. I knew."

"And you didn't turn him over to the police?"

"No, I didn't."

"Good God, man. What were you thinking?"

The beers arrived.

Del took a long sip, then set the bottle down. "He lied to Randy and me about what he was up to. By the time we found out, it was already done."

"So what? He belongs in prison."

"I know."

"Then why didn't you report it?"

273

"Look, you're a defense attorney. You know life isn't always a matter of action and appropriate reaction."

Ray stared at him. He drummed his fingers on the table. "This reporter he knifed, was it premeditated?"

"Yeah, I think so. Randy and me, we just thought he was trying to scare her."

"And you were okay with that?"

He nodded.

"Why? I mean, this is so . . . out of character. Nothing like the Del Green I know."

"Maybe you don't know me as well as you think you do. Maybe nobody knows anybody. Look, Ray, she was digging into that old murder case in Iowa. We wanted her to stop."

"Why would you care? Unless one of you killed her."

Del's eyes drifted around the room.

"Christ! That's it? That was why he tried to murder her? He thought she might dig up some information that would convict one of you?"

"Yeah," said Del, taking another sip of beer.

"Ethan was arrested for the murder, but he was acquitted. Are you all trying to protect *him*?"

"I can't answer that, Ray."

"Can't or won't?"

Del shook his head.

Now Ray was getting mad. "And my daughter——"

"She and Cordelia drove down to Iowa and talked to the people their reporter friend had planned to interview."

Ray groaned. "Sounds like Jane."

"Larry got them to back off, according to what Randy told me."

"How?"

"I don't know, but obviously he felt they didn't really get the message. And then when Gunderson regained consciousness, I think he just went tilt and grabbed your son."

Ray had no idea why Jane hadn't come to him with what she knew. Maybe she'd been trying to protect him, to see if the reporter's information had any validity before she came to him with her suspicions. Jane was the exact opposite of Peter—too goddamn independent, too capable and self-sufficient for her own good.

"Look, Ray, here's what you gotta understand. Randy and me, we met Larry in Vietnam. He saved both our lives more than once." Del went on to explain how, after they came home, Randy had invited them to stay with him at his parents' house in Waldo, Iowa. Del didn't have anything else to do, so he took him up on it. Same with Larry. "You ever been in combat, Ray?"

"No. What's that got to do with any of this?"

"Everything." He tipped his bottle back and finished the beer.

Ray pushed his across the table. "Take it. I don't want it. But keep talking."

Del sucked in a deep breath, let it out slowly. "It was the early seventies, man. I can only tell you what it was like back then from my viewpoint. When Randy got back to Waldo, they gave him a parade. A fucking parade! When I got back to Detroit, people spit at me. Randy was a local hero, I was a baby killer. When I heard about the parade thing, I made sure I was in uniform when I got off the bus in Waldo that spring. Otherwise, I woulda been just another nigger. At least with the stripes on my arm, most people had to make a pretense of respect. See," he said, pulling his chair closer to the table, "a lot of people thought I murdered Sue."

"Did you?"

He shook his head. "No, I loved her."

"Love——as in romantically?"

"Nah, more like a sister. But people got the wrong idea because they saw us together. The night she was murdered, we walked out of a bar together. Arm in arm. Down the center of the street. I was drunk and didn't care. In fact, I wanted people to see us. I was as black as night and she was as white as a summer cloud, and we were friends. The goddamn world was changing and I wanted that town to look it in the eye."

"But if you'd just met her," said Ray, "how could you love her?"

He smiled, pulled Ray's beer closer to him. "Randy, he used to get letters from her every week. Sometimes he'd read them to us, sometimes he wouldn't. Nobody ever wrote me and I got to thinking, hell, maybe if I got Sue's address, sent her a letter, that she'd write me back. Course, I knew Randy wouldn't like it, being the jealous kind. So, when I finally got up the nerve to write her, I told her that she seemed like a nice person and that I was superlonely, that I'd like to hear from her——but that if she did write me, I suggested that she type the letters and use a different name. That's how it started. We got to be great friends that year. By the time I made it to Waldo, I felt like she was part of my family." He laughed. "Better than family. Nobody back in Detroit ever wrote me a goddamn thing."

"Let me get this straight," said Ray. "Because you were friends, people saw you together, they assumed you murdered her? Even for racists, that's a stretch."

"Actually, it's not, but I won't argue the point right now. No, it was more than that. If Jane did her work down in Waldo, you're going to hear about this sooner or later, so I might as well explain it now, tell you the whole truth." He took a sip of Ray's beer. "It was my dog tags. The cops found them in the field where Sue was strangled, close to the tree where they found her body. They'd already arrested Ethan, but they called me in for questioning. Larry came up with this plausible explanation, and since I was scared out of my mind, I used it. He told me to tell the cops that we'd been horsing around in that field earlier that night. Wrestling. And that my tags had come off then. We all met at a bar that night in town."

"Who exactly?"

"Me and Larry, Ethan, and Randy and Sue. Larry backed up my statement, told the cops that I was so pissed that I'd lost my tags that I wanted to go back to the field and try to find them, but Larry talked me out of it, said we'd go back in the morning when we could see better."

"But that wasn't true."

"No. Like I said, Sue and I left the bar together that night. I walked her to the front door of her house and said I'd see her in the morning. She seemed really down, but wouldn't tell me why. She was like that sometimes, kept things to herself. I thought maybe it was the war. She was totally against it. She'd gotten into an argument with Larry that night. Larry was a huge supporter of what we were doing in Vietnam and made fun of the candlelight peace vigils and sit-ins she was always attending. At one point, I thought she was going to throw her beer at him. Anyway, as I was walking across the front lawn back to Randy's parents' place, her brother came up to me. He'd been in the garage working on his car. He didn't like me, didn't like it that I was a friend of his sister's. He'd been drinking, too. Seemed like everybody in town was drunk that night. Grant—that was his name—had just graduated from high school and registered with the draft. I knew he had a low draft number, and I also knew he was scared shitless about being sent to Nam.

"He came out of the garage, demanded to know what I was doing with his sister. I told him to go fuck himself. I kept walking across the field where we used to sit. I finally stopped because he wouldn't shut up, must have stood there for almost a minute listening to him yell a blue streak. He told me I was a sick killer. Asked if I was proud of that. Said that people like me deserved to rot in hell for playing along with our evil government and agreeing to go fight innocent people. You get the drift. I got sick of it after a while and told him to go home and play with his toy car, leave me the hell alone. Well, that did it. He rushed at me, shoved me to the ground. He was stronger than I thought he'd be, and scrappy as hell, but I pinned him. I was about to beat the crap out of him when Sue showed up. I guess she heard him yelling at me from her upstairs window. She ordered me off him, so I got up. But as soon as I did, he came at me again. I think that's when he yanked my tags off, although I can't be sure.

"Sue got between him and me, finally got him to back off. He ran off. She was so embarrassed. She apologized over and over again for his behavior. As I was walking her back to her house, her brother sped past us in his piece-of-shit car, honking and cursing. He was a real piece of work. Anyway, I said good night again and then headed for Randy's place. It was a warm night, so I lay down in the grass by the barn, stayed there until sunup."

Ray listened to the story. Del sounded like a man telling the truth, but there was no way he could be sure. As a defense attorney, he'd met a lot of persuasive liars in his day. "You didn't go anywhere else that night?"

"Nope. I saw Randy come in a while later."

"What about Ethan?"

"I don't know. He said he stayed until the bar closed."

278

"And Larry?"

"No idea. I was dead to the world by the time he said he got back."

"Are you telling me Larry could have done it?"

"He swears he didn't."

"And you believe him?"

"I did, at the time. Now I'm not so sure. But you can believe that Larry, Randy, and me were the prime suspects after Ethan. None of us wanted to spend the rest of our lives in prison for something we didn't do. The case went cold. Sure, we all wanted to know what happened to Sue, but not at the risk of our freedom. That's why we've always kept an eye out for someone digging into that old murder case. There are people in that town would would still love to put my ass in jail for her murder."

"You know that for a fact?"

"I do."

"And now Larry has abducted my son."

"Randy told me that there's a warrant out for his arrest on a Colorado murder charge, and of course, if Melanie Gunderson remembers what happened to her, she can ID him, so that's attempted murder on top of the murder charge. Larry's in deep, Ray. Maybe Randy's right. Maybe he has flipped out."

"That's really what I want to hear about the guy who's just kidnapped my son."

Del turned the beer bottle around in his hand. "That's why we have to play this carefully. You don't want your campaign manager—or your ex-campaign manager—making the papers because of an old murder case, which then led to your son being abducted."

"I don't give a rat's ass about the governor's race, I care about Peter!"

279

"And I get that," said Del, pushing the bottle aside. "But here's the deal. Randy and I know Larry better than anybody else. If there's any way to talk him down from this, we're the ones who can do it. I understand your concerns. I'm a father, too, but give us some time to see if we can defuse the situation without anybody getting hurt."

"You think that's possible?"

"Yeah, I do. Absolutely."

Ray had dealt with criminals all his adult life. If a man had nothing to lose—and that defined Larry Wilton—he was at his most dangerous. If Ray contacted the police and they even made one small mistake, he might never see his son again. But then, there was no guarantee that Del and Randy would handle things perfectly, either.

The waitress came over to the table, asked if they'd like another beer.

"No thanks," said Del, handing her a ten and telling her to keep the change.

As she walked off, Ray fastened his eyes on Del. "Before you clean out your desk, cancel all my events until further notice. I don't care what excuse you give. Then tell Mar Rios that she's been bumped up to your job."

"Think about that a minute, Ray. Are you sure canceling your speaking engagements is a wise idea? The press is going to smell blood, no matter what cover story I give them, especially if they also know I've been canned."

"Just do it. All I can think about now is my son. Now, here's the bottom line. I've been around a long time, Del. Longer than you. I know how to play hardball with the best of them, so listen up because I'm only going to say this once. You've got two days. Call me tomorrow with an update. You better have one. If you lied to me about any of this and I find out, if something happens to my boy because of you and Randy and your psycho friend, I'll come down on you so fast and hard there won't be anything left of you but a grease stain on a rug."

31

Larry sat splay-legged in the backseat of the rented Ford Taurus while Peter drove. Every so often Peter would feel something cold touch his ear. A gun. It was Larry's way of making sure he remembered to be a good boy, as Larry put it, which meant to do what he was told and keep his mouth shut. Larry didn't like a lot of extraneous talk, unless he was the one doing the talking.

Peter had listened closely to the call Larry had made a few minutes ago. Every so often Larry would take a slug from the bottle of Jack Daniel's he'd bought at a liquor store in Moose Lake. The more he drank, the more his mood seemed to improve. Peter had no idea who he was or what he was talking about, but the longer the conversation went on, the clearer it became that he was a man running from the law. Jane had been involved with him in some way, and so had Cordelia. Several times it seemed as if Larry was talking to Peter's father. All Peter knew was that he'd landed in the middle of something bad, with no help in sight.

At first Peter thought Larry wanted nothing more than his car, that he'd let him go as soon as they were out of town, someplace deserted. They'd found that deserted spot, all right, just north of Cambridge, but instead of setting Peter free, Larry had cuffed Peter's hands behind his back and then sat outside next to a tree talking on his cell phone. Larry ate a bunch of candy bars there, too, reading a porno magazine while Peter sweated it out in the front seat. It was only after the last phone call that Peter truly realized what was going on. This wasn't a bad guy hijacking a car, this was Peter being abducted, and that knowledge turned his blood to ice.

It had grown dark by the time they reached London Road in Duluth. They were heading straight for the freeway up to Two Harbors. Peter was keeping track of the odometer readings. Larry probably thought they were in the middle of nowhere, but Peter was familiar with the North Shore and hoped that somewhere down the line, it might give him an edge.

After cruising through Two Harbors, Peter checked the rearview mirror and saw that Larry had screwed the cap back on the bottle and was sitting up. Peter got the feeling they were getting close to their destination. They passed Superior Shores, a resort condominium complex, and followed Highway 61 up to Silver Cliff. Once they'd passed through the tunnel, Larry slid over to the left side and stared out the window. The lake was somewhere to the right of them out in the darkness. Most of the smaller resorts were on the lake side of the highway, near the water.

A few minutes later, Larry told Peter to slow down. Once again, Peter checked the odometer. Just over a mile later, Larry ordered him to turn left onto a dirt road. They bumped along in silence for three quarters of a mile until they came to a small clearing, where Larry told him to stop.

"We're almost home, Petey," he said, laughing, shoving the back door open. He made Peter stand by the front bumper while he cuffed his hands behind his back again. Switching on a flashlight, he jabbed Peter in the back with it and said, "Now we walk."

"Where are we going?"

"No questions, just move it."

They pushed through the brush into the trees. Larry wasn't very good at holding the flashlight steady, so Peter couldn't always see the ground in front of him. He slid into a couple deep water-filled holes and nearly toppled over. All the while, he could feel bugs crawling up his pants legs.

"I don't suppose you brought along any bug spray," he said.

Larry hit him in the head with the flashlight. "Shut up."

What felt like hours later, but was probably only ten or fifteen minutes, they came to a clearing.

"There she is," said Larry, washing the flashlight beam over an ancient, completely trashed travel trailer. "Home sweet home."

When they walked closer, Peter saw that the tires were all flat. The trailer looked almost organic, like it had grown from some bizarre seed. Graffiti covered most of the rusted and cracked exterior. The two windows in the front were both broken.

"It's a Shasta," said Larry, his voice full of an odd sort of reverence. "My parents owned a Shasta back in the sixties. Course, this one could use a little work. Couldn't believe my luck when I found it. I mean, it's fucking perfect. No rent. No landlords. Lots of peace and quiet." He pushed Peter into the already open door. They stood in the darkness for a few seconds while Larry fired up a lantern.

The inside of the trailer was even worse than the outside. Not only did it smell moldy and rank, but the water damage was so bad that part of the roof near where the stove vent had once been was completely caved in.

Peter looked around him and saw that the appliances were all missing. Against the back wall was a long bench. A sleeping bag was tied into a roll in one corner. Next to that were two backpacks. One looked empty, the other stuffed full. A old Coleman stove sat on a counter in what was once the kitchen. On the floor were a couple of banged-up coolers. The only table was a piece of plywood attached to the wall by hinges and propped up at the end by a two-by-four. Two folding chairs sat on either side of it and a bunch of porno magazines were spread across the top.

"All the comforts of home," said Larry, dropping the gear he'd been carrying to the floor.

Peter turned to stare at him.

"First rule of basic training," said Larry, picking up a baseball bat and tapping it menacingly against the palm of his hand. "Never look the drill sergeant in the eye."

"What?"

Larry slammed the bat into Peter's stomach, propelling him backward over the coolers.

"Next rule," said Larry, standing over him. "Speak only when spoken to."

Peter waited for the pain to subside, then gazed up at him with terrified eyes.

"You need another lesson, boy?"

Peter quickly looked away.

"Next rule. When I ask you a question, you answer and then say 'Thank you, Drill Sergeant.' "

Peter blinked. His heart was beating so fast and loud he wasn't sure he'd heard him right.

"Understand?"

"I think so," said Peter.

"I think so *what?*"

"Yes, I understand. Thank you, Drill Sergeant."

Larry smiled. "Get up."

Peter struggled off the coolers.

"Sit here." Larry pulled out one of the folding chairs.

Behind him, Peter could hear Larry fiddling with a zipper. Then something began to buzz.

"Now sit still," said Larry.

Peter felt the buzzing noise hit the back of his head. He ducked away.

"It's a hair trimmer, asshole," said Larry, showing it to him. "Now, sit up straight and don't move. Can't have a beard or long hair in boot camp. We gotta get rid of it, clean you up good and proper. Maybe I'll make you look like one a them skinheads." He laughed.

Peter's eyes darted around the dank interior. He couldn't believe this was happening.

"Tomorrow, we start basic training, so you better get a good night's sleep. Oh, and just so you know, you're writing a letter tomorrow. Your sister and your dad don't believe I've really got you. Can't have them thinking ole Larry lied to them, now can I."

"No. Thank you, Drill Sergeant."

"Just shut up."

32

He's been *what?*" said Cordelia, sounding just short of apoplectic.

"Kidnapped," repeated Jane. She was driving through the pouring rain on I-94, heading back to Minneapolis on her way to talk to Sigrid.

"What the hell does Wilton want?"

"Our silence. And Melanie's."

"Melanie doesn't remember a thing."

"There was no point in telling him that. He knows as well as we do that her memory could come back anytime. He also doesn't believe we'll leave it alone. Maybe we missed something down in Waldo, Cordelia. Maybe there really is something that proves who Sue's real murderer was."

"So, he's going to hold Peter for what? A week? A month? He can't hold him forever."

"He says he needs time to put some sort of plan together. His getaway, I assume."

"And then what?"

"I don't know. That's why we've got to find my brother, before Larry does something stupid. I'm on my way to talk to Sigrid now. I called Nolan, left him a message. My dad and I both want him to weigh in on what he thinks we should do. How's Mia?"

"She fell asleep on the couch in the study around eight. That poor kid is exhausted. I covered her with a quilt. With any luck, she'll sleep until morning. Teacake is asleep on the couch right next to her, Mouse is stretched out on the floor, and Blanche is curled up at her feet. I haven't seen Lucifer or Melville all day. I think they're plotting something."

"Did you and Mia have fun together?"

"Of course. We made monster cookies, chocolate sodas, played checkers—she beat me three times and Cecily twice. We drew self-portraits. But what am I going to tell her if she wakes up and Peter isn't here?"

Jane had been thinking about that nonstop since she left Randy Turk's house. "I guess we make something up. Like, maybe he was called away on a business trip."

"Boy, that's going to be a hard one to sell. He gave her his promise that he'd be back."

"And he will be," said Jane, "just not tonight."

Jane parked behind Peter and Sigrid's apartment building and then dashed through the rain to the rear security door. She'd called from the road, so Sigrid was waiting for her, ready to let her in.

"You know something?" said Sigrid, grabbing Jane by her arm before she could reach the stairway.

"Let's go up to your apartment."

"No, tell me here. Has he been in an accident? Is he—"

"No," said Jane. Tension swelled between her shoulders. This was a conversation she would give anything not to have. "He's okay, as far as I know. Please, Siggy. We need some privacy." She could see a look of confused bewilderment pass across Sigrid's face. "Come on."

Jane led the way upstairs. The apartment door was open a crack so she walked in. Her jean jacket was damp, but she didn't take it off. She sat down on the couch.

Sigrid stood over her. "What is it? Where is he?"

"Please, Siggy. Sit down."

"Tell me."

"Okay. He's . . . been abducted."

"What?" Her first reaction was to laugh. "Is this a joke?"

Jane shook her head.

"While he was in Chicago?"

"No, after he got back. Sometime today." Jane explained everything she knew. By the time she was done, Sigrid was sitting on the couch, staring impassively down at her wedding ring. She opened her mouth to speak, but closed it again.

"I think I know some of what you're feeling," said Jane, reaching for Sigrid's hand. "I'm feeling the same thing. Dad's talking to Del right now. Maybe he'll find some information that will help us. Siggy? Are you okay? What can I do? You want some water?"

"Water? Are you serious? Get the brandy. It's in the kitchen."

"Are you sure—"

"How often does my husband get kidnapped? I think we could both use a drink."

Jane found a nearly full bottle in the cupboard and brought it back with two shot glasses. Setting everything down on the coffee table, she poured them each a shot.

Sigrid downed it, poured herself another, downed that, then poured herself a third, which she held in her hand.

Before Jane could touch hers, her cell phone rang. "Hope that's Nolan." When she answered, she found that it was. "Hi. Are you back from New Jersey?"

"Flew in two nights ago. How did Peter make out with the girl?"

"Okay. But there's a problem." She gave him an abbreviated version of everything she'd told Sigrid, ending with Peter being kidnapped.

"I knew you weren't down in Iowa for your health."

"Got any opinions on what we should do?"

"Call the police. Have them put out an APB on Wilton's truck."

"I knew you'd say that. But Randy and Del think they can defuse the situation without anybody getting hurt. If the police make one wrong move, my brother is a dead man."

"Yeah. I've heard that a million times. Let me think about it. I'll call you."

"Thanks," said Jane. "Think hard, and call me soon." She flipped her phone closed.

"Has he got any brilliant ideas?" asked Sigrid, downing the third shot.

"Not really. If we could just catch a break." The comments Larry had made about Peter being soft, about turning him into a good soldier, bothered Jane almost more than anything else. She might be wrong, but Larry seemed to enjoy twisting the knife during that conference call, which left her with the distinct impression that he had a sadistic side.

"I can't believe this is real," said Sigrid. She started to laugh again, caught herself, then laughed even louder. "You know,

Peter and I, well, we haven't been seeing eye to eye on much lately. I'm sure he's talked to you about it."

"A little."

"It started out as an argument about whether or not we should have children. You know all about that. But, to be honest, it's gone further than that now, at least it has for me."

It wasn't what Jane wanted to hear.

Sigrid poured one more shot, then set the bottle behind her on the end table. "I feel like a traitor, talking about him when he's . . . he's—" She tilted her head back, closed her eyes, started to cry. Wiping a hand across her cheeks, she went on. "God, how can this be happening?"

"He'll come home, Siggy. I believe that with all my heart."

"I want to believe that, too. I do . . . so much. I was thrilled when he called about that job in Chicago. He sounded so excited. He's a great photographer. It suits him perfectly. He can work behind the scenes, but he can still be creative." Looking over at Jane, she said, "Do you mind if I talk to you about this?"

Jane could hardly say no. Sigrid seemed to need to talk. "Sure, go ahead."

Sigrid downed shot number four.

"I think you should slow down."

"Not every day your husband gets kidnapped."

"I know, but—"

"See, I want him to get that job in Chicago. That way, it could be a fresh start for both of us."

"You'd go with him then?"

She shook her head.

"Are you saying you want a divorce?"

"I'm saying that Peter . . . he's the greatest guy in the world. He's smart, funny, good-looking, sweet, caring, but . . . he

291

doesn't have a lot of ambition. What he wants out of life is . . . how do I say this . . . it's less than what I want. His dream is a house with a picket fence and a bunch of kids in the yard and a dog running around and me in the kitchen."

"I think that's a little simplistic."

"Okay, maybe, but not by much. I don't want any of that, Jane. It just seemed to me like now might be the best time to call it quits. All we have is this apartment. Sure, we've both bought some furniture, but he can have it all, I don't care. I'll always love him, Jane. And if he'll let me, I'll always want to be a part of his life, but not as his wife."

Jane didn't know what to say. Her stomach was already in knots, and this just made it worse.

"It's like . . . you knew me back when I was getting my undergrad degree at the U. I dated lots of guys, even some women. I never wanted to be tied down to just one person."

"But you wanted to marry Peter."

"I did. He was one guy I didn't want to get away. I figured, if other people could do it, if my friends could marry and be happy, so could I. I mean, I not only fell in love with your brother, I fell in love with his family. You and Ray. You two are *so* important to me. I don't ever want to lose either of you. But—" She leaned back. "See, I want more. I don't want to spend my life as a couples counselor, just eking out a living. I haven't told anyone this because I just learned about it a couple of days ago, but I've been accepted into the doctoral program in social psychology at Stanford. It's the number one university in the country in psychology. I've also been reading about this program M.I.T. offers. It's a one-year master's in political science. I want to somehow combine the two. I'm fascinated by how social psychology could be applied to geopolitics. Working at the UN is my dream. I want to write, to research, to explore new ways for governments to work with each other."

"But couldn't Peter be a part of that?"

The excitement in Sigrid's eyes faded. "How do I make you understand. You're going to hate me, Jane. You and Ray, you're everything I admire. You've created lives that are meaningful, lives based on your passions."

"I think you're looking at us a little unrealistically."

"I don't."

Poor Peter, thought Jane, living his life around workaholic overachievers when all he ever wanted was an ordinary, sane existence. She could see now more clearly than ever why, out of all the women he'd dated, he'd picked Sigrid to marry. She must have felt like home, like what he'd always been used to.

Sigrid's eyes dropped to the bottle of brandy next to Jane. "Have you ever fallen out of love?"

"Oh, God."

"I'm sorry, but it happens. Even when you don't want it to, even when you try your damnedest to prevent it. I mean, I still love your brother, but not the way I should, not the way he deserves."

The alcohol had no doubt caused Siggy to say more than she wanted to, not that it mattered. It was all the truth. It had been awhile since Jane had had a heart-to-heart with Sigrid. She regretted that now.

"Peter and I, we've got a good physical relationship. That's what's kept the marriage going, but it's nothing to build a life on. In a strange way, this running argument we've had about having a child has kept us together. It's been something to talk about. Peter knows I want to go for my doctorate, but he never wants to discuss it. He just doesn't get why I can't be satisfied with my master's, just work my job, and enjoy life. He's creative, and he likes what he does, but it's his free time, his personal life that makes him happy. Last year he was all excited about taking the two of us on a Caribbean cruise. I can't tell you how little interest I have in that. Work, meaningful work, is where it's at for me."

Jane did understand. But where did that leave Mia? All this time, Peter had been operating under the assumption that reuniting Sigrid with her daughter was the magic bullet for all of them. Clearly, he hadn't been listening to his wife even a little. Mia's entrance into their lives would change everything.

"I'm sorry, Jane. I've been bending your ear about something that's really beside the point at the moment. I'll do anything to help find Peter. Just tell me what to do. I may not stay married to him in the long run, but if I ever lost him, I'm not sure I'd survive it. I know that doesn't make any sense."

"Yeah, it does," said Jane, exhaling a soft, frustrated sigh.

"I'll call my supervisor in the morning and tell him I need to take some time off."

The phone in the kitchen rang.

"Maybe that's Peter," said Sigrid, rushing to answer it.

Jane doubted it. She got up and stood in the doorway.

"Oh, hi Ray," said Sigrid. She listened for a few seconds. "Sure, I appreciate that. But I don't think I should drive. I've had some brandy." She listened again. "That would be great. It won't take me long to get ready. Half an hour is good." After she hung up, she turned to Jane and said, "Your dad doesn't think I should be alone tonight. He wants me to stay at his place."

"He's coming by to pick you up?"

She nodded. "Like I said, what a great family."

Walking Jane to the door, Sigrid asked, "Are you going to be okay?"

"Not until Peter's back home and safe."

"Yeah. I know."

They hugged, then said good night.

When Jane got back to Linden Lofts, she sat in her car in the back parking lot and called Kenzie. She might as well break the bad news to her now. She wouldn't be coming down for the Memorial Day weekend. At least it wasn't business that had nixed their plans this time. It was late, going on midnight, but Jane figured that even if she woke her, Kenzie would understand.

"Hey, babe. It's me. Were you asleep?"

"No, just reading."

Jane could hear her yawn. "I'm afraid I've got some bad news."

Silence.

"Kenzie?"

"You're not coming."

"No."

"I knew it. I just knew it. I told you how important this was to me. I've been planning it for months. You know, I've really had it with your compulsive need to work all the time. Don't I ever get to come first?"

"Of course you do. But it's not about work. It's about my brother."

"What about him?"

"He's been . . . abducted."

"*What?*"

"A psycho grabbed him. I don't know where he is, or what this guy is planning to do with him. I'm scared out of my mind."

"I'm sorry. I—"

"Look, I can't talk right now. I'll . . . call you later."

"Jane, you've got to forgive me. I just went off. I didn't mean—"

"Nothing to forgive. Go to sleep. We'll talk in the morning." She shut off the phone and threw it on the floor. Getting out of her Mini, she stood for a moment, hands on the hood, trying to force the anger out of her system. Tears welled in her eyes, but she refused to let them come. It wasn't Kenzie's fault, it was hers. She should have talked faster. But what if it had been her job? Was that the end of the world?

She stood there a minute more, trying to back away from her emotions, then looked up and surveyed the parking lot. The rain had finally stopped. Hearing the sound of laughter, she turned and watched two men run past her on the footpath along the river road. That's when she saw it. Larry's truck. It was parked on the street directly under a streetlamp. It was as if the cosmos had reached down and pointed at it with a lighted finger.

Jane rushed up to it, checked the doors and windows, but everything was locked tight. She looked inside and saw some junk on the seats. Was Peter being held someplace near here? Or—what if Larry hadn't used his truck to grab Peter. As she mulled it over, she realized that Larry must have been waiting for her brother when he came out of the Linden building after dropping off Mia. They must have driven away in the car Peter had rented in New Jersey.

Jane sprinted to the rear door of the Linden building and let herself in with her key. Entering Cordelia's loft a few minutes later, she found Cecily in the living room, lying on the couch reading a fashion magazine.

"Where's Cordelia?"

"Asleep. Mia woke up a while ago and was pretty upset that Peter hadn't come, so Cordelia took her up to her room for a lit-

296

tle talk. Last I looked, they were both out cold with various cats and dogs littering the room." She hesitated. "Jane, I need to tell you how sorry I am about Peter."

"Thanks."

Mouse trotted down the steps. Jane crouched down and gave him a hug and a scratch. She was so incredibly glad to see him. "I don't think I'll be getting much sleep tonight, so I thought I'd take Mouse and we'd head over to the Lyme House, burn the midnight oil trying to figure out some way to find my brother."

"Good luck," said Cecily. "Really, if there's anything I can do—"

"Tell me where Cordelia keeps a hammer."

"In the junk drawer in the kitchen."

"Junk," said Jane. "Why not." She found it underneath a kitchen timer, two yo-yos, and a bunch of take-out menus. Nolan might advise against what she was about to do, but she didn't care. If there was something in that truck that might give her a clue to where Larry had taken her brother, she intended to find it.

Back outside, Jane let Mouse run down to the riverbank while she made quick work of smashing the front window. Thank God it was late and most people who were out for a night on the town were up on First Avenue or Hennepin. She brushed the glass off the front seat, then started to sift though the junk, piece by piece. Candy wrappers. Crumpled-up fast-food bags. There were a bunch of catalogues and a few magazines. An empty package of Trojan Magnums. She picked everything up and put it in an empty Wal-Mart bag, including the contents of the glove compartment.

"Come on, boy," she called, seeing that Mouse was sitting down on the footpath, sniffing the night air. "Let's go for a ride."

They drove across town and made it to the Lyme House just before one. The upstairs dining room was closed, but the pub on the main level was still open. Jane unlocked her office door and let Mouse inside. He jumped up on the couch in front of the cold fireplace and made himself at home, while she headed down the hall to the pub and pulled herself a pint of ale. She said hi to one of the bartenders, spoke to a few regulars, and on her way back grabbed herself a bowl of popcorn.

After closing and locking the door, she sat down behind her desk. She didn't want any interruptions. She checked her cell phone and saw that Kenzie had called back twice. She just couldn't deal with that right now.

Dumping the contents of the sack on the desk, she turned on the lamp and began going through everything. Two of the magazines were porn, one was all about guns. She dumped those in the trash. Most of the contents of the glove compartment had to do with the recent purchase of the truck. But there was a Minnesota map that Jane put in a separate pile to look at more closely. The last two magazines were law enforcement supply catalogues.

Jane took a sip of her ale, then paged through the first one. Nothing stood out until she got to the section on body restraints. Larry had circled a pair of Smith & Wesson handcuffs, a pair of leg irons, and something Jane had never heard of before— transport restraints, a combination of the two connected by a heavy-duty chain. None of it made her feel any better about Larry or his intentions toward Peter.

She pulled the Minnesota map in front of her and stared down at it, hoping Larry might have marked a destination. And there it was. He'd circled three cities in red ink. Fergus Falls. Duluth. And Grand Rapids. Obviously, these were big areas to search, but Jane couldn't help but feel her pulse quicken.

298

After studying the map a few more seconds, she put it aside and started to go through the bits of paper she'd picked up from the floor of the truck. One was a receipt from a gas station in Battle Lake, near Fergus Falls. Another was from a motel in Hill City, just south of Grand Rapids. There was a receipt from Judy's Cafe in Two Harbors. Another from Betty's Pies up on the North Shore. Jane knew that area of the state best.

Elbows on the desktop, hands buried in her hair, she tried to think it through. Where would Larry try to hide her brother? And why had he circled those three towns? Jane's mother had always loved Lake Superior. Superior wasn't your average Minnesota lake, it was more like an inland sea, and so for the few years that Jane's mom had lived in Minnesota before her death, she'd insisted that the family spend time during the summer on the North Shore. Jane's dad had continued the tradition, taking Jane and Peter up to various cabins and resorts from Duluth to Grand Marais when she was in college and Peter in junior high. She knew the shore well and so did Peter. But if Larry had taken him to somewhere around Fergus or the Grand Rapids area, she was in the dark.

"It's your fault," she whispered.

The impact of the words dissolved her.

If she hadn't gotten mixed up in that cold murder case in Iowa, none of this would have happened. Ever since their mother had died, Jane had felt like Peter was her responsibility. She couldn't let him down in a mundane, ordinary way. Oh, no. She had to do it in a life-threateningly huge way.

As she thrashed around for a life raft in her self-induced purgatory, Mouse nosed the side of her leg. She hadn't heard him get up. She put her hand down to pet him, but he nosed it away.

"What's wrong?" she said, looking down at him. As she

299

pushed her chair back, he jumped into her lap. "Whoa." He'd never done it before.

"Oh, buddy," she said, her eyes instantly filling with tears. The feelings she'd been suppressing all night finally came pouring out. She cried against his fur. "Thanks, Mouse," she whispered, holding him tight.

33

Peter didn't sleep much that night. Larry cuffed his hands behind his back, but this time, he added leg irons, and something
he called a bull strap tether—a piece of heavy leather that
hooked the back of Peter's handcuffs to the leg irons. Larry wasn't
taking any chances. While he snored away inside his sleeping bag
at the back of the trailer, Peter shivered on the floor under the
broken windows. Terror mixed with the chill night air kept his
mind alert.

When he was pretty sure Larry was asleep, he tried to get up.
Larry flew at him, racked the slide of his semiautomatic pistol,
and pressed it to Peter's temple. Peter thought it was all over,
but instead of shooting him, Larry kicked him in the stomach a
bunch of times to work off some steam, then told him that if he
tried to get up again, he'd take him outside, tie him up, cut him,
and let him play Russian roulette with the northern Minnesota
wildlife population.

Peter didn't move for the rest of the night.

Before sunup, Peter, untethered now, was standing outside the trailer, feet together, arms at his side, eyes forward, chin up. Every muscle in his body ached.

What seemed like hours later, the sun had finally risen above the trees and now struck him square in the eyes.

As he stood sweating in the morning sunlight, a fly landed on his nose.

"Well, now, ain't that a good case in point," said Larry. He sat cross-legged on the ground about fifteen feet away, smoking a cigarette. "That fly, he don't care that you're in formation. Looks like one of them big bad blackflies, too—the kind that bite."

Peter's head felt like it was stuffed with cotton. He hadn't had anything to eat or drink since yesterday morning and it was starting to take a toll. He clenched his jaw, tried to will the fly away.

Larry got up, ambled over to where Peter was standing. "I'm gettin' tired of this, Petey. Drop and give me twenty."

Peter didn't know what he meant. Since he couldn't speak without being asked a direct question, he had no way of finding out.

"You hard of hearing, boy?"

"No. Thank you, Drill Sergeant."

"Then do it!"

"I don't know what you mean, Drill Sergeant."

Larry pressed the gun up under Peter's chin. "Push-ups, you retard! Ever heard of them?"

"Yes. Thank you, Drill Sergeant."

"*What?*"

"Yes. Thank you, Drill Sergeant!"

He cupped a hand around his ear. "I can't hear you."

"Yes, thank you, Drill Sergeant!" Peter yelled.

"That's better. Now, get to it."

Peter sank to his knees. He might have been able to do twenty push-ups with ease six months ago, but after he'd been fired from his job, he let his membership at the local health club lapse. He stretched out. The first ten weren't a problem. By twenty, he was getting winded.

"Gimme twenty more," said Larry.

Peter went at it again. His muscles were screaming at him to stop.

"Now, flip over and give me fifty sit-ups," said Larry. He sat down in the doorway of the trailer.

Peter eased onto his back. He didn't exactly complete the fifty quickly. As he struggled through the last ten, Larry yelled at him to "pick it up." Peter had never truly hated anyone before, not the kind of white-hot hate you saw in movies, but he was beginning to understand it—the desire for total annihilation.

"Get up," said Larry.

Peter eased over, tried to move into a crouch, but lost his balance and fell forward to his hands and knees. He ran his tongue over his cracked lips.

"I need water," he said.

Larry was up instantly. The butt of his gun connected with Peter's head, forcing him backward. The pain was so intense that for a few seconds, he couldn't see or hear.

"Get up!" screamed Larry.

Gritting his teeth, Peter struggled to a sitting position, feeling hot blood ooze down his cheek. When he hoisted himself up, he felt so dizzy that for a moment, he thought he might fall.

"I guess it is time for a little R&R." Larry pushed him through the door of the trailer, told him to sit at the table. "You're going to write that letter, Petey."

Peter pulled out one of the folding chairs and sat down.

This time, instead of cuffing him Larry tried something new. He wound duct tape around Peter's upper arms, and then around his lower legs, leaving his hands free so he could write.

"Here's the situation. You dad seems to need some proof I really got you. Write somethin' only you would know." He pulled a battered steno notebook and two Bic pens from his backpack. Tearing off a sheet of paper, he set it down in front of Peter. And then he retreated to the rear of the trailer, where he sat propped against his rolled-up sleeping bag and began to write something himself.

Peter had been thinking about the letter all night. This might be his only chance to tell his dad and Jane where he was.

Hi, all.

My cell phone number is: 756-624-2979. I'm a Libra.

It's really Peter, not my evil twin. That's a joke.

Let me make some points that prove it's me.

My mother's maiden name was Lind.

On my next birthday, I turn 37.

I left the dry cleaning in the bedroom closet—Sigrid's red dress and my blue suit.

They got the and stain out of the dress finally, which should make Sigrid happy.

I rode my dirt bike over to Jane's house three nights ago for dinner. We had fried chicken.

Steve promised to come on Saturday with the trailer to pick up the old gas stove.

My favorite play is Into the Woods by Stephen Sondheim. Favorite food, steak. Favorite dessert, lemon meringue pie. No favorite color.

I wish I hadn't been in such a hurry with my life, wish I had
taken more time to enjoy it.

I love you all,

Peter

When he was done, he looked up. Larry was still working on whatever he was writing. Peter took the chance to read through the note one more time. There was only one word he'd written that might set off Larry's alarm bells, but he'd tried to hide it the best he could.

A few minutes later, Larry finished up. He tore the page he'd been writing on out of the notebook and stood. "Done, Petey?" He removed a couple of envelopes from his backpack, then moved up to the table and grabbed Peter's note.

Peter held his breath.

"Hmm. Yeah, guess this is okay. Thought maybe you'd plead a little."

Peter stared straight ahead.

"Tell me your dad's address. Or your sister's. Don't matter." His pen was poised over the envelope, ready to write.

Peter gave him Jane's address.

"Okay." He stuffed the note inside and licked the back of the envelope. Flipping open one of the coolers, he reached inside and took out a bottle of water. "Drink it fast," he said, setting it down on the table. Peter didn't need any encouragement. He sucked it back in a matter of seconds. He could have drunk two or three, but Larry had already closed the cooler.

Larry locked Peter up again in the handcuffs, leg irons, and used the bull strap to connect him to a piece of the reinforcing bar holding the trailer together. When he was finished, he stuffed the pistol in the back of his belt and rubbed his chin.

"You really do look like a skinhead," said Larry, laughing.

Peter dropped his gaze to the floor.

"I'll be gone for a while. But never fear, I'll be back by to-night, Petey. Say your prayers. Boot camp goes thermonuclear tomorrow."

Randy was almost finished with his morning run when his cell phone went off inside his jacket. He stopped along the side of the road and checked the caller ID. No information popped up.

"Randall Turk," he said, watching a car drive past. One of his neighbors. He waved.

"Hey, bro," said Larry.

Randy's frustration ratcheted into the stratosphere. "Where are you?"

"At the moment, in Cambridge."

"What are you doing there? Where's Peter? Is he okay? You haven't hurt him, have you?"

"Not much."

"What's that mean?" Randy began walking back toward his house. It was only a short distance.

"Let's talk turkey, Turk." Larry laughed at his joke. "I grabbed Petey to buy me some time, but you and me, we both know I also did it to keep you from spillin' your guts to the cops."

"If you don't shut up about that weak link crap——"

"Tell me it ain't crossed your mind."

"It hasn't."

"Liar."

"Look, let Peter go. You've got my word of honor that I won't talk to the police. I'll even help you get away. Whatever you need."

"Just what I was hopin' you'd say."

Randy trotted across his lawn and up the steps to the deck outside the kitchen. Dropping down on a chair, he said, "What do you want?"

"Money."

"You already took that fifty thousand."

"Not enough. I need more."

"How much?"

"Remember when we was hoistin' a few down in Stillwater that one time years ago and you started shootin' your mouth off about how much money you made in the nineties with investments and shit, so much that you got yourself one of them Swiss bank accounts?"

"Yeah, I remember." Randy rarely bragged. But around Larry, especially when he'd been drinking, he did. He regretted it now.

"Well, I been thinkin' what's the easiest way for you to get me the money. Tomorrow I should have a brand spankin' new passport, driver's license, SS number. I'll be a whole new me!"

"You planning to run?"

"Over the border to Canada, and then off to Europe. Always wanted to visit Paris. But to stay lost, like you and me both want, I'm gonna need me some serious greenbacks. A couple hundred thousand should do it. You got that much?"

Randy would have begged, borrowed, or robbed a bank if it meant getting rid of Larry. "I can handle it."

"Great, man. Great. Next stop, South America. Hear an Americano can live pretty cheap down there. So, if I go to Switzerland, can you have your banker get me the cash?"

"You don't want to travel with that kind of money on you."

"No?"

"I'll open a bank account for you, transfer the money in. You'll have to go to my bank in Zurich and sign, give them your new identification, but once that's done, you can do wire transfers from then on. They'll explain everything."

"You're my man."

Randy could hear a catch in his voice.

"Do you know what your new name's going to be?"

"Elmer Hall, from Lava Hot Springs, Idaho. Won't know anything else until tomorrow."

"You can't call me any more, Larry. It's too dangerous."

"Yeah, been thinkin' about that, too. So I got me a Yahoo account. You don't even need to write it down to remember it. It's wildmanwilton1971@yahoo.com. You can leave messages for me there. Let me know where to go, who to talk to. Just remember, don't send it from your computer. Send it from the library or someplace neutral."

"And before you go, you'll free Peter, right?"

"Abso-fucking-lutely, dog." He paused. "So, I guess this is the last time I'll talk to you this side of the grave. Just wanted you to know that . . . that I love you, man. I purely do. You and Del have been my only real family. I'll pay you back one day, I promise."

"Don't worry about that," said Randy. "You let Peter go and we're even."

"Brothers to the end," said Larry.

"Yeah, brothers to the end," repeated Randy.

"Bye, man. Don't forget me."

Randy checked his watch. If he called his account manager in Zurich right away, he might still be there.

An hour later, Randy came out of his office. Through the windows in the living room he could see Ethan out by his truck in the drive, getting ready to leave for the day. They hadn't spoken since the night before. Randy couldn't leave it like that.

Katie had left for school just as Randy had headed out for his morning run, so if he and Ethan got into it, as they sometimes did, Katie wouldn't have to suffer through it.

Walking across the lawn, Randy caught Ethan's eye.

"I don't wanna talk," said Ethan, turning away.

"We have to."

Ethan lifted a five-gallon container of gasoline into the back of his truck. "I heard you talking to your banker. You're giving Larry more money?"

"You shouldn't be listening at my door."

"I got ears! I got eyes!"

"He's my friend. Or, at least, he was once."

"You got bad friends, Randy."

"What's eating you? You won't even talk to me anymore."

"I talk."

"Not the way we used to. Not the way I want us to."

Ethan wrapped both hands around the back of his neck, looked down at the concrete. "I can't stand it anymore."

"Can't stand what?"

"Me!" He walked to the other side of the truck, stood with his arms pressed against the passenger door.

"What's wrong?"

"Everything."

"You can tell me," said Randy, leaning next to him on the hood.

"No. I can't."

"Why?"

"Because I did something bad. Something I never told you. And now, if I tell you the truth, you'll hate me."

Randy felt fear like the prick of a knife sliding down his backbone. "What . . . didn't you tell me?"

"What happened."

"What happened *when*, Ethan?"

"The night Sue died."

"What about that night?"

"She was going to talk to you, tell you she couldn't marry you."

"She did talk to me," said Randy, listening to the rhythmic pounding of his heart, wondering if this was the moment when it would finally stop.

"That's why I got drunk that night. I couldn't stand it. I thought she was going to tell you why. But she didn't."

"Didn't what?"

"Tell you why she wouldn't marry you."

"She said she didn't love me."

"That's part of it."

"What's the other part?"

"Me. Sue and me, we were in love. It happened while you were in Nam. I didn't mean for it to happen. I'm sorry, Randy." He broke down, covered his eyes with his arm and began to sob.

Randy stared at him. He couldn't quite get his mind around it, but he knew Ethan wouldn't lie about something like that. Randy was surprised at his reaction. He felt nothing, not the least bit angry. But then, as he stood there watching his brother wrapped in his private hell, sadness expanded inside of him so hard and fast that it almost cut off his breath. Such a waste, he thought. All of it. Such a pointless, useless waste.

"That's why, if I killed her—"

"You didn't, Ethan."

"But you don't know that," he cried.

"I do know it. I know who killed her and it wasn't you."

Ethan looked up, wiped the back of his hand across his eyes. "You know?" he said, looking stunned.

"I always have. I just can't talk about it."

310

"It was Larry, wasn't it." His eyes turned suddenly cold.

"No."

"Yes it was! You're protecting him, just like you always do."

"Del, Larry, and me, we all protect each other. That's the way it is. But I'm telling you the truth. You didn't hurt Sue. Deep down, you *must* know that."

Ethan stood motionless for a few seconds, then walked around to the back of the truck and shut the rear hatch. "I gotta go think about this."

As he opened the driver's side door to get in, Randy took hold of his arm. "I'm sorry, Ethan. When Sue died, you lost a lot more than I did. I never realized it. If you'd told me about the two of you back then, you're right, I probably would have been furious. But I'm not now. I'd do anything to change what happened, you have to believe that. You and Sue deserved a life together. But . . . there's nothing I can do about it now."

Starting the engine, Ethan looked up at him. "You could tell the truth," he said. He yanked the door shut, pulled out of the drive, and drove off.

34

Jane cracked an eye, looked around for a few seconds, then eased her upper body off the desk. She ran both hands through her hair, massaged her neck until the reality of the room reasserted itself.

She was in her office at the Lyme House. She must have fallen asleep. Glancing at her watch, she saw that it was a few minutes after seven. The last time she remembered looking at the time was just before five. She'd been thinking about running upstairs to get herself some coffee. Apparently, she never made it.

Mouse was fast asleep on the braided rug in front of the couch. She'd taken him outside around three for a short walk along the west side of Lake Harriet. When they got back inside she'd stretched out on the couch to try to get some rest, but she'd been too tense. Her eyes just kept popping open. Eventually, she returned to her desk to MapQuest the areas of the state Larry had circled. She was working out what she wanted to tell Nolan.

On weekdays, Nolan usually got up anywhere between seven and eight, but it took three or four cups of strong black coffee and a substantial breakfast before he was, in his words, "fit to carry on a conversation that didn't involve snarling." Jane figured she could use some coffee herself.

"Mouse?" she said softly.

His tail began to thump against the rug.

"Let's get out of here."

She cleared everything off her desk into a paper sack, then turned off her desk lamp and locked the door behind her.

After all the rain last night, it was a damp morning. She thought about taking Mouse for a run, but she didn't have the energy. Instead, they got in her car and drove up the hill to her house.

Once inside her kitchen, Jane put on the coffeepot and then ran upstairs to shower while the coffee brewed. Returning to the kitchen dressed in a pair of old jeans, sandals, and a dark green and black rugby jersey, she poured herself a cup of coffee and stepped out onto the back porch with her cell phone. Mouse was out in the yard, sniffing along the fence. Just as she sat down, the phone rang.

"Hello?" she said, not bothering to check the caller ID.

"Janey, it's Dad. I just got a call from Randy. Wilton phoned him a little while ago, said Peter was doing okay and that he'd release him soon."

"How soon?"

"He didn't say, but Randy thought it would be a day or two, not much more. I got the impression he might be paying Wilton some sort of ransom."

Jane assumed that somewhere along the line, money would change hands. "But Randy didn't say that directly?"

"No."

"I wonder why?"

"He plays things pretty close to the vest, Janey. Always has. I figure Del was right. Since they know Wilton better than you or me, they know best how to handle him. Apparently, Wilton got Peter to write us a note, so we should have that—hopefully—by tomorrow. At least we know he's still alive."

It wasn't enough.

"I fired Del."

"No kidding. What about your campaign? Don't you have some speaking engagements scheduled for today?"

"Everything will be canceled until further notice."

"Won't that create problems?"

"Probably. But I can't think about that right now. We've got to get Peter home. I didn't get much sleep last night. Neither did Sigrid. But the letter will help some, assuming it's Peter's handwriting."

Jane quickly filled her dad in on what she'd found in Larry's truck. "I think he's been looking for a place to hide. My guess is, he found it. That's where he's stashed Peter. I'm ready to hit the road right now, go looking for them."

"Talk to Nolan first," said her father.

"Yes, Dad, I will."

Her father got a call interrupt, so they said good-bye.

Jane sat for a while sipping her coffee, watching Mouse nose a ball around the yard. The day loomed long and empty in front of her. What she needed was a focus, something that would make her feel like she was helping, a way to feel close to her brother.

Nolan called as Jane was letting Mouse back into the house. Everything she'd discovered came spilling out. Nolan said he wanted to do some checking around, told her to stay put until he got back to her. He made her promise to stick close to home, and then said good-bye.

For the next hour, Jane busied herself digging out old picture albums. She wanted to show them to Mia, keep her connection to Peter strong even though he wasn't around.

Her land line rang just after ten.

"Here anything more about Peter?" It was Cordelia.

Jane explained what her dad had just told her.

"Well, at least it isn't bad news."

"How's Mia?"

"Good. Could be better, I suppose, but she thinks Peter got called away on business. For the moment, she's resigned to stay with me and Cecily. Oh, I should tell you that Mel's had a little bit of a setback."

"What kind of setback?"

"Her blood pressure spiked and the doctors are having a devil of a time bringing it down. I just got back from the hospital. Been there since six."

"Awfully early hours for you."

"Kids mean early hours. It's good practice for when Hattie gets back."

Jane was sorry to hear about Mel. She'd already been through so much.

"Hey, you wanna go shopping with us today? Mia needs more clothes. Peter got her a few things, but—don't take this the wrong way, Janey—he doesn't have much taste when it comes to kids' clothing."

Jane smiled. "Where are you taking her?"

"Thought we'd run out to Southdale. At the moment she's watching a movie, eating some cereal. Teacake is sitting next to her, hoping she spills something significant."

"She watches movies even if she can't hear?"

"You've heard of subtitles, yes? She's enraptured."

"And what's she watching." Jane already knew.

"*Mildred Pierce*. And after that, we'll watch *Notorious*. Then, *Sorry, Wrong Number*. *Casablanca*. *Double Indemnity*. *Laura*. *This Gun for Hire*. The possibilities—and my film library—are endless. I mean, the child is ten. Ten! And she hasn't seen any of the classics. It's a travesty, borders on child abuse in my opinion. While she's living with me, she will receive the full benefit of my bounteous film, theatrical, fine cuisine, and cultural background. It's the least I can do."

And it kept Mia's mind off Peter, thought Jane. Thank God for Cordelia.

"We'll pick you up. Maybe we can have lunch somewhere along the way."

"What time?"

"It will take me about an hour to make myself breathtaking. So, how about we sail by around eleven."

Jane spent the day shopping and getting to know Mia a little better. Peter had already pointed out that she was slow to warm up to strangers, but Cordelia had clearly won her over. With Cordelia in the lead and Mia right next to her, they charged through the shops, trying on this and that, piling up the purchases.

All during the afternoon Jane kept checking her cell phone to make sure it was on. It only rang once—her manager at the club needing some information. Jane had hoped Nolan would call back with some brilliant way to find Peter, but it never happened.

Cordelia dropped Jane back at her house around six that night.

St. Croix Falls Public Library
710 Hwy 35 South
St. Croix Falls WI 54024

stcroixfallslibrary.org

She was exhausted, but still so wired that she wasn't sure she could sleep. She watched the car pull away from the curb, waved at Mia, then walked up the sidewalk to the front door. Maybe it was exhaustion, or maybe it was depression, but she was so weary she could hardly move.

Mouse greeted her with his usual enthusiasm. She opened the door in the kitchen to let him out into the yard, but stopped as she was about to open the screen door on the porch. Kenzie was sitting in the wicker rocker.

Mouse circled around twice, then rushed up to her, wagging his tail and bouncing on his front feet.

"Hi," said Kenzie, standing up. She seemed ill at ease, folding her arms over her chest, then unfolding them and pushing her hands into the pockets of her jeans.

"Come on, Mouse. Go outside." Jane opened the door and he bounded out into the yard. Turning to Kenzie, she said, "What . . . I mean, how did you get here?" Kenzie was the last person she expected to see tonight. It was a seven-hour drive between Minneapolis and Chadwick, Nebraska.

"I left right after my morning class. I have to be back by three tomorrow afternoon because I'm teaching a practicum at four." She moved a few steps closer. "You wouldn't take my phone calls last night. I had to talk to you. Had to apologize. I was way over the line, Lawless. I couldn't leave it like that." She paused, lowered her sunglasses.

Jane could see the puffiness under her eyes.

"Will you forgive me?"

"I already told you. There's nothing to forgive."

"Not true. I hurt you. That's something I never want to do."

The evening sun flickered in through the trees, casting a golden light on the yard.

317

Jane was so glad to see her that she felt herself moving toward her as if Kenzie were the magnet and Jane the helpless iron filing.

"You're crazy to drive all this way," she said, wrapping Kenzie in her arms, kissing her, holding her tight. "Nothing is your fault."

"Have you heard anything more about your brother?"

They sat down on the couch.

"Just that Randy Turk, one of Wilton's war buddies, may have paid him a ransom."

"How are you doing?"

"Not well."

"I had to come, Lawless. I just needed to be with you."

Jane looked away, then began to cry.

"I'm here for you, babe. For the rest of your life, if you'll let me."

Peter was asleep in the corner of the trailer when the door opened and woke him. Trudging in with a grocery sack and a rifle strapped across his back, Larry set the sack down on the counter, then pulled the rifle strap over his head.

"Look at this, Petey. I bought it off a guy in Moose Lake for next to nothin'." He laughed, slapped his thigh. "Don't seem fair, somehow." He looked the rifle up and down, sighted it at Peter. "Not bad. Not bad at all. It's a Ruger semiauto. An older one, but it's in great shape. I'll have to take it apart and clean it, but hell, I like cleanin' guns. You never know when you're gonna need a little extra firepower." He sniffed the air. "God, it stinks in here. You pee your pants?" He pointed at Peter and winked. "'Spose you want more water. But it'll just make you pee some more." He held his nose. "Shit, let's get some dinner cookin'."

He fired up the Coleman stove. Once it was going, he pulled a cheap pan out of the sack. Setting it on the flame, he ripped the

318

plastic off a pound of hamburger and tossed it in, breaking it apart with a stick. When it appeared to be heated through, he tossed in a can of baked beans.

Peter sat in the corner and watched. It smelled good, but he didn't hold out much hope that Larry intended to share. He'd glanced outside and saw that the sun had moved around to the west. He must have slept most of the day. He didn't feel any better for it.

Larry removed a bottle of whiskey from the sack and unscrewed the top. "Thought I'd celebrate tonight. It was a good day, Petey. I'm gettin' all my ducks in a row." He rubbed his hands together, gave the mess in the pan another stir, then turned off the flame. Setting the pan on the table next to the bottle, he pulled up a chair and sat down.

"I like that rental car of yours. It's comfortable—better than my truck." He pulled the sack over to him and rummaged around until he found a plastic spoon. Shoveling the food into his mouth, he continued to talk.

Peter turned his head away. He was so hungry his stomach felt like it was digesting itself.

"I'm an asshole," said Larry. "Always have been."

Peter tuned him out. When he tuned back in again a few minutes later, Larry was scraping out the last of the food. The bottle of whiskey was down by a third. Larry was feeling no pain.

"So, I figure I killed six people since I come home from Nam. Only one I regret was a woman." He burped, looked down at Peter. "You ever kill anybody?"

"No," said Peter, gazing up at the broken window.

"What'd you say, boy?" Larry got up and kicked him hard in the thigh.

Peter clenched his teeth, waited for the pain to subside, then said, "No, thank you, Drill Sergeant." He said the words with no energy. He figured Larry might kick him again, but instead, he leaned back against the counter, crossed his arms over his chest.

"I expect you don't like me very much, Petey."

Peter didn't think it required an answer.

"Boo hoo is all I can say." He picked at his teeth with a toothpick, studied Peter for a few seconds, then turned around and lit the lantern. "I want you to see something." He rummaged through the sack again and came out with a small pink hand mirror. Holding it up in front of Peter's face he said, "Look at yourself."

Peter blinked a couple of times before the image registered. When it did, his eyes opened wide in horror. The face staring back at him was a man he'd never seen before. His head was almost bald, and his face shaven, but his beard was so heavy that it had partially grown back. He looked mean, hard. There was a deep gash next to his left eye that trailed dried blood down the side of his face. The man staring back at him looked like a thug.

"Who is that guy?" asked Larry. "You know him?"

"No," whispered Peter. "Thank you, Drill Sergeant."

"I'd say we've made some progress turning you into a man. But we got a long way to go and not much time." He picked up the rifle. "Hey, I just got me a brilliant idea. Let's play a war game." He took another swig from the bottle. "Here's the rules. I'm gonna let you go, Petey. I'll take off the cuffs, count to ten, and let you run into the woods. If you get away, good for you. If you don't, maybe I'll shoot you or maybe I'll just beat the shit out of you. Either way, it's the best chance you're gonna get."

"You're going to kill me? Thank you, Drill Sergeant."

Larry laughed so hard, he doubled over. "Yeah, I'm gonna kill you, Petey. That surprise you?"

Peter didn't answer.

Larry shook the key to the cuffs out of the plastic cup on the counter. After unlocking Peter's restraints, he pulled him to his feet, pressing the end of his pistol to Peter's temple. "Think I'll leave the duct tape on your upper arms. Makes it more interesting."

Peter was so bent from lying in one position all day that he could hardly stand. Larry shoved him out the door and he landed on his stomach. His right leg was asleep. He rolled over on his back, tried to rub some feeling back into it.

"I'm counting," said Larry. He was holding the rifle again, the pistol shoved into his belt, but he didn't close his eyes. "One . . . two . . ."

Peter scrambled up and hobbled into the woods. Adrenaline began to work its way into his muscles. Still limping, he jumped over a log, headed into a section of thick brush. If he could just find a good hiding place, he might be able to wait it out. It was getting dark. If Larry couldn't find him, he might give up, think Peter had escaped. He couldn't outrun the rifle. Hiding was the only chance he had.

He pushed deeper into the woods. He could hear Larry singing "A Hundred Bottles of Beer on the Wall" somewhere behind him. He tried to rip the tape away from his upper arms, but it was so thick, he couldn't get it to tear. It didn't slow him down that much, so he gave up. As he flew through a clearing, his eyes darted in every direction, looking for a hole or a big log he could hide under.

And then he saw it. It was a pine tree. One of the broad lower branches was broken, still connected to the trunk but resting on the ground. Its needles were so dense, he couldn't see through it. With one last burst of energy, Peter skirted a boulder and dove behind it.

Larry was still singing behind him somewhere.

Peter curled up and waited, trying to steady his breathing, to control his twitching muscles, to focus his mind on nothing but survival.

That night, with just a thin crescent moon in the sky, darkness fell like a heavy curtain. Peter spent the time counting out the seconds, then minutes. When it seemed to him that several hours had passed, he moved slowly into a crouch. Larry could be out there, just waiting for a twig to snap or the crunch of stones, but if Peter didn't make a move before sunup, he'd lose his one chance. Larry had been drinking. Maybe he'd fallen asleep somewhere and was dead to the world. Or even better, maybe he was just dead.

But as Peter was about to crawl out from behind the branch, he heard Larry start up with his singing again. Only this time, the sound was close. The beam of a flashlight washed over the woods to the right of him.

"Fee fi fo fum," Larry called, laughing into the damp night air. "I smell the blood of a dirtbag." He was holding his pistol, waving it around in the air.

Peter wondered if this was a lucky guess, or if Larry had known where he was all along. He burrowed himself back down, as far into the earth as he could get without making a noise. The beam of light flew over his head but didn't linger. He heard Larry's boots tramp around not far from him, then saw them pass right by the tree.

"Come out, come out wherever you are," Larry cooed.

A bullet ripped into the earth about a foot in front of Peter's head. His heart stopped.

"Pssst. Hey, Petey, let me tell you somethin'. One of the reasons

322

I was such a good soldier over there in Nam was because I could smell Charlie. Always knew he was close even if I couldn't see him. Charlie had this real strong smell of weird sweat and fish. Now you, on the other hand, smell like vomit and piss. Kind of hard to disguise, know what I mean? I been sittin' on a rock about twenty feet away this whole time, just waitin' for you to make a move so I could chase you some more, but hell, don't seem like that's gonna happen. You got ten seconds to come out from under that tree. You don't come, I start firing."

Peter's mind went numb. Shivering with cold he clawed the dirt in front of him, hauled himself out from behind the branch. As soon as he was up, Larry shined the light in his eyes, blinding him.

"God but you're a pussy, Petey. You agree with that statement?"

Peter couldn't seem to focus. Nothing seemed real.

"You agree!"

"Yeah."

"Yeah what?"

"Yeah, I agree." He put a hand in front of his eyes to block the light. "Turn it off."

After that, it was all a blur. He felt Larry slam him to the ground, then press the gun hard into the small of his back.

"Well now, little Petey, it might just be judgment day in the big woods. Do I kill you, or just mess with you a little more? Decisions, decisions."

35

Jane was up the next morning before Kenzie. She pulled on a navy crew neck sweater over a pair of powder blue jeans, and she made sure to wear the boots Kenzie had given her. Once downstairs, she fixed coffee and had just taken a carton of eggs and some bacon out of the fridge when Kenzie walked into the kitchen.

"How'd you sleep?" asked Jane, smiling over her shoulder.

"Better than I did the night before." She sniffed the air. "The coffee smells good."

"Can't send you off without a decent breakfast."

"Come here," said Kenzie, pulling Jane into her arms, brushing her hair with a kiss. "I'm sorry."

"You already said that."

"I know."

When Kenzie didn't elaborate, Jane drew back. "Are you sorry *generally*—as in the 'life sucks' sense?"

Kenzie's eyes searched Jane's. "I didn't tell you why I got so twisted about the Memorial Day party this weekend."

"Sure you did. You think I'm a workaholic and it pisses you off."

"Well, there's that, yeah. But there's more." She hesitated. "This isn't exactly the way I pictured having this conversation. See, I had it all planned. Before the party, I was going to give you an engagement ring. I've had it for months. I was just waiting for the perfect time."

Jane felt something clench in the center of her chest. "You want to get married?"

"Yeah. It's possible now, you know. Even legal. Not here, yet, but I thought we'd drive up to Winnipeg or Thunder Bay— assuming you said yes." Again, she hesitated. "You would say yes, wouldn't you?"

"I'm speechless." It wasn't an answer.

"We don't have to do it right away. We could just be engaged for a while. But it's not like this comes out of the blue. I mean, we've been together for a couple of years. I want to spend the rest of my life with you, Lawless. You feel the same way, right?"

Jane stared at her a moment. "I do. More than anything."

"Man," said Kenzie, drawing a hand over her forehead in mock relief, "I thought there for a minute you were going to turn me down."

"No, it's not that," said Jane. She couldn't explain her reaction, not even to herself.

"But we should do it right," said Kenzie, stroking Jane's arm. "This was just a test run. I didn't bring the ring with me. Besides, you've got too much on your plate right now."

"Yeah, I do."

"So we'll table this until later, okay?"

325

"Sure," said Jane. They kissed and then held each other. Maybe Jane held on too tight, but she didn't care. "I love you," she whispered. She had to make sure Kenzie knew that, that she would never doubt it.

"I know," said Kenzie. "Somehow, in this crazy world, we got lucky."

Kenzie left to drive back to Nebraska just before eight. Jane spent the next couple of hours vacuuming the house, cleaning the bathroom, wiping down the kitchen cupboards, and studiously refusing to think about Kenzie's marriage proposal. She knew she'd have to figure out why she'd reacted the way she did, but not now.

She talked to Nolan for a few minutes. He'd checked out Peter's rental car, got the license number and a full description. It was a white Ford Taurus. Four door. He'd spoken to a couple of his police buddies, unofficially put out the word that the car had been stolen. Jane wasn't sure it was the best idea, but it was a done deal, so she let it drop. The problem was, Nolan pretty much confirmed what she already knew. When it came to finding Peter, there was no magic bullet. As they said good-bye, Nolan said he'd be in touch.

Mainly, Jane was just waiting for the mail. She didn't know when Peter's letter would come—or if it would come to her or her father—but she wanted to be there the moment the mail arrived. She dug the lawn mower out the garage and was about to fill it with gas when she saw the mail carrier cut across her drive on the way to her mailbox.

Racing around to the front of the house, she caught him just as he was looking in his bag, pulling out her letters.

"I'll take it, Dave," she said, holding out her hand.

"Oh, sure thing." He came back down the steps. "You expecting something important?"

"Yeah, hope so."

"Have a good day."

"You, too," she said, flipping quickly through each item. And there it was, second to the last. A small white envelope. No return address. It wasn't Peter's handwriting on the outside. She assumed it was Larry's. The postmark was from Cambridge, Minnesota. She figured, if Larry was smart, he wouldn't mail the letter from anywhere near where he'd stashed Peter.

Jane sat down on the steps, setting the rest of the mail next to her, and ripped the envelope open. Inside was a folded piece of steno notebook paper. She read through the note. It was Peter's scrawl, all right, but it made no sense. She read it through a second time.

Scooping up the mail, she ran around to the back of the house and entered through the screen porch. Mouse trotted along after her as she entered her study. The first call she placed was to her father.

"I got it. Peter's letter."

"Is it his handwriting?" asked her dad.

"Yes."

"What's it say?"

She read it to him.

"I don't get it."

"I think he's trying to tell us something, but it's in code."

"That just sounds like a bunch of gobbledegook. Have you talked to Nolan?"

"I'll call him next."

"Fax me a copy. Sigrid will want to see it. So do I."

She called Nolan. "Nothing in the note is real. Our mother's maiden name wasn't Lind. He's not a Libra. I mean, I can go right down the line. He hates steak. He didn't ride his bike over to my house three nights ago. He doesn't even have a bike. And if he had a favorite pie, which I doubt, it wouldn't be lemon."

"I thought the note was supposed to prove to you it was him," said Nolan. "That was the whole point of it."

"So why all the fiction?"

"You're right, it's got to be a message."

"Yeah, but how do we figure out what the message is?" Jane dropped her head in her hand.

"My guess is, he's trying to tell us where he is. What was the postmark?"

"Cambridge."

Nolan was silent a moment. "Fax it to me."

After sending the fax to her father and Nolan, Jane got herself a cup of coffee and sat down behind her desk to work on it.

By lunchtime, she had a bunch of word lists, but she was no further along than she'd been when she started.

Deciding to take a break, she called Cordelia. "How's Mia today?"

"Actually, pretty good," said Cordelia. "I'm about to leave for the hospital. Cecily's taking her swimming at the downtown Y this afternoon."

"Sounds like you've got it all handled," said Jane, feeling incredibly grateful.

"Doing our damnedest. Any updates on Peter?"

Jane read her the note.

"Lord."

"It's a code."

"Think so. How's it written?"

328

"What do you mean?"

"Is it all one block of writing, or is it in paragraphs?"

"Paragraphs."

"How many?"

Jane took a look. "Counting the 'I love you' at the end, twelve."

"Rats."

"Why do you say that?"

"I read a book once about an Englishman who was great at cracking codes. Seems it's the numbers that give the message structure. I mean, what about that fake phone number? Except, there are only ten numbers in a phone number, so that's a dead end."

"Maybe not. I'll keep working on it."

"Call me when you've broken it, Janey. I know you will."

"Thanks for the vote of confidence."

After saying good-bye, Jane looked for a few seconds at the phone number. Had Peter just made it up, or was Cordelia right? Did it point to something in the text?

If she took away the sentence the number was in, and then re-moved the "I love you all" from contention, that left ten paragraphs.

"756-624-2979," she whispered.

She wrote another list, the selected words pulled out of each paragraph with the exception of the first and the last. And then she read it out loud:

> *twin*
>
> *points*
>
> *Lind*
>
> *turn*

left
dirt
rode
trailer
Woods
hurry

"My God!" She shivered in recognition. She knew right where he was. "Thank you, Peter!" She called her dad, but he wasn't answering. Most likely, he'd gone out to discuss Peter's note with some legal or law enforcement buddy. She left a message. Then she called Nolan. He didn't answer either. "Strike two," she said, waiting for the answering machine to give him the update.

"I know where Peter is," she began. "He's up near a place that used to be called Twin Points, on the North Shore of Lake Superior. It was a resort about fifteen miles northeast of Two Harbors up on Highway 61, but it's been torn down, so don't look for a sign. You've got to go by the mileage. If you screw up, people in the area will know where Twin Points used to be. It's a public access beach and boat launch now. Here's what you do: As you're going north out of Two Harbors on Highway 61, go approximately fourteen miles and then start looking left for a dirt road. Take it and drive back into the woods. Maybe his rental car is parked somewhere along the way. He's being held captive in a trailer in the woods. It's a big area, but this narrows it down. He said to hurry. I can't wait, Nolan. I'm heading out to Flying Cloud. My dad's not using his Cessna at the moment, so I'm taking it. It's the fastest way up there. When you get this, call me. I'll already be on my way, but I need you to follow. I don't want to do this alone, but if I have to, I will." She cut the line.

"Mouse," she said, getting up, "I'm leaving. I'll call Evelyn and have her come get you. You be a good boy." She grabbed her keys and her billfold and burst out the front door.

Peter hadn't slept the first night in the trailer because he was terrified—and because of the cold. Last night, hate had kept him awake.

The sun had been up a long time before Larry finally snored himself into semiconsciousness. He moved his legs, then rolled over on his side. Peter figured he'd have one huge hangover when he got up, which would make him meaner than ever. He knew now, without a doubt, that this was his last day on earth. He'd given up hope of being found. It was just him and Larry. Peter didn't quite understand how Larry had mesmerized him, but he had. Maybe it was shock. Sure, Larry had a gun, he'd kept Peter locked up tight, but as he thought about it, there had been a couple of times when Peter could have tried to get the jump on him. If Larry took the cuffs off him today, it would be a different story.

Larry swung his feet off the rear bunk a little while later. When he looked over, he saw Peter staring at him.

"Hey, soldier. You ain't supposed to look me in the eye."

When Peter's lips turned up in a slight smile, he felt them crack. "What are you going to do about it? Kill me? You're going to kill me anyway."

Larry nodded, then laughed. "I 'spose that's right." He got up, walked nearer, gazing down at Peter with a mixture of curiosity and doubt. "Something different in your eyes today, boy."

"I'm in the army now."

"Yeah," said Larry, rubbing a hand over the stubble on his face. "Yeah." He turned away, opened the cooler and took out a

331

beer. Cracking the top, he tipped his head back and guzzled the contents, then crushed it and tossed it on the floor.

"I want one," said Peter.

"What'd you say?"

"I said I want a beer. I'm thirsty."

"Shit." Larry glared at him sideways. "Oh, I 'spose. Why the hell not?" He cracked open another one, crouched down, and held it to Peter's lips. When Peter was done drinking, Larry pulled the can away, but he kept his eyes on Peter. "What's wrong with you?"

Peter shrugged. He could feel the beer loosening him up.

Larry stared at him a minute more, then got up. "Okay, we got some work to do." He checked his watch. "But first I drive into town. Might even have to drive back to Duluth. Gotta find me one of them Internet cafes and check my e-mail." He winked, then shoved the pistol into the back of his belt, picked up the rifle, and left.

Peter closed his eyes. He prayed for one chance. Just one. This time, he'd know what to do.

36

On the way to the airport, Jane called Information and was put through to the small airfield in Two Harbors. She learned that she could tie the plane down there, as well as refuel. Everything she needed—except for one thing. She asked if there was a rental car company near the field. The man she spoke to said no, but he gave her the name of a car dealership in town she could call. He told her that if she phoned ahead, they would have a car waiting for her when she arrived.

Jane made all the arrangements on the way to the field. She raced through her preflight check and then taxied out to the runway. The FCC didn't allow the use of cell phones while in flight, so for the next few hours, she would be out of contact with Nolan and her father.

The weather was good, so Jane made it up to the Arrowhead by the middle of the afternoon. She set a cruising altitude of twenty-three hundred feet, but she dropped it when she saw that she was approaching Two Harbors. It wasn't long before she spied the red rock beach to the right of the plane. Years ago, it had been part of Mrs. Lind's resort—Twin Points. Jane didn't know what the real name of the beach was. It was just the name she and Peter had given it when they were kids.

She flew up past Split Rock Lighthouse, then did a slow 180 back to Twin Points. She dropped more altitude and saw a couple of dirt roads that might be the one her brother had referred to, followed them with her eyes, but didn't see a white car parked anywhere. The land below her was full of creeks and dense with tree cover, but there were also lots of clearings with nothing but low brush, rocks, and grass.

Jane flew over the same section three times before she spotted the trailer. From the air, it looked tiny. It was nestled into a stand of pine, barely visible from the air, which was why she'd missed it twice before. She calculated the distances she needed to find it from the ground, then headed back to Two Harbors, feeling hopeful for the first time in days. Now if that car she ordered would just be there, waiting for her, when she touched down.

"Keep digging," ordered Larry.

Peter was about one foot down in the dirt, carving out the pit he assumed would be his grave. Larry had removed his cuffs when he got back from town, but the semiautomatic pressed to the back of his neck at all times had given Peter no opening. He seemed more cautious of Peter now.

Peter dug another shovelful of dirt and rock, tossed it next to the hole. Larry was standing a ways away, too far for Peter to throw the dirt in his face, but close enough to be accurate with the gun if Peter tried to bolt. They were approximately a hundred yards behind the trailer.

"Come on, bitch," said Larry. "Move it." A small plane had flown over a couple of times and it had made Larry jumpy.

Peter dug a few more seconds, then leaned heavily on the shovel. "I need water."

"You need to do what I tell you," snarled Larry.

"I can't," said Peter, sinking to one knee. So many days without anything in his stomach, with all the exertion and the fear, his body was shutting down. He felt light-headed, and at the same time like he weighed a million pounds.

"Get up!"

Peter tried. He hoisted himself to his feet using the shovel, but that was his limit. "I can't."

Larry seemed momentarily at a loss. "Fuck," he shouted, motioning for Peter to move out of the shallow pit and back toward the trailer.

Once they were inside, Larry said, "I should just kill you now." He hooked the cuffs back up, then the tether.

"Why don't you?"

"Don't want any blood in the trailer, retard." He took out a can of beer and set it on the table. "You can look at that while I finish *your* job. Think about what you'll never taste again."

Jane checked her cell phone as she drove along Highway 61, headed north. Nolan had called twice.

First message: "Jane, stay put. I'm coming right over."

Second message: "You're crazy, girl, you know that? Okay, I'm leaving now. If you get this, stay in Two Harbors. I'll meet you at the airport. Under no circumstances—repeat—under no circumstances will you drive out there by yourself! Wait for me!"

Jane smiled, but she knew it wasn't funny. She was risking her life, but saw no other choice. Nolan was at least half an hour

335

away, if he made good time. Half an hour might be the difference between life and death. She punched in his number. He answered on the first ring.

"Where are you?"

"About five miles north of Two Harbors."

"I told you to wait for me!"

"I couldn't."

"Jane, stop right now. Pull over."

"Where are you?"

"I'm just leaving Duluth. I'll be there in twenty minutes, tops."

"Let me tell you where to go."

"Are you stopping?"

"Just listen." She gave him the directions. Just as he was about to scream at her again, the cell connection died. Sometimes it was hard to get or stay connected this far up the shore, and sometimes a finger inadvertently pressed the wrong button. She dropped the phone and pushed the gas pedal harder. Peter said to hurry. She believed he meant it.

Jane took the wrong dirt road the first time around. It ate up precious time, but she finally figured out her error. She got back on the highway and drove another half mile. She found the rental car parked off to the right, a blue tarp thrown over it and anchored to the ground. Larry wasn't taking any chances.

Now, crouched in the brush, she watched the trailer. She listened, but all she could hear were birds and the wind in the trees. She assumed Peter was inside, but Larry could be in there, too. That was the problem.

Creeping along the edge of the woods, she approached the front of the trailer. She stepped up on a rock and peered through one of the broken windows. The interior seemed to be empty. She could see signs of life: a camp stove, a lantern, the remains of some uneaten food on a table.

Easing down off the rock, she edged up to the door. It was wide open. She looked over both shoulders, then took three steps one at a time. The smell inside nearly gagged her. She looked quickly to her left and then to her right. The interior light was minimal. If she hadn't been looking for her brother, she would have missed him.

Two feet poked out from behind a cooler. She stepped closer and saw a body slumped back against the wall, where a refrigerator had once been. At first she wasn't sure who it was.

The man's eyes opened, shifted, drifted, then shifted to her face.

"Peter?" she whispered. The horror of his condition cut straight to her core. Everything she'd imagined he'd been through was written on his face and body, only ten times worse. She knelt down, touched the scar near his eye.

"Water," he whispered.

She turned, saw the can of beer, grabbed it off the table and opened it. She held it to his parched lips as he drank huge gulps. Rivers ran down his chin. "Key," he said. "Get the key for the cuffs." His eyes traveled to a plastic cup on the counter.

Jane got up. A few moments later he was free.

"Where's Larry?" she asked, knowing that if he caught them, they'd be trapped.

"Out in the woods digging my grave," he said, rubbing some life back into his wrists and ankles.

"Your . . . *grave?*" she repeated.

"Help me up."

As she did, she saw the vomit stains on his shirt, the urine stains on his pants. She was transported to another universe, one that was a stinking, seething sty. "Can you walk?"

"Yeah. I think so." He opened the cooler, took out a water and drank it down.

"Follow me, I've got a car."

He steadied himself on the counter, nodded. His eyes looked glassy, unfocused, like all the life in them had been vacuumed out.

Waiting a heartbeat, Jane eased back down the steps and crept back along the way she'd come. Sinking down in the brush, she looked around, saw that Peter was coming out the door. He waved at her, motioned her on. She worked her way slowly back to the edge of the woods. When she looked behind her again, Peter was gone.

A shiver of panic blew through her. "Peter," she whispered, her eyes darting in every direction.

This time, she ran flat out back to the door. She ducked inside, but he wasn't there. As she inched around the far end of the trailer, she saw him. He was about thirty yards ahead of her, pushing fast through some brush on his way to a section of pine. But what made her tremble was the rifle in his hand. She rushed after him, stumbled over a rock, righted herself, and kept on going. She knew where he was headed, what he was about to do. She couldn't shout his name because that would alert Larry that he was coming.

He was less than twenty yards ahead of her when she saw him sight the rifle and fire. She heard so many rounds crack the sky apart that she stopped counting. When she finally reached him, she saw that Larry was on the ground, half in, half out of the hole he'd been digging. The shovel was still in his hands, as if he'd tried to use it to block the bullets. Blood oozed from

338

wounds across his chest, arm, and head. His eyes were open and staring at nothing.

"Peter!" she screamed. She gulped air, turned to him, saw the cold, even look in his eyes.

"Give me the rifle," she said, grabbing his arm.

"No." He shook her hand off.

"Peter? Please! You've got to give it to me. It's Jane."

"I know who you are. I need it, in case he moves."

"He's dead, Peter."

"I can't be sure."

Jane saw something flash in the woods just ahead of her. She tried to make out what it was, but nothing moved.

Hearing branches snapping behind her, she turned as Nolan rushed up. He looked sweaty in his rumpled dress pants and white shirt, angry as hell. But something else, too. Wary. Unsure. His gun was drawn. She was about to tell him he didn't need it, when he shoved her behind him.

"Peter? It's Nolan."

Peter kept his eyes on the lifeless body, didn't reply.

"How you feeling?"

"Me? Never better."

"It's over now, son."

"Maybe."

"It's over, Peter. Look at me and tell me you know that."

Peter licked his lips, walked over to Larry, kicked him a couple times. He waited a second, then bent down, pulled Larry's head up by his hair, looked him in the eyes. When he seemed confident that Larry was dead, he dropped the head. "Okay," he said, getting up. "It's over." On his way past Jane and Nolan, he laid the rifle on the ground. "We can go now," he said over his shoulder.

Gripping Jane's arm, Nolan said, "Wait for me. You can walk back to the car with him, but don't drive away. Promise me." He squeezed her arm hard.

"Promise."

"He's in shock. He'll come out of it, but I don't want you to be alone with him until he does."

"What are you going to do?"

He lifted an arm, wiped the sweat off his forehead. "I'm going to make this crime scene disappear."

37

Two Nights Later

Peter waited until he thought Sigrid was asleep, then pushed back the cotton blanket and got out of bed. Moving over to the open window in the bedroom, he stood naked in the moonlight, breathing in the sweet night air. Coming home had been a bizarre experience. In the short time he'd been gone, his reactions had changed, his senses altered. He was like a man in an old sci-fi movie returning from outer space, not entirely sure how the aliens had changed him, but knowing that they had. He was pretty confident he was still himself, not some alien creature who merely looked like him, but, in a profound way, he couldn't be sure.

Nolan had convinced Jane that Peter had been in a state of shock when he'd killed Larry. Maybe they both needed to believe that, but it wasn't true. He knew exactly what he had to do and he'd done it. He'd been bone tired and had wanted nothing more than to get it over with. They'd mistaken his tiredness for shock. He supposed he owed his freedom to Nolan, and for that, he was grateful. But it wasn't like he regretted killing Larry, no matter what the consequences might have been—or might still be. In a certain way, he realized he owed Larry as much as he did Nolan. They'd both been instrumental in setting him free. He'd learned a lesson about control. It was all an illusion. You got on the bus the day you were born and you couldn't get off, no matter where it took you, until you took your last breath.

As he stood looking down at his arms and legs, at how smooth and clean he was, how fresh he smelled, it was like seeing someone else's body. Yesterday morning, he'd stood in front of the refrigerator just to remind himself he could eat or drink anything he wanted—anytime he wanted. Sigrid had come in, asked him if something was wrong. He said, no. Everything was fine. And then he thought: maybe this was what it felt like to come home from war. People expected you to be the same person. They asked a few questions, but mainly, they wanted the return of the status quo. But where did that leave the poor asshole who'd had his intestines ripped out through his mouth, because that's what Peter felt like. He knew things now he would never talk about, but all of it was inside him. Not necessarily good things, either, but not all bad.

Peter's hair had grown out just enough that he hoped he wouldn't scare Mia tomorrow. His full beard was gone, too. In its place he was keeping the two-day-growth look. He liked it, felt it suited him more than the beard did—the new him.

He'd told Sigrid last night after dinner about Mia. He wasn't the least bit frightened or anxious about her reaction. Quite honestly, he didn't care. She'd either be okay with it or she wouldn't. Either way he intended to love Mia with every last ounce of his badly battered heart. He wondered if Mia would

342

see the change in him. He'd heard that when one sense died, others got ramped up. She sure did watch people closely. She might be able to tell, to sense the difference, but he doubted she had the sophistication to understand the full ramifications. Hell, he was only beginning to see that himself.

It was really kind of funny when he thought about it. He could see things now that he couldn't before. Like, he knew Sigrid was going to leave him. She didn't love him anymore. She'd assumed they would have sex tonight because that's what they did to pretend they still had a marriage, but Peter had no intention of sleeping with her ever again. Besides, she'd be gone soon. He and Mia would have to learn how to be single together. Peter intended to protect Mia from anything cruel or brutal. Whatever it took. Whatever that meant.

Yes, he thought, running his hand over the bruises on his thigh, three days in a trailer with a psychopath did change a guy.

When he turned away from the window and saw his reflection in the mirror, he smiled.

38

Happy Memorial Day," said Cordelia.

"I guess we can use the term 'happy' again," said Jane.

Cordelia had pressed Jane to tell her every last detail of the rescue mission. Jane had explained most of it, but she hadn't said anything about the murder. That whole afternoon had been surreal. When she and Peter got back to her rental car, while Nolan was burying Larry in the woods, she'd leaned against the back bumper of the rented Chevy and unloaded the contents of her stomach. Peter had put a comforting hand on her back, stood next to her without comment. She remembered wiping an arm across her mouth, her gaze sliding along the ground until her eyes came to rest on his. She felt woozy, bruised, furious. He must have read all that in her face. But all he'd said was, "Feel better now?"

The lie they were putting out there was that Larry had escaped. Since nobody was about to go looking for him, it seemed a safe enough cover. But no matter how hard she tried, Jane simply couldn't get her mind around the fact that her brother had murdered a man in cold blood, and then just walked away. Somewhere, somehow, there had been a huge disconnect between the man who'd walked into that trailer and the one who'd walked out. She'd been up every night since they'd come home, drinking probably more than was good for her, trying to come to terms with what had happened. Maybe he had been in shock and didn't know what he was doing, but that explanation didn't satisfy her.

Nolan had sworn both Peter and Jane to secrecy about the murder and its aftermath. Jane couldn't even tell her father the full truth. Only three people would ever know what really went on during that rescue, and that's the way it had to stay. But without Cordelia or her father to talk to about it, Jane was beginning to feel the terrible weight of the secret.

"When are Peter and Sigrid coming over?"

"They should be here any minute."

Mia had spent the night at Jane's house last night. Everything was a hard transition for the little girl, but the dogs eased some of the rough spots. Mia knew she would be meeting her mother this morning, as well as being reunited with Peter. Jane could tell she was nervous, but she figured that was normal.

"So what's the plan?" asked Cordelia.

"For Peter and Sigrid? I guess they take Mia home and get on with their lives. Peter said he can buy faked adoption papers."

"Boy, that's something I never thought I'd hear come out of your brother's mouth."

"Yeah, I know. What you don't know is that Sigrid told me she wanted a divorce."

"She actually said that?"

"She has lots of plans for her life, none of which include my brother—or Mia. But now, everything's changed. I have no idea how it will all play out."

"Wow, that's really piling on. I mean, after all Peter went through. And now a divorce? How's he dealing . . . after what Larry did to him?"

"I want him to see a therapist, but he says he doesn't need to. Says he's fine."

Cordelia snorted. "Right. Has he told your father about Mia yet?"

"No, I don't think so. Unless he called him this morning. There's no rush because Dad's back to campaigning—trying to make up for lost time. Besides, Peter wants to bring Mia by Dad's house himself, introduce her in person. He can't tell him the truth about how he found her. Neither can we." More secrets, thought Jane.

"What's he going to say?"

"He'll tell Dad that he and Sigrid have been working on adopting Mia, but that they didn't want to break the news until it was a done deal."

"Well, you can count on my discretion, Janey. My mouth is officially zipped. Hey, I hear your father's giving a speech in St. Paul this evening. Some sort of Democratic fund-raiser. I'll have to miss it."

"Are you at the hospital?"

"In the waiting room. The doctors are doing their morning checkup with Melanie."

"How is she today?"

"Sitting up. They even had her walking yesterday."

"And the blood pressure?"

"It's down some. Not where they want it, but it's headed in

346

the right direction. I want to take care of her when she gets out, Janey, but she's so damn independent. She's already talking about going back to St. Cloud."

"Sounds like someone else I know."

"Who?"

Jane cleared her throat.

"Her health has been badly damaged. This is just my opinion, but I think it will be a long time before she can go back to work."

Jane took her cup of coffee and walked out into the living room. Mia was lying on the floor, coloring in a sketchbook with the new megaset of crayons Cordelia had bought her. Mouse and Teacake were tussling on the rug in front of her.

"You hear anything more about Hattie?"

"I won't know anything until Octavia returns from Italy in late June. I expect that the shit, pardon my Italian, will hit the fan right about then."

Jane smiled at Mia, bent down to see her drawing up close. It looked a little Jackson Pollock, not exactly a pretty picture.

"I think I better get going. Wish I could be there to see Mia finally meet her mom."

"I'll give you the play-by-play later tonight."

"Ciao, babe."

Walking over to the windows in the living room, Jane looked out at the street. Still no car. Instead of wandering around downstairs doing nothing, Jane decided to go up and strip the sheets off Mia's bed. She touched Mia on the shoulder and pointed to the stairs.

Mia nodded that she understood.

Entering the guest bedroom a few seconds later, she looked around. Mia hadn't packed her suitcase, so Jane figured she'd help out. She took the pants and shirt she'd been wearing yesterday and folded them up. She assembled everything on the bed, then opened the case.

"What have we here?" she said, seeing that Mia had collected three apples, two bananas, a box of crackers, an unopened package of Havarti cheese, and half a salami. Jane dug a little deeper and found a serrated chef's knife, which gave her a moment's pause, a gold necklace that Kenzie had given her for her birthday last year, one of Cordelia's favorite silk scarves, and the framed picture of Peter that Jane kept down in her study. As she thought about it, she realized she shouldn't be surprised. At least when it came to the food and the photo of Peter, Mia was simply taking care of herself. The necklace, scarf, and knife, however, were a different matter. For all Mia's outward sweetness, she was really an unknown quantity. After years in a child welfare system, there had to be some scars, some damage.

Right then, the doorbell rang.

Racing downstairs, Jane told Mouse and Teacake to get back. Mia wasn't the only one who was nervous.

Jane opened the door.

"Where is she?" asked Peter, standing outside wearing a new white polo shirt and light blue Dockers.

Jane's head tilted to the right.

"Okay, let me go in first," he said to Sigrid. "And then I'll introduce you."

"I'm a wreck," said Sigrid, pushing a strand of hair away from her face.

"Me, too," said Jane. She wanted to ask Sigrid what she thought of Mia's sudden return to her life, but that conversation would happen later.

"Everything's going to be fine," said Peter. He ran a hand

down the front of his shirt, then stepped inside. He moved to the edge of the living room and crouched down.

Mia frowned when she saw him, but then the light of recognition dawned in her eyes. She leapt up and ran into his open arms.

"God," he said, picking her up, spinning her around, "you're what kept me alive. Seeing you again was all I wanted."

Jane glanced sideways at Sigrid, saw the tightness in her expression. She couldn't help but wonder what Sigrid thought of the bond that had already formed between Peter and her daughter.

Peter set Mia down, then spoke slowly and clearly so she could read his lips. "I missed you. I'm sorry I had to go, but I'm back now, and I want to take you home with me."

She nodded, threw her arms around his neck.

He held on to her until she backed up. "Mia," he said, straightening the red bow on her dress, "there's someone I want you to meet. Remember I told you that I was taking you to see your mother? Well, she's here. Would you like to meet her?"

Mia gazed over Peter's shoulder, chewing her lower lip. Finally, with her eyes lowered, she nodded.

Peter motioned for Sigrid to come in.

Bending at the waist, Sigrid smiled, waited for Mia to look at her. When she did, Sigrid said, "I'm so so *so* glad that you're here, and that you're coming to live with us."

Mia looked at Peter, then back at Sigrid. She turned and picked up the sketchbook and a crayon. "Are you my *real* mom?" she wrote on a clean page.

Sigrid nodded.

"And is Peter my real dad?"

When Sigrid didn't respond, Peter took the crayon and wrote, "In every way that counts, sweetheart."

"Why did you go away?" wrote Mia, squinting up at Sigrid.

Sigrid hesitated. "I guess . . . I guess I got lost, honey. For a long time. But now, thanks to Peter, I've found my way back to you."

"You're my real family?" wrote Mia, looking at Peter and Sigrid, then up at Jane.

"Yes, sweetheart," said Peter, putting his arm around her and giving her a kiss on the cheek.

Jane started to laugh, but ended by choking back her tears.

39

Randy and Del stood in the shadows at the far edge of the ballroom as Mar Rios, Ray's new campaign manager, introduced
him. She'd already primed the crowd with her signature mixture
of laid-back humor and passionate politics. The sound of ap-
plause roared in the hall as Ray stood up at the head table and
moved over to the podium. Mar shook Ray's hand, clapped him
on the back, and then sat down.

Randy elbowed Del in the ribs. "Come on," he whispered,
"follow me."

They used the elevators outside the ballroom to take them
down to level A in the parking garage. Standing in the semidark-
ness next to a concrete pillar, Randy handed Del an envelope.

"What is it?"

"It's from Larry," said Randy. "Believe it or not, the guy came
through for us after all. I expect this is his parting gift to his old
buddies. And it's a whopper."

351

"Meaning?"

"It's a full confession. In the note, he says he was the one who murdered Sue. He describes the night, what happened, everything."

Del opened the flap, but didn't take it out. "Man, I never thought he'd do that. Never, not in a million years."

"Figured it was important for you to have the original," said Randy. "Just in case."

"Thanks, man. I hear you."

"I made a copy for myself. Store yours somewhere safe. You never know when the cops might come calling."

Del seemed dazed. He pressed his fingers to the side of his temple. "When did you last hear from him?"

"Four days ago. I arranged a money transfer. Once Larry let Peter go, he was planning to head up through Canada, fly to Zurich, and meet up with my account manager. So far, he's been a no-show."

"Four days is a long time."

"I know." Randy had pretty much come to the conclusion that something had happened to Larry, although he'd never be able to prove it. "You know, I think Larry was insane."

"Always or just recently?"

"Always," said Randy.

"You think he'll ever contact us again?"

"He better not."

They watched a woman close and lock her car and then walk quickly to the elevators.

"I'm sorry you lost your job," said Randy.

"Don't worry about it. I'll land on my feet."

"Yeah, you always do." Randy stood there, squeezing the back

352

of his neck. It seemed like he should say something more about what happened back in Waldo, but nothing came to him.

"Feels like something has ended," said Del. "Something huge."

"It will never end for me," said Randy.

"I know, man. She was your girl. I should've never gone back to her house and made her come out again and talk to us that night. I just . . . just wanted us to all have a chance to cool off, part friends, you know? But it didn't work out that way."

"No, it didn't."

They gripped each other hard.

Del stuffed the envelope in his suit pocket. "Why don't we go find ourselves some dinner?"

"Can't. Not today. Maybe next week."

"Sure. Hey, what do you hear from Sherrie?"

Randy cleared his throat, looked off in the distance. "She filed for divorce. Got the papers today."

"Ah man, that sucks." He searched Randy's eyes. "You okay?"

"I been better."

"But you're okay."

"Yeah. I'm fine."

Before they said good-bye, Randy put a hand on Del's arm. "You think Lawless is gonna make it?"

"Honestly? Yeah, I do. Come next November, I think he's gonna be our new governor."

"Good luck, man."

Del patted his suit coat pocket. "Don't need luck, now that I got Larry's confession."

Randy took I-94 to Stillwater, then turned north on Highway 95, heading back to his home in Marine on St. Croix. The sun

353

had set behind the tall limestone bluffs. In the growing twilight, he could just make out the river far below him as he sped along the winding road.

Something Larry had said to him a million years ago about the "fucking pearly gates" had somehow lodged in his mind and wouldn't let go. In the last few days, it had almost become a mantra. Except, a mantra was supposed to bring you peace. These words did just the opposite.

Randy felt jittery. He turned on the radio and heard an NPR voice talking about Iran. No way was he going to listen to that crap. He switched to an oldies station. The song "Wait Till the Midnight Hour" was playing.

"Jesus," he said, snapping it off. Who the hell ever listened to Wilson Pickett anymore? It was a Vietnam song. Memories flooded his thoughts. And then he remembered Larry's comment again. Maybe it was time. Maybe this was the door and he should finally walk through it. At that moment, he knew with total certainty that Larry was right, he *had* been the weak link. So why wait for fate to choose the time, when he could take control, force himself to have the conversation he'd been dreading his entire adult life. It was madness, for sure, but then, maybe like Larry, he'd always been mad.

On the next curve, instead of slowing and turning, he pressed the pedal to the floor, shot straight ahead through the metal barrier, and sent himself flying, floating, rushing toward the river. With his last conscious thought, he begged his daughter to forgive him.

Epilogue

Late Spring, 1971

*T*hree young men on a northern Iowa back road, cutting through the pit *of night. The moon is down, but their soldier's eyes guide them in the darkness. They swerve and stumble, but push ahead, away from the field, where a dead woman lies with her back comforted against a willow.*

Two of the men are shaking, broken, sobbing. One is astonished. He feels as if he's wired to all the electricity in the universe, glowing in the dark. The men assume combat silence as they search for cover. Beer and Jim Beam boil in their veins. What they don't know but will soon find out is this: the young woman's murder will forever weld their pasts to their futures and their lives to each other.

The one called Delavon sees it first. An abandoned, falling-down barn that lists heavily to one side. He points.

"No way," says Larry, coming up behind him. He squints at Delavon, smiles to himself. Black skin and a moonless night. All Larry can see is the white around Delavon's round eyes and his perfect teeth. He's like a cartoon ghost. "A puff of wind and we're buried in old lumber," says Larry.

"Fine," says Delavon, setting off through a cornfield. "Go find yourself one of them holes you're so partial to."

Larry waits a beat, then grabs Randy around his waist before he falls over, drags him into the field.

"I wanna die," mumbles Randy.

"You will," says Larry. "Count on it."

They all drop to the ground just inside the barn door.

Delavon raps Larry on the arm. "Flick your Bic. Let's see what we got."

The interior is empty except for a rusted pitchfork lying in the dirt a few feet away.

"Smells like cow shit," says Larry.

Randy falls on his stomach. He's alive but he shouldn't be. He should be back there in the field with Sue. He should have seen it coming. He was drunk. They all were. "I'm gonna puke," he says.

Delavon watches him crawl away, empty his guts in the corner.

Larry cuts the flame, thinks about lighting a cigarette.

"What happened?" says Delavon, a kind of wonder in his voice.

Larry leans back against the door frame. He figures if the building starts to collapse, he can scramble out. "Was just a fluke, man. She had one of them fragile-type throats. Just a little pressure, and . . . snap." He scratches his stomach. "What can I say? Death makes me feel . . . purely alive. Nothing else comes close."

"You're sick!" screams Randy from over in the corner.

"Yeah, man, but I'm breathin'."

Randy crab-walks back to them, flips on his back. He lies there watching the scene in his head. "I loved her," he says, grief grabbing at his throat.

"So did I," says Delavon. He's done crying, but he still feels a few chest chokes.

Randy sees her float through the darkness toward him. She tells him she can't marry him. She doesn't love him. His skin feels too tight.

356

"Fuck. Fuck!" Delavon shouts the word at least a dozen times as he feels around beside him in the dirt.

"What?" says Larry. He's impatient as he taps out a menthol cigarette.

"My tags. They're gone."

Larry lights up. "If they're back in that field, your ass is grass."

"It already is. Who do you think they're gonna pin Sue's murder on? Not the beloved town war hero——not when they got themselves a real live nigger to string up."

"This place ain't exactly in love with this boy, either," says Larry, breathing smoke into the darkness.

"That's why we all gotta stick together," says Delavon. "Come up with a good cover story."

"Hell, we weren't even there," says Larry. He shrugs. "There ain't no witnesses, so who's gonna say we were?"

"If I left my tags back there, it's gonna be kinda obvious I'm lying. But hell, maybe they got ripped off when Sue's brother jumped me."

"Good," says Larry. "Use it. We'll back you. Right, Turk?"

Randy is too far away to hear the question. He's still back in the killing field, his hands around Sue's neck, squeezing and squeezing until the terror leaks out her eyes and they turn flat and indifferent. Larry and Delavon pull him off. They stand around in the ferocious silence, unsure what to do. Until Randy breaks and runs.

Larry flicks a bright spark of cigarette ash next to his boot. "We are so freakin' fucked."

Randy rolls on his side. "I can't do it. I can't live with myself. First light, I'm gonna turn myself in."

"Hell you are," says Delavon.

"You do that and they're gonna haul all our asses in," says Larry. "We're in this together, whether we wanna be or not."

"If I tell them what really happened——"

"You think they'll believe you?" says Delavon, eyes narrowing. "They love you, man. They'll figure you're still being a hero, protecting your psycho war buddies."

"No," says Randy.

"Yes!" shouts Delavon.

"He's the weak link." Larry snaps his half-smoked cigarette away. "Always has been."

"I can't live with myself," bawls Randy.

Larry climbs over Delavon and straddles Randy's body. With both hands, he grabs Randy's shirt, yanks him up off the ground. "Sure, man," he says, his face inches from Randy's. "We understand. You're the professor, the college guy. You got delicate sensibilities. So go ahead and tell the truth. We'll even cheer you on. When you get to the fucking pearly gates, man, tell Saint Peter whatever shit you want. But until then, you keep your mouth shut. That's the way it's gotta be. We clear?"

Randy looks around, knows he can't fight them both. He closes his eyes. "Clear," he says, feeling the word crush him.

CPSIA information can be obtained
at www.ICGtesting.com
Printed in the USA
LVOW10s1924240817

546241LV00001B/42/P